My Sister's Prayer

Books by Mindy Starns Clark and Leslie Gould

COUSINS OF THE DOVE
My Brother's Crown
My Sister's Prayer

THE WOMEN OF LANCASTER COUNTY SERIES
The Amish Midwife
The Amish Nanny
The Amish Bride
The Amish Seamstress

Other Fiction by Mindy Starns Clark

THE MEN OF LANCASTER COUNTY
(WITH SUSAN MEISSNER)
The Amish Groom
The Amish Blacksmith
The Amish Clockmaker

THE MILLION DOLLAR MYSTERIES
A Penny for Your Thoughts
Don't Take Any Wooden Nickels
A Dime a Dozen
A Quarter for a Kiss
The Buck Stops Here

STANDALONE MYSTERIES
Whispers of the Bayou
Shadows of Lancaster County
Under the Cajun Moon
Secrets of Harmony Grove
Echoes of Titanic
(with John Campbell Clark)

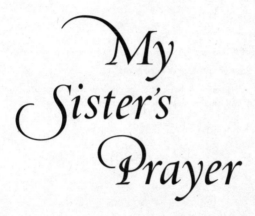

My Sister's Prayer

MINDY STARNS CLARK
and LESLIE GOULD

HARVEST HOUSE PUBLISHERS
EUGENE, OREGON

Scripture quotations are taken from

The Holy Bible, New International Version®, NIV®. Copyright © 1973, 1978, 1984, 2011 by Biblica, Inc.® Used by permission. All rights reserved worldwide.

The New King James Version®. Copyright © 1982 by Thomas Nelson, Inc. Used by permission. All rights reserved.

The King James Version of the Bible.

Cover by Garborg Design Works

Cover photos and images © darkbird77, jocrebbin / Thinkstock; canicula / Bigstock

The authors are represented by MacGregor Literary, Inc.

This is a work of fiction. Names, characters, places, and incidents are products of the authors' imaginations or are used fictitiously. Any resemblance to actual persons, living or dead, is entirely coincidental.

MY SISTER'S PRAYER
Copyright © 2016 Mindy Starns Clark and Leslie Gould
Published by Harvest House Publishers
Eugene, Oregon 97402
www.harvesthousepublishers.com

ISBN 978-0-7369-6290-2 (pbk.)
ISBN 978-0-7369-6291-9 (eBook)

Library of Congress Cataloging-in-Publication Data

Names: Clark, Mindy Starns, author. | Gould, Leslie, author.
Title: My sister's prayer / Mindy Starns Clark and Leslie Gould.
Description: Eugene, Oregon : Harvest House Publishers, [2016]
Identifiers: LCCN 2016009530 (print) | LCCN 2016015846 (ebook) |
ISBN 9780736962902 (softcover) | ISBN 9780736962919 ()
Subjects: LCSH: Sisters—Fiction. | Life change events—Fiction. | GSAFD:
Christian fiction. | Romantic suspense fiction.
Classification: LCC PS3603.L366 M95 2016 (print) | LCC PS3603.L366 (ebook) |
DDC 813/.6—dc23
LC record available at https://lccn.loc.gov/2016009530

Printed in the United States of America

16 17 18 19 20 21 22 23 24 / LB-KBD / 10 9 8 7 6 5 4 3 2 1

CHAPTER ONE
Maddee

*T*he cry for help came as I was coasting toward the bicycle rack at the far end of the building. I'd recently assigned a new custom ringtone—a few bars of the old R&B classic "Rescue Me"—to my sister, Nicole, so the moment I heard it trilling from my pocket, I knew exactly who was calling. Pretty sure I also knew why, I decided not to answer right now. One crisis at a time was about all I could handle.

Aiming toward an open slot in the rack, I rolled to a stop, careful not to scuff the suede of my new shoes as I climbed off. By the time I'd locked up bike and helmet, grabbed my purse, muted my phone, and started toward the Learning Commons, the music had ceased, though it still reverberated in my head.

I would indeed rescue my sister if that's why she was calling, but first things first. Right now I had to focus on the appointment I'd come here for. Nicole I could take care of later.

At the door, I caught my reflection in the glass and paused to straighten my blouse. I also tried to fix my hair, which had been smushed flat on top by the helmet and made frizzy at the ends by the wind. Growing irritated as I fruitlessly fluffed and smoothed, I had to remind myself that one of the reasons for using a bicycle during the workday was exactly this, to give me helmet hair and windblown clothes and otherwise mess with my precisely coiffed and coutured exterior. Thanks to a disturbing conversation I'd recently had with my grandmother, I was determined to conquer my more perfectionistic tendencies, and the bike riding was part of that. I'd already been at it for two weeks now, but thus far all it had really accomplished was to make me waste time at each destination as I desperately tried to put myself back together again.

Thoughts of Nana giving me fresh resolve, I stopped fooling with my hair and went into the building. Detective Ortiz had asked me to meet her on the second floor, third classroom on the right, so I headed there now, the pointed toes of my Via Spiga pumps clicking on each step as I ascended the stairs.

The second floor hallway was quiet and empty, classes still in session behind the closed doors. A glance at my watch told me I was a few minutes early—just enough time for a quick dash to a bathroom mirror.

Or not, I scolded myself, resisting the urge. I continued on down the hall to the door of the designated classroom. Peeking inside, I saw that it was nearly full, with Ortiz standing at the front giving what she'd said on the phone was a guest lecture for the criminology department. The students seemed to be listening intently, which didn't surprise me. As a working detective, Ortiz could bring a wealth of knowledge and experience to Virginia Commonwealth University's criminology department. No doubt she had a lot to teach these students.

I leaned against the wall as I waited for the class to end, my mind consumed with questions about why I'd been summoned here today. Detective Ortiz was in charge of an ongoing investigation I was connected with, but all she'd said on the phone was that we needed to talk in person. Considering that our past few interactions had been via phone or email, I had to assume this was indicative of some new development, which was exciting.

The investigation involved an incident that had taken place nineteen years ago, when my sister, our two cousins, and I were kids and had been witnesses to a crime scene. Back in the '90s, during a family reunion at our grandparents', we four girls had gone hiking in the woods next to their estate, making our way to a small, deserted hunting cabin where we sometimes played. When we went inside, we were shocked to discover a dead man—a murder victim—lying on a cot, a knife protruding from his chest and blood pooled around him on the floor.

Terrified, we'd run screaming back through the woods to our families, who promptly called the police. But by the time they arrived, listened to our tale, and then hiked all the way back out to the cabin, the dead body was gone and the mess cleaned up, leaving behind not a hint of foul play.

We girls were stunned, especially once the adults decided that we'd merely been victims of our own overactive imaginations and that we hadn't seen what we thought we had. The four of us knew that wasn't true, but there was no convincing the grown-ups—not even our own parents, much to our shock. But with no body or blood or murder weapon to be found, there was no way to prove our claims.

Not surprisingly, the whole matter—both the gruesome sight we'd witnessed and the fact that no one believed us afterward—had left scars on all our psyches. But then, about four months ago, my cousin Renee had come up with an idea. She conducted a forensic-type test in the old cabin using a chemical known to show blood traces, even really old ones. That test proved a tremendous amount of blood had been on the floor at some point in the past, exactly where we'd said it was. After so many years, the four of us were vindicated at last. The evidence from that one test, combined with our statements, was enough to convince the police to take another look.

Detective Ortiz had been working on the case ever since, having our findings retested and analyzed, tracking down leads, and attempting to piece together the few shreds of information she had to go on. We still didn't know who the victim had been, much less who killed him or why or how the body managed to disappear so quickly, but Ortiz was obviously diligent and methodical, and my sister, cousins, and I all had faith that she would eventually solve this puzzle.

In the meantime, as the only one of us living locally, I had become the de facto liaison between the Talbots and the police. I didn't mind, though I sure hoped I'd been asked here for good news.

My thoughts were interrupted by the sounds of doors opening up and down the hall. Students began trickling out, and soon the door next to me opened as well. I waited for the rush to pass by and then stepped into the classroom. Detective Ortiz stood at the podium, gathering her notes.

"Hello, Detective," I said, moving toward her and shaking her hand. "Good to see you again."

"You too, Maddee. How's the family?"

"Eager," I blurted out, thinking how ready we all were for closure on this matter that had hung over our heads for nearly twenty years.

My heart sank as the detective let out a small sigh. Clearly, she hadn't asked me here today to tell me of some new development. She had bad news for me, so bad that it had to be delivered in person.

"I'm sorry I don't have time to take you for coffee," she said, her eyes averted as she grabbed a briefcase and stuffed her teaching notes inside, "but I need to get back to the office soon. I'm sure you do too."

I nodded, unable to speak. *Please don't pull the plug.*

"Why don't we have a seat?" She motioned to a nearby worktable with several chairs around it. "It doesn't look like there's going to be another class in here right now."

We sat across from each other, and I realized I was holding my breath as I waited for her to speak. She paused to pull a file from her case and then met my eyes. "I'm sorry, Maddee, but I have to tell you something you don't want to hear."

"No," I whispered.

She nodded. "You know how hard we've been working this case, but it's been one dead end after another. At this point, things have ground to a complete halt. There are no leads left to follow, nothing else to test or examine. Nada."

"So the trail's gone a little cold," I said. "Nineteen years is a long time. You said yourself it wasn't going to be easy. You can't just give up."

"We're not giving up. The case will remain open. But you need to know that as of last Friday, it's officially inactive. We can't expend any more resources on it at this point."

"Resources? Detective Ortiz, a man was *murdered*."

She exhaled slowly, sitting back in her chair and meeting my gaze. "We don't know that for sure."

Before I could respond, she cut me off. "Yes, between your eyewitness accounts way back then and the evidence we collected from the scene a few months ago, we do know a man was in the cabin, that he'd been stabbed, and that he lost a lot of blood. But unless you girls checked his vitals before you ran off, we can't say with absolute certainty he was dead at the time."

I thought about that for a moment, my head spinning. "He wasn't breathing. Wasn't moving. Besides, no way could anyone lose that much blood and survive—much less clean up the mess on his way out."

"I know. But this is a crucial element, Maddee. We don't have a body. I mean, really, no victim, no crime. Frankly, I'm surprised the chief let me work this one as long as he did."

I leaned toward her across the table. "What about DNA? Your people recovered enough dried-up old blood from the floorboards to run tests. You got the results. You said so yourself."

"Those tests return genetic markers, not names. Not identities."

"So you compare those markers with some database to find a match—"

"Done. We tried every state and federal database available to the Commonwealth of Virginia and received not a single hit."

I sat back, defeated.

"We worked this case from other directions too, you know," she continued, her tone kind but weary. "Slogging through old missing persons reports, old hospital records, old cold cases, trying to find something relevant. We canvassed neighbors, worked through scenarios, and attacked the forensics with every tool at our disposal, but in the end we have nothing except proof of blood and a DNA profile. We can't know for certain he was dead. We can't figure out who he was. With no body and no weapon, we've taken it as far as we can."

"So this was all for nothing."

The detective reached out and placed a hand on my wrist, giving it a squeeze. "Not true. Don't forget, at least you were vindicated. There *was* blood there, lots of blood, and you girls proved it. Where it was and how it was disbursed directly corroborate your account of what happened. That's not much, but it's going to have to be enough. For now at least."

I swallowed hard, working to keep tears from my eyes. Everything she said made sense. It was just really painful to hear. Vindicated or not, the four of us were still going to have to live with some very big, apparently unanswerable questions. And the thought of telling that to my sister and cousins broke my heart.

"Is there anything at all about this case that I could pursue myself?" I asked softly. "More records to dig through or people to question or online searches to conduct? Anything?"

Detective Ortiz shook her head, pushing a lock of straight, shiny black hair behind one ear. "I'm afraid not. We've already covered every base there is."

I nodded, looking away, knowing that couldn't be true. Surely there was some angle she'd missed, some approach that could turn up something.

"How about the records from your investigation?" I asked, gesturing toward the manila folder. "The case file. Could I get a copy of that? I'd like to go through it myself to see if anything jumps out at me."

"No, sorry," she said, looking startled at the thought. "I mean, you're allowed a copy of the initial police report, of course. But not the evidence reports or the notes or anything like that."

Desperate, I decided to play on her sympathies. "You probably don't know this, Detective, but my sister was in a really bad car accident."

Her eyebrows raised. Clearly, that wasn't what she'd expected to hear. "Nicole? When? Is she okay?"

"About six weeks ago. She's not great. She has multiple fractures in her legs, two cracked ribs, and a whole bunch of nasty cuts and bruises. Anyway, I think she'll be coming to stay with me for a while as she continues to recuperate. Something like this could give us a project to work on together, especially if we had access to the things you've done thus far."

Her face tightened. She knew what I was trying to do. "Well, I'm sorry about your sister, hon, but you'd better get out your scrapbooking supplies or take up crocheting because this is one project I can't help you with."

"Are you sure?"

She studied me for a long moment and then seemed to relent, though more out of weariness than anything else. "Well, we can probably give you copies of a few things that don't have to be kept confidential, but I'll need to go through the whole file first and talk to the chief. We'll share what we can."

I could tell she was trying, and I immediately felt bad for using my sister's misfortune this way. "I appreciate that. We all appreciate everything you've done."

"Thanks." She slid her chair back and reached for her briefcase. "I guess that's about it. I'll let you know if by some wild chance we get a break in the case." As we stood to go, she met my eyes and added, "But...I'm sorry, Maddee. Don't count on it."

Once I was back outside, I took a look at my phone. Nicole had called two more times while I was with Ortiz, though she hadn't left any messages. She had, however, sent a text. Taking a seat on an empty bench near the bike rack, I opened it up and read:

This. Woman. Is. Driving. Me. Crazy.

I smiled in spite of myself. Poor kid. I could sympathize. Our grandmother could be trying at times, and Nicole had been staying with her for two weeks now. To be honest, she'd lasted longer than I had expected her to.

After her car accident and subsequent surgery, Nicole was in the hospital for two weeks, followed by an inpatient rehab facility for two more. From there, we'd moved her into Nana's house just west of Richmond, near Subletts. With both of her legs in casts, Nicole couldn't walk and had to be tended to around the clock. So Nana, with her expansive home and legion of hired help, had been the logical choice for taking her in. Our parents, who lived in Suffolk about an hour and a half away, both worked full-time, so they weren't the best choice. And though I was happy to help out, and my home was the most convenient, being in Richmond proper and the closest to her doctors and physical therapists and such, I also worked full-time. We all agreed Nana's would be best—all except Nicole, of course, who had balked. She loved our grandmother, but Nana wasn't always the easiest person to be around. She could be critical, especially of Nicole, who had made a mess of her life in so many ways.

Prior to the accident, my sister had been living in the seediest section of Norfolk, addicted to drugs, and running around with all the wrong people. Since the accident, she'd been a prisoner of her own injured body, cut off completely from the methamphetamine she lived for and forced into sobriety, cold turkey. That was the silver lining in all of this. Perhaps now, finally, she would be off drugs long enough to get some perspective and change her life for the better.

In the meantime, she still had much pain to endure. A few weeks ago, when Nicole was still in rehab and I'd been charged with getting her on board the Nana plan, I'd told her that if she would stick it out as long as she could, when it got to be too much for her I would figure out a way to shift her over to my place instead.

"So why not just start there and skip Nana's altogether?" she'd pleaded, her bruised eyes making her look like a sad raccoon.

I explained that I'd only been at my job for two months, not nearly long enough to have earned any time off, and that the first few weeks of her care were going to be quite time-intensive. "You're better off with Nana in the beginning. I can't be there for you enough, but she can."

"Seriously, Maddee?" Nicole whined. "She'll be all up in my business twenty-four-seven."

"No, she won't. She'll be in charge of your care, sure, but only in an administrative sense. She'll hire a daily aide to do the hands-on stuff."

"Okay, so why don't I just move in with you, and we get an aide to come help me there instead? Then I would be where I want, but you wouldn't have to miss any work on account of me."

I raised an eyebrow. "And you'd pay for that aide how?"

Nicole's face reddened. We both knew that at the time of her accident, she'd had no job or any means of support. Thus far, Nana's wealth had been a huge blessing, providing Nicole with the finest care at the best hospital from the top doctors. But the only way to ensure Nana's continued generosity was to do this next part on her terms—and her turf.

Helplessness filled my sister's eyes as she finally seemed to accept the inevitable. "You know she's going to drive me crazy, right? What happens when I can't stand it any longer?"

"Then I'll come get you, like I said."

Nicole swallowed hard. "You promise?"

"Yes—but only if you promise to stick it out first for as long as you possibly can."

"Fine," she muttered. "I promise."

Nicole had kept her word. Now it seemed it was time to keep mine. And though I was hesitant to take her in, a part of me was excited at the prospect. She and I had been separated for so long by the life choices she'd made. Surely this was our chance to reconnect and forge a new kind of relationship, the sort I'd always wanted.

I thought for a moment and then began to type.

Sorry, was in a meeting. Will swing by tonight so we can figure things out.

After a moment, I got her response:

I'll be counting the minutes. And by counting, I mean sweating, praying, biting my tongue, and doing everything I can not to bop this woman over the head with her own day planner. Would you believe she brought in a hairdresser this morning to fix "that disaster you call a hairdo"? Like that's something I felt like fooling with right now! Arg! Come as soon as you can. Please! I can't take it anymore.

Chuckling, I responded:

Will do. Back to work for now. See you tonight.

I was still smiling as I took off toward my office on Cary Street.

Though much of Virginia was a wonderland of vivid fall colors by mid-October, here in Richmond we wouldn't reach our peak for another three or four weeks. For now, there were just hints of orange and yellow and brown among the green.

The bike ride took eight minutes, long enough for my mind to wander from the situation with Nicole back to Ortiz. As I sailed down Main Street and then cut over to Cary, I focused on coming up with a new ringtone for the detective. Until today, it had been a line from a Barbalettes song: *Gonna solve this puzzle for you.*

So much for that. The time for optimism was over.

There were plenty of song lyrics that would work for a cop, like *Put your hands up* or *You've stolen more than my heart*, but I needed something specific to our situation. Thanks to my near-encyclopedic knowledge of even the most obscure '50s girl bands, I finally thought of a perfect choice, a little-known gem by Tammy and the Smash. I made it to the office with seven minutes to spare, just enough time to buy the ringtone I wanted and edit it down to one line: *I've done all I can but it's over now.*

"That's what you think, Detective," I said as I assigned the clip to her number in my contacts. She might believe this investigation was finished, but I wasn't giving up that easily.

CHAPTER TWO
Maddee

The sun was nearing the horizon as I headed out on the twenty-minute drive to Nana's. My afternoon had been so busy at work that I hadn't had time to dwell on the full implications of the change I would be instigating tonight, but as I pulled onto the highway, my earlier elation about taking in Nicole was slowly replaced with anxiety and a gnawing in my gut that told me to move slowly, to be careful.

Nicole's addiction was at the heart of the issue. Years ago, it had driven her from us and into a difficult and miserable existence. Six weeks ago yesterday, it had led her to climb into a car while high on meth and go for a drive along the back roads south of Virginia Beach. It had caused her to wrap her car around a tree at fifty miles an hour and nearly die of blood loss while waiting for help to arrive. The thought of almost losing her made my hands tremble on the steering wheel.

Addiction was the enemy, but did I have what it would take to help her face such a powerful foe? Sure, she'd been clean now for forty-two days. She'd already gone through the initial physical withdrawals, but that meant nothing in the face of a habit that had overwhelmed her life for years, starting at a young age. It went further back than that first, quick joint behind the middle school cafeteria, that initial sleepover with the friend who'd stolen a bottle of vodka from her parents' liquor cabinet. In fact, I believed the roots of my sister's addiction could be traced all the way back to that day in the Dark Woods, when at just six years old she'd been exposed to a grisly, horrifying crime scene.

She started acting out soon after. Refusing to believe our claims about what we'd seen in the cabin, our parents simply called her behavior a "phase." Mostly, they just placated her, giving her whatever she wanted. But as she grew, placating turned to enabling, which went on for years.

It wasn't just my parents, either. I'd enabled her as well, consumed by my guilt over what had happened and my inability to protect my baby sister way back when. It wasn't until I was in college and well on my way to becoming a psychologist that I'd learned about the nature of addiction and about boundaries and how best to help a loved one who was an addict, no matter the root cause. For a good five years now, I had been applying all of that knowledge to our relationship, drawing healthy lines with my sister. But now that she was moving in with me, could I stay strong? Could I hang on to all that I'd learned and maintain the kind of tough love she needed—especially considering how pitiful and helpless she was right now?

Bottom line, I would have to care for her and love her while still guarding my own heart. She wouldn't get the casts off for at least three weeks, possibly more, and after that she would need even more weeks of intensive physical therapy before she could walk normally again. But once she was fully ambulatory, she might very well walk right back into a life of drugs.

It is better to trust in the Lord than to put confidence in man.

Words from the Psalms popped into my head, a reassurance from God that this wasn't my problem but His. As I took the exit for the road that would bring me over the James River, I was comforted by that truth.

Settling back into my seat, I enjoyed the rest of the drive. Once on Huguenot Trail Road, I took in the beauty of the passing landscape as

I drove westward. It was darker now but still light enough to see the tall trees that lined both sides of the street and the massive homes that peeked out here and there between them in the distance. I turned onto Willow Lane and neared Nana's house, which was one of the biggest in the area. As I eased up her driveway and around the curve, the impressive sight came into view.

A three-story red brick Colonial set amid acres of graceful wooded land, the Talbot estate was a testament to our Huguenot heritage and its legacy of talented craftsmanship combined with a strong work ethic. Our ancestors had come to this country back in the early 1700s, and though they had started modestly, over time they had established and grown the family business, Talbot Paper and Printing, until it had become one of the largest and most well-respected paper and printing companies in the nation.

Nana met me at the door herself, leaving behind a whiff of Calèche perfume after she kissed my cheek. She looked lovely though tired, as if not even the most artfully applied concealer could hide the dark circles under her eyes. Those circles had been there since the accident.

She seemed to have taken it harder than any of us, and though I knew that was due in part to her love for her youngest granddaughter, I had a feeling it was as much about the shock of it all. Wealth tended to cushion one against many of life's uglier realities, but in the space of a single, near-fatal crash, Nana's cushion had been jerked away, forcing her to face the fact that bad things happened, and most of them were totally out of her control. For someone like her, life was all about control, about engineering and organizing and dictating all the details into their proper places. I wasn't all that different from her, if I were being honest, yet another reason for my bicycle plan.

"How's she doing?" I asked, giving a smile and a thanks to the maid who magically appeared to take my jacket.

"I hope you didn't come straight from work," Nana replied, ignoring the question as she eyed my dark-wash jeans. I'd worn them with a pair of Franco Sarto ankle boots and a hunter green V-neck top, and I thought the outfit looked great, its colors complementing my long auburn hair.

"Don't get me wrong," she added, seeing the expression on my face. "You look impeccable, as usual. I just didn't realize blue jeans were suitable for—"

"They're not, Nana. I went home and changed first."

"Oh, good. And at least everything else is perfect, as always. Well, almost." She patted down some imaginary loose strand on the side of my head and then took my elbow, leading me across the solarium toward the study. "Speaking of hair, wait till you see your sister. You won't recognize her." Lowering her voice, she added, "That hideous bleached-blond disaster is gone forever, thank goodness."

Poor Nicole. How she had managed to stick it out even this long was beyond me.

I held my tongue as we reached the door and gave it a quick knock. My late grandfather's study, which hadn't been used much since his death almost a year ago, was currently serving as Nicole's temporary bedroom. Fortunately, it was large enough to accommodate her massive hospital bed as well as her wheelchair and other medical devices.

Our knock was answered by Inez Valero, the aide who cared for Nicole each day. She handled everything from dressing to feeding to bathing and more, and I could only hope Nana would let her continue in that role once we'd shifted things to my house.

Inez greeted me warmly before leaving the room to give us some privacy. I looked to Nicole, who was pale and thin but had a definite sparkle in her eyes that hadn't been there last Sunday when I'd visited after church. This was the glow of *relief*, no doubt.

I moved over to the bed and gave her a hug, careful not to jostle her healing ribs. I resisted the urge to smooth her gown and tuck in her blanket and otherwise mother her. She would always be my baby sister, but at twenty-five she was no baby and hated being treated like one.

"Hey, you," I said softly.

"Hey back," she replied. "Is it time for our racquetball game already?"

I laughed.

"Well?" Nana exclaimed, stretching the word outward and upward. "What do you think?"

It took a moment for me to realize she was talking about Nicole's hair. I hated to admit it, but there was no denying she looked a thousand times better. The two-toned dye job had been replaced by carefully foiled and highlighted blondish-brown locks. The style was cute too, a shoulder-length bob with long layers that curved in at the bottom.

"She looks amazing," I said.

"Thanks," Nicole replied. "I think this shade of blond is the perfect complement to my orange-and-yellow legs."

With a huff, Nana turned and left the room, no doubt the very response my sister had been going for. Nicole's vibrantly colored fiberglass casts had been a source of embarrassment to our grandmother since she first saw them at the hospital. "What's wrong with good old plaster of paris?" Nana had cried. "At least it's white, unlike this ridiculous pair of oversized Popsicles."

"Oh, Mom, it's what all the kids are doing these days," my father had said, trying to calm her down but causing a quick jab to my gut. How many times had he uttered that sentiment?

"She's drunk? Oh, well. It's what all the kids are doing these days."

"Moving in with some guy? I suppose that's the way kids are these days."

"Arrested for possession? It's okay, honey. I think it happens to a lot of kids these days."

Shaking those thoughts from my mind, I focused on the girl in front of me. "How are you feeling?" I asked. "Think you'll be up to making the big shift by Saturday?"

To my surprise, Nicole's face fell. "Saturday?" she whimpered, and in that moment I realized she'd thought I would be taking her back with me tonight. How very much like my sister to expect the thing she wanted without giving any thought to the complicated logistics involved.

Trying not to sound aggravated, I explained I needed time to shift stuff around in my apartment and make room for her, plus we'd have to get a bed delivered, plus Nana and I needed to work out the details of her care.

She huffed. "Fine. Just don't leave me here any longer than that."

"I won't, I promise—as long as you're sure you still want to come once you hear my ground rules."

A hardness passed across her eyes, but she was in no position to refuse. If she really wanted out of here, this was the price she'd have to pay.

"Go ahead," she said with a heavy sigh.

"I just have three rules, but they're nonnegotiable. First, no visitors or phone calls except those preapproved by me—and I'm not approving anyone who might come in and slip you some drugs, so don't even ask."

"How am I going to call anyone anyway?" she retorted. "My phone got busted up in the crash."

"You have the burner phone Nana gave you."

"Yeah, but without my contacts, what good does it do?"

I hesitated, realizing she'd never bothered to memorize her friends' numbers. I would check the activity on her device periodically just to make sure, but I had a feeling rule one was probably a nonissue for now. Deeply relieved, I continued with my list.

"Second, you'll do thirty meetings in thirty days. Between Narcotics Anonymous and Celebrate Recovery, I've found plenty to choose from. You can start next week."

"Next *week*? My casts don't come off for another month."

"Doesn't matter. Nana said the doctor just cleared you for moderate activity."

"Yeah, but he meant like physical therapy. Not trudging down to some church basement to talk about my feelings and sing 'Kumbaya' with a bunch of other losers."

She was trying to be funny, but her words broke my heart. "You're no loser, Nicole."

"Yeah, yeah," she said. "What's the third rule?"

"As soon as your casts come off, you'll get a job—preferably with me. I talked to my supervisor this afternoon and lined one up for you if you want it. It's just clerical-type stuff, but you can work from a seated position, it pays hourly, and the schedule would be flexible enough to accommodate your meetings, physical therapy, and endurance level."

She didn't reply.

"And that's it. Respect my home and my things, and in return I'll happily share with you what I have. I'll take the best care of you I know how, and I'll do it without judgment or criticism or, uh, hairdressers. If you play your cards right," I teased, "I might even teach you how to knit."

"Why stop there?" she snapped. "We could plant some grass and watch it grow. Maybe hold turtle races down at the nursing home."

Despite her sarcasm, I couldn't help but smile. "What do you think, sis? Do we have a deal?"

Nicole was quiet for a long moment, and though I couldn't read her expression, I had no doubt what was going through her mind. This line I had drawn in the sand made me both her dearest friend and her greatest enemy.

"Maybe," she said at last. "But I want it on record that you're a big meanie."

I chuckled. "I am. And I'm so sorry. But that's how it has to be for now, you know? Boundaries and all that?"

She shrugged, looking away.

"So is it a deal?" I cajoled, reaching out and taking her hand in mine. "I'll get you all your favorite foods. Pop-Tarts. Strawberry milk. Macaroni and cheese." Leaning closer, I added, "You can pick the board games. You can control the remote. You can even eat the marshmallows out of the Lucky Charms, and I won't say a word."

Again she met my eyes, but this time I could see she was trying not to smile.

"Okay, I accept. I'll be a good girl," she said.

And in the moment, at least, I believed her.

Convincing Nana to go along with the plan ended up being not nearly as difficult as I had expected. A part of her seemed relieved, and that made me nervous. If she felt overburdened by Nicole's care in a mansion this big with a full staff and everything, how much harder was it going to be for me in my tiny carriage house with just a single daytime aide for help?

Then again, Nana wasn't exactly a spring chicken. Perhaps at her age just the responsibility was burden enough—and that was something I felt fully equipped to handle. My new job as an individualized education program coordinator had turned out to be a lot less demanding than the one I'd held for the past year in my postdoctoral internship at a children's clinic. That internship had kept me running from morning to night. In comparison, this new job was a walk in the park, a true nine-to-fiver that had felt almost like a vacation thus far—which was something I sorely needed after the craziness of the past year. But I knew that once I finished catching my breath, this new job would likely grow less than satisfying. I wanted to work with children, but these days I spent most of my time with reports and papers and other adults. Eventually, if things didn't change, I would need to move on.

Right now, however, this current situation might prove to be a real blessing because it freed me up as much as possible to focus on my sister. This time a year ago, no way could I have taken care of her. But now, I would be available from five in the evening till nine in the morning and all day Saturdays and Sundays, no problem.

And wasn't that just how God worked? Here I'd been concerned about my employment not being challenging enough when, in fact, that was exactly what I needed in order to care for Nicole.

By the time Nana and I finished hammering out the details, including Inez's continued employment for the time being, I was feeling good about everything.

"One last matter," Nana said as she settled comfortably into her chair. "Do you remember how much you girls enjoyed reading the journal of Catherine Talbot?"

"Of course." The journal had been written by my eleven-greats grandmother in 1685 when she was just eighteen years old, during a time that Huguenots were being persecuted in France for their faith. It told of her courage and determination and had made for a fascinating and inspiring read.

"Well," Nana continued, "it recently struck me that there's something else you really should see that is related to Catherine. Information about her daughters."

"Her daughters?" I thought for a moment. Though Catherine's journal only covered the span of a few months, we knew she'd gone on to have six children in her lifetime. Her son, Emmanuel Talbot, had been the first male in the family to come to America, though I seemed to recall hearing he'd been preceded here by two of his sisters.

"Some of their old letters have been preserved in the family archives," Nana said. "I was reminded of them last summer when Renee was researching the pamphlet."

Back in July, my cousin had solved a centuries' old family mystery involving a pamphlet—and met the man of her dreams in the process. I smiled now, thinking of Renee and her good fortune. Blake had recently moved to Seattle to be near her, and the two were happily dating and more than likely headed toward marriage.

"Last week I was thinking about the relationship between you and Nicole, and those old letters came to mind. I think the two of you ought to read them."

"Sounds great. The letters were written by Catherine?"

"No, *to* her by her grown daughters once they emigrated to Virginia."

I thought for a moment. "They're not in French are they, like the journal was?"

"No. Catherine and her husband fled from France to England, if you recall. Their children were born and raised there." Nana sighed, and I could see how tired she was. "Anyway, once things settle down around here, I'll dig them up for you. Considering the story they tell of two sisters making their way in the New World, I think you and Nicole would enjoy reading them together."

"That sounds wonderful, Nana. We'd love to."

By the time she and I finished our conversation, Nicole was asleep and Inez had gone home, so I left without telling my sister good night. I drove away with a lightness in my heart I hadn't felt in a long while. I was intrigued by the ideas of the letters, yes, but mostly my thoughts were on my sister. Not only was the real Nicole back—for now, at least, I reminded myself—but it struck me how nice it was going to be to come home to someone at night, to not have to eat alone. To bond with her again.

Just don't trust her, said the voice in my head. *Bond, yes. Love, yes. Trust, no.*

I whispered a quick prayer, fully aware that taking Nicole in could turn out to be either a tremendous blessing or the biggest mistake of my life.

CHAPTER THREE
Maddee

I woke Thursday morning to the sound of rain tapping against my bedroom window. The pitter-patter made me want to pull up my blankets and sleep some more. A glance at the clock told me I didn't need to be up for another fifteen minutes, but when I closed my eyes again, all I could see behind my lids was a to-do list of the many things I needed to accomplish before Nicole could move in.

I sat up and looked over at the stained glass window. Despite the rain, a sunbeam must have been piercing the clouds because greenish-blue light was dancing on the wall across from it as it did most mornings. The sight always gave me instant peace, reminding me of the complexity of the inexplicable union between man-made things, like glass, and God-made things, like light.

This tiny building, first constructed more than a hundred years ago, had been done and redone several times throughout the years. My landlady, Vida Zimmerman, had been the last one to make changes, renovating the interior to take advantage of the building's earlier charm. She'd uncovered as much of the original structure's wood as possible, exposing beams and tearing out carpets and polishing the floors until they glistened. Then she'd painted and furnished the place in light, muted tones, making it feel open and airy despite its small size. Up here in the bedroom, the pale blue walls were a perfect complement to the light that refracted through the stained glass.

Charming as it all was, no one would call this place spacious. The downstairs held a kitchen, living room, and bathroom, all quite small. The upstairs consisted of just the bedroom. It had come furnished with a single bed, a dresser, and a bookshelf, to which I had added a small arm chair by the window and a cedar chest at the foot of the bed. The closet wasn't huge, though I managed to make it work by installing a floor-to-ceiling shoe tree in a corner.

Looking around the peaceful space now, I whispered a prayer of thankfulness. Then I headed down the narrow staircase to the kitchen to start the coffeemaker. In minutes, the rich scent of ground beans filled the room. As the machine bubbled and slurped, I stood in the wide doorway between kitchen and living room, contemplating the space. If I ditched the coffee table, shifted the TV to one side, and pushed the couch all the way against the wall, there might be enough room for Nicole's hospital bed, though it would be tight. She wouldn't have a closet or dresser, but clearing off the bookshelves temporarily should make room enough for her things. There was also the matter of privacy, thanks to the open floor plan. Maybe I could rig a curtain of some kind. Glancing at my watch, I knew these were matters I would have to deal with tonight after work. For now, I needed to focus on getting dressed for the day.

By the time I was ready to go, the rain had stopped and the sun was fully out, which meant I could bike to work. As I headed off down the road, I thought back to Nana's comment that had started me on this anti-perfectionist, self-improvement plan in the first place.

It happened six weeks ago. I had been at the office just wrapping things up for the day when I got the call from my mother, saying Nicole had been badly hurt in a car accident south of Norfolk. Frantic, I raced southeast on I-64 and was well on my way when Mom called back to say that Nana had just arranged to have Nicole airlifted to Richmond's VCU Medical Center, the number one hospital in Virginia. I turned around at the next exit and sped back the direction I had come, making it in record time.

There we were told that though my sister would need surgery on one of her legs the next day, the primary concern was to get her safely through the night first. She'd lost a lot of blood, and her condition was precarious at best. While she hovered between life and death in intensive care, all any of us could do was wait and commiserate with one another and pray. Even my eighty-three-year-old grandmother insisted on sticking it out till morning.

Hours past midnight, Nana awoke from a light sleep in the chair next to mine. I asked if I could do anything to help make her more comfortable, and she said thanks, but no. Then, giving me an appraising look, she added, "Have I ever told you, Maddee, that out of all my grandchildren, you're the only one who always looks impeccable? Your hair, your face, your clothes, everything. You can't imagine how satisfying it is that at least one of you understands how important that is."

Considering the situation, I found it inconceivable that she would bring up something like that at a time like this. What kind of person was she?

My shock turned to mortification, however, when I realized that not thirty minutes before, after using the restroom, I had paused to freshen my lipstick, brush my hair, and run a purse-sized lint roller over my blazer and slacks. Forget what kind of person was she.

What kind of person was *I*?

For the next hour, as she dozed off again beside me in the ICU lounge, I ruminated on that question.

I knew why I was always so careful with my appearance. The time I spent making myself look my very best surely came out of the years I'd spent looking my very worst. I was the classic ugly duckling as a child and teenager, shooting up to my current height of five feet eleven inches when I was only thirteen. Besides being abnormally tall, I was skinny and gangly, my teeth in braces, my face freckled, my hair a frizzy red mess. For many years, I spent almost every waking hour feeling like a hideous freak of nature.

Then the strangest thing happened. During my senior year of high school, my figure filled out, giving me curves in all the right places. Thanks to the time I put into various high school sports—swimming, track, basketball—my arms and legs grew tan and shapely. I found a decent stylist who knew how to work with hair like mine and showed me how a good cut with lowlights, the right products, and a well-done blow-dry could work miracles. The braces came off, and even the freckles on my cheeks slowly faded, giving me a more porcelain complexion, one I learned to enhance with just the right amount of makeup. I began to explore fashion, learning to play up my assets. Despite my height, I developed a fondness for heels, sometimes very high heels, and between that and the clothes and the hair and the face, before long people began saying I looked like a fashion model.

On the inside, of course, I was still and would always be the ugly duckling, but on the outside I had transformed into a swan. And I enjoyed it to the hilt. Throughout college and grad school, my part-time jobs were always at whatever my current favorite clothing store happened to be just for the employee discount. These days, I was more selective as I slowly built a professional wardrobe made up of quality pieces, but I was totally shoe crazy and owned at least seventy different pairs.

I did look impeccable all the time, as Nana had said, and that was understandable, given my history. But as I sat there that night with my sister's life hovering in the balance, I realized that the ugly duckling-to-swan thing wasn't the whole story.

My personality was part of it too. I was by nature orderly, conscientious, meticulous, and in charge—or, as Nicole liked to put it, I was a super-organized neat freak with an innate need to control the world. No doubt that played into this issue of mine.

But at last I recognized a third element of my incessant quest for perfection: the trauma we'd endured as children at the cabin in the woods. That experience had taught me at a young age that I dare not drop the ball ever again lest disaster strike. Of course, that was ridiculous, not to mention exhausting. Yet always in the back of my mind was the thought that if I just planned carefully enough and acted responsibly enough and looked good enough and worked hard enough that I could do better next time, that I could keep bad things from happening to my sister and myself.

Yet here I was sitting in a hospital at four a.m., forced to admit that all the lipstick and lint rollers in the world couldn't have prevented Nicole's accident nor have any impact on whether she lived or died now. Control was an illusion.

In the end, Nicole made it through the night, thank the Lord. And the very next day, I decided to work on fixing the part of myself that erroneously thought by controlling the little things I could control the big things. Step one was to force myself to not be so hypervigilant about my looks. And though I had a ways to go before I would actually embrace the helmet hair, at least I was trying. As I neared my office in downtown Richmond now, I took in the beauty of the city streets, glistening from the recent rain, and felt the air in my lungs and the pull of my leg muscles as I pedaled. In that moment, I was reminded how one change for the better could be that first domino tipping over, starting a chain reaction that would bring multiple benefits.

It was a lesson I planned to hang on to, especially when the going got rough.

My day at the office was packed, but I managed to take a quick break midmorning to arrange for the delivery to the carriage house of a hospital bed, one smaller than the behemoth currently being used at Nana's, along with a rolling tray table. I had just finished that call and was about to return to my work when I heard a song by the Peterson Twins coming from the depths of my purse, a tinkly music box-type intro followed by the words, *My grandma.*

"Hey, Nana. What's up?"

"I'm sure you're busy, Maddee, so I won't keep you," she said in her usual efficient phone voice. "I just needed to let you know that you have an appointment with Nicole's doctor tomorrow at four o'clock."

"Four? Tomorrow?" I pulled up my calendar, trying hard to suppress my annoyance. "I'm tied up then. I didn't know you'd be scheduling things for me. I don't think I can make it."

"It will just be a quick fifteen-minute consultation. You're lucky he had an opening because you really need to see him before Saturday, you know. You have to be up to speed on your sister's condition by the time she moves in."

I pinched the bridge of my nose as she went on to give me the specifics of where to go and whom to ask for.

I sighed when she was finished. "All right. I'll try to shift things around."

"Very good. Give me a call once the appointment is over if you don't mind."

I did mind, but I agreed anyway, knowing that with Nana the path of least resistance was almost always the best—or at least the quickest—option.

That evening when I got home, as I turned in from the sidewalk and coasted to a stop under the covered portion of my small patio, I spotted a tuft of silver hair peeking up from the other side of the fence. My landlady had a garden behind her house, where she loved to putter around. Her efforts paid off. She was still reaping the fruits—and the vegetables, for that matter—of her summer labors, including squash, beans, cabbage, and sweet potatoes.

"Hey, Miss Vida," I called out as I locked up my bike and helmet. "How are you doing?"

"Maddee? Is that you, darling? Come on over here. I have a big, fat cantaloupe with your name on it."

I grinned as I crossed the tiny patch of grass and pushed open the gate in the fence.

Though she was up in age, Miss Vida was an agile woman with a ton of spunk, and I'd liked her since the day we met back in August, when I'd accepted my new job and was looking for a place to live. Once

I found the carriage house, I searched no further, and the whole situation had turned out to be even better than expected. She was the perfect landlady—never intrusive, always helpful, and a lot of fun besides.

At the moment she was over by the watermelons, gently lifting one of the smaller green orbs and shoving a handful of straw underneath before laying it back down again.

"So they don't rot as they're growing," she explained when she saw my curious expression. "Anyway, help yourself." She tilted her head toward the bench beside the back door, which was piled high with her bounty.

"Whoa! Nice." I reached for the only cantaloupe in the pile, a specimen so gorgeous my mouth was already watering.

"I'm getting tired of the things, and I thought you might enjoy it instead."

"You spoil me," I said, tucking it under my arm. "Thank you."

"Don't mention it. How's your sister doing?"

"Actually, I saw her last night. It looks as if she's finally ready to make the shift. I'll be bringing her here on Saturday." I had already mentioned two weeks ago that I might end up moving Nicole in with me as she recovered, and Miss Vida had seemed pleased with the idea.

Now she sat back on her heels, her face lighting up. "Oh, how wonderful! Imagine having two lovely young Talbot ladies living right behind me."

I felt a surge of guilt because I still hadn't told her the whole story, how my sister was a drug addict and there was always a chance she might fall into old behaviors while she was here. Of course, if she did, she'd be out the door, but I still thought Miss Vida deserved to know, just in case. Swallowing hard, I launched in with an explanation, but she soon stopped me with a wave of her gloved hand.

"I already know about all of that. But don't you worry. It's not a problem with me. In my opinion, everyone deserves a second chance, even tweakers."

"Tweakers?"

"Yes, isn't that the word for it?"

"For what?"

"Sketchers. Addicts. Meth heads."

I couldn't help but laugh. "First of all, how do you even know those terms?"

She shrugged, returning her attention to the next watermelon as she explained. "From my volunteer work down at the crisis center. Trust me, hon, we see more than our share. Most of them are decent folk who somehow lost their way and went down the wrong road for a while."

"And how did you know about Nicole? Did my grandmother tell you?" Miss Vida and Nana knew each other through the historical society, where they were both on the board of directors. That was, in fact, how I'd learned of this rental in the first place. But Nana was usually so tight lipped about Nicole's issues that I couldn't believe she would have mentioned them to anyone, much less a casual acquaintance, and definitely not in a group setting.

"Nope. My rabbi's brother's..." she paused, thinking, "...yoga instructor is dating your grandmother's...housekeeper. Or something like that."

I laughed. "Of course. The South at its finest."

She smiled.

"Anyway," I continued, "knowing that, you're sure it's all right with you? It'll only be for a few months, and I'll totally understand if it's something you're not comfortable with. I'm not even sure *I'm* comfortable with it, but I feel that I need—"

"Maddee." Once again, Miss Vida cut off my stream of words. "Of course it's okay with me. Family comes first. Always. I trust you to keep an eye on her with all that stuff."

"Oh, don't worry, I will," I said firmly. "Thanks again."

"No problem. Just let me know how I can help."

"Actually, I could use two quick favors."

"Name them, doll."

I explained about the hospital bed being delivered in the morning and asked if she'd be around to let them in. I also wondered if there was anywhere she could temporarily store the coffee table, TV stand, and a few boxes, which would make more room in the carriage house. She seemed fine with both requests, telling me to stick anything I wanted into her guest room and asking where the bed should go when it got here.

"About the only place it can go, which is the middle of the living room."

"You got it, doll. Now, go enjoy your cantaloupe. I'm sure you must be counting the minutes till you can kick off those high heels and put your feet up. I truly don't know how you wear those things every day."

Smiling, I stepped out of the gate and latched it behind me. "Oh, I have higher heels than these, including a pair of leather-and-suede booties with five-inch stilettos."

"Five inches? *Oy, vey!* You'll have to wear those the next time I need a lightbulb changed."

We both laughed as I headed to my door.

Once inside, I sliced up the cantaloupe, made myself a cup of tea, and sat down at the little kitchen table to enjoy both. When I was finished, I washed my dishes and headed upstairs to change. The room was stuffy from the day's heat, so I slid open the front window, letting in the breeze. Though I would have loved nothing more than to sit and relax for a while, listening to the distant squeals and laughter of the children playing in the park up the street, I knew with all I had to do there wasn't time. My sister would be moving in the day after tomorrow.

I had a feeling nothing was ever going to be the same.

Chapter Four

Maddee

I started with the shelves in the living room, carefully packing everything away into boxes, which I lugged next door along with the furniture I'd asked about. After that, I rigged a big sheet across the living room doorway, making it secure enough that it wouldn't fall down from repeated opening and closing. Fortunately, my front door was on the kitchen side of the sheet, as were the stairs, so that would ensure some measure of privacy for my sister. Once done, I pulled the curtain to one side and tied it to the banister so it wouldn't be in the delivery people's way.

I spent the rest of the evening planning our meals and making out a grocery list. Tomorrow night would be for shopping and other final preparations, and then Saturday would be the big move.

Once I was satisfied with the downstairs, I headed up to my room, tired but pleased that I'd managed to accomplish everything on tonight's agenda. It was quiet up there as I readied for bed, the park down the street empty now that the sun had gone down. It was just as well. Though I usually loved the sound of kids playing, sometimes it had the opposite effect, sending a pang of longing through my chest, a deep ache for children of my own.

All my life I'd wanted a bunch of little ones running around and a loving husband at my side, but here I was at twenty-seven without a single prospect. I hadn't necessarily expected to be married by now, but I'd at least hoped to be seriously dating, moving along the path in that direction. Lately, I'd begun to wonder if I would ever find anyone at all. It was hard enough to meet a decent guy, harder still to find one who was also a man of faith and character. I'd tried the usual routes—church events for singles, mixers at local student unions, and putting the word out among my older church friends. But every single guy who came along was either too pious, announcing his deeds with trumpets like the hypocrites in Matthew 6, or too secular, claiming to have a solid faith over dinner and then trying to get cozy in the car afterward. No thanks to either extreme. Despite my desperation, I was determined to hold out for a man who walked the talk—serving humbly, living kindly, and trying always to be Christlike.

After putting on my pajamas, I moved to the chest at the foot of my bed and opened it up, releasing the cedar scent of my lifelong hopes and dreams. Inside, beneath a stack of knitted baby blankets, were clothes I had sewn as a teenager for my "someday children." I pulled out one of the little outfits now, a tiny white sailor dress with a navy blue anchor embroidered on the front and matching navy hat and pants. So fun to make, so cute to look at, so sad to hold in my hands and realize I might never have a daughter of my own to put it on. Could I live with that? Could that possibly be God's will for my life? Surely not. Otherwise, why would He have filled me with such a burning desire to be a wife and mother?

My thoughts were interrupted by the sudden sound of a woman's voice from the kitchen. Startled, I put down the clothes and moved over to the stairs. I was about to call out when the sound repeated itself and I realized what I was hearing. It was Tammy and the Smash, proclaiming, *I've done all I can but it's over now.*

Detective Ortiz. I laughed at myself as I descended the stairs and retrieved the cell phone from my purse, catching it just in time.

"Good news," she said when I answered. "The chief has given me the go-ahead to share parts of the case file with you. We just need to get together to go through everything. How's Monday evening?"

"Perfect." My pulse surged at this tiny glimmer of hope—and then I remembered that Nicole would be living here, which meant I wouldn't be in a position to go anywhere.

"Any chance you could come to my place?" I asked, explaining the situation. I was relieved when she said yes, though she declined my offer to stay for dinner. We chose six p.m. and concluded the call.

Phone in hand, I headed back upstairs, encouraged by this latest development and glad that my sister and I would have a project to work on after all, common ground that would perhaps not just help us to bond, but also heal some of those wounds from the past.

"I think this'll be good for you," my supervisor said the next day when I told her I'd be moving Nicole in with me this weekend. "It'll force you to be more flexible."

"I'm flexible," I replied, trying not to sound offended. We were in Debra's office, a space so perpetually overfilled with books and papers that it gave me anxiety just to step inside. Debra herself, however, was a lovely person, and I respected her opinion. A single mom in her early forties, she had a no-nonsense demeanor and a look to match, her brown hair cut in a neat bob, her clothes mostly solids with simple lines, her shoes stylish if vaguely orthopedic.

She rolled her eyes. "Maddee, your filing cabinet is alphabetized, color-coded, and recorded on a separate file you keep on your laptop."

"I'm sure a lot of people do that—"

"You rearrange your coworkers' lunches in the break room fridge."

"Well, it looks better when all of the coolers are on one shelf and the bagged lunches on another."

She watched me through narrow eyes until I gave a sheepish grin. "All right, I'll give you that one."

"Your sister is recovering both physically and mentally. Her medical needs won't run on a schedule. You won't know what to expect or what might come up. That's a good thing. Like I said, it'll teach you flexibility."

"Yeah, well, that's Nicole," I replied. "Bringing chaos to my order."

She smiled. "And in return, maybe now you can bring some order to her chaos."

Order to her chaos.

The words had a nice ring and stayed with me the rest of the morning.

At a quarter of four I unchained my bicycle and helmet from the U-rack outside and headed for the doctor's office on East Marshall. It was near the hospital, less than a mile away, but suddenly I realized that between here and there was a steep hill I would have to climb. My new bike was nothing fancy, an inexpensive women's seven-speed I had chosen primarily because of its oversized chain guard to protect my good slacks and its color of robin's egg blue with tan accents. Whether it had the ability to tackle this mini mountain, I hadn't a clue.

A good thirteen minutes later I finally made it, though I was breathless and sweaty and completely disheveled as I locked up my bike and helmet and strode toward the building. For once I didn't even bother with primping because I knew it would take a lot more to fix this mess than a quick peek at my reflection in a glass door. With only two minutes to spare I fought dueling inclinations: be on time but messy or be late but look good? I prided myself on both punctuality and polish, but because I was trying to scale back on the latter, I went with the former. Walking quickly past the women's restroom, I headed straight for the elevator and took it to the third floor. I then made my way down the hall to the door marked *River City Orthopedics, Austin Hill, MD.* Stepping inside, I reached the desk at four o'clock on the dot.

As I was checked in, a part of me hoped the doctor was running late so I could make a quick visit to a mirror first, but the nurse waved me around the desk and led me down the hall to a corner office. The room was empty at the moment, but she told me to have a seat and that Dr. Hill would be right with me.

She wasn't exaggerating. Before I could even dig a pocket mirror from my bag, he came striding in the door.

"Sorry to keep you waiting," he said as he entered the room and crossed over to his desk. "I'm Austin Hill." I had expected an older guy, but from the back at least he seemed young, not to mention tall and muscular.

Then he turned around. My face immediately grew hot, startled as I was by this guy's incredible good looks. He had to be one of the most handsome men I'd ever seen. It was almost laughable, the chiseled jaw straight from a cologne ad, the green eyes worthy of the silver screen. The thick blond mane, cut and styled as precisely as the hair in a salon poster.

"Ms. Talbot, is it?" he said, placing the file he was carrying onto his desk, flipping it open, and having a seat. "Let's see what we have here."

He skimmed the pages in front of him for a moment and then glanced up at me, at my two good legs, a puzzled expression on his face. "You don't look like the Nicole Talbot I operated on six weeks ago."

I blinked, trying to gather my wits about me. "Um…no." I cleared my throat. "I'm Madeline Talbot, uh, Maddee. Nicole's older sister."

He sat back, swiveling in his chair. "Oh, that's right. I knew you were coming in. Your grandmother set this up. She said you needed to speak with me ASAP and faxed over a release from Nicole so I could freely discuss your sister's condition with you." He closed the file and crossed his arms over it, leaning slightly forward and fixing his gaze on me. "How can I help you exactly?"

Added to my general speechlessness was a surge of confusion. How could he help me? I thought he was supposed to be leading this show. After hemming and hawing for a minute, I explained I wasn't sure, but that I would be taking over my sister's care on Saturday, and my grandmother had said I needed to be brought up to speed on her condition first.

"Huh." He, too, seemed perplexed. "Well, I'll tell you what I can, but I'm a little confused. You really ought to be having this conversation with her internist, or even just her regular doctor. I'm the one who did the surgery on her leg, and I'm in charge of the follow-up for that, but otherwise I'm not involved with her case. Your grandmother knows that. I wonder why she wanted you to see me specifically."

Before I could reply, we were interrupted by a light knock at the door and a nurse who needed him. Flashing me an apologetic smile, he excused himself, saying he would be right back. Then he walked out, leaving behind a faint scent of wood and citrus, probably one of those expensive colognes from the Nordstrom in Short Pump.

While he was gone, I seized the opportunity to do what I could with my appearance, smoothing my clothes, running a quick brush through my hair, wiping a tissue under my eyes for mascara smears. I dabbed on some lip gloss but didn't dare whip out the lint roller in case he returned midroll. I finished by checking my face in my pocket mirror and then tucked it away and folded my hands in my lap, trying to look relaxed.

When he still wasn't back, I let my eyes wander around the room, taking in all that I saw, starting with the multiple framed degrees hanging near the desk. University of Pennsylvania. Johns Hopkins. The guy was definitely credentialed.

He was also quite neat, the ceiling-to-floor bookshelves along the back wall tidy and organized, with clusters of medical books—in alphabetical order—perfectly aligned and separated by tasteful *ojets d'art*, including what looked like a prehistoric bone of some kind mounted on a brass base. There were also several framed photos featuring three adorable little blond children ranging in age from two to six. In one they were jumping into a pile of leaves and laughing. In another, he was holding a boy under each of his arms while the girl sat grinning atop his shoulders. Nowhere did I see a family photo that included a wife, but that didn't mean there wasn't one.

My eyes went to the far shelves, which were lined with a wide row of neatly labeled binders. Above that rested several plaques. *Patients' Choice Award 2012. On Time Doctor Award 2016.* The latter made me smile, pleased to know there even was such a thing.

Then I gasped, thinking of one possible reason why Nana may have wanted me to see this man specifically. Was this a fix up? Obviously, with all this punctuality and organization, he and I had a lot in common. And he was out-of-this-world gorgeous. But would she really take advantage of a grave medical situation just to play matchmaker? Before I could decide, Dr. Hill came back into the room, apologizing for the delay.

"Better watch out," I teased, "or they might rescind your big award."

He glanced where I gestured and then laughed. "Yeah, that's a kick, isn't it? An On Time Doctor Award?" He returned to the leather chair behind the desk. "Though it's a shame something like that even has to exist, you know? Why should doctors be celebrated for not making people wait? My time is no more valuable than anyone else's." A tinge of pink flushing his perfect cheeks, he added, "So says the man who just made you sit here twiddling your thumbs for five minutes. I'm sorry about that."

"It's fine. I was having fun looking around. Your children are precious."

Again he looked where I gestured, this time to the shelves behind him. "Oh, those aren't my kids. Niece and nephews. They're a handful, but I love 'em. You?"

"Me?"

"Kids. Do you have kids?"

"Oh. No. I'm not married." I held my tongue, resisting the urge to add that I wasn't even dating anyone. I didn't want to sound aggressive. Or pathetic.

Feeling my own face flushing now, I tried to get us back on track, asking if there was anything he could tell me about my sister's condition that would help me take better care of her. He responded in full-on doctor mode, talking about the healing process and bone repair and immobility, and it was all I could do to pay attention when his perfect lips were moving so beautifully over perfect teeth in that perfect face. What a man.

Before I knew it, he was wrapping things up and asking if I had any questions even as he pushed back from his desk.

"No, I think I'm good," I said, scrambling for the handle of my bag, which had fallen sideways on the floor at my feet.

By the time I stood up, he had come all the way around the desk and was standing directly in front of me. Rising to my full height plus today's three-inch closed-toe wedges, I still had to look upward to see into his eyes.

"Oh, my," he said, locking his gaze on mine. "I do like a tall woman."

"Really? What's her name?"

He laughed. "Ah, and a funny one too."

Were we actually flirting with each other?

Almost as if remembering himself, he took a step back and replaced the sexy grin with a more professional demeanor. "Bottom line, Maddee, you sister's prognosis is good as long as she's diligent with the physical therapy."

"Thank you. That's great to hear." I reached to shake his hand goodbye, but he held on to it for a few seconds too long before letting go.

"She's blessed to have someone like you in her life," he said.

My cheeks grew warm again. "I'm blessed she's in mine."

Another long pause, our eyes still locked together. "Listen, before you go, stop at the front desk and make sure we have your contact information on file. If we need to reach you, it would help to be able to call directly."

My pulse surged. *If we need to reach you.* Was there an extra layer to that request?

"Will do. Thanks, Dr. Hill."

"Austin. Please," he said, swinging open the door. "Considering you're not the patient here, I think first names are in order."

"Austin," I replied with a smile and a nod, message received.

Then I turned and walked away, unsure how I managed to get anywhere while floating three feet off the ground.

Somehow I focused on my work and got through the rest of the day. Tonight was reserved for shopping, but I had to run home first to switch out the bike for my car.

The sun had already set by the time I got there, which meant I was already behind schedule. I ran inside to drop off my things and grab the car keys, but when I flipped on the light, I gasped, startled at the sight in front of me.

The bed. Of course. How had I forgotten? There in the middle of my living room, rolled up against the couch, were Nicole's hospital bed and tray table. A small thrill ran through me. My baby sister would be here tomorrow.

As I walked around the bed, observing its knobs and buttons, trying to figure out how it worked, the thrill began to subside. This wouldn't be a weekend sleepover with games and candy and bonding. Nicole was a recovering addict. She could have died in that car accident. We'd barely interacted with each other in years, at least not beyond a superficial level. This experience was going to be unpredictable and unnerving. How we would learn to trust each other again, I didn't know. The old family letters Nana had told me about came to mind, and I wondered if those two Talbot sisters had ever faced anything like this.

Growing suddenly somber, I sat on the vinyl mattress and reminded myself that nothing here was under my control. Only God could take this crazy situation and turn it into something good for both Nicole and me. I closed my eyes and prayed for help and guidance and strength, surprised when tears filled my eyes at the end. Blinking them away, I rose and busied myself gathering purse, keys, phone, and lists. I headed for the door and then turned to give the room one last look. The bed was here. Tomorrow, Nicole would be here.

For better or worse, this was actually going to happen.

CHAPTER FIVE

Celeste

1704

*D*eep in steerage on the *Royal Mary*, Celeste Talbot pressed her palm against the ruby ring tucked inside her skirt, launching a new wave of guilt. For the hundredth time she wondered how Maman and Papa had reacted to her note about leaving for the New World. She wondered if they realized when they read it that their other daughter, Berta, was gone too. And the ring. How long before they discovered that it was also missing?

The bunk she shared with her sister creaked with the rocking of the ship, which was now more like the gentle rocking of a cradle than the fury they had endured for the last week. Berta groaned, and Celeste put her hand to the girl's forehead.

The fever had returned. Celeste dropped to the filthy floor, knowing her sister desperately needed to see the doctor.

But how would they ever pay for it? Besides Berta and the ring, all Celeste had left was a simple porcelain brooch from Jonathan that wasn't worth anything, a pittance of money, and one wool blanket. Everything else had been stolen several days into the voyage by some fellow passenger. Celeste had been trying to be a Good Samaritan, tending to those who were sick as best she could, when she realized one of the sickest—a young woman tucked away in a bunk on the far side of steerage—was her own sister. In her shock and the rearranging that followed, Celeste had neglected her belongings and someone had snatched them.

Now it was time to sell the ruby. There were plenty of first-class passengers who might be interested in such a purchase, and she could use some of the money to obtain food and another consultation with the surgeon.

Berta shifted in the bunk, and Celeste raised her eyes to meet Spenser Rawling's. He was a kind young man who had stayed near their sides since Celeste first discovered her sister. He'd jumped in to help right away, carrying the ailing Berta over to Celeste's bunk, and then soon after when Celeste realized that in all the confusion she'd been robbed. In the dim light neither Spenser nor she could find who had taken her property, and though they complained to the first mate—a big, burly man by the name of Hayes—he blamed her for not taking better care of her things.

Since then, Spenser's cheekbones had grown as hollow as hers and Berta's, but his square jaw helped give the impression that he wasn't as famished. And his confidence that they would all survive had given her an inkling of hope even as her internal storms, as powerful as the gales that had threatened to tear the *Royal Mary* apart, battered her soul.

Celeste didn't know what she and Berta would have done without Spenser during the long crossing. The voyage had taken three weeks more than the anticipated seven. In steerage, men, women, and families were all mixed together, and Spenser bunked within sight of Berta and Celeste, ready to come to their aid as needed. Throughout the voyage he'd protected them from harm, and when Celeste couldn't get to the food line, Spenser went for her. What the ship provided was horrid—stale biscuits, thin porridge, and meat with maggots—but it kept them alive, even the little bit Berta could keep down. When the steerage kitchen ran out of food during the last storm, Spenser shared the hardtack he'd brought from home. Celeste usually gnawed it dry as he did, but she softened it in water for Berta, getting it down her sister as best she could.

The thought of the first-class passengers above, enjoying decent meals, tormented Celeste. She'd done this to Berta.

When Celeste had decided to sneak away from home and sail to America on the *Royal Mary*, she'd had no idea nearly two hundred humans would be packed in worse than cattle, with little sanitation, water, or food, and rarely any fresh air. Though her family could have well afforded a first-class ticket, she hadn't much money of her own and had been forced to sign an indentured servant contract in exchange for a place in steerage. At least she'd had Spenser's help, thanks be to God. He wasn't the sort of person she would have given a second thought to back home, but she was grateful for him now.

Spenser stood, pulling his brown hair back in a leather tie. "I'll go get water." He'd had to steal it from the first deck the last few times. Perhaps the storm had filled the barrels—though whether he would be allowed access to them or not was another matter.

"Thank you," Celeste said. "When you get back, I'll buy food." There were rumors of passengers on the upper decks who would sell some of their leftovers to the starving wretches below.

Spenser raised his brows, and his hazel eyes questioned her. He knew she was nearly out of money. She'd been holding on to the little she had left for when they docked, to provide for her and Berta until they reached Jonathan. But if she could find a first-class passenger to give her at least a portion of what the ruby ring was worth, she'd have more than enough for food and medical care.

The ring had belonged to her great-grandmother, a French noble-woman, who had passed it on twenty years ago to Celeste's mother, Catherine. The way the story went, Catherine had married quickly, just before fleeing France, and forgot to tell the pastor ahead of time that they had no ring. But when that part of the ceremony came, her groom surprised her by pulling one from his pouch. Catherine's grandmother had slipped it to him in secret prior to the ceremony so he could give it to his new bride.

Catherine had always promised that ring to Celeste, her oldest daughter, who dreamed of Jonathan sliding it onto her finger during their wedding. Her heart thumped at the thought of him. If only he were with her now instead of in Williamsburg, awaiting her arrival.

As Spenser headed toward the ladder, carrying the water bucket they shared between the three of them, Celeste leaned closer to her sister and whispered, "Berta, I'll get you the help you need. I promise."

Celeste had boarded the ship on the Thames of her own free will, signing on with the captain as an indentured servant with a four-year contract to cover her passage to the New World. The captain would be selling all of the contracts when they reached Virginia—but Jonathan would buy hers as soon as she got to Williamsburg, where he was stationed as a lieutenant in the British Army. They had gone over the plan in detail before he'd left London early last February.

Berta, however, had not boarded the ship by choice. She said she'd spotted Celeste sneaking away from home and followed her down to the docks, where she'd been abducted and forced on board, her signature forged on an indentured servitude contract. Celeste wasn't sorry for having embarked on this journey herself, but she was sorry, terribly sorry, for the consequences of that action. If she hadn't gone down to the docks that day, Berta wouldn't have followed her, and if Berta hadn't followed her, then she wouldn't have been kidnapped. It was that simple. Berta's current misery was primarily Celeste's fault, and she would feel guilty about that forever.

Due to the darkness of steerage and the number of people crammed from one end to the other, Celeste hadn't even known her sister was here until they had been at sea for several days. By then it was too late to do anything, and poor Berta was so seasick that she could barely speak.

Spenser had seen Celeste struggling to move Berta and had scooped the girl up, carrying her down the narrow aisle, holding her close to his chest to protect her as Celeste directed him to her bunk. His tenderness and dedication to Berta were evident as he offered her herbs for nausea that he'd brought from home. They seemed to help—a little, anyway—but then Berta had developed a fever, one that came and went through the last weeks of travel. The surgeon claimed it was all part of the seasickness and that Berta would recover once the ship docked, but Celeste was sure it was something much worse. True, she believed her sister suffered greatly from the motion of the sea, but something else was wrong.

Celeste shivered at the thought of the danger Berta was in. Jonathan would have to buy her sister's contract as well. She hoped he had enough money for both of them. The crossing had nearly killed Berta. The girl would most likely never be able to return home because that trip could prove fatal.

If only she hadn't followed Celeste that day! Celeste couldn't imagine the anguish their parents felt at having both of their daughters disappear.

Shouts startled her. As several men from steerage stumbled to the ladder, Spenser came bounding down from the deck.

"Land!" he yelled.

Celeste struggled to her feet, bumping her head on the bunk above.

Spenser, the empty bucket swinging from his hand, jumped over two men on the floor. "Celeste! Berta! Land!" Both his strength and litheness surprised her, considering all they had gone through.

Celeste stood and then swayed as she reached out her arm. Spenser grabbed it and pulled her into an embrace. Tears filled her eyes. He was nearly starving, but his arms were strong as he held her tight. For a moment she relaxed against him. Berta would live. Celeste would find Jonathan. All would be well.

A tear escaped. She leaned in closer and laid her head against his chest as a sob burst from her throat. All these weeks she'd stayed as stoic as she could, focusing on her sister. But now that safety was in sight, tears poured down her face.

"Everything will be all right." Spenser held her until she gained control. Then he wiped away her tears. At his touch, she stepped back, alarmed that she'd let down her guard. He'd been nothing but honorable, but she didn't want to give him any ideas.

Surely sensing her awkwardness, he turned his attention to the bunk and stepped past her to kneel beside it. "Did you hear, Berta?" Speaking softly, he reached out to brush a lock of hair from her face. "We made it. You'll be off this ship and on solid ground before you know it." It had been obvious since that first time Spenser held Berta and carried her across steerage that he'd been captivated by her beauty. Hugging Celeste meant nothing. She'd been foolish to fear he might think otherwise.

"I'm going to go summon the surgeon again," Celeste said to Berta, thinking of the many who had died—from disease or dysentery or who knew what else—during the trip. What if Berta were near death now when they were so close to land?

Spenser cleared his throat. "I'd hang on to your money and give it a day or two first. If the seasickness is the worst of Berta's problems, she'll recover once she's on land. If the fever continues, hopefully you can find a better physician than the ship's surgeon. I wouldn't waste any more money on him."

Spenser wouldn't risk Berta's life. Celeste couldn't help but think his advice seemed sound. She would wait. She needed to save every penny she could—and especially the ring, if possible.

"I'll go back up," he added, "to get water and see if there's anything else I can find out." Celeste watched him go. He had a job waiting for him with a carpenter just outside of Williamsburg, which was exactly where Celeste and Berta needed to land as well.

Before Jonathan had come to Celeste's parents' inn outside of London, Celeste had never given thought to emigrating to the American colonies. Some in their congregation of Huguenots—French Protestants who had found refuge in England—had chosen to relocate to Virginia, but Celeste's parents hadn't been interested. Papa was a printer by trade, though he'd had to sell his share of the family business in Lyon twenty years earlier before fleeing from France. Once in London, his intention had been to open a new print shop there, but that hadn't worked out thanks to the English government's strict restrictions on the owning of printing presses. Instead, he was forced to find some other type of business in which to invest. In the end, he'd done as many of his fellow Huguenots had and opened an inn. Once it was up and running and fully functional, Celeste's mother had moved to the helm, freeing Papa to take a job as a printer for the *London Gazette*.

When other Huguenots began heading to Virginia, Celeste's brother, Emmanuel, tried hard to convince their father that they should go too, saying he could open his own print shop there. As the oldest son, much of the family's future rested on him.

"And what would we print on?" Papa had replied. "There are no paper mills in Virginia."

"So let's open a paper mill instead," Emmanuel insisted. He was three years younger than Celeste but quick on his feet and always full of ideas.

"Why would we do that? There's no need for paper because there aren't any printers in Virginia."

Celeste giggled. Papa had taken his son's logic and twisted it back on itself.

"So we do both," Emmanuel cried, ignoring their father's teasing. "I know that would be twice as expensive, but what about Uncle Jules?" Their uncle, a successful businessman, had remained in France. "I'm sure he would invest as well if need be."

Papa shook his head. "I'm sorry, son, but it can't work. The population there isn't large enough to produce the quantity of rags we would need for making paper. No paper, no printer. We're staying in England."

Celeste knew that Papa had other reasons for not emigrating, including the fact that there was no freedom of religion in Virginia. "We'd all have to become Anglican," he had explained over dinner one night. There was also the matter of the African people who were being kidnapped and enslaved, he'd added. The colony was quickly becoming dependent on their labor. "I'm afraid the Huguenots who are already there—if they stay—will end up becoming entwined with that miserable business. The mulberry seedlings they took with them in hopes of producing silk aren't growing. They'll soon have no choice but to grow tobacco, but it takes so much labor to produce the crop that a profit can't be earned unless one uses enslaved humans to do the work."

Berta let out a soft moan, tearing Celeste away from her thoughts and back to her sister. She brushed Berta's dark hair from her face and then dabbed at her hot forehead with a cloth. Once the moaning ceased, her mind again went to home.

After their father made it clear that none of them would be going to Virginia, Celeste hadn't given the colony another thought. She would soon marry George Barré, a young man in their congregation of Huguenots. They had known each other since childhood, and it had always been assumed they would wed. He was good and kind and helped out at the inn when needed. Although his father was a weaver,

George would probably work at the inn once they were married. Weaving didn't pay what her family's business could provide.

Celeste would continue helping her mother, both in the inn and attending to her younger brothers—Alexander, Frederick, and William. She'd been like a mother to them their whole lives, and she wanted nothing more than have her own brood of children someday. Celeste had had no concerns back then. She was content, unlike Berta, who had been restless her entire life.

All of that changed, however, the afternoon Celeste first saw Jonathan Gray. Her heart skipped a beat at the memory. She was in the garden the first moment he appeared at the inn's back door. He was in uniform, and his blond hair was pulled back from his face, revealing chiseled features and a perfect mouth. His blue eyes brightened at the sight of her, and when she curtsied, he gave her a sweeping bow in return, his black hat in his hand.

Just an hour later, as they sat side by side on the garden bench that late autumn day, she already felt as if she'd known him her entire life. That, in turn, made her wonder what she'd ever seen in George. Comparing him to Jonathan was like comparing a candle to the sun. Jonathan was mature and disciplined and had a plan for his life. After he'd told her about his mother's death when he was six, his father's passing ten years later, and the subsequent loss of most of the family fortune, she felt more sympathetic toward him than she had anyone in her entire life. He'd had enough money left to buy a commission and become an officer, but he said that was all. In his duties, he'd been as far away as America.

"There are more opportunities there than you could ever imagine," he said. "And everyone *belongs* no matter what their station is in life. Does that make sense?"

Celeste nodded, enthralled. She asked if he would go back to the New World.

"I'd like that more than anything, but I'll be assigned here for the next three years at least." Then he thought for a moment as he took her hand. "Actually, since meeting you, I've changed my mind. I'd rather stay than go."

Her heart raced in a way it never had with George. Jonathan squeezed her hand and pulled her close.

Soon she was slipping away from the inn to meet him at the market or to fit in a quick stroll along the Thames. In no time, Celeste felt that she would be willing to follow Jonathan to the ends of the earth—though there was no threat of having to. He had no plans to go anywhere. The problem was in convincing her parents to allow her to marry him. They wanted all their children to wed other Huguenots and preserve their faith and heritage, but Jonathan was Anglican. She broached the topic once, without giving specific details, and her parents made clear their expectations, as usual. All Jonathan and Celeste had were stolen moments together.

Not that she felt good about that. She wasn't usually the type for sneaking around—though, as it turned out, Berta was. Celeste was slipping back into the house one night just as her younger sister emerged from a window. They spotted each other at the same moment, and Celeste gasped. Berta, however, simply stood up straight, shot her a challenging look, and dashed off into the darkness. Obviously, she had a young man of her own—a fact that didn't surprise Celeste. Berta had always been impulsive and reckless, not to mention secretive. And her beauty guaranteed no shortage of handsome admirers. What niggled at Celeste now, in the steerage of the *Royal Mary*, was that after years of wishing Berta would grow up and rise to a certain level of behavior, she realized she had lowered herself to Berta's instead.

Regardless, Celeste couldn't seem to stop. Even when she and Jonathan weren't together, her mind was consumed with thoughts of him—and of how she might possibly convince her parents to give their blessing.

Before she could come up with a plan, however, Jonathan's orders changed. They had been seeing each other only two months when he learned he was being sent to Virginia with new orders and the promise of a land grant. How could he refuse? He would bring honor to his family again, but even more importantly, he would be able to support a wife and children.

In the time before he left, Jonathan was busy preparing to leave so

Celeste didn't see him as much. But the night before he sailed, he came by the inn and begged her to follow him on the very next ship. She hadn't made up her mind—until then. She'd never loved anyone the way she loved Jonathan, and she couldn't imagine how she ever could. Celeste had intended to leave a week later on the *Royal Mary*, the ship Jonathan had recommended. But it was full, so she'd had to wait until its next voyage, more than three months later.

Berta moaned again and shifted in her bunk. Celeste hoped Spenser would return soon. A damp rag would be so much better than the dry one she dabbed against her sister's sweaty forehead.

A few minutes later a man on the floor cried out, and she heard Spenser say, "Sorry, mate. I forgot you were there." He was back with the water.

Celeste sighed. Oh, to be out of the confines of steerage. She didn't know how any of them had survived the horrible conditions. Spenser held the bucket steady, and Celeste spooned the liquid into Berta's mouth. Thankfully, her sister swallowed. After she and Spenser drank too—the water was still brackish, so Celeste had to force it down—she dipped the rag in the bucket and sponged Berta as best she could. The stench of steerage had seeped into every pore of their bodies. Celeste couldn't imagine how bad she smelled. She was determined that she would find a way to wash before Jonathan saw her.

"See if you can sneak on deck." Spenser unwrapped a piece of hard-tack, most likely his last, and handed her a portion. "Take a look at the New World, Celeste. It's beautiful." He grinned. "I'll stay with Berta and try to feed her." Spenser's feelings for Berta couldn't end well given his station, but there was no reason to worry about that now.

"Thank you," Celeste said and then cringed at her judgmental atti-tude, acknowledging that she and Berta were currently in the same social class as Spenser. But they wouldn't be for long. And they hadn't been before. They were from French nobility, although her mother said that was all in the past.

She struggled to her feet, waited for her head to clear, and then moved toward the ladder. She nibbled the hardtack as she went, grate-ful for Spenser's generosity.

Celeste struggled up the ladder a rung at a time, and soon she was through the hatch, blinking at the bright sky and gulping in the salty air. The sailors up on deck were so jovial about soon landing that they took no notice of her. The rush of the sails unsettled her for a moment, along with the blinding light, but then she began to relax under the heat of the July sun. She crossed to the port side and shaded her eyes. She could make out the silhouette of trees in the distance, not a village or structure in sight. The New World was a wilderness, she knew. Only a few towns existed. Still, she longed to see some sort of settlement.

"This is all part of the Carolina colony," a voice said behind her. "We were blown off course to the south, but we'll reach Virginia by the middle of the night."

She turned her head, expecting to be sent below deck once the man realized she wasn't a first-class passenger. It was Captain Bancroft with a spyglass in his hand. Not more than a decade older than her eighteen years, he was handsome with his dark hair and blue coat with gold braiding. "How are you faring, Miss Talbot?"

"Fine, thank you, sir," she answered, curtsying to him, surprised he remembered her name. She'd been shrill and beside herself when she'd confronted him about Berta's abduction, but he'd calmly explained there was nothing he could do at the time.

His first mate had chimed in that indentured servants frequently claimed they had been abducted, especially ones as ill as Berta, but the captain had shushed him. His expression kind, he'd told Celeste he was sincerely sorry for her troubles and promised to look into the matter as soon as the voyage was over.

"When do you anticipate that we'll reach the James?" she asked now.

He stepped to her side. "So you know your colonial rivers?"

"Yes, sir. I need to get to Williamsburg."

"We'll stop in Norfolk first. That's where the market for indentured servants is. Farther north, most are wanting slaves. They're tired of having to free their laborers."

Surely the captain understood that her contract wasn't to be sold in Norfolk with all the others. Celeste tried to keep her voice calm. "And then the ship will continue on to Williamsburg?"

"Yes. We have goods to deliver."

"Oh, then that's perfect. My betrothed will purchase me there, along with my sister." At least she hoped Jonathan would settle Berta's debt too.

"Are you certain? We've heard that story before."

"It's the truth. I swear it."

He shook his head. "I'm sorry, Miss Talbot, but I'm in this to make money."

Celeste bristled. She understood that, but their situation was an exception. She squared her gaze on him. "My sister was kidnapped. Perhaps you've forgotten our conversation." Over and over she'd imagined Berta being drugged and then carried on board and stashed on the far side of steerage. The kidnappers must have slipped away before anyone else boarded. Those in the bunks around Berta assumed she was sleeping, and by the time she came to it was too late to do anything about it.

"No. I remember it well."

"My betrothed is a member of the King's army."

"Yes, I remember your saying that too."

Celeste couldn't match Captain Bancroft's calmness as hard as she tried. Shaking from hunger and exhaustion, she said, "Once we can prove Berta was abducted, Jonathan will press charges."

"Against me?" He touched his chest with the flat of his hand. "On what grounds?"

"Buying stolen property."

"I run a reputable business, I can assure you." The captain shook his head, sadness settling on his face. "Can your sister identify the kidnappers?"

"They slipped a bag over her head before she could see them."

"And she didn't recognize their voices? Or anything about them?"

"No." Celeste grasped the railing. "They were strangers."

"So it's her word against—" he frowned. "The contract."

"Exactly. The contract will give it away. It will state who kidnapped her."

He shrugged. "*If* they signed their names."

Celeste shivered, realizing how naive she'd been all these weeks to think they could prove Berta had been forced aboard against her will simply by reading a piece of paper.

The captain leaned a little closer and whispered, "Was she in trouble with the law?"

"Of course not!"

"Is your family in debt? Would someone have arranged her sale and then chosen to make it look like a kidnapping?"

"No!" Celeste's voice had grown shrill again. No one in her family had known she was leaving or that Berta was going to follow her down to the docks. And neither Papa nor Emmanuel, the only two with any legal rights, would ever betray Berta—or anyone else—in that way. They were moral men. Their family was not in debt. And they *loved* Berta unconditionally, difficult as she could be at times.

Besides, there had already been too much loss in their lives, heart-wrenching separations for Papa and Maman from those they had been forced to leave behind—such as Uncle Jules and Maman's beloved Grand-Mère—when they fled France for England years ago. Celeste knew her father would never put himself or his wife through anything like that again, especially not involving one of their own children. The thought of any man doing such a thing to a loved one made her ill.

"Please forgive me, but I've seen more surprising things than that happen, believe me." He frowned again. "We'll find out what the contract says once we dock."

Celeste exhaled. "Thank you." He did seem to be a fair man. Surely he would do the right thing. Still, she couldn't help but think that if their roles were reversed, her spirited sister would have done a better job presenting her case. He tipped his hat and continued on down the deck toward First Mate Hayes and the ship's wheel.

Celeste turned back toward the land. Yes, her sister could be annoying at times, but after weeks of infirmity, Celeste found herself missing Berta's mischievous and daring ways. If she were well, she wouldn't have allowed Celeste to worry so. She would have joked and laughed with the people around them. She would have seen the fun in the adventure of the crossing despite the miserable conditions.

Berta *had* to get better. Celeste couldn't bear the thought of losing her only sister.

The sky turned a fiery orange with streaks of pink just above the trees, but Celeste couldn't enjoy the New World it illuminated. Tears stung her eyes again—and for more reasons than Berta's health. She had always been a good daughter. Helping in the inn. Caring for her brothers. Worshipping with her family in their church. Accepting George's pursuit of her. She'd done everything that had been expected of her.

Until she met Jonathan.

The colors streaming across the sky intensified as the sun dipped lower. She would try not to think about the consequences of her choice. She had never meant for Berta to follow her.

Celeste had always been so level headed. So compliant. So responsible. Berta, on the other hand, was the unpredictable one. Brave, yes, but impulsive. Reckless, even. Anyone who knew them would have thought Berta had been the cause of all this trouble. This time, however, the fault lay entirely with Celeste. The "responsible one" had been impulsive and reckless—and now here they were. Her only defense was love, a love so searing that it burned her heart like a brand.

The sun disappeared, leaving nothing but a glow at the horizon. Spenser often snuck up on the deck at night to watch the stars, and then he'd come back down and describe the constellations to Celeste. One night he said her parents must have loved the heavens to have named her after them. "More than that," she had replied. "They called me Celeste as a reminder that they'll spend eternity with the loved ones they left behind in France."

Despite having a name that derived from "celestial," she'd never had much interest in the stars—except to hear Spenser describe them. But if she stayed on the deck a bit longer now she might see the stars herself for the first time in ten weeks. She couldn't allow herself to linger, though. She needed to get back down to steerage and to her sister.

A sense of hope settled over Celeste for just a moment. But as dusk fell, she once again felt unsure about what tomorrow might bring. Making her way toward the hatch, she tried to pray everything would be made right, but she couldn't form the words.

Surely all of it would work out just fine as soon as they reached Jonathan.

CHAPTER SIX

Celeste

Early the next morning, the *Royal Mary* crossed into the Chesapeake Bay and then eased up the James River, finally docking at Norfolk. Now Celeste stood on the wharf, her bundle at her feet and both arms around her sister, waiting for Captain Bancroft to show them the contract. She'd had to remind him twice.

Berta leaned heavily against her. Celeste's own legs were so unsteady she nearly buckled under the extra weight. It didn't help that the summer morning was already hot and painfully humid. Sweat beaded along her hairline. Nearby seagulls fought over scraps of food. Sailors unloaded cargo from the ship, lugging it past them on the wooden walkway.

Behind the wharf was the town, so small she could practically see the whole thing from where she stood. First was a tavern, then a few warehouses, and beyond those were several streets lined with shops and homes. Wagons and carriages rolled along the cobblestones. At the far end was a fortified building flying the flag of England. Norfolk was barely a village.

A group of men were gathering on the wharf, talking and laughing among themselves. Celeste returned her attention to her sister. "How are you faring?"

"All right." Berta was still pale and weak, but at least she wasn't out of her head as she had been for much of the voyage. Her fever had broken shortly before dawn, and she'd been coherent ever since, a good sign that perhaps she was past the worst of it.

"We're on land now, right?" she asked weakly, lifting her head to look around.

"Close to land but still on the wharf," Celeste replied, surprise sounding in her voice. Did Berta not remember making her way down the gangplank, supported by both Spenser and Celeste, just a short while before?

"I know we're off the ship, but this must be some sort of floating dock. Can't you feel it rocking and moving?"

Celeste smiled, relieved. "That, dear sister, is what's known as 'sea legs.' I've got them too. The wharf isn't moving; it just seems that way. According to what one of the deckhands told Spenser, this happens a lot—and it can take a while for the feeling to go away."

"Really?" Berta returned her head to her sister's shoulder. "How very strange."

Celeste hoped the fresh air and solid ground would help Berta to feel better soon. Perhaps the surgeon was right. Perhaps Berta had simply had a horrible case of seasickness, and now that they were in the New World and off the ship for good, she would keep getting better. Perhaps the fever was simply the way her body had responded to the shock she was enduring.

Spenser waved from the end of the dock and held up a loaf of bread and three apples. The sight of fresh food made Celeste's mouth water. He also seemed cleaner, as if he'd found a place to wash up. Perhaps he'd jumped into the harbor and rinsed himself off in there.

She waved him over. He had just reached her when a thud of boots on the dock behind Celeste caused her to turn.

"Just as I suspected." Captain Bancroft held a document in his hand. "'Berta Talbot,'" he read aloud. "That's your sister's name, correct?"

"Yes."

He held the contract so she could see it. It was Berta's name all right, but the signature wasn't hers. It couldn't be. Celeste had to admit that it wasn't too far off, but it wasn't exact. The perpetrator must have made a point of observing and copying her actual signature as best he could.

"It's a forgery," she announced to the captain, sounding more certain than she felt.

He grunted, looking back at the page. "Perhaps she could show me hers then?" He nodded down the dock toward several stacked crates that an older man was using as a table. "That's where I'll be attending to my paperwork. Take her over and we'll have a look." He marched off, contract in hand.

Celeste scooped up their belongings and then looked to Spenser, who helped support Berta as they made their way to the crates.

"What's going on?" he asked.

"Just as I thought, someone forged Berta's signature." Celeste nodded toward the captain. "But he wants to see what her signature looks like."

Captain Bancroft gestured toward a piece of paper and a quill on the crate. "Please," he said to Berta. "I'd like to sort this out once and for all."

She nodded and extended a shaky hand, doing her best to pick up the quill. Finally, Celeste grabbed it, dipped it in the ink, and then positioned it in Berta's hand. "Go ahead," she said.

Berta leaned over with Celeste still supporting her, but her hands were shaking so badly that when she pressed the quill to the paper, she splotched the ink all over it. Trying again, she started to make a "B," but then she pressed too hard and tore the paper.

"Can she even write?" the captain asked.

"Of course. Since she was a little girl."

Their parents believed strongly in education and had brought in tutors for all of their children. Berta hadn't been as studious as Celeste, but she'd certainly learned the basics of reading and writing, in both English and French.

"Perhaps she hired someone to write her name for her," the older man said. "That happens sometimes."

"No," Celeste replied. "There's no reason she would have done that. She's quite capable. She's just very weak right now. Not six hours ago she was nearly incoherent with fever."

Berta tried again, and this time she managed to write out her name. Sort of. The signature looked familiar, but the letters were wobbly and uneven as if written by an old lady rather than a young woman.

The captain picked up the paper and studied it closely then held it next to the contract, his eyes going from one to the other.

"Taking her current condition into account," he pronounced, "I'd say these are a match."

"What?" Celeste cried. Berta didn't even bother to protest. She had collapsed with exhaustion against her sister. Celeste struggled to stay on her feet. "How can you say that?"

He held the pages in her direction. "How can you not?"

She couldn't deny there was a resemblance. However, Celeste knew Berta wouldn't have signed it, and yet she couldn't prove her sister hadn't.

The older man nodded, seconding Captain Bancroft's opinion.

"I'm sorry, Miss Talbot," the captain added, "but it's time to start the bidding." He gestured toward a group of men who had lined up along the wharf and seemed to be waiting.

Celeste's free hand flew to her throat. "We're to be traded like cattle?"

He frowned. "No. Your indentured servant contracts will be sold in a respectable fashion. Surely *you* signed your own contract? Or were you kidnapped too?" This time, there was sarcasm in his voice.

Celeste swallowed hard, nearly overcome. "No, my contract is legitimate," she managed to utter. She turned away, her mind in a whirl.

All along she'd pictured the ship landing at Williamsburg and Jonathan being there, searching the dock for her and then sweeping her up in his arms when she disembarked. He would buy her contract himself, fulfilling her financial obligation just as he'd promised he would, and then they would tear it up together.

Now there was no way for him to even know that she had made it to the New World. Somehow, she would have to get word to him, after which he would need to come all the way to Norfolk to buy not just her contract but Berta's too.

She looked at Spenser. "Stay close to us, would you? You'll have to be the one who tells Jonathan. Can you do that for me?"

He nodded solemnly.

"Good. Once our contracts are sold, make sure you get all the information you can about the person who is buying us."

"No one's buying you, Celeste. They're buying your contracts," he reminded her sympathetically. "You won't be enslaved. It's your labor that's for sale, and only for a specified amount of time."

She nodded. That was exactly what she had told herself over and over back in England when she'd made the arrangements for herself in the first place. Her hands had been shaking nearly as bad as Berta's when it had come time to sign her name, but somehow she'd managed to calm down and complete the transaction, driven as she was by the thought of Jonathan waiting for her across the sea.

Spenser led her and Berta away from the old man and the captain, and as they walked he offered them both a piece of bread and an apple. Celeste ate hers as quickly as she could without being unladylike, and Berta managed to take a few bites. They were both filthy, but at least Celeste had been able to comb out her sister's matted hair, braid it, twist it up on her head, and cover it with her cap.

Soon the men were allowed to come closer, where they began to examine the indentured servants, male and female alike. A middle-aged fellow with a long stride and an air of authority stopped at Celeste and asked if she'd had experience as a maid. "I can fulfill those duties," she answered. She had never had to clean much herself, but she had instructed the maids in the inn for years.

"These two beauties are sisters," Captain Bancroft said as he approached the man.

Celeste's face grew warm. Both she and Berta had their mother's dark eyes and hair, but Berta was by far the more beautiful of the two.

Then the captain said, "They must stay together."

Celeste's heart was warmed at his order. He was watching out for them.

The man crossed his arms. "The smaller one appears ill."

"She's just seasick, sir," Celeste piped up. "Once my sister gets her land legs again, she'll be all right." It would be a tragedy if they were separated, and Celeste couldn't help but be grateful for the captain's kindness in the matter.

The man nodded and continued on down the dock, inspecting the other young women. But after a short time he returned to talk to the older man who kept the books, nodding toward Celeste and Berta as he did.

Spenser stepped toward the crate. He seemed to have adapted to land right away, no sea legs at all for him. A few minutes later he returned. "His name is Constable Wharton. He has a house up on the last street of the village."

"You'll tell Jonathan?"

"Yes, I promise. I'm sure he'll come to get you—both of you. You'll be in Williamsburg before you know it."

Celeste wanted to hug him, but instead she simply looked into his eyes and murmured a soft, "Thank you."

He smiled down at her and then at Berta. "God willing, I'll see you ladies again soon."

Berta managed a smile, and she whispered her own words of gratitude. The two shared a tender look until Constable Wharton directed Celeste and Berta to follow him. They shuffled along behind, trying to keep up. Both wore their cloaks, even though the day was growing hotter by the minute. Celeste hefted up her blanket and the meager belongings it held, missing the small chest she'd started out with, the one that had been stolen. Nervous, she released her sister for a moment and verified with a pat of her hand that the ring, brooch, and money were all secure in the pouch tucked between her petticoat and shift.

The walk along the wharf was a struggle, and they had to stop every few steps. Finally, they made it to the loading area, where the constable directed them toward a wagon.

Celeste had expected a carriage, considering the man's position. He certainly seemed wealthy. Perhaps he did have a carriage but just didn't want to use it for transporting servants.

Celeste was helping Berta up onto the bench when someone yelled, "Wait!"

She turned and squinted toward the wharf. Spenser waved. Another man, who looked as if he'd just rolled out of bed, was swaggering alongside. The constable also turned and looked, shading his eyes from the morning sun.

Celeste couldn't imagine what Spenser wanted. She hadn't forgotten anything.

"Is there a problem, Mr. Horn?" Constable Wharton asked as the men drew near.

"No," the older man replied. He had a tattered felt hat pulled over greasy dark hair, and he wore a wrinkled vest and an old pair of breeches, a small whip hanging from his belt. "But I'd like to talk with you about the young woman who speaks French."

The constable glanced at Celeste. "We both do," she said, although Berta, with her ear for sounds, spoke it best.

"Why wasn't I told?" Constable Wharton asked.

Celeste shrugged. "You didn't ask."

"I'm looking for a girl to help at Edwards's inn," Mr. Horn said. "His cook only speaks French, or so she pretends." He scowled. "Edwards needs to take her down a notch or two. He thinks he needs a translator."

"The ship's captain insisted that the girls stay together," Constable Wharton said.

Celeste nodded her head.

Spenser made eye contact with Celeste and said, "The inn is in Williamsburg."

"Who will get the money for the contract?" the constable asked. "Bancroft or me?"

"Why, you, sir," Mr. Horn answered.

The constable turned toward Celeste. "I can get another maid in a few weeks. My wife wanted two, but she'll be happy that whichever one of you who comes with me speaks French. She's been wanting a tutor."

"You should go," Berta whispered. "I'll stay here."

"No!" Celeste said. "I won't leave you."

"It's the prudent thing to do," Berta responded. "I can't bear the thought of getting back on the ship. Tell Jonathan to come get me as soon as he can." She coughed after she spoke and dragged a sleeve over her mouth.

"The innkeeper has allowed a fair sum of money. Most likely more than what you bought the contract for," Mr. Horn said. This time he smiled widely, showing tobacco-stained teeth. He seemed to be some sort of broker.

"I'll allow it," Constable Wharton said. "As long as the younger one really does speak French too."

Berta nodded. *"Oui."*

"We're both fluent," Celeste said. "Our parents are French. I'm sure my sister would be happy to give your wife lessons."

Constable Wharton turned toward Mr. Horn. "You have a deal. Deliver the payment when you return."

"Don't let Jonathan leave me here for long," Berta said, a little louder this time.

"Shh." Celeste hoped Constable Wharton hadn't heard. "We'll come back as soon as we can. I promise."

Berta pursed her lips.

"Go on. Get moving," Constable Wharton said to Celeste. "We don't want to waste the entire day."

She quickly told her sister goodbye and then jumped down from the wagon. Constable Wharton immediately snapped the reins, and the horse took off. Celeste jumped back, a sense of dread sweeping over her. It had always been her responsibility to protect Berta no matter how foolish her sister's actions were, but this time Celeste had been the foolish one.

Berta glanced over her shoulder, a look of despair on her face, as the wagon bounced over the cobblestones. She gave Celeste a halfhearted wave and then turned back toward the road ahead.

Celeste swallowed hard. It wouldn't do to cry. Not in front of Mr. Horn and Spenser. Berta had been grateful for Celeste's care while on the ship, but perhaps now that she was feeling better she would come to blame her sister for her plight. And rightly so. Celeste had led her on a devastating journey whether she had realized it at the time or not.

Mr. Horn started back toward the wharf, but Spenser waited with Celeste, and together they watched the wagon roll down the cobblestone street. It wasn't until it turned away from the bay that they began walking back to the ship.

Chapter Seven

Celeste

C eleste stood on the starboard side of the ship, staring at the thick trees that grew nearly down to the river's edge, shivering in her damp clothes even though the sun was high in the sky and the day was hot. She'd done her best to wash them once she reboarded, but she was still dirty—and now she was cold too.

The river was wide and muddy and slow. Thankfully, enough of a breeze blew that the sailors could catch the wind and propel the vessel upstream.

Creeks and marshes cut into the river, and occasionally a cleared field could be spotted, but mostly all Celeste could see were trees. She couldn't help but think of the Thames back home and the half a million people living along its banks. What a contrast that was to this wilderness.

Spenser stepped to her side. "Well? What do you think?"

"I grew up in London. I'm not used to living where there are so few people."

Spenser grinned. "You'll have to get used to it. There are fewer villages here than in West Kirby, where I come from."

"West Kirby?"

"On the River Dee, not far from Liverpool. My father moved there from Scotland before meeting and then marrying my mother."

"You said he was a carpenter?"

"Yes. As are my brothers and I." He paused a moment and then added, "My father was an educated man. He brought a small collection of books from Scotland and did his best to instruct us. About the Bible, of course, but also about plants and the stars and languages and such." He grinned. "My French was never any good, although my Latin isn't too bad."

Celeste laughed, thinking it had been the opposite for her. "Why didn't you stay in West Kirby?"

He shrugged. "My parents both died two years ago. When I heard a carpenter outside of Williamsburg was in need of an apprentice, I decided to take the position."

"But why? I mean, why leave home at all?"

He shrugged. "I'm the youngest of five boys. There wasn't enough business to support all of us. And I'm the most adventuresome. I've wanted to see the New World since I first heard about it. With me gone, that left more work for the rest of them."

So his choice to come to America had been based on logic and reason—a vast contrast to hers, which had been completely illogical and without reason, driven solely by love.

Spenser continued. "Matthew Carlisle, the man I'll be apprenticing under, runs a sawmill too. He also needs help with the machinery, and I've always wanted to learn more about that sort of operation."

Celeste nodded. Virginia might not have enough rags to make paper, but it certainly had enough trees for lumber.

"Was there no young woman for you back home?"

Spenser smiled again, leaning against the railing. His hazel eyes sparkled as he looked up at her. "No girl in her right mind would be interested in marrying a fifth son." He lowered his voice. "I'm hoping to keep that a secret now that I'm in Virginia."

"Perhaps that sort of thing doesn't matter here," Celeste whispered back.

Spenser laughed. "Maybe not. But I've heard that there are far more men than women, so perhaps this place has a different kind of competition."

Celeste agreed, relieved she wouldn't have to worry about such things.

"How long have you known your soldier?"

"Long enough," she replied. Her face grew warm even though she was chilled.

"Forgive me. I didn't mean to offend."

"You didn't. I'm tired, that's all. I met him last year." It had been mid-November when Jonathan first came to the inn. She'd only known him a couple of months, but it seemed like much longer. She'd never felt so alive with anyone before—or so sure that running off to marry him was the right thing to do. Until she discovered Berta on the ship.

Spenser didn't press her for more details, and when the captain approached, he stepped away.

"I see you found a means to get to Williamsburg after all." Captain Bancroft stopped with his hands behind his back.

She nodded.

"Good," he said. "I've been feeling horrible about your sister."

"We'll soon have it all sorted out."

Captain Bancroft bowed and then, before continuing on toward Mr. Horn, he added, "We'll dock in half an hour."

The two men spoke for a few minutes. Both seemed serious, but then the captain smiled and slapped the broker on the back. Mr. Horn simply nodded before returning his gaze to the forest as the captain left him.

Celeste also turned back toward the trees. A small stream bubbled into the river. A crane landed on the water. A fish jumped, even in the heat. She pondered what the forest might be hiding. Somewhere there were tobacco plantations. And native people.

Farther up the James there was a falls and then a Huguenot settlement, but they wouldn't go that far. She would become Anglican instead, like Jonathan, and leave her childhood faith behind. Difficult as that would be, it was part of embracing this New World.

Celeste was on the same ship that had carried her across the Atlantic, but this trip up the river with the freedom to remain on deck and so few aboard now seemed like a Sunday adventure compared to the crowded and stormy crossing of the ocean.

Except for the first few days on the ship, before she discovered Berta, this was the first time Celeste had been without family. Growing up, Berta had often embarrassed or frustrated Celeste with her antics. Spying a mouse during services and then climbing up on the bench while screaming. Flirting with George, as if he might be interested in her rather than her older sister. Faking illnesses so she could stay in bed daydreaming instead of doing her chores.

But there had also been times when Celeste lived vicariously through Berta. Except for Jonathan, Celeste had never had the audacity to speak with customers at the inn the way Berta did. Or ask questions of strangers. Or sing loudly during services. Celeste truly believed she should be seen but not heard, while Berta wanted to be seen *and* heard. Yet Celeste could be truly amused by her sister too, like the time they were at the market and Berta joined a visiting French singer in performing *airs de cour*.

Despite their differences, Celeste had always felt extremely loyal toward her sister, as if she should be able to guide her through an easier route in life—until Celeste decided to follow Jonathan. In so doing, she had unknowingly led Berta on a perilous journey that nearly killed her.

The *Royal Mary* rounded one last bend before anchoring in the river. The process of unloading the cargo from the ship to the small fleet of flat-bottomed boats took some time, and then the passengers transferred as well. Celeste settled down on a bench in the back of the last boat with Spenser and Mr. Horn. Soon they were being propelled by the incoming tide up a waterway called Archer's Hope Creek, according to Mr. Horn, while the pilot used a long pole to navigate. Once they reached the landing, Celeste could see a warehouse and then wagons hitched to oxen, waiting to be loaded. She assumed at least one was for carrying passengers, but maybe not because the others started walking. Clutching her bundle, she peered through the trees down the narrow road, looking for signs of the town.

"Get going," Mr. Horn said.

"We're walking?"

"Yep. It's not much more than a mile."

"Along a road?"

He snorted. "Some might call it that. The way's passable—the wagons manage to make it."

Obviously seeing her surprise and dismay, Spenser offered to carry her bundle. She declined. He had a small trunk and satchel of his own. She'd seen some of their contents on board, including paper and pens, a few books, and some herbs and salves.

She started walking, listening to Spenser ask Mr. Horn about himself as they went. He said he'd been born and raised in Jamestown but eventually moved to Norfolk, where more of the trading was done.

At first, by "trading" she thought he meant the term generally, as in goods and services. But as the conversation continued, she realized he was talking about the trading of *people*. Mr. Horn wasn't just a broker for indentured servants. He also brokered slaves. The realization turned her stomach. It was one thing for him to deal in indentured servants, who knew freedom was just a few years away, but an entirely different matter to buy and sell people's lives against their will, with no hope of freedom at all.

The road grew smaller until it wasn't much bigger than a trail. Broken shells covered parts of the soil, probably in an attempt to create a hard surface, but recent rain had turned the red soil into mud, and the shells had sunk into ruts dug by the wagon wheels. Celeste followed Spenser, regretting that she'd attempted to wash her clothes. The hem of her dress was soon caked with the claylike mud, while the heat was nearly unbearable. A hum of insects filled the forest around them, and mosquitoes stung at her neck and arms. The only blessing was that Berta hadn't come with them. The trek in the heat would have done her in.

Soon they reached a creek covered with two planks of lumber. Celeste tottered across one.

"Are there no decent roads in this wilderness?" she muttered when she reached the other side.

Laughter welled up behind her. Celeste didn't expend the energy to look back.

"There's a lot missing in this wilderness," Captain Bancroft said. "You'll soon forget all about the comforts of London." He laughed again. "Williamsburg is actually the hub of all the roads in Virginia, roads to nearby plantations and even across the peninsula to York. But you're right. What the colonists call roads we would call muddy trails back home."

Each time Celeste stopped to catch her breath, Spenser waited with her. One time she could see a shack through the woods and hear a pig grunting in a nearby pen. The property certainly wasn't a plantation.

The distance grew between Celeste and Spenser and the others, including Mr. Horn and Captain Bancroft. Celeste pushed herself to keep going, anxious to see Jonathan. Sweat dripped down the backs of her legs. She swatted at mosquitoes every few steps as she clutched her blanket bundle. After a while Spenser took her burden and carried it along with his own. She was grateful for that, and for her hat, which kept most of the sun from her face.

They had lost sight of the others when a wisp of smoke appeared above the trees. Celeste guessed it was from a home in the village. Soon the acrid scent of burning wood reached them. Then came the sight of more smoke, all rising above the trees. She guessed, by the lowering sun, that it would soon be time for supper.

Her stomach growled. They'd had no dinner to speak of on the ship, just hard biscuits and water.

Her thoughts drifted to Jonathan, who currently lived at the barracks. Their plan was for her to stay at the local inn until the wedding, after which they would rent a cottage.

The trail opened up to a wider street, but it was just as muddy. First there was a farm with a white house and several outbuildings on a hill. Then they passed the College of William and Mary, a large brick building, and soon after a church also made of brick. Next came what appeared to be a courthouse, with stocks and a pillory out front.

Most of the homes were small, but a few were stately. The village seemed to be well planned with wide streets and large lots, gardens, and even orchards. The rat-a-tat of a snare drum caught her attention. As they kept walking it grew louder. Spenser pointed left, to a wide, open area.

A group of soldiers marched on the green toward Captain Bancroft, Mr. Horn, and some sailors. She gasped and quickened her steps. Her heart raced at the thought of seeing Jonathan.

For this moment she'd crossed the Atlantic, sacrificing everything she'd ever known. Her heart pounded as she clutched at her skirts and pressed on, determined to appear as cheery as possible. She'd endured so much—but it would soon be over. She scanned the soldiers, who had stopped marching and were now standing at attention in the village square. She searched the crowd but couldn't find him as the commander dismissed the unit.

She approached Captain Bancroft, who was talking with a soldier.

"When will Lieutenant Gray return?" the captain asked.

"Soon," the officer answered. "He's on patrol to the south, toward the Carolinas."

"Ah," the captain said, glancing toward Celeste. "How unfortunate. There's a young lady here to see him."

Celeste curtsied. "I'm Miss Talbot."

"Major Cole," the officer answered. "How are you acquainted with the lieutenant?"

Celeste's mouth grew dry. Jonathan must not have told his superior about her—but then again, perhaps that wasn't how things were done here.

"I know him from London," she answered, aware that Spenser stood behind her. Her throat began to tighten, and she swallowed hard. She was exhausted, yes, but she would not shed any tears. Not now.

"I believe she's betrothed to the young lieutenant," Captain Bancroft explained.

Celeste doubted her face could grow any warmer than it already was, but she felt herself blush anyway. "Yes," she answered, "that's correct."

"Is that right?" The major crossed his arms. "Well, then, several of us are anxious for the lieutenant to return." He glanced at the soldiers who were near. A few chuckled. Celeste's face grew even warmer.

Major Cole nodded at Captain Bancroft in a knowing way, one Celeste guessed was probably a judgment of her. Jonathan would have to set everyone straight when he returned.

Mr. Horn took her elbow, more forcefully than he needed to. "Come along to the inn," he said. "The sooner you take over your duties, the better."

"Where will you be staying?" she asked Captain Bancroft. "I would like to send a letter back with you, to my—family." She nearly choked on the word.

"At the inn, where you'll be working. Have it to me by morning."

"Thank you." She looked at Spenser.

"God be with you," he said, his eyes concerned. He handed her the blanket bundle.

"And with you," she replied. "Thank you for everything. I don't know what we would have done without you."

He smiled. "I'll look for you when I come into town."

"I'd like that," she answered. He turned away and headed across the green, his small trunk balanced on his shoulder.

Mr. Horn nodded toward the street.

She followed him. Ahead, a sailor pushed a handcart filled with goods. They passed a smithy, where smoke—perhaps the same smoke she'd seen from the trail—rose into the sky. Next came several white houses trimmed with green paint, and then a cobbler shop and a dressmaker.

The village wasn't without amenities.

The street dipped down into a ravine and then back up to the inn, a long, two-story whitewashed building with gables and a sign hanging from the eaves. *The Publick House Inn.* Mr. Horn took her around to the back of the large lot, where she saw a garden, a small orchard, a few stables, some sheds, a privy, and a chicken coop. Two buildings stood about thirty paces from the back of the inn, and Celeste guessed they were the kitchen and the laundry, similar to her parents' property. Both needed to be far away enough that if they caught fire the inn itself wouldn't burn.

At the edge of the garden, grape vines spilled over a trellis. Raspberry bushes grew alongside a white picket fence. In front of the fence was a small, partially open hut with bundles of herbs hanging from the ceiling. On the other side of the fence was a bench. Several men were clustered there, smoking pipes and talking.

Mr. Horn nodded to the smallest shed that stood on a little knoll. "There's a spring here on the property. That's why the garden flourishes."

Celeste nodded. Her parents had a well on their property, but the hauling of water still took one of the servants a big part of the day.

"The kitchen is there." The man pointed to the building with the biggest chimney. "We'll find Mr. Edwards—the innkeeper—first."

The broker climbed the back steps to the inn. As he opened the door, a loud cheer exploded. "Sounds like some of the sailors are already here," he said.

Celeste followed him into a wide passageway, and then she peered through the doorway to the right into a dining room. Sailors, soldiers, and civilians crowded around rectangular tables. Celeste searched the crowd for Jonathan, hoping he'd returned sooner than expected, but she didn't see him. To the right was a long counter with a leather-bound ledger on it. Celeste knew such a book would be expensive in London, and she couldn't imagine how much it would cost in the New World.

Mr. Horn continued on to the next room, another dining room, where the tables were smaller and not as crowded. All the walls were whitewashed, as was the fireplace. It was a trick Celeste's parents had used too—the flames from the fire reflected off the white bricks, creating more light and cutting down on the need for candles. But on this hot night, the fire wasn't lit.

A man, perhaps a few years older than her father, served pewter plates of stew. He was short and plump and had a full head of white hair. The broker called out a hello. The man turned, frowned, and then put the last plate down. He ambled toward them, speaking to the broker. "Is Captain Bancroft on his way too?"

"Aye," the broker said. "With more sailors, I'm afraid."

"We'll do our best to feed them."

"How's that wretched cook doing?" Mr. Horn asked, shoving a hunk of bread in his mouth.

"Just fine."

Mr. Horn gestured toward Celeste. "Well, I got your translator like you wanted, but I'm telling you it won't solve your problems. That cook just needs to understand who the boss is."

Ignoring his comment, the man turned to Celeste. "You speak French?"

She nodded.

He seemed relieved. Then he said, "Forgive me. I'm Mr. Edwards."

Celeste bobbed a curtsy. "Miss Talbot. How do you do?"

He chuckled. "At the moment? Heartily glad to see you." He swiped his hands together. "We'll talk later." Quietly he added, "For now, go tell Cook to stop heaping so much food on each plate. I've tried to explain, but she can't seem to understand. As soon as she has more plates filled, bring them in."

Celeste nodded, glancing down at her muddy skirt.

Mr. Edwards shrugged. "No one cares what state your clothes are in. We'll fix that soon enough."

"The girl will need some supper first." Mr. Horn's thoughtfulness surprised Celeste.

"Of course," Mr. Edwards said. "How rude of me. Instruct Cook, eat, and then serve the food."

She wanted to ask him if he had paper and a quill she could use but decided now wasn't the best time. She wished she'd asked Spenser for some of his before they had parted ways.

Celeste gave the two men a brisk nod and then headed to the back door and down the steps. She crossed the yard to the kitchen building, but when she stepped inside she was blasted with heat. The back wall was completely covered by a brick fireplace, inside of which a fire crackled, heating the contents of two enormous black pots that hung above the flames, steam rising from them both.

Standing in front of the fireplace, dwarfed by its enormous size, was a small African woman, her hair wrapped in a thin, blue scarf.

"*Bonjour.*" Celeste placed her bundle on a chair and paused to look around. At least the room seemed functional and well stocked, with two separate worktables and plenty of baskets, plates, pots, and pans.

Sacks of food filled a row of side shelves. A steep staircase led to a loft, probably where the cook slept. Celeste couldn't imagine how hot it was up there.

She returned her attention to the woman, who wore an apron over a gray dress. Her brown eyes shone, but she didn't speak. Celeste introduced herself in French and proceeded to explain the innkeeper's directions.

The woman frowned but didn't reply.

"What is your name?" Celeste asked.

"Sary," she muttered, turning back to the fireplace and dishing up a bowl of stew from one of the pots. Celeste stepped close to take the bowl, nearly overcome by the heat.

She was fully aware of all it took to run an inn—a cook, kitchen maids, a scullery maid, housemaids, a laundress, gardeners, and stable boys, but the only one present at the moment was this one tiny woman.

Sary handed over a spoon and motioned for Celeste to sit at the table, so she settled in one of two chairs across from a hunk of raw meat. Only the very wealthy in England ate venison, but perhaps it was more common here in the New World. At her parents' inn, they served cold meat and bread and pudding in the evening, while a hot stew would have been served much earlier in the day.

Digging into the stew now, Celeste couldn't place the seasoning or the other ingredients—large yellow kernels and some sort of chunks of orange tubers. She held up her spoon and asked in French, "What are these?"

Sary shrugged. "American vegetables."

They were different than any vegetables Celeste had eaten before. There was one bite of meat in the mix—it was very good, and she longed for more. She quickly ate the rest of the stew as Sary took several loaves of bread from the brick oven at the end of the fireplace. Once Celeste finished her food, Sary started filling more plates with the stew. Celeste quickly told her not to dish up too much. Sary frowned and continued with her work, reducing the size of the servings somewhat. She nodded toward a tray and then the bread. Celeste placed the loaves on the tray. Sary added the plates of stew and nodded toward the inn.

"Go," she said, in English, placing Celeste's bowl in a wooden bucket on the other end of the table.

Passing through the back door with the tray took a moment of concentration, but Celeste managed it. She then delivered food and cleared tables. When she returned to the kitchen for more plates, she was glad to see that Sary did have help after all, including a servant girl who was now at the table washing the dishes, and an African man who was busily hauling water.

Later, back in the inn after everyone had been served, Mr. Edwards stopped Celeste in the passageway near the counter and asked her if she'd done this kind of work before.

"My parents own an inn near the Thames on the outskirts of London, toward Westminster."

"How long have they been in business?"

"Nearly twenty years."

Mr. Edwards raised his bushy eyebrows just as someone summoned him from the dining room. "I'll be right back. Rest a minute."

Relieved, Celeste plopped onto the chair next to the counter and tried to ignore her aching feet as she thought of home. Her parents had used family money to purchase the inn, and her father's parents had helped operate it until their deaths, living in the family quarters at the far end of the large building. A substantial staff was also employed, many who were Huguenot too.

The French were known for their good food, good wine, and hospitality. When it became clear the family wouldn't be able to open a printing press or paper mill in London as they had back in France, they decided that owning an inn would be the next best option. Maman had grown up in a stately manse in Lyon, where her grandmother had taught her how to manage a household. She applied all she knew to running the inn and learned more along the way. Because of the family's economic means and French nobility, they were considered gentry even though they were immigrants.

Mr. Edwards returned to the counter. "Are you educated, Miss Talbot?"

"Yes."

"I see," he said, even though he looked as if he didn't. A puzzled expression stayed on his face as he told her, "There should be a basket of food on the table in the kitchen. Please take it to the jail. We supply all of the meals there."

She stood. "Where is the jail, sir?"

"Northeast of here." He gestured to one side, saying, "Head in that direction. You'll find it."

Celeste felt unsettled about delivering anything to a jail. "To whom do I give the basket?"

"Constable Jones. Knock on the door to the house. He'll be waiting."

The last rays of light were disappearing behind her as Celeste hurried up the street, trying to keep the large basket steady. At the intersection, she crossed another street and spotted a small brick building with a courtyard beyond, surrounded by iron bars. Surely this was the jail. She hurried up the front steps, ready to knock, but the door swung open before she had a chance.

"You're late." A portly man with dark hair and sallow skin stood in front of her. He licked his lips as he took the basket. "Smells good. What is it?"

"Stew."

"Is that all?"

Celeste shrugged. "Bread too, perhaps."

He took the basket from her, pulled off the cloth to look inside, and frowned. "No bread, just stew," he huffed, tossing the cloth back over the top. "I sure hope Edwards gets that cook back in line. She's the best around when she wants to be."

Celeste didn't respond.

The man stepped back and closed the door.

As Celeste headed down the steps, a voice called out from the area of the courtyard, "Jones! Leave some supper for us. It's your duty to make sure we're fed."

She stopped by the gate and looked through the bars into the courtyard, where she saw the doors to two holding cells. She darted away quickly, shivering even though it was still muggy and hot, guessing that delivering meals to Constable Jones and the inmates at the jail would be part of her regular routine.

The sailors and soldiers became unruly as the hours wore on, and finally the innkeeper told Celeste to help Sary finish cleaning the kitchen.

"Then go to bed, up in the loft," he said. "I hope you don't mind sharing sleeping quarters with Sary."

"Of course not. My parents taught me that we are all one in Christ Jesus, as it says in Galatians."

With a look of relief, Mr. Edwards replied, "Good. I'm hoping Sary will warm up to you. The last maid didn't speak French, but they roomed together and seemed to get along, at least until…"

Celeste cocked her head, but the innkeeper didn't finish his thought. She changed the subject. "Could I write a letter to my parents tonight for Captain Bancroft to deliver?"

"Paper is expensive," the innkeeper said. "Perhaps the captain would deliver a verbal message."

She approached the captain in the dim light, but she could easily see that he was drunk. Changing her mind, she quickly retreated to the kitchen. An hour later, Celeste followed Sary up the stairs, carrying her bundle that she'd stashed next to some shelves in the kitchen. A breeze blew between two open windows, and the loft wasn't as hot as she'd feared. Sary immediately collapsed on her pallet. Celeste was too tired to talk anyway, but she was interested in Sary's story. Perhaps another night when they had energy enough to speak.

Celeste took off her skirt, stockings, chemise, and stays, then she pulled her pouch out from under her petticoat and tucked it below her pallet. She didn't think anyone would steal it, but she couldn't take a chance. It held everything she had of any value—the ring and brooch and a little money. She would tie it back around her waist in the morning.

She slipped out of her petticoat and collapsed onto the cot wearing only her shift. She'd never worked so hard in her life. Jonathan had to return soon.

CHAPTER EIGHT
Celeste

The swish of a skirt near her head woke Celeste. Sary headed for the ladder. A bird sang outside, and the first rays of light streamed through the open window. Surely they weren't required to rise at dawn after going to bed past midnight.

"Now?" Celeste asked in English and then quickly translated. *"Maintenant?"*

"Oui," Sary answered as her head disappeared.

Celeste stood slowly, thankful for the cool breeze. In the corner, on a crate, stood a pitcher and basin on a small table. Sary must have fetched the water already, or else someone else brought it up. Celeste washed her hands and face and dressed quickly. Then she wrapped the strings of the pouch around her waist, tying them tightly before tucking the pouch between her petticoat and shift. As she slipped her feet into her shoes, she realized they were falling apart after yesterday's walk. She had no money to replace them. Slowly she descended the ladder.

The fire had already been built up, and an African boy of about twelve poured water from a bucket into a pot, the one Celeste had cleaned stew from the night before. She introduced herself to the boy in English. He kept his head bowed but said his name was Benjamin. Sary picked up a bag filled with some sort of grain—it was yellow like the kernels from the night before.

In French, Celeste asked Sary if she had a piece of paper and a quill she could use. The woman shook her head. "What do you need?" the boy asked in English.

Celeste explained that she wanted to write home and then said, "I can pay a small amount if you can find me paper and ink." She fished a coin from her pouch and handed it to him.

"I'll be back." He took the bucket with him.

Sary stirred the grain into the water, and Celeste began placing bowls on the table to be filled. She couldn't imagine the sailors up so early. She hoped she would have time to write the letter and get it to Captain Bancroft before he left for his ship.

Sary took two teapots from the shelves. A few minutes later a bleary-eyed and unshaven Mr. Edwards entered the kitchen with two pitchers from the night before in his hands. "Good day to you," he said to both women. "The sailors are clamoring for food." He put the pitchers on the table and then looked directly at Celeste and then the porridge.

His face fell. "Why isn't Sary cooking eggs?"

Celeste asked the woman.

She shrugged and in French answered that there weren't enough, according to Benjamin. "The hens must be upset," she added as she started ladling porridge into bowls. Mr. Edwards appeared frustrated but didn't challenge the explanation.

He shuffled over to the spice cupboard by the shelves. He took out a key, unlocked the door, and removed a white canister, which Celeste guessed was tea. There were other canisters in the cupboard, probably for sugar and salt and other spices. There was also a medium-sized crock, which Celeste guessed was full of honey. Her parents kept tea, spices, and sweeteners in a locked cupboard too.

Mr. Edwards measured tea into each pot on the table, and then Sary dipped boiling water out of the cauldron and poured it into the pots. Once she was finished, she pushed them to the middle of the table to let them steep while Mr. Edwards returned the tea and relocked the cupboard. Then he wrapped a rag around the handles of each teapot, lifted them off the table, and left the kitchen. It seemed to be a ritual that was probably repeated every morning. Back home, they made the tea in the dining room.

Benjamin returned a few minutes later with the supplies she needed. The paper was crude and the ink was thick, but Celeste did her best to scratch out a letter. She simply wrote that she and Berta were both safe and she was sorry for acting out of character, but she loved Jonathan and planned to make a life with him. She didn't have time to explain about Berta, how she'd been abducted and forced aboard against her will, so for now she would just have to let her parents assume that the two girls had fled together. She would add more details in the next letter.

At the bottom, she signed her name. To add "Your loving daughter" above that seemed incongruous. She put aside her quill and spread sand over the paper, let it rest, then dumped it into the fireplace. Next, she folded the paper, wrote her father's full name followed by the words *London Gazette* on the front and repeated the process with a little more sand. After the ink had dried, she lit a candle and sealed the paper as best she could by pressing a spoon into the dripping wax.

Celeste tucked the letter into the waistband of her skirt, grabbed a tray, loaded the bowls, and headed out the door. She struggled to balance the tray as she climbed the stairs to the inn and then tilted it slightly to get through the door. Once inside, she looked for Captain Bancroft but couldn't find him. She passed out the bowls to the men around the table, many of whom already had a small cup of tea.

The second time Celeste entered with another tray of the porridge, Captain Bancroft was seated at the table with his first mate. Thankfully, Mr. Edwards was back in the kitchen. Celeste pulled out the letter. His eyes grew large. "My, you are resourceful, aren't you?"

"I try to be," she answered. "Remember, this is for Mr. Talbot at the *London Gazette*."

First Mate Hayes reached for the letter. "I can deliver it when I place the advertisement for our next voyage."

Celeste glanced at the captain. He shrugged. "Very well."

She surrendered the letter. The captain had so much to attend to. Hayes probably would have more time to make such a delivery. After offering her thanks and a curtsy, Celeste hurried back to the kitchen to retrieve yet another tray of food.

She had returned to the inn and was just about to go through the door when she heard a familiar voice.

She froze. *Jonathan?*

Juggling the tray awkwardly, she twisted to one side and peeked through the door, her heart filling with joy and relief as she spotted her beloved in his uniform. He looked as tall, handsome, and impressive as ever as he moved toward Captain Bancroft.

"I was afraid I'd miss you." The captain rose to shake Jonathan's hand. Lowering their voices, the two men began to converse, though Celeste could no longer hear their words.

As excited as she was to see Jonathan at last, she found herself faltering, stunned at how casually the two men were interacting.

They know each other?

She hesitated, confused, her mind racing. Why hadn't the captain said as much during one of their conversations? All those times she'd gone on about her betrothed, Lieutenant Jonathan Gray, never once had the captain said, "Oh, yes. I'm acquainted with the man. In fact, we're friends." Then again, knowing now what a small place Williamsburg was, it didn't surprise her that the two were acquainted.

Heart pounding, she moved through the doorway, the tray still in hand. But in her eagerness she stepped too quickly and tilted the tray too far to one side. Immediately, the bowls began sliding away from her. Coming fully into the room, she managed to right the tray—only to have the bowls slide in the other direction, toward her. Before she could do a thing, one slid right off and landed on her shoulder, splattering porridge all over her and the floor. Another bowl followed and another until the tray was empty.

Mortified, she didn't even glance Jonathan's way. Instead, she just fell to her knees and began gathering the bowls. By the time she stood, every eye in the room was on her.

"Foolish girl." Mr. Edwards's face had turned red, but his voice was surprisingly calm.

Swallowing her pride, Celeste glanced at Jonathan. His blue eyes were as vivid as ever, but his face had grown pale. "Celeste! What… what are you doing here?"

"Mr. Edwards bought my contract."

He opened his mouth, but no further words came out.

In that moment she wanted nothing more than to fall into his arms, but she knew it wouldn't be proper—not to mention that she was covered in porridge. Instead, she just gave him a meaningful look and tilted her head toward the side, as if to say, *Meet me out back, where we can share a proper greeting in private.*

But first she had to clean up the mess she'd made in the dining room. Moving as quickly as possible, she deposited the bowls and tray in the kitchen, grabbed a bucket of water and a rag, and then ran back toward the inn, brushing away clumps of porridge from her hair and clothes as she went.

By the time she got to the dining room, rag and bucket in hand, Jonathan was already gone. Panic rising in her throat, hoping he would know to wait, she worked as fast as she could, scrubbing furiously. Once she'd finished, she hurried out back, but he was nowhere to be seen. Confused, she flung the dirty water onto the ground and stepped around the side of the inn, looking out toward the street.

There he was, on the other side of the fence, near the bench.

Unfortunately, Captain Bancroft was with him, the two men deep in conversation. No doubt, the captain was explaining the situation with Berta.

Celeste placed her bucket and rag on the ground and hurried around the fence toward them.

As Jonathan turned, Captain Bancroft bowed. "Miss Talbot. Lieutenant Gray. I'll leave the two of you to speak in private."

Looking up into Jonathan's blue eyes, Celeste hoped for a kiss—even a hug. She needed some sign of his affection. She stepped closer, but he didn't reach for her. Or bend his head to kiss her. He wouldn't even meet her gaze.

"The captain explained what happened."

"Do you two know each other?" Celeste asked.

Jonathan's face reddened. "He introduced himself just this morning." He cleared his throat, still not meeting her eyes. "Did Berta say why she followed you onto the ship?"

Crestfallen, Celeste answered. "She didn't come of her own free will. She was abducted and forced aboard."

He exhaled. "Who would do such a thing?"

Celeste shook her head. "We have no idea. Once you buy our contracts, we can figure out a plan." She hoped Jonathan could settle things with Mr. Edwards immediately. She didn't want to have to endure another minute of servitude. Then, as soon as he did, they could head to Norfolk together and rescue her sister.

His face grew red. "About your contract...I wasn't able to save the money I'd planned to."

"I thought you already had the money." She couldn't be certain of his finances. At times it seemed his family had lost everything, but at others it seemed he had some funds tucked away.

"I had expenses..."

Mr. Edwards stepped around the side of the inn. "What's going on?" He seemed more confused than angry. "Miss Talbot. Why aren't you working?"

"We were discussing Lieutenant Gray's plan to buy my contract from you."

"Who said it's for sale?"

Celeste's hand went to her throat. Surely the man would allow it once Jonathan had the money. And she hoped that would be soon.

Mr. Edwards turned toward Jonathan. "You can afford to hire any maid for your new house. I don't know why you'd want this one. She's clumsy."

"Maid?" Celeste stuttered. "No, we're betrothed."

Mr. Edwards's eyes narrowed. He shook his head. "Miss Talbot," he said. "Please get back to work."

"Please, sir, with your permission, I need another moment." She turned quickly before Mr. Edwards could reply. "J-Jonathan," she stuttered. "Explain who I am to you—"

"Some complications have arisen." He kept his voice low. "We need to talk this through, Celeste, but not now."

She swallowed hard. "When can we talk?"

"Soon."

"Miss Talbot, I need you to finish serving breakfast." Mr. Edwards's voice was firm. "No matter what's going on between the two of you, I bought your indenture. You need to uphold your end of the bargain."

She knew he was right. She gave Jonathan one last look. He frowned and turned away. Her stomach fell. This wasn't the man who had vowed to love her forever. Who had begged her to follow him to America.

She stumbled off as Mr. Edwards demanded, "What did you promise the girl?"

Celeste stopped and turned, wanting to hear Jonathan's reply. But he didn't say a word. Instead, he simply left, marching toward the town square as the rat-a-tat of the snare drums started up again.

The beat heightened her anxiety. She swallowed, trying to calm herself even as her fears grew in intensity, along with the drumming.

Not until breakfast was finished and the crowd was gone did Mr. Edwards see to Celeste's clothing situation. He appeared at the kitchen proffering a skirt, chemise, cap, petticoat, shift, apron, and straw hat. They weren't new, but at least they were clean and pressed.

"After you change, go down to the cobbler and get fitted for a pair of boots," he said. "You'll need them by the time winter arrives. The shop is across from the square."

She bit her tongue to keep from responding that she wouldn't be in his service by then. Somehow Jonathan would find a way to make all of this right. He'd promised her on his life that he loved her and would care for her, always.

"Put your dirty clothes in the laundry house. The housemaid will get started on them soon."

She thanked Mr. Edwards and hurried up the ladder. Once she had completely stripped, she scrubbed herself as best she could with the lukewarm water. When she was dressed, her pouch tucked inside the clean petticoat, she carried the pile of dirty clothes to the laundry house and then headed down the street to the cobbler, hoping she would see Jonathan again.

None of the soldiers were in sight. Or the sailors. It seemed Captain Bancroft and his crew had returned to the *Royal Mary*. She prayed that Hayes would actually deliver her letter. A wave of grief swept over her at the thought of her family. How could she have decided so carelessly to leave them forever?

After the cobbler fitted her feet, she waited for a moment in the street, looking in every direction for Jonathan again. Dejected, she turned back toward the inn when someone called out her name.

She stopped.

"Celeste!" It wasn't Jonathan. It was Spenser in a wagon filled with furniture. Two horses pulled the load.

She waved and hurried toward him.

"I'm headed to the barracks," he said. "I thought I'd ask about Jonathan."

"I saw him this morning."

He leaned toward her as he grasped the reins. "He already bought your contract, then?"

Celeste wrinkled her nose. "We didn't have a chance to speak for long. We still need to sort things out."

"Oh, that's too bad. I thought the new clothes meant your new life had begun."

"These are just work clothes from Mr. Edwards." She looked down at her apron. They were the simplest she'd ever owned. "I'd better get back."

Spenser sat up straight. "It's good to see you."

She nodded in agreement and then bid him farewell. She moved quickly down the street, knowing Sary needed her help.

Once she arrived, Mr. Edwards instructed Celeste to tell Sary to fix the rest of the venison into another stew and make sure not to burn the bread. It took several minutes for Celeste to find Sary, who was in the drying shed, hanging fresh herbs.

When they returned to the kitchen, Sary told Celeste to chop the vegetables while she braised the meat. Then she tossed everything into a pot of broth. Benjamin came in with more water and filled the second pot on the fire while Sary stirred the stew. The savory smell made Celeste's stomach ache.

Sary cleared the table and soon the stable boy came in. Behind him was a housemaid, a young Irish woman who introduced herself as Aline. She was pretty, with auburn hair and lively brown eyes. After her came Benjamin and a man who was likely his father. Sary served them all, and then Mr. Edwards came in and said a blessing before everyone started to eat.

"Miss Talbot, you'll have your meal once your work is done," he said to Celeste before grabbing two pitchers and heading back to the inn.

Celeste followed him with plates of stew and the bread. A few businessmen sat at the tables, all speaking in respectful voices, a scene entirely different from the rowdiness of the night before.

An hour later, as she cleared the last of the dishes, the front door to the inn opened. Spenser stepped inside and motioned to her. Celeste glanced at Mr. Edwards, who was across the room, sitting at a table with two other men. He sighed but then nodded his head.

"Sorry," Spenser said. "I debated whether to tell you this or not, but when I delivered the furniture to the barracks I asked the supply officer about Lieutenant Gray."

Celeste pursed her lips together.

Spenser whispered. "Should I continue? I won't if you don't want me to."

"No, you should," she said, even though her first instinct was to cover her ears with her hands and run away.

"I have no way of knowing whether this information is accurate or not," Spenser said, "but the supply officer told me Lieutenant Gray has been courting a young woman in the area."

Celeste felt as if she'd just fallen overboard the *Royal Mary*. "Courting?" she managed to sputter.

Spenser nodded, the expression on his face pained. He reached out to steady her. "But like I said, I don't know that it's true." She nodded again at his muffled words, her ears stopped with fear.

Spenser continued. "Perhaps when you see Jonathan, you can ask him about the—"

"No need to ask the lieutenant," Mr. Edwards interrupted, standing near them now. "It's true."

"Who is she?" Celeste leaned her hand against the wall to steady herself.

"Ask him yourself," Mr. Edwards said. "But I've seen him with a young woman plenty of times. That's why he bought the carriage."

Celeste gasped. Had he spent the money he'd saved on that? She managed to thank Spenser and assure him he'd done the right thing to tell her. "I'd better get back to work," she added.

Mr. Edwards nodded, and Spenser slipped out the door. Perhaps Jonathan had already been given the land grant and that was the reason for the carriage. Perhaps he was only being kind to the other young woman. That's what she tried to tell herself as she scrubbed the dishes in the unbearably hot kitchen, sweat dripping down her cheeks like tears.

Chapter Nine

Maddee

"Well, look at that. You're alive after all," Nana said as she opened her front door on Saturday morning. Her face was pinched, and I realized she was peeved with me.

I glanced at my watch. "I'm not late. We said between ten and eleven."

"I'm talking about yesterday, Madeline."

Uh-oh. Full name and everything.

With a huff, she turned and crossed the solarium to the living room, where she sat in her usual chair and returned to what she'd obviously been doing when I arrived, going through Nicole's medications and getting them organized into a travel case.

And today had started out so well, my heart light despite the burden I was about to take on, my soul filled with purpose and a sense that this was God's plan for me to care for my sister. I wasn't going into this blindly, and I knew there would be at least some drama ahead, but I hadn't expected it to come right away—and especially not from my grandmother. What was going on?

"I assume your appointment went well?" Nana asked through tight lips. "With Dr. Hill?"

Ah. Of course. The hunky doctor.

"So it *was* a setup," I replied, crossing my arms. "I thought so. Shouldn't *I* be the one who's put out with *you*? After all, you did ambush me."

She bristled. "I would hardly call that an ambush. I was trying to do you a favor. Obviously, you didn't see it that way or else you would have called afterward like you promised you would."

I sighed heavily, telling myself Nana wasn't really mad about this. She was worried and probably sad and even a little hurt about Nicole leaving. She had to find somewhere to direct all that emotion, so she'd turned a minor irritation with me into a major event.

"You're right, Nana," I said, stepping into the room. "I'm sorry. I should have called. Honestly, with all I've had going on, it just slipped my mind. But I do apologize."

"Well…thank you," she said, mollified. "I only wanted to hear from you because I was excited to know what you thought of him."

I took the seat to her left. "I understand. But the next time you set me up, how about a little warning first? I rode my bike there, and by the time I got to his office, I was an absolute mess. I doubt I made much of an impression."

She waved off that thought with a flip of her hand. "I'm sure you're wrong there. I have no doubt he was quite taken with you. I assume it was mutual?"

I shrugged. "He's certainly one of the most handsome men I've ever seen, but we weren't together all that long. I don't know anything about him."

"I do. His mother and I have worked together on a number of charity events, and he's all she can talk about. He sounds like a wonderful young man, and he's from a very fine, very old Virginia family."

"Oh. Well, then. Let's ring out the wedding bells."

She gave me a sharp glance but softened a bit when she saw my smile and realized I was teasing.

"He's one of the top orthopedic surgeons in the country, and I'm the one who arranged for him to do your sister's operation. That's when I got the idea about matching up the two of you."

"So you set up some bogus appointment, hoping it would spark a love affair?"

"Don't be sarcastic, Madeline. The two of you have a lot in common. You're both churchgoers, in the medical field, high achievers, well educated, from good families…" Her voice trailed off, and then she hesitated for a moment before adding, "I probably shouldn't tell you this, but according to his mother he has, quote, reached that age where he's ready to find someone and settle down, but he wants lots of children and has yet to meet a woman with similar ideals."

I swallowed hard. "Lots of children?"

She nodded. "Now are you interested?"

I smiled. "I wasn't *not* interested before, Nana. I found him very appealing, very attractive. But I highly doubt it was mutual."

She looked at me, her eyes narrowing. "You're not that gawky teen anymore, you know. You have to remember that. Trust me, Maddee, you are every bit as beautiful as he is handsome."

Heat rushed to my cheeks. True, there was a big difference between the ugly duckling inside my head and the swan I saw in the mirror each day, but no way was I in his league. The reigning Miss America was barely in his league.

"You think I'm exaggerating?" she asked, sensing my skepticism.

"I think you're biased," I replied, leaning forward to give her a peck on the cheek. "But I love you. And I do appreciate your trying." I rose, clapped my hands together, and added, "Now how about we get this show on the road so I can take my sister off your hands?"

With so many elements to tend to, it took more than two hours to make that happen. First came a lesson from Inez about the proper way to get Nicole in and out of the bed, the wheelchair, the bathroom, and the car. At my home Inez would be coming only on weekdays, and only while I was at work. The burden of Nicole's care would fall to me on evenings and weekends, so that meant learning to do these things correctly lest I end up hurting her or myself in the process.

Next came a lesson on tending to her various other needs, such as icing her ribs and elevating her legs. Throughout it all, Nicole was cooperative but quiet, though I couldn't tell if that was because she was tired and in pain or because she resented being treated like such an invalid. Either way, we managed to get through it. Then, as Nana and I sat in the living room and went through the medications, upcoming appointments, medical info, and more, Inez finished gathering up Nicole's things and loading them into my car.

At last we were ready to transfer the patient herself. As I returned to the study and took in the sight of her, my heart lurched. In the middle of that ridiculously large bed she looked so tiny and helpless, her arms frail and thin as they hung at her sides, her face sunken from all the weight she'd lost.

"I think, at long last, we're ready," I said.

Her face lit up for the first time all day. With a glance behind me, she lowered her voice. "You're really breaking me out of this joint?"

"Sure am."

"Not a minute too soon." She pushed herself up from the mattress, looking as if she could leap from the bed and take off running through sheer force of will.

Of course, Nana fussed over Nicole all the way down the front walk as I rolled her wheelchair to my car, saying how she'd hired a transport van for the move but that Nicole had insisted on her canceling it.

"I'm tired of being some weirdo, coddled patient. I just wanted a nice, normal ride in a car with my sister."

Nana clucked her tongue, but I came to Nicole's defense. "You can't blame her for feeling that way," I said lightly. "Besides, I could use the practice getting her in and out of the passenger seat."

With both of her legs in casts, we soon realized she wouldn't fit in the front and would have to ride in the back instead. Inez did the lifting and lowering, setting her down and carefully sliding her across the seat until both legs were in. As I stood watching, it startled me how small Nicole had gotten. The medium-sized T-shirt I'd bought her after the accident now hung on her like a poncho, and the waistband of her shorts couldn't hide the sharp pair of hipbones underneath.

"She's so thin," I whispered to Nana, alarmed, but she assured me that though Nicole had barely eaten at first, her appetite had been coming back a little more each day.

Inez tucked pillows behind Nicole and then stood up straight beside the car, the doors closed but the windows down, her face red with exertion as she caught her breath.

"See?" Nicole called from her bizarre perch on the backseat. "Just a nice, normal ride in a car with my sister."

I laughed, though Nana did not.

"Don't forget the wheelchair," she directed, even though Inez was already rolling it around to the trunk. "And her fan. Inez, did you remember the fan?"

"No, I forgot," she replied easily as she worked. "I'll get it in a sec."

Turning to me, Nana explained, "Your sister has night sweats sometimes because of the pain. The fan helps."

I could see how difficult this was for our grandmother, her eyes almost desperate, her hands working furiously at a wad of tissue. Impulsively, I reached out and wrapped my arms around her in a big hug. She didn't resist, and I could feel her weight relaxing against me as I patted her back and assured her that Nicole was going to be just fine.

"Please don't worry." We pulled apart. "I think this is going to be a very good thing for both of us."

"I do too," she said, dabbing at her eyes with the tissue. Myriad emotions shone on her face, everything from concern to fear to relief. "It's just hard for a lot of reasons."

"I know." I waited as she pulled herself together.

"I'd like to visit weekly. How do Saturday mornings sound to you? I could stop in after Bible study."

"That sounds great, Nana. I'll put it on the schedule."

With a brisk nod, she took my arm and walked me slowly toward the front of the car.

"I found the letters I told you about. The sisters' names were Celeste and Berta. I'll have copies made this week and bring them with me when I come next Saturday."

"I'd *love* that." I stopped at the door and pulled out my keys. "I'm sure Nicole would too."

"Would too what?" Nicole asked, tilting her head to look up at us from inside the car.

"Maddee can tell you about it while you're driving." Nana looked from me to Nicole, an odd expression on her face, as if she had more to say. But then she seemed to let it go. Turning, she simply leaned in through the back window and planted a kiss on Nicole's forehead, a sweet and surprisingly tender gesture from a woman who rarely initiated physical affection.

"You'll both be in my prayers," she said, giving me a smile and a pat on the arm. And though I detected a catch in her voice, she managed to hold herself together.

Inez had come back out from the house and was putting the fan in the trunk. She slammed the lid and then gave me a thumbs-up.

"I'll see you two on Monday," she said to me before taking Nana's arm and leading her out of the way.

"Wait, one more thing," Nana called out just as I started up the car and put it into gear.

"Enough already," Nicole muttered under her breath from behind me.

"What's that, Nana?" I replied sweetly through the open window even as I discreetly slid a hand back and gave my sister a pinch.

"I've hired a very special physical therapist to do Nicole's home visits. He'll be starting on Monday."

I hesitated, assuming that by "special" she meant obscenely expensive and used by all the right people. Either that, or he was another drop-dead-gorgeous option for marriage and multiple procreation. I was about to ask for clarification when I felt a sharp pain at my elbow and realized I was being pinched in return.

"Just go!" she hissed.

"Sounds great. Talk to you later," I called to our grandmother.

We started off at last, the two of them watching and waving as we headed down the long, winding driveway. All was quiet inside the car until we pulled onto the road, at which point Nicole let out a whoop of joy from behind me, so loud it hurt my ears.

"I'm free! I'm free! I don't believe it! I'm free!" She pounded against the back of my seat for emphasis.

"Okay, okay. Cool it with the fists. Trying to drive here."

"Sorry. I'm just…it's not that I'm not grateful to her. I am. But there aren't words. You have no idea." She let out another whoop, only this one ended in a long, drawn-out exhale. Poor thing. I smiled, pleased I could be the source of such happiness and relief.

When I'd thought of this trip, I had pictured us chatting all the way home, but now with me in the front and her directly behind, it was hard to carry on much of a conversation. I told her what Nana had said about bringing over the letters, but after that our words grew less frequent until eventually we were silent, and that was fine. We would have plenty of time for talking in the days and weeks to come. She'd grown so quiet, I had a feeling she'd fallen asleep on me anyway. After such a crazy morning, she was probably exhausted.

Settling back in my seat, I took in the view of the James River as we crossed the bridge. Something about the silence in the car felt deeply pleasing to me, as though I were a busy mom after a long shopping trip with a toddler who conked out in the car seat on the way home. It wasn't just a restful silence but a *protective* one, my charge tucked in safely behind me and everything right with the world.

Fifteen minutes later, I was turning onto Monument Avenue when I heard a dinging sound, followed by a *zip* and a *bonk* and then a burst of applause. It wasn't a ringtone I remembered having installed, but I reached for my phone just the same, trying to catch it before it woke up my sister.

Only my phone wasn't there. Startled, I twisted around to take a look, and there sat Nicole with my phone in her hands, head bent in concentration, fingers busy on the screen.

She was playing some kind of game. On my phone.

"Where did you get that?" I asked, tilting the rearview mirror so I could see her face.

"From your purse," she responded, not bothering to look up. Another dinging noise, followed by a casino-like jingle.

"My purse?"

"Yeah. And by the way, you really should turn on password protection. You never know when someone might take your phone."

She continued on with her game, not even hearing the irony of her own words. Unbelievable.

"Nicole," I said, trying to keep my voice even, "what did I say to you about respecting my things? I wasn't kidding with all that."

"I know you weren't."

"And yet here you are, playing on *my* phone. What part of respect do you not understand?"

"Oh, come on, Maddee. Do you know how badly I miss my apps? It's just a game—"

"Games, calls, texts, whatever. You could be surfing the Internet trying to buy me a brand-new set of color-coded organizational binders, but it wouldn't make a difference to me. If you try to use my purse, phone, laptop, tablet—*whatever*—without asking first, I'm taking you straight back to Nana's, no questions asked."

"What? Why?"

"Because you're not respecting my boundaries, and I can't have that." I sucked in a breath and counted to ten. Maybe I was overreacting, but her action had really startled me. Was this how it was going to be? Her violating my space, my privacy, my things, and then acting as if I was the one with the problem?

"Fine," she huffed. "No phones, tablets, laptops, PalmPilots, Walkmans, Gameboys, beepers, fax machines—."

"You think the sarcasm is helping?"

She grunted. "Fine," she said again, this time handing the phone to me over the seat. "I promise I'll be good. Just please don't make me go back there."

"I'm not making you do anything," I reminded her. "Actions have consequences, Nicole. *Your* actions. How this plays out is entirely up to you."

I glanced at her in the rearview mirror, but she was looking off in the distance. After a long moment, she spoke.

"I can't go back there, Maddee. I didn't say anything to you before, but it wasn't just Nana getting on my nerves. It was the nightmares. They've always been worse at her place, you know that, but they were nearly unbearable this time."

I studied my sister, considering her words. If she was telling the truth, then I didn't blame her for needing to leave. She had struggled with horrific nightmares for years, ever since that day at the cabin in the woods. On the other hand, she was smart enough and manipulative enough to know that this was exactly the sort of tidbit that could get to me in a way that nothing else could. Her dreams had tormented me throughout my childhood too, one more thing I couldn't protect her from. She knew how I felt and was probably using this now to try and get me to soften the rules simply out of compassion and guilt.

Whether she was playing me or not, I could practically feel the tightrope under my feet, that delicate balance between wanting to trust her and knowing I had to protect myself at every turn.

"Just…respect my things. Please. I don't want to take you back there any more than you want to go."

She didn't respond, and the silence hung heavy between us as I took the roundabout onto Franklin Street. We were nearly home, and the last thing I wanted was for us to start off on the wrong foot.

"Sorry to be so harsh," I said finally. "But if you recall, it is on record that I'm a big meanie."

She grunted, but I could hear the hint of a chuckle. "I'm sorry too. I won't touch your phone again without asking."

"Thank you."

"You're welcome." After a long moment, she added, "You know you want that color-coded organizational binder set, though."

Chapter Ten

Maddee

"You live *here?*" Nicole asked as I put the car in park and turned off the ignition.

I'd found us a spot directly in front of a gorgeous, three-story Georgian house with thick white pillars, a decorative pediment, and a row of dormers across the top.

"No, but I'm allowed to park here," I replied, relieved we'd gotten something so close to home. Sometimes the best I could do was a couple of blocks away. "We're right around the corner."

I climbed out, popped the trunk, grabbed and unfolded the wheelchair, and then opened the car door to lean inside, holding my arms out toward my sister.

Nicole and I gripped each other's wrists, Red Rover-style, and then I pulled, gently scooting her toward me across the seat. As I did, her two brightly colored casts shot out on either side of my legs like twin cannons rolling into place along a parapet. When she was as far as she could go, we released our grip and I got into a different position, managing to lift, pivot, and lower, transferring her successfully from car to wheelchair.

"Man, that's exhausting," I said, trying to catch my breath as I raised her legs and set them onto the elevated leg rests. "I don't know how Inez does this all day long."

"Yeah, well, try it with two cracked ribs and then tell me about it," Nicole replied, her voice strained. She smiled as she said it, but I could see she was hurting.

Fortunately, the curbs along here were low, so once I'd retrieved my bag and locked the car, it was easy to get her up onto the sidewalk—except that my purse kept sliding down my arm as I pushed the chair.

"Want me to hold that for you?" she asked as it slid down yet again.

"Thanks," I said, lowering it onto her lap.

"No, thank *you*," she replied. "I'm thinking if you look the other way, between here and your place I could probably score a couple quarters, a tube of lip gloss, and a breath mint."

"Don't push it, Peanut," I replied, surprised at how easily the old pet name tripped off my tongue. The two of us had lived such separate lives for so long, and yet now that she was sober again, it was almost as if the old Nicole was back.

Despite her pain, she was looking all around as I pushed her down the sidewalk, taking in everything like a prisoner fresh out of lockup. Even if she hadn't been so confined of late, this neighborhood was a truly beautiful part of Richmond, its streets lined with historic homes, their graceful exteriors painted in shades of vibrant yellow, sage green, or navy blue. There were doors and shutters of reds and purples and whites. Some yards had small pumpkin patches, their succulent vines curling around picket fences and spilling out onto the brick sidewalk. Others had lush pots of chrysanthemums lining their front steps, the fiery flowers bursting with life.

When we came to the corner, I paused for a moment to take in the stately redbrick home across the street—Miss Vida's sprawling colonial with its wraparound porch and intricate stained glass windows.

"And here we are," I said.

"Get *out*! You told me it was super small."

"Yeah, this isn't it," I said with a chuckle. "That is." Leaning forward, I pointed toward the carriage house tucked behind, peeking out like

a shy toddler from the back of her mother's legs. Size-wise, the structure was almost embarrassing, but what it lacked in space, it made up
for in style.

"It's adorable," Nicole said diplomatically as I pushed her closer.

"Well, it's little, but it's home."

Once inside, though there wasn't much to see, I gave her a quick
tour, starting with the kitchen and then the bathroom.

"My room's up there," I said, gesturing toward the stairs. "And this
is where you'll be staying."

With a flourish I pulled aside the privacy curtain to reveal the living room, all set up and ready for its new inhabitant.

"This is for me?" she asked, taking in the bed with its crisp, powder
blue linens and lacy white coverlet, the plant stand I'd draped with a
small tablecloth and pulled into service as a bedside table. Atop that
was a small vase of yellow daisies and a wicker basket filled with things
I thought she might enjoy—magazines, a deck of cards, some candy
bars. There was also a coloring book and crayons, and I was about to
make a joke about that when I looked down and realized she had tears
in her eyes. She brushed them away sheepishly.

"Sorry. I cry a lot these days. Probably has to do with not being high
all the time. Forces you to feel things, you know?"

"Yeah, I get that," I said, surprised at her admission. I knew that for
her to even say such a thing was a positive sign.

"Speaking of drugs," she added, "what time is it?"

I took in her pale face and hunched posture and realized her meager pain meds had worn off. As a recovering addict, the strongest thing
she could take for all of her injuries was prescription-strength ibuprofen, but at least that was better than nothing. She needed to eat something first, though, so I rolled her over to the table and pulled from the
fridge the lunch I'd already prepared for her. It was one of her old favor-
ites, ham on rye with mustard, and a side of potato salad

"Oh, Maddee, that's so sweet. But I'm just not hungry."

"Sorry, kid. You can't take the pills on an empty stomach. Try to eat
as much as you can while I unload the car. Then you can have your
medicine and shift over into the bed for a while."

"That would be nice. I'm wiped."

It took three trips to bring everything in, but by the time I was done, my sister had managed to polish off half the sandwich and a fair amount of the potato salad.

From the travel case Nana prepared, I pulled out the bottle of ibuprofen and then watched as Nicole's trembling fingers plucked the little tablets from my palm. She swallowed them down, tipping her head backward, eyes closed, as if willing the feeble medication to work faster and stronger. I looked away, not wanting her to see the distress on my face. On the one hand, I wanted more than anything for her to stay sober, even if it meant suffering now. On the other, I couldn't stand seeing her in this kind of pain.

We managed to get her into the bed, but it took such an effort that she just lay there, breathing heavily, sweat dripping from her hairline.

"It's hard," she said between gasps, "even the little things."

Without thinking, I brushed the hair from her face. She didn't push my hand away. Instead, she closed her eyes.

"We'll unpack your stuff later," I said softly. "You just rest for now."

"Okay," she mumbled.

By the time I slid her privacy curtain back into place and took one last peek, she was already sound asleep.

After eating my own lunch and giving Nana a quick call to let her know we'd made it and all was well, I spent the next three hours upstairs in organizational heaven. I'd bought a new whiteboard and a pack of dry erase markers, which I used to draw a calendar. Then I filled in our schedule for the next few weeks, including my work hours, Inez's visits, Nicole's doctor and physical therapy appointments, and so on. With that as the framework, next I slotted in her NA and Celebrate Recovery meetings, grateful that there was so much to choose from in the Richmond area. Between me and Inez, we should be able to get her to one or the other every single day.

Later that afternoon, once Nicole was awake, I showed her my masterpiece of scheduling. She burst into laughter.

"Aw, man! Some things never change. You're giving me flashbacks, Maddee. Wow."

"Excuse me, but this was a lot of hard work."

"I'm sure it was," she replied, still laughing. "And I appreciate it."

"Uh-huh."

"But, wow. It's just so…you."

"So me?"

She wiped at her eyes. "Yeah. Like, remember our Barbie beauty parlor? I was happy just washing the dolls' hair and stuff, but you had to create a tiny little appointment book for the front desk—and then you got mad if any of the dolls showed up late."

"Yeah, yeah."

"Or how about when we decided to set up a classroom for our Polly Pockets? You insisted on keeping attendance records. You made topic outlines." Another peal of laughter. "You even handed out report cards!"

"Hey," I said, trying not to sound offended. "Can I help it if that was my idea of a good time?"

She tried to wind it down, wiping at her eyes as the last few chuckles bubbled from her throat. "It hurts to laugh, but I just can't help it," she said, arms wrapped around her rib cage, holding it tight.

"Well, laugh all you want," I replied, retrieving the hammer and a stud finder from a kitchen drawer. "You could use some structure in your life."

She didn't respond, and as I found a stud, hammered in the nail, and hung the board up the wall, I realized my comment may have come out sounding harsh. When I was finished, I turned to look back at Nicole, but she didn't seem hurt, just contemplative.

"You're right about that," she said. "Guess I'm as unstructured as they come."

"Yeah, and I guess I do tend to go too far in the other direction." I gave her a wink. "Maybe between the two of us we can strike the right balance."

"Maybe," she replied. After a beat, she added, "Just don't alphabetize my toiletries, okay?"

~

The rest of the afternoon went smoothly, a wonderful mix of chatting and reminiscing and just hanging out. I pinned back the curtain so she could keep me company from the bed while I made our dinner, and at one point she mused that she could probably start helping with the preparation once she recovered from today's activity.

"I couldn't stand there and do dishes," she said, "but if I'm in the chair I could roll up to the table and chop vegetables."

"That would be great," I replied with a smile. "I've always wanted a sous chef."

Once supper was ready, she ate better than expected, polishing off almost a full plate of spaghetti and a wide slice of garlic bread. Afterward, we finished unpacking her things, ending with a small but brand-new Louis Vuitton suitcase.

"Nana strikes again?" I asked, holding it up.

Nicole grinned. "I know, right? Wait until you see what's in there."

I turned it on its side, unzipped the cover, and then began pulling out the contents one item at a time, astounded at the shopping choices Nana had made for her granddaughter. Two satin bed jackets with elaborate lace trim. A velvet robe, monogrammed in gold thread with Nicole's initials. Three pairs of old-lady slippers, all stiff, scratchy, and terribly expensive. She hadn't done as bad with two regular outfits, though I couldn't imagine Nicole wearing either. My sister was a jeans and T-shirts girl, but these were really nice tops and slacks. I recognized one as a Stella McCartney, a silk crepe de chine blouse that had surely cost a fortune. Too bad it was size 2, petite, or I would have gladly traded for it.

Once everything was folded and put away, I felt kind of bad that we'd made fun of our grandmother that way, especially considering how generous she'd been in buying these things. Maybe it had been worth it as a team-building exercise, bonding us together in the face of a common enemy.

"What about your own things from your apartment in Norfolk?" I asked as I tucked the empty suitcase under the bed.

Nicole shrugged. "Nana sent one of the maids over there last week to get all my stuff and close it out. I didn't care. No reason to pay rent on a dump I'm not even using."

"But where is everything?" I asked, ignoring the dump remark, though I'd seen the place and knew the term was accurate.

She shrugged. "The apartment came furnished, so I didn't have that much. Just one or two boxes, but I ended up throwing most of it away." She looked pensive for a moment, and then she added sheepishly, "You know, anything of value got sold off a long time ago. Like, who needs a lamp when you can trade it for weed?"

A lump in my throat, I turned and busied myself with adding water to the flowers.

After such a pleasant afternoon and evening, getting Nicole ready for bed that night was a sobering experience. She was just so incredibly thin, so terribly injured. I actually had tears in my eyes while giving her a sponge bath. At least I managed to hide them, and I pulled myself together once she was dressed and tucked in. As I refilled her water glass and set it on the little table, she quickly drifted off to sleep, her chest rising and falling in a peaceful rhythm.

Lowering myself into the wheelchair beside the bed, I watched her. One of her small arms poked out from between the sheets. I took her hand in my own and held it, surprised to find how cold it was despite the red flush on her cheeks.

All I could do was be here for her. And pray. Closing my eyes, I prayed for her health and her heart and her sobriety. I prayed for myself too, for patience and wisdom and the right words at the right times. Then I laid her hand back at her side, pulled the covers more tightly around her, and slowly headed up to bed.

The next morning, Miss Vida surprised me by knocking on the door and offering to stay with Nicole so I could go to church. And though at first I declined the offer, she was so persistent—and Nicole seemed willing enough—that I decided to take her up on it. It was a beautiful day, and I knew I'd love nothing more than to slip away for an hour or so and recharge my spiritual batteries.

By the time the service had ended, I was feeling refreshed, rejuvenated, and ready to jump back into the Nicole situation with vim and vigor. My church was only a ten-minute walk from home, and I was just starting back when I heard someone call my name. I turned around to see a man walking toward me from across the street.

"Maddee? Hi, it's me."

The encounter was so out of context that it took me a moment to realize that this tall, handsome man coming my way was Dr. Austin Hill. Today he was resplendent in a dark tailored suit with a gray shirt and navy tie. I wasn't quite so done up, but at least I wasn't a disheveled mess this time. I'd worn one of my favorite dresses, a simple maroon sheath, with a gold cuff bracelet and a pair of black suede pumps. Self-consciously, I wet my lips and ran a hand over my hair.

"Dr. Hill," I said when he reached me, trying not to sound as confused as I felt.

"Sorry. I didn't mean to throw you. I was just coming out of church when I spotted you and thought I'd say hello."

"Church? Here?" I asked, gesturing to the glass-fronted, contemporary building behind me. The place was pretty big, but I couldn't imagine why I hadn't seen him inside.

"No, over there," he replied, turning and pointing to a far more traditional church up the street, its twin Gothic Revival spires protruding into the brilliant blue sky. Well-dressed parishioners were filing out from the doors, some gathering in clusters on the sidewalk to chat.

"It's so good to see you." The way his eyes lingered on mine, I almost believed him.

"Back atcha," I blurted out, and then I immediately blushed, mortified. *Back atcha? Where had that come from?*

"So, you go here?" he asked, ignoring my idiocy and gesturing toward my church building.

I nodded.

"Huh. Talk about ships passing in the night. We've probably crossed paths before and don't even remember it."

Oh, I would remember, I thought but didn't say. Nothing about this man was forgettable.

We shared what might have been an awkward silence except that it wasn't awkward. Our eyes locked and held for a long moment, and for some reason words didn't seem necessary.

"Anyway, now that we've run into each other," he said, placing a hand on my arm, "may I take you to lunch?"

"No," I said more quickly than I had intended. "I mean, I can't. Not today. I have to get back to Nicole. She moved in with me yesterday."

"Oh. Sure. Another time, then." He removed his hand and stepped back. "Mind if I call you?"

"Call me what?" I retorted, trying to be funny but once again just sounding like an idiot.

At least he had the decency to smile. "On the phone. For a date."

"Ah," I replied, feeling the heat burning at my cheeks. "Sure. That would be great."

"Super." With that, he turned to go.

So did I. Grinning broadly, I headed in the opposite direction. My heart pounded all the way home—but not from the exertion of walking.

Chapter Eleven
Celeste

Celeste worked with Sary in an exhausted fog for the next couple of days, trying to distract herself from thinking about Jonathan. He hadn't come back into the inn, although other soldiers had. Spenser hadn't returned either.

Besides giving her orders and telling her to translate instructions to Sary, Mr. Edwards didn't talk much with her. A couple of times he opened his mouth as if to say something, but then he would just shake his head and walk away.

Sary didn't talk much either, certainly not in English but also barely in French. When she did speak, Celeste had to concentrate on understanding her accent, which was so different from Maman's. But Sary didn't seem to have any trouble understanding Celeste.

Several times a day, Sary checked her herbs in the drying hut. Celeste was sure they didn't need that much attention and soon discerned that it was a place of comfort for the woman. Probably a chance to collect her thoughts, be alone, and escape the chaos and heat of the kitchen. Mr. Edwards had mentioned that Sary had been very particular about where the shed was placed. Clearly it was important to her.

113

All of their interactions had to do with cooking until Celeste's third night above the kitchen, curled up on the pallet on the floor. Grief overcame her as she thought about Berta. Her entire life she'd cared for her younger sister and brothers. True, Berta had been the most challenging sibling, questioning everything over and over, but Celeste had always looked out for her sister. Until now.

Celeste bowed her head, intending to beg for God's protection over her sister, but no prayer came. Instead, she turned toward the wall and choked down her sobs as best she could. Exhausted, alone, and desperate to know why Jonathan hadn't kept his promise, she gave in to her tears. A couple of times Sary flopped over on her pallet and cleared her throat. Celeste tucked her head under her blanket to hide her crying.

The next morning, Sary motioned toward the pitcher and basin.

"Merci," Celeste answered.

As she washed, Sary stood near the ladder but didn't descend the stairs. She asked in French if Celeste missed home.

"Oui."

Sary nodded and climbed down the ladder. When Celeste joined her a few minutes later, the woman pointed to a piece of bread and jam. "For you," she said in English. "Then see to the chickens."

Celeste nodded. She'd fed the chickens the last few days and gathered the eggs. She enjoyed leaving the kitchen and going to the coop.

When she returned with the eggs, encouraged by Sary's kindness, she asked in French how long she'd been a cook.

"My entire life," she said, explaining that her mother was a cook on a large plantation in the West Indies. "I wasn't fit for the big house, so my mother kept me by her side. I grew up in that kitchen. My sister served in the house, though."

"How old are you now?" Celeste asked.

Sary shrugged. "I'm not sure. Maybe twenty-five."

"Do you have children?"

Sary's face grew slack and she turned away.

"I'm sorry…"

Sary waved her hand as if it didn't matter, but Celeste could tell it did. The woman began cracking eggs into a pan. Sometimes she hummed while she worked, but not today.

After they finished cleaning up the dinner things, the gardener brought in a large basket of small cucumbers. Sary sighed. Celeste guessed they needed to make pickles.

"Go get the master," Sary said in French, probably needing him to unlock the spice cupboard for the salt.

Later, Celeste went out to the garden to see if there were more cucumbers to fill the small barrel Sary was using to make the pickles. The midsummer garden was far ahead of where the garden back home would be. Bush beans grew up a trellis. Cabbage and broccoli flourished, along with squash, parsnips, and greens. Tall stalks of what she'd been told was corn grew along the far end. She filled the basket with cucumbers and then stood, straightened her back, and wiped her brow with her apron as Mr. Edwards marched past to the chicken coop and then stopped. He turned back, saying he needed her to go down to the blacksmith to pick up an order.

Celeste put her hand on the small of her back, not used to the labor she'd been doing. "All right."

"Take the handcart. It's behind the chicken coop."

Celeste followed him, put the basket in the cart, and then pushed it around the coop. As she did, she heard Mr. Edwards talking to the gardener about manure. The garden was one of the best in the village that she'd seen, and Celeste could tell a lot of work went in to it. Every morning Benjamin and his father hauled water from the well to the orchard and garden for several hours. Their hard work paid off. Farmers brought meat, milk and cream, and some produce to the inn, but Mr. Edwards did well with what he grew on his own property.

Celeste left the cucumbers in the kitchen with Sary and told her she would return soon. By the time she reached the blacksmith shop, sweat dripped from her face. July had to be the worst of the hot weather, surely. She maneuvered the cart down the narrow pathway to the back of the smithy. Open shutters let in the air, but the heat was even worse than in the kitchen at the inn. An open brick furnace stood in the middle of the building, and a young boy operated billows, blowing air onto the fire. Two blacksmiths were working. The younger one, most likely an apprentice, asked what she needed.

"Mr. Edwards's order," she said.

As the younger man left the fire and turned toward a workbench, Celeste heard the older one ask if he'd finished the piece for Lieutenant Gray. Her head snapped up.

"Yes," he answered. "He said he'd pick it up this afternoon."

"Did he say when?" Celeste asked the young man as he approached her with a large iron pot.

He squinted at her. "What are you asking?"

"Did Lieutenant Gray say when he would stop by? I've been hoping to speak with him."

He handed over the pot, which was heavy. "Who are you?"

"Miss Talbot. I know the lieutenant from back in England."

"Aren't you Mr. Edwards's new kitchen maid?"

"For the time being."

The man raised his eyebrows. "I heard he bought your contract."

Celeste's face grew warm. Williamsburg was a small place. It wasn't surprising everyone knew her business.

"For the time being," she answered again, barely adding a mumbled "Thank you" as she wheeled the cart away. Humiliation warmed every inch of her skin.

She had a difficult time pushing it down the narrow pathway toward the street and put all of her weight into it, only to topple it over, the pot clattering onto the hard earth. She quickly righted the cart and wrestled the pot back in, dropping it the last few inches. Thankfully, Mr. Edwards wasn't nearby to see how she treated his property. Tears stung her eyes. Essentially, she was his property too, at least for the time being.

Once she reached the street, the cart moved more smoothly, and she forced her sad thoughts away.

Ahead, a group of soldiers stood in the middle of the street. One, with his back to her, had blond hair. Celeste pushed the cart faster.

As she approached, another soldier elbowed the blond. He turned.

It was Jonathan.

He quickly stepped away toward the cobbler's shop.

"Jonathan! Wait!" Celeste called out.

The soldiers began to laugh. "You're a rascal!" one of them yelled.

Celeste was beginning to agree.

"Please stop," she begged, overcome with embarrassment at airing her problems in public.

He turned slowly. "I only have a minute."

She pushed the cart to his side. Out of breath, she said, "I've heard rumors…that you've bought a carriage and…you've been courting someone else."

"I'd given up on your coming, Celeste. You said you'd be on the next ship—I thought you'd changed your mind."

"The next ship was full. I took passage on the one after that, but we hit rough weather and were delayed." He'd begged her to come. Couldn't he have waited a few more months? "So it's…true…" she stammered.

He shrugged.

"Courting another?" the soldier said. "I thought you were to marry Miss Mary Vines soon, Gray."

Jonathan frowned and stepped closer to Celeste. "I need to explain things to you. Her father owns a plantation between here and York. He's giving me land."

"What about your land grant?"

He sighed. "That was part of the problem. There's been a delay, and it could be a few years. If I'm ever going to acquire land in my family's name, I'll have to marry for it."

"What am I to do?" Celeste asked, despair coursing through her. "And now I have my sister to care for too. I only left Berta because I was sure that if I could only get to you, you would help us."

He kept his eyes on her. "I feel horrible about all of this, Celeste, but please understand how difficult this is for me too. I did wait, but after some time it seemed your promise to come hadn't meant any-thing. That was when I began seeing Miss Vine…" His voice trailed off.

"I came as soon as I could!" Yes, it was some months after they'd planned, but it wasn't that long. "Jonathan, how…how could you do this to me?"

"Believe me, I wouldn't have if I'd had any idea you were on your way."

He reached for her hand. She let him take it. His skin was warm against hers, reassuring for just a moment, but then it only reminded her of everything she'd lost. His love, most of all.

She pulled her hand away, afraid she might collapse in the middle of the street. "What now?"

"I'll try to sell the carriage to pay for your contract."

That was honorable, at least.

"And then?"

His eyes fell beyond her. "That's it. I don't have anything to offer you. No land. No future."

"All of that doesn't matter." Celeste felt a measure of hope. "I came to be with *you*. To be your wife. We could survive in a cottage if we needed to—"

He shook his head. "It's not that simple. I can't support a family on my soldier's pay. You deserve more."

Her heart fell again, and her knees nearly buckled.

"Celeste, I never intended for this to happen. You have to understand—"

She let go of the cart again, and the pot clattered to the ground, landing on a rock. As she struggled to get it back in, Jonathan bent down to help her. "I'm so sorry," he said, his watery blue eyes meeting hers. "Can you ever forgive me?"

She let go of her side of the pot and stood quickly, ashamed that she still had feelings for him. She grabbed the handle of the cart as he settled the pot inside it.

He met her gaze. "Please, Celeste. I care too much about you to think you'll be angry with me the rest of your life. Doesn't your faith require forgiveness of you?"

She frowned. It wasn't as if she'd been practicing her faith much since she'd met him. But he was right. She'd been taught to forgive as God had forgiven her.

She swallowed hard and then said, "Yes, I forgive you." But the words brought her no comfort. Just saying them started a flood of tears she couldn't stop.

Not wanting to make a fool of herself, she pushed forward with the cart, causing the other soldiers to scatter. She continued down the street, weaving from side to side, her sight bleary behind her tears. Jonathan didn't follow.

She stopped a moment and wiped her eyes before continuing on. She hoped he'd keep his word and buy her contract, and then she would do her best to buy Berta's with the ruby ring. But she had no idea what they would do next. They had no money to get back home—and no guarantee Berta would survive the trip even if they did.

"There's not much of a market for carriages around here, I'm afraid," one of the soldiers said loudly. "He won't get what he paid for it."

Celeste didn't look back or respond in any way. The less she said, the better.

She'd been jilted. It was as simple as that. And it hadn't ruined just her life but Berta's too.

Before Jonathan, she would have prayed for guidance. But now she couldn't. Had she prayed at all since she met him that day in her parents' garden? She couldn't recall doing so. She'd been so set on pleasing him, on attaining what she wanted. She'd recited prayers she knew, but she hadn't prayed directly to the Lord, hadn't asked for His help.

And now she didn't feel as if she could, not after what she'd done. The thought of her sister, all alone in Norfolk, made her sick. So did the thought of both of them in Norfolk, with no means of support. But at least they would have each other. No matter what had happened with Jonathan, she had to get back to Berta.

As Celeste served ham slices and corn bread to a room full of soldiers that evening, she couldn't help but notice that Jonathan wasn't among them. Was he off courting the plantation owner's daughter? *Miss Mary Vines.* Celeste felt a wave of anger toward the woman. But then she sighed. None of this was her fault. She wouldn't hold a grudge against her. Perhaps Celeste wasn't able to pray, but she needed to do all she could not to make her situation even worse.

Her thoughts returned to Jonathan. It was raining. Had his precious carriage become stuck in the mud?

She chided herself again. Bitterness toward Jonathan wouldn't help either.

She concentrated on her work as best she could. In the first dining room, several important-looking men sat around one of three tables. Celeste recognized Constable Jones from the jail, shoveling bluefish in a cream sauce into his mouth. He didn't acknowledge her. Then again, she'd seen him an hour earlier when she delivered the evening meal. She imagined he'd shoveled that into his mouth too.

Everyone, including Mr. Edwards, seemed to think that Sary's cooking was better since Celeste arrived. A variety of meals were coming out of the kitchen, all delicious. Business had picked up because of it. Celeste wasn't sure Sary would consider Celeste a friend, but it seemed she was trusting her more and more. For her part, Celeste was grateful for Sary's presence in her life. She'd gained some measure of comfort in spending so much time with the woman.

The diners were discussing a new slave code and how it would impact the need for indentured servants. They all seemed to defer to the man at the head of the table, who wore a long, dark wig and appeared to be not much older than her father.

"We'll definitely see a decrease in the number of indentured servants," the man said. Celeste wanted to listen to the rest of the answer, but just then Mr. Edwards motioned to her from the door.

Once she was in the passageway, he whispered, "Tell Sary to finish up the bread pudding. The governor is looking forward to it."

"The governor?" Celeste glanced back into the room. "The one with the black wig?"

Mr. Edwards nodded. "Who else would it be?"

Celeste shrugged. She'd guessed he was a businessman but hadn't suspected the governor. Papa, with all of his curiosity in the way the world worked, would be interested to know she'd served the man.

When she reached the kitchen, the Irish housemaid, Aline, sat at the table sipping cider. After relaying the instructions to Sary, Celeste asked Aline about the governor.

"Francis Nicholson is his name. I hear he has a temper." She lowered her voice. "And he's had his struggles with some. The old families and that sort of thing, so they say." Aline took another sip and changed the subject, saying how busy she'd been that afternoon. "But it's been a good day. Every day here is the best of my life."

"How is that?" Celeste asked.

She held up her empty mug. "I'm not starving. Or dying of thirst. Believe me, a full stomach makes for a happy girl." Aline was thin, but she did look healthy. "Having Mr. Edwards buy my contract was the best thing that ever happened to me. He's like the father I never had."

Celeste pondered that. Obviously, she could have done so much worse too when it came to a master.

A half hour later, while she served the pudding, the governor commented that she must be new to the inn.

"Yes, sir." She slid a pewter plate onto the table in front of him.

"And how are you liking Williamsburg?"

"Very well, thank you." She knew to keep her answers short.

He looked up, meeting her eyes. "Where do you hail from?"

"London, sir."

He cocked his head. "And what brought you to serving in this inn?"

"My parents own an inn, sir. I know the business." That was the shortest answer she could come up with, considering her circumstances.

"Are you not an indentured servant?"

She served the man next to him as she spoke. "Yes, I am." The governor seemed kind, but she didn't want to share any more of her humiliating story.

After they finished their bread pudding, Celeste wished Governor Nicholson a good evening, and then he and his guests left the inn. Unfortunately, the soldiers stayed, growing rowdier as the evening wore on. Finally, Mr. Edwards sent Celeste to the safety of the kitchen. She admired that about the man—he seemed to take her well-being into account.

As she washed the plates and Sary scrubbed the pots, the thought of Jonathan's betrayal ate away at Celeste. By the time she reached her bed, sadness overwhelmed her again. She still loved him. If he came to the inn tomorrow and said he had made a big mistake, that he loved her and wanted to marry her, she would forgive him everything. Out of habit she knelt beside her pallet as if to pray, but again no words came. Instead, tears flooded her eyes. She tried to stop them for Sary's sake, but the sobs kept coming. In the darkness, Sary sighed and asked her what was wrong.

Celeste explained briefly about Jonathan, finishing with his promise to sell the carriage.

"Don't believe that he'll help you. He needs the carriage to look wealthy enough for the landowner's daughter."

"He said he would—"

Sary sighed again. "And what else has he promised?"

Celeste began crying again.

"At least you came here by choice," Sary muttered before flopping over onto her other side. Soon her breathing changed.

Celeste stayed awake, knowing she'd offended Sary, who had probably been forced away from her entire family with no choice. Celeste had stepped onto the ship under her own free will.

Her situation wasn't nearly as helpless as Sary's, regardless of whether Jonathan sold the carriage or not. Of course it wasn't. Her indenture was only for four years—and at least she had some rights within that arrangement. Enslaved people, on the other hand, had no rights at all and were condemned to their fate forever.

Nevertheless, in this moment, four years felt nearly the same as forever. She simply had to get some help. She knew there were Huguenots north of Williamsburg. Perhaps some lived in the village too.

She would think about Sary's predicament later. Right now she needed to focus on finding help to free Berta.

Chapter Twelve
Celeste

"Are there others in Williamsburg who speak French?" Celeste asked Mr. Edwards the next morning as she cleared the last table. Except for two old men in the corner, the breakfast crowd had left.

"A few. Why? Are you wondering why I didn't just hire one of them to be my translator?"

"No," she answered, but his question did make her curious. "Why didn't you?"

"I needed a new kitchen maid for one thing. So I thought I might as well get someone who spoke French to make things easier with Sary. She's the best cook I've ever had." He paused for a moment.

"What's wrong?"

"I don't mean to speak ill of the dead," he said in a softer voice. "Benjamin's mother was the cook before Sary."

"What happened to her?"

"She died of a fever just before Christmas last year." Somber, he paused for a moment and then added, "Mr. Horn leased Sary to me

123

after that. I didn't want to have to give her up just because she doesn't speak English."

"What? You lease her?"

He nodded. "Mr. Horn owns her. But I needed a cook."

Celeste wasn't sure how to respond, realizing the assumption that she'd made. But it was no wonder she'd thought that, considering the others he owned. As she finished loading her tray, she said, "I was asking about anyone who might speak French because I'm in a bit of a predicament. As you know, I followed Lieutenant Gray here from my home in London."

Mr. Edwards nodded.

"But things haven't..."

"Turned out the way you expected?"

"Yes." She went on to tell him about leaving Berta in Norfolk to come to Williamsburg, thinking that Jonathan would buy her contract and then help her rescue Berta.

Mr. Edwards ran his hand through his white hair. "And now he won't help?"

"He said he'd try to sell his carriage to buy my freedom."

"Did he, now?"

"He did, but I'm not sure he'll be able to. That's why I asked about any French-speaking people in the area. My family is Huguenot—French Protestant."

Mr. Edwards nodded. "There's a group up the river past the falls. At a place called Manakin Towne. It's on the edge of the frontier. Quite a primitive area."

Celeste nodded. "I've heard about that group. I'm wondering if any of them could help us."

Mr. Edwards shook his head. "I doubt it. Some lost all they had when one of their ships sank on the river a few years ago. Many haven't figured out a livelihood yet, although I heard some have started growing tobacco. Most are living in huts." He began to wipe down a table. "Many have left for Carolina, although not all." He moved to the next table. "As far as the French around here, they worship as Anglicans with the rest of us."

"Of course. I'm guessing all of them would."

"Yes. But the ones at Manakin Towne are allowed to speak French in their services, even though the church is Anglican."

Celeste's heart skipped a beat. The congregation her family worshipped with back in England had been allowed to speak French—and stay Calvinists.

He picked up the rag and leaned against the table. "Now, down in Carolina, in Charles Town, the Huguenots are still allowed to have their own church."

Celeste found that appealing, but it was much too far away to do her any good. "Perhaps you could tell me who speaks French in the village. They might be of some help to me."

Mr. Edwards stood up straight, and he seemed to be putting some thought into his answer. After a long pause he said, "Those two men in the corner do."

"Really?"

"Yes. Take a moment and talk with them, but then get back to work."

"Thank you!" Celeste said to Mr. Edwards with a smile, and then *"Bonjour,"* as she approached the men. Each was reading an old copy of the *London Gazette*. It seemed the paper was shipped over for the colonists to read. She swallowed hard as she thought of her father. He'd most likely helped print that very copy.

She cleared her throat and said, *"Je m'appelle Mademoiselle Talbot."*

The first man, who was nearly bald, introduced himself as Monsieur Martin. The other, with thick gray hair and lively brown eyes, introduced himself as Monsieur Petit.

Celeste switched to English, not wanting Mr. Edwards to become suspicious of what she might be saying, and explained what had happened to her and Berta, leaving out the part about Jonathan jilting her. They would probably hear about that soon enough if they hadn't already.

"I'm hoping there might be someone who would be kind enough to help me figure out a way to relocate my sister to Williamsburg, or at least closer. Perhaps you or someone you know could buy her contract so she could relocate. Do you know of anyone? Around here? Or up at Manakin Towne?" At least there Berta would be with other Huguenots.

The two men glanced at each other. Then Monsieur Petit said, "I think the Frenchmen there are struggling to get by and probably not in a position to help."

"How about around here?" Celeste's face grew warm with the humiliation of having to beg.

The two men looked at each other again. Monsieur Martin turned to her and said, "We'll ask around. Perhaps our wives might have an idea or two."

Celeste thanked them and then hurried out the back door to the kitchen, avoiding eye contact with Mr. Edwards, feeling shamed that she'd had to ask for help at all. A wave of grief washed over her. She'd been such a fool to leave the safety of her family for the New World.

Neither of the Frenchmen came back into the inn over the next few days. "They usually come in regularly," Mr. Edwards said the fourth day. "What did you say to scare them away?"

Celeste insisted that she hadn't said anything to offend them, but maybe she had. Perhaps they felt obligated to help when they couldn't—or didn't want to. Perhaps they were avoiding her. Or perhaps there was simply nothing they could do.

Day by day, Celeste and Sary established a working rhythm. Sary rose first, then Celeste. By the time they descended the stairs, Benjamin had the fire stoked. Sary started the food and Celeste took over making the tea. Most days they worked silently, but bit by bit Sary shared a little more of her story. She was born in the West Indies and raised on a plantation. Her master died two years before and left a lot of debts. To settle what he owed, the oldest son sold Sary along with several other slaves, and she ended up on a ship to Virginia. Celeste had heard that cooks were the most valued of those who were enslaved and demanded a high price.

Celeste appreciated hearing more about Sary's life in the West Indies—the spices they used for cooking, the beautiful turquoise sea ever-present in the distance, and more. One day Sary had a faraway look in her eyes and said, "It was my life. My home. All that remained was taken from me in one horrible day."

When she didn't elaborate, Celeste talked some about her own life in England and her family and then the voyage to America with Berta. Sary listened intently, nodding a few times as if she empathized. It wasn't until one evening when Celeste finished sharing a story about her youngest brother that she realized Sary, even though she teared up while listening to Celeste, had never mentioned any family other than the brief mention of her mother and sister. She never spoke of a husband or children. Not a word.

Before each meal was served in the inn, the staff gathered in the kitchen to eat. Mr. Edwards always said a blessing and then the others ate while Sary and Celeste dished up for the patrons waiting in the inn for their food. Little by little, Celeste was learning about the other staff. Benjamin's father, Joe, doted on his son. Aline had worked in the kitchen sometimes before Celeste arrived, but she preferred her other duties. She would often try to chat with Celeste, but there was no time in the kitchen. One morning, however, as Celeste hurried to the drying hut with orders from Sary to collect sprigs of rosemary, Aline stepped out of the laundry. She asked how Celeste was getting on with the cook.

"Very well."

"She despised me when she first arrived," Aline said. "I couldn't do anything right."

"Really?" Celeste couldn't imagine Sary treating anyone badly. With silence maybe, but not with hate.

"I may not have been very welcoming, though. We were all in mourning."

"Oh?"

"Cook had just died."

Celeste nodded. She knew about that.

"And Miss Annabelle."

"Miss Annabelle?"

"Surely you've heard of her."

Celeste shook her head.

"Mr. Edwards's daughter. She was the reason he came to Virginia. She was married to a major here, but he died up north. She opened the inn, and Mr. Edwards came with financing and to help her."

"Oh," Celeste managed to say again. She'd had no idea.

"Mr. Edwards is a widower. Miss Annabelle was his whole world. So, you can see, we were all out of sorts when Sary arrived. And with her not speaking English or anything, and she'd been injured too—which Mr. Edwards didn't realize at first—it was all very difficult."

"No doubt," Celeste said, wondering what had happened to Sary. She held up her empty basket. "I need to get to the drying hut."

"Wait," Aline said. "That's not the only tragedy we've had. The kitchen maid right before you—"

"Good morning." Mr. Edwards stood on the back stoop, a mug in his hand.

Both girls returned the greeting, and then Aline stepped into the laundry while Celeste bobbed a curtsy and headed on to the hut.

The next morning, Mr. Horn came to the inn dripping wet from a summer downpour soaking the village. Steam rose off him as he took a seat. Celeste overheard him say he'd come from Norfolk again and had then been at the Vines's plantation, delivering several new field hands. She wondered how far it was to the plantation, how far Jonathan traveled to see his betrothed.

"How is your kitchen maid working out?" Mr. Horn asked over the din of the conversations and the clanking of metal spoons against pewter plates.

Mr. Edwards simply answered, "Very well." The communication with Sary had gotten better with Celeste translating, and that meant that the meals were coming out of the kitchen faster and with portions more to Mr. Edward's liking. Everyone seemed happier.

"And the cook? She still acting uppity, or did you take care of that?"

Celeste wondered what it was about Sary that irritated Mr. Horn. He'd leased Sary to Mr. Edwards. What did he care how she acted now?

That was between her and Mr. Edwards—and he didn't seem to have problems with Sary's work performance or her attitude, not anymore.

"Everything's fine," Mr. Edwards said, busying himself with setting the table.

"These indentured girls are getting harder to find," Mr. Horn told him over the clanging of the crowd. "The constable in Norfolk is looking for a maid again."

Celeste gasped.

Mr. Edwards gave her a harsh look, probably for eavesdropping. She continued on with her work, but when Mr. Edwards stepped into the other room, she approached Mr. Horn. "Why is the constable looking for another maid?"

"The last one died."

"No!" Celeste placed her hand on the table to steady herself. "That's where my sister went, remember? Surely it wasn't her."

The man looked up, an expression of annoyance on his face. "She was ill, right?"

Celeste nodded.

Mr. Horn sighed. "I hope he doesn't expect a refund. Or a discount on the next girl I find. But he probably will."

Celeste struggled to breathe. Mr. Horn didn't seem to notice.

She stumbled away from the table, broken by the news and the man's callous disregard for her sister's life. She never should have left Berta in Norfolk. Obviously, she was much worse than Celeste had realized. It hadn't been just seasickness.

Where had Berta been buried? Who had cared for her in the end? Had she suffered terribly?

Mr. Horn must have told Mr. Edwards about Berta's death, because later, when all of the patrons had left, he approached Celeste and said, "I'm sorry for your troubles."

"Thank you."

"It really is a shame…" Mr. Edwards ran his hand through his thick white hair. The wrinkles around his eyes seemed extra deep.

Celeste nodded. He knew grief too. "I'd like to go talk to Constable

Wharton," Celeste said. "To find out how my sister died and where she's buried. I promise I'll come back." She had nowhere else to go.

Mr. Edwards shook his head. "I can't allow that. Besides, you can't travel by yourself."

"I know someone who might be able to go with me."

"Not Jonathan."

She shook her head. "Spenser Rawling. He works for the carpenter, just outside of the village. He has proven to be a good friend."

"How would you pay for the boat ride?"

"I have a small amount of money. Enough to get us there," Celeste answered, looking him in the eye. "But I was hoping I could borrow some from you for the return trip." She had no idea how she would reimburse him except to sell the ring.

"That's what I was afraid of." He pursed his lips together.

"You can add what I owe to my contract. I'll work longer to pay it off if I can't come up with another means."

When he didn't respond, Celeste continued stacking dirty plates into a basket. When it was full, she headed toward the passageway.

Mr. Edwards cleared his throat from the desk in the foyer. Without looking up, he said, "I know what it's like to lose someone I loved. Ask this young man, Mr. Rawling, if he can go with you. If he can, head straight to the landing. The boat Horn came on is scheduled to leave this afternoon. Just make sure to give Sary her instructions before you leave." He went on to tell her what he wanted done for the next few meals. "Aline can help serve while you're gone. Oh, and pick up your boots at the cobblers." He glanced down at her pathetic slippers. "You'll need them in this mud." Then he said, "Wait here just a moment." He retreated to the small room he used as an office and then returned, holding out his hand. "Here's the money for the passage. Pay me back when you can, even if it's in four or five years."

"Thank you," Celeste said, curtsying slightly as she balanced the tray, her heart filled with gratitude. Once again, Mr. Edwards had shown he was a kind man at heart.

Celeste went straight to the cobbler's. The boots fit perfectly, and gratitude toward Mr. Edwards swept through her. When she got back to the kitchen, Benjamin and Sary were washing dishes, so she quickly carried her tattered shoes up to the loft and then came back down.

She spoke to Sary first, in French, explaining Mr. Edwards's instructions and about her plans to be gone for a couple of days. She repeated what she said to Benjamin, in English, adding that he would need to deliver the meals to the jail while she was gone. Then she asked, "Can you tell me how to get to the carpenter's shop?"

He offered to show her, but she refused, saying he needed to stay and help Sary instead. He seemed disappointed but explained where the shop was, outside of the village, down a trail just wide enough for a wagon.

Celeste followed Benjamin's directions, heading to Botetourt Street and toward the beat of the snare drums. It seemed the soldiers were constantly drilling. As she passed by, she scanned the group marching toward their tents, but didn't see Jonathan. When she reached the creek, she followed along the bank to the east. The road was narrow, and branches from the catalpa trees hung low, ready to tug at her straw hat. Cattails grew in the marshy area on either side of the creek, and every once in a while a fish jumped. Celeste slapped at the mosquitoes that buzzed around her as she walked, holding her skirt above the mud. Finally, alone, she let her tears come. Their mother had told Celeste and Berta, from the time they were little girls, how blessed they were to have each other. Maman hadn't had a sister, but she'd had a cousin—Amelie—who had been as close as any sister ever could be. But then Amelie had died, leaving behind a baby girl, right before Maman and Papa had fled to England from their beloved France.

Even with Maman's urging, Celeste hadn't always appreciated her sister or their friendship. Berta claimed Celeste was bossy and unfair. Celeste felt Berta was impulsive and unwise, not to mention lazy. True, there had been times of affection and camaraderie between them, but not nearly enough. Why hadn't Celeste valued her sister more?

And now, just like Amelie, Berta had died. Celeste stopped a moment under a tree with star-shaped leaves and wiped her face on her apron. It wouldn't do any good to be a babbling fool when she asked Spenser for his help. Once she reached the meadow, she followed Benjamin's instruction to veer to the left, along the creek. Ahead was the sawmill. She quickened her steps, hoping Spenser wasn't out making a delivery.

CHAPTER THIRTEEN
Celeste

Celeste pushed open the heavy door of the carpentry shop and stepped inside, breathing in the comforting scent of sawn wood that hung in the air. The workroom was full of unfinished furniture—tables, chairs, bureaus, washstands—pretty much everything imaginable. She recognized pieces made of oak and walnut, but some of the other woods she wasn't familiar with.

"Yes?" a voice asked that wasn't Spenser's. It took her eyes a minute to adjust to the dim light and make out the man standing in the rear of the shop, a mallet in his hand, tall and middle aged, with red hair.

"I'm looking for Spenser Rawling."

"He's down at the mill. I'm Matthew Carlisle. I'll walk with you." He put the mallet down and made his way through the shop, weaving around pieces of furniture. She followed him to the door and down the path. The wheel turned as water from the creek flowed over it. The mill was open on both ends—really just a makeshift roof over a wooden structure. The thick scent of sawdust hung in the air.

Celeste stepped to where she could look inside. Spenser and another man directed a log through a saw, powered by the water wheel. She retreated back from flying bits of wood and the noise.

"Spenser!" Matthew called out. "You have a visitor."

Spenser smiled at the sight of her, but then his smile faded, probably in response to her expression. Matthew stepped up to the log, taking Spenser's place. In a moment Spenser was beside her.

"It's Berta," she said.

"Is she worse?"

Celeste couldn't speak for a moment. She swallowed and tried again. "She's passed."

Spenser's face grew pale.

Celeste managed to relay what Mr. Horn had said.

"Was he absolutely certain Berta was the one who died?"

Celeste nodded. "He seemed to be."

"Did he see her? Confirm it?"

"I don't think so," Celeste said. "He said it was the new maid. And that the constable was looking for a replacement."

Spenser frowned.

"What are you thinking?"

"That we should go to Norfolk and find out for sure."

"Yes, that's what I want to do. Go and talk to Constable Wharton. Find out how she died. Where's she's buried. I came to ask you to go with me."

"Mr. Edwards will allow it?"

Celeste nodded. "He even loaned me money for our return trip."

"I have enough to cover my own passage. I don't want you paying for mine and adding more to your debt. That won't do."

Celeste put her hand to her throat. "Thank you," she said. He truly cared about Berta. Her heart felt sick for the loss he must be feeling too.

"I'll ask Matthew if I can go."

"See if you can leave now. Mr. Edwards said we should try to get on the boat that's leaving this afternoon. The one Mr. Horn is taking."

It was past noon when Celeste and Spenser reached the boat, and by the time they arrived at Norfolk, the sun was setting and the day had grown cold.

"We should go straight to the constable's house," Celeste said. Maybe he would let them spend the night in his stable. It would be scandalous, but they didn't have the money to stay anywhere else. She trusted Spenser, no matter how things might look.

They followed Mr. Horn off the boat. Celeste knew which direction the Wharton home was, but that was all. When they reached the end of the dock, Celeste asked Mr. Horn how to find it.

"Go to the last street and then turn left," he said. "It's the biggest house that way."

Celeste and Spenser headed toward the loading area, turning left at the exact same spot she'd last seen Berta. If she hadn't gone on to Williamsburg, would her sister be alive? As Spenser quickly linked her arm in his, she realized just how unsteady she was.

They continued on, looking at each house they passed, trying to decide which was the biggest. Celeste pulled her cloak tighter even though it was still warm, grateful Spenser had come with her.

The very last house had to be it. It was brick, three stories high, with both a barn and stable. Celeste and Spenser walked up to the door. Before they could knock, the door swung open, revealing an older woman.

"Oh, my," she said, slamming it shut.

Celeste stepped back, alarmed. Perhaps they looked like beggars. Spenser knocked. There was a commotion on the other side of the door, and then it opened again. This time Constable Wharton stood in front of them, minus wig or hat. His hair was short, gray, and thin, and he didn't look nearly as authoritarian as he had before.

He glanced from Spenser to Celeste as if he'd never seen them.

"I'm Berta Talbot's sister," Celeste said. "We met before."

"Ah, that's right. I can't see you well in the dim light. What are you doing here?"

"Mr. Horn told me what happened. About Berta." Celeste couldn't say anything more. Death occurred all the time, but she still couldn't believe Berta had been taken.

Spenser stepped forward, a serious expression on his face. "We're hoping for some information—"

Celeste blurted out, "Where is she buried?"

The constable pursed his lips and held up his hand. "Wait here," he said. He disappeared behind the half open door. "Where's the housekeeper?" he called out. And then, "Did the maid that spoke French die?"

Celeste grabbed Spenser's arm.

"Why didn't you tell me?" The constable's voice was loud and annoyed.

Celeste couldn't make out the response of whomever he was conversing with.

"That's what I thought," he answered. He came back to the door. "Mr. Horn gave you false information. A different maid died. Your sister is alive—but barely, and most likely not for long."

Celeste's knees grew weak, and she leaned against the open door, nearly falling into the house. Spenser steadied her. "I need to see her," Celeste managed to say.

"Go around to the kitchen. The housekeeper will meet you."

Spenser started down the steps. "We have to take her with us," Celeste said, following him.

"Let's see how she's doing first. She may not be up to traveling."

The housekeeper, the same woman who'd slammed the door in their faces, met them by the kitchen and led the way to a shed on the far side of the barn. She opened the door and motioned for Celeste to go inside. Spenser followed—but the housekeeper didn't.

"Berta," Celeste said.

The waning light didn't reach the far corner of the shed, but the sound of a groan led Celeste to her sister. She knelt beside her. "Can you hear me?" she asked. Berta didn't respond. Celeste's eyes began to adjust as she placed her hand on her sister's hot face.

Berta made another sound and then managed to say, "Water?"

"I'll get some." Spenser slipped back out of the shed.

"Are you in pain?" Celeste asked.

"No." Berta stirred, shifting toward the wall. "Not anymore."

"Has a physician seen you?"

"Yes. He said there was nothing he could do."

"Have you been eating?"

"Cook brings broth now and then."

"Why are you out here instead of in the house?"

"They were afraid I had measles because I have a rash."

"Measles?" Celeste cried. "But that's impossible. You can only get it once, and you already had measles a few years ago."

"I know. I told them as much, but they didn't believe me."

Celeste sighed in frustration. "Well, you and I both know it can't be that."

"True," Berta replied. "Though I do think it's the same illness I had on the ship—not the seasickness but the fever. It seems to come and go."

"Maybe it's typhoid," Celeste said, turning toward Spenser as he ducked back into the shed with a cup. "Can't typhoid fever cause a rash?"

He nodded. "And sometimes the fever goes away but then comes back with a vengeance. All in all, it can last for months."

It didn't appear as if anyone had been caring for her. Celeste had to get Berta out of the shed and away from the constable's house. He'd proven unfit to protect those he was responsible for. And because it couldn't be measles—and it obviously wasn't smallpox—there was no need for quarantine.

"Do you think you could travel?" Celeste asked her sister.

Berta groaned.

"The ship ride up the river is nothing like across the ocean."

Berta pulled her arm over her head and didn't answer.

"I'll be right back," Celeste said. She grabbed Spenser's hand as she passed by him and pulled him out the door. "I'm going to go talk to the constable and ask him if I can buy Berta's contract."

"With what?"

She pulled her pouch out from under her petticoat and retrieved the ring, holding it up.

"Oh, Celeste. But it's all you have left, right?"

She nodded.

He didn't hesitate. "Of course you should use it to buy Berta's freedom."

"It means we won't have any means to get back to England."

"She would never survive a trip back anyway."

She knew he was right.

"Tell the constable you'll give him the ring for Berta's contract as long as he also provides you with an extra amount of money to care for her until she regains her strength," Spenser said. "You won't be able to do your work and nurse her. You'll have to hire someone to do it."

Celeste nodded. That was a good plan.

"Do you want me to go with you?"

Celeste considered it. The constable might be more willing to negotiate with a man instead of her. And she was afraid in her anger over Berta's lack of care that perhaps she would alienate him. She'd never seen Spenser lose his temper. Regardless of how fond he was of Berta, she doubted he would now either. "Yes," she said. "Please."

"Tell me about the ring," Spenser said as they started toward the house.

"It belonged to my great-grandmother, a baroness in France. Her husband gave it to her while they were still in Paris. She gave it to my mother."

"A Parisian heirloom," Spenser said. "Any idea how much it's worth?"

Celeste shook her head. She imagined it was quite valuable, although her mother certainly never bragged about it being so. She shook her head. "I have no idea."

Instead of heading to the house, Spenser stopped at the kitchen. The door was open, and the cook was scrubbing the last of the pots in the dim light. "Excuse me," Spenser said. "Do you have a minute?"

"No."

"We won't interrupt your work. I just have a few questions."

The woman scowled, but Spenser stepped into the building. "Are there other maids here besides the ill one?"

"Yes. A kitchen maid, who has conveniently disappeared at the moment, and a housemaid."

"Do you know what the constable plans to do with the ill one in the shed out back?"

"That one's been nothing but trouble. He'll sell her contract if she doesn't die first."

Celeste shivered but managed to hold her tongue.

"Is there a lady of the house?"

"Madame Wharton."

"Madame? Is she French?"

The cook made a disgusted face. "She fancies she is and wants me to fix French dishes." She dropped her voice to a whisper. "But it's all a show."

Celeste felt a measure of hope, remembering what Constable Wharton had said about his wife wanting to study French.

"Interesting," Spenser said. "Thank you." He nodded toward the house. "If we knock on the back door, will the constable speak with us?"

"You can try, but he retires early. He may already be in his bedchamber."

Spenser kindly thanked her and led the way to the back door of the house. He knocked soundly, and a waiflike maid appeared. At their request, she went to find the housekeeper, who said the constable would talk with them in the morning.

"S'il vous plaît," Celeste said. "Could we speak with Madame then, instead?"

"Wait here," the housekeeper said. A few minutes later she returned. "She'll see you in the salon."

Chapter Fourteen
Celeste

Celeste and Spenser followed the housekeeper through a formal dining room with a cherrywood table and matching chairs, down a passageway, and then to an elegant room on the right. The last rays of sunlight came through a bank of windows, which the housemaid was in the process of opening to let in the evening breeze. A woman, probably in her midtwenties, rested on a settee. A lamp was lit on a mahogany table beside her. The walls were covered with textured paper, and the ceiling was painted a light blue. Clearly, Constable Wharton was a wealthy man.

The woman wore a gown made of fabric printed with bluebirds, probably from London, and her blond hair was piled on her head in a stylish fashion. Her lips were as thin as she was, her cheekbones sharp, and her gray eyes deeply set.

"Bonsoir," the woman said. In just the single word, Celeste could detect her thick English accent.

Celeste curtsied and then said in English, "We've come to check on my sister. The maid out back, in the shed." She couldn't hide the hint of anger in her own voice.

141

The woman pursed her lips.

Spenser stepped forward, a concerned expression on his face, and partially blocked Celeste. "We're very grateful that you've cared for Berta, even though she hasn't been able to serve you."

The woman smiled a little.

Spenser looked around. "You have a fine home here. The finest of any I've seen since arriving in the colony."

She nodded in agreement. "My husband has many profitable business interests besides being the constable."

Celeste stepped forward. "My sister was kidnapped and forced into servitude. She's too ill—"

Spenser interrupted her. "As I was saying, we appreciate your care for Berta, but thankfully we're now in a position to take her off your hands." He shot Celeste a warning look. "It's too much to expect your busy household to care for her."

Madame Wharton frowned. "My husband purchased her contract."

Celeste started to speak again, but Spenser bumped his arm against her. "That's true," he said. "We are very aware of the financial commitment that has been made."

"We'll soon have to purchase another servant—or a slave." Madame Wharton leaned forward. "My husband feels that he was misled. That she was already ill before—"

Celeste interrupted. "He knew she suffered from seasickness."

"But this illness has been far worse than recovering from that. I, myself, was very ill on our trip over, but I recovered in a fair amount of time. Something else is wrong with her. Only once did she feel well enough to help me with my French, and then once she revealed she had a fever and a rash, we found other accommodations for her. She has measles." The woman's face turned down into a pout.

Celeste started to argue but then realized it would be pointless. If the woman hadn't believed Berta, why would she listen to her? "Is that what the other maid had?" she asked instead, her voice low. "The one who died?"

"*Oui.* That's why this one is not in the house."

Celeste bristled. "Yes, I am aware of the practice of quarantining. But that doesn't give you the right to shove her out in some filthy shed and just abandon—"

"We'd like to take her away from here before she grows any worse," Spenser interjected much more politely. "We'll make arrangements for her care in Williamsburg."

The woman pursed her lips again. "You'll need to discuss it in the morning with my husband."

Spenser's sweet talk had gotten them nowhere. Celeste wiggled her pouch from the waist of her skirt and opened it, first pulling out the brooch. She wished it had some sort of monetary value, but porcelain had no real worth beyond the sentimental. She dug in the pouch again, pulled out the ring, and stepped to Spenser's side. "My sister and I are from a good family in London. We have loving parents. By no fault of her own, she—"

Madame Wharton met Celeste's gaze with cold, heartless eyes. Celeste realized appealing to the woman's goodness wasn't going to work.

Celeste took a deep breath. "I'm willing to buy her contract," she said, holding out her hand.

"I'm not interested in cheap jewels."

Spenser shot Celeste a cautionary look. She ignored him. "Of course, it's worth far too much to simply trade it for my sister. I would need money back in return for her care."

The woman laughed. "Surely you're toying with me."

Celeste slipped the ring onto her own finger. "My great-grandmother was a baroness in France. Her husband gave her this ring in Paris eighty years ago." She held the ring close to the lamp, and the light caught the stone, making it shimmer.

"Oh," Madame Wharton said, easing forward, her hand going to her bosom. She stared at the ring and then said, "You must talk with my husband."

"We need to return to Williamsburg first thing in the morning," Spenser said. "We may not have time."

The woman shrugged. *"C'est le vie."* Again, and for such a simple phrase, her accent was atrocious.

"Thank you for your time," Spenser said, turning toward the door. "We'll find our way out."

Celeste followed him, the ring still on her finger.

"Wait."

They turned toward her.

The woman stood. "It is beautiful," she said. Celeste noticed that she wore no rings. Madame Wharton walked to the desk and opened the bottom door. She returned with a packet. "This is all I have."

Celeste opened it up. She guessed the money was probably for household expenses and that it would last at least a few months to pay for Berta's care. She glanced at Spenser. He shrugged.

"*Merci,*" Celeste said, taking off the ring. "But I need her contract. With your signature." She knew that the woman's approval probably wouldn't stand up in a court of law—she had no rights to her husband's property, but she hoped Constable Wharton wouldn't pursue getting Berta back, not when he thought she'd soon be dead anyway.

"I'm not sure where the contract is."

"Try the desk," Celeste suggested, making a fist around the ring.

Madame Wharton rifled through three drawers. Eventually, she withdrew a document and held it up to her face, reading it slowly. "Berta Talbot," she said.

"Yes, that's right," Celeste answered. "Does your husband have a seal? Or a stamp? Some sort of symbol of his approval? Could you mark the contract with it?"

The woman nodded and opened the top drawer. Again, Celeste doubted that if the constable pressed the matter that the document would hold up in court, and she could only hope he wouldn't pursue them.

Spenser would have to be listed as the new owner of the contract. She asked quietly if he agreed to that as the woman dripped wax onto the page and then stamped it with some sort of a seal from the top of the desk. Spenser nodded, and they both stepped forward.

The woman pointed to the ink and quill on the desk. For a moment Celeste wondered if Spenser could sign his name, but then she remembered he'd studied Latin and French. He signed quickly, *Spenser Rawling*. His penmanship suggested that he was indeed educated. Once Celeste had the document and packet of money in her hand, the woman said, "Take your sister tonight. Don't stay here with her. I want you long gone by the time my husband wakes in the morning."

"Of course," Spenser said.

Madame Wharton extended her hand. Celeste spread her palm out again and glanced down at the ring. It paled in worth compared to Berta. She gave it to the woman, clutching the document and packet tightly in her other hand.

A smile spread across Madame Wharton's face as she slipped the ring onto her finger. It was loose, but she didn't seem to notice. Then she looked up. "You need to go."

They quickly exited into the long passageway. By the time they reached the dining room, footsteps fell behind them. "Wait!" a voice whispered.

They stopped, and the young maid appeared. "I overheard what you said about the girl out in the shed. That she was kidnapped."

Celeste nodded.

"So was I! No one would believe me. Not even the constable. And especially not Madame Wharton."

"What did they say?"

"That lots of indentured servants make that claim."

"That's what we've been told too," Celeste said. "Where were you taken from?"

"London. A year ago."

Celeste reached for her hand. "Have you written to your family?"

The girl shook her head. "I have none, not really. I was caring for a distant cousin's children. She sent me down to the dock on an errand, and the next thing I knew I woke up on a ship far out at sea."

Celeste's heart filled with concern for the young woman. "Do they treat you well enough here?"

Her eyes filled with tears. "They do. I get enough to eat—something I never had in England. Thankfully I've been healthy, unlike your poor sister. But it just isn't right..."

"Of course it isn't." Celeste wished she could say more—that she would try to help or she would report the kidnapping or something. But what could she do? Especially when it was the constable's own household. "Thank you for telling us. If I can think of anything to do, I will."

The girl shook her head. "I don't expect you to do anything. I just wanted you to know. I'm sorry I couldn't care for your sister. They wouldn't let me."

"Thank you for trying." Celeste felt for the girl. "God bless you." Celeste reached out and patted her arm.

As they hurried out the back door, she thought of all of the sad stories of women in the New World. This girl's. Sary's. Berta's. Her own. Women torn from home and all that was familiar against their will. Celeste couldn't help this girl, but she could be Sary's friend. And she could do everything in her power to see Berta back to health and be the sister she was meant to be, at least to one of her siblings.

They spent the night in the constable's field under an oak tree. Celeste wrapped Berta in her cloak, and then Celeste curled beside her sister, pulling hers over the two of them. Spenser kept watch out under the stars. Before Celeste fell asleep, he pointed out Aquila and then Hercules. Though she couldn't see them through the heavy canopy of leaves, she drifted off to him naming other stars, her arms around her sister, grateful that such a man cared for Berta.

They left at first light, Celeste leading the way while Spenser effortlessly carried Berta in his arms. The fields glistened in the dew that had fallen during the night. By the time they reached the road, the sun was rising over the bay. Celeste's boots were wet from the grass, and she shivered in the cool morning, but the pink and orange of the sunrise lifted her spirits. There was always hope—hope Berta would survive, hope they would find a way to return to England. Or perhaps hope that Jonathan would change his— She stopped herself. There was no use setting herself up for more disappointment.

Berta would marry Spenser and stay. That was as it should be. After completing her commitment of servitude to Mr. Edwards, perhaps Celeste could eventually find her way home.

She swallowed hard and turned her gaze to Spenser and Berta. He stepped carefully down the cobblestone street. Her sister kept her eyes closed, but Celeste doubted she was sleeping. She regretted thinking before that Spenser wasn't good enough for Berta. She couldn't imagine a more caring man for her sister to marry.

Her heart began to beat faster, and she increased her pace, leading the way. She'd judged Spenser on a false scale. How foolish she'd been in so many ways. In this New World, he had a skill that was needed. He would be able to provide for a family. They might never be wealthy, but neither would they starve. Celeste shivered again. She hoped she wouldn't either.

When they reached the wharf, a woman selling loaves of bread appeared. Celeste didn't want to spend any of the money Madame Wharton had given her, but they had to eat. She pulled a coin from the packet and bought a crusty loaf.

"Where did you get money?" Berta managed to ask.

Celeste shushed her and led the way to the end of the wharf. Once they reached the boat, Spenser lowered Berta beside a barrel. Celeste tore off a chunk of the bread and held it up for her sister. She made a face and shook her head.

Celeste handed it to Spenser, and then she tore off some bread for herself.

"That was good of Madame Wharton to allow you to take me," Berta said to Celeste.

Celeste nodded as she chewed.

"I would have thought her too greedy to do such a thing. In the little bit of time I spent with her, all she talked about were her possessions and the constable's businesses."

Celeste tore off another piece of bread and then handed the rest of the loaf to Spenser.

"Aren't you going to tell her?" he whispered as he took it. Celeste shook her head. She couldn't bear to admit that she'd traded the ring. To do that, she would first have to confess that she had stolen it from their mother's bureau.

She bent down toward her sister. "The housemaid said she'd been kidnapped in London. Just like you."

"Oh?" Berta said. "I hadn't heard that."

Celeste handed the last bit of bread to Berta. "Try it," she urged.

She took a bite, shook her head, and passed it back. "I won't be able to keep it down."

If Berta were to recover, she would need sustenance. Celeste knelt beside her and took her hands in hers. "We'll find help for you. And good food. There are orchards in Williamsburg. And gardens. Eggs, milk, beef, chicken, and lamb. Fish from the river. You'll get your health back." She paused, searching her sister's face. "I'm so sorry. None of this turned out the way I thought it would."

"What are you saying?" Berta asked. "Jonathan wasn't willing to buy out my contract too?"

Celeste blinked back tears. She would have to tell Berta about Jonathan's rejection sooner or later—but not in front of Spenser. Surely he already knew the details of how everything turned out, but she didn't want his pity. It would be easier in private, with just Berta.

"No, it's complicated," Celeste said. "I'm still…bound to my contract. I'll explain it all later."

Berta nodded and closed her eyes, obviously too ill to press for details.

A few minutes later, the captain appeared on the deck of the boat that would be taking them up the river. Soon a few more passengers arrived. Several loads of goods were wheeled by in carts. Mr. Horn appeared, leading two African women. Both were younger than Celeste and dressed in tattered clothes.

The man nodded as he passed by. "Looks like I was wrong about which girl died," he said to Celeste.

"Thankfully so," she answered through gritted teeth. Did he not care at all about the pain he'd put her through? She grieved for the girl who had died and wondered if her family would ever know.

He led the two slaves onto the vessel, a cargo boat known as the *York*, which was piloted by a Captain Doane. The first mate motioned for the other passengers to board, and Spenser scooped Berta up again. Once they were on deck, they huddled near the bow of the boat, Berta between Spenser and Celeste. The fresh air would be much better for her than going below. For now, the sun warmed them.

As Celeste soaked in the moment, gratitude flowed through her. Berta was alive, her contract bought. Now they just needed to get back to Williamsburg and safety before Constable Wharton realized what his wife had done.

CHAPTER FIFTEEN
Celeste

After the *York* arrived at the landing, Berta was allowed to ride in one of the wagons on the road to Williamsburg while Spenser and Celeste walked alongside it. It hadn't rained that day, so there was less mud than before.

Smoke rose from an unseen cabin to the left, out of the trees. Celeste wasn't sure how anyone besides those who grew tobacco made a living in Virginia. The red soil didn't grow much. Watching Benjamin and Joe work in the garden showed her the effort it took to produce vegetables, let alone a crop. The chicken manure helped. That worked for a garden but would be hard to support an entire field.

The land didn't seem to have as many opportunities as Jonathan had implied. Then again, he could have misled her. Celeste shivered. No, she would try to continue to think positively. Yes, she was disappointed in him, but she had no reason to believe he'd deceived her. He'd truly believed she wasn't coming. That and the false promise of the land grant had unsettled him.

Spenser, as he walked along, stepped closer to the wagon and asked Berta if she was all right.

She nodded. She had her eyes open now, taking in the scenery. Spenser had tucked his coat around her even though the day was now hot and humid.

Celeste mulled over whom she could ask to care for Berta. Even if Mr. Edwards would allow her to stay above the kitchen with Celeste and Sary, she wouldn't be able to check on her sister throughout the day. And it would be hard to get Berta up and down the loft ladder.

Berta couldn't go with Spenser to the carpenter shop either. There would still be no one to care for her, plus it would be scandalous for Berta to live with three men. Perhaps a woman in town would be able to help. Celeste would ask the Frenchmen first to see if they had any ideas.

As the trees thinned and the village appeared, Berta raised her head a little more. "This is Williamsburg?"

Celeste nodded.

"I expected it to be bigger. It isn't anything like what I imagined."

"Who described it to you?" Celeste asked, wondering if someone in the Wharton household had been up the James this far.

"Oh, I had a few ideas just from what people mentioned, is all."

Celeste didn't press for more of an answer than that. The rat-a-tat of the snare drums soon filled the air, reminding Celeste of Jonathan and his rejection of her once again. After they passed the green—which she searched for Jonathan out of habit, to no avail—they continued on down the street.

She told the wagon's driver to head to the Petits' house, and then she explained to Spenser as they walked how she had met the French-speaking Monsieur Petit in the inn and had asked him and his companion if they knew of anyone who might be in a position to take Berta in.

"And did he?" Spenser asked.

Celeste hesitated. "Not exactly. But he did agree to ask around. Perhaps he's found someone by now and can tell me where we should take her." She didn't add that her biggest hope was that if she showed up on his doorstep and pleaded her case, the man and his wife would agree to take in Berta themselves.

Not wanting to delay the wagon's driver for too long, she rushed to the door, gave it a knock, and asked the maid who answered if monsieur or madame were home.

"Just a moment," the girl replied. While she was gone, Celeste turned and gave the wagon's driver a wave, hoping he had a few minutes to spare. He nodded in return.

She was again facing the door, still waiting, when she heard someone behind her yell out, "Jonathan!"

With a gasp, she twisted around to see Jonathan's carriage approaching from the rear—and he wasn't alone. A young woman perched beside him on the bench. His Miss Vine, no doubt.

"Jonathan!" someone cried again, and Celeste realized that was Berta's voice—though she had no idea how the girl had been able to call out so loudly, sick as she was.

He'd obviously heard it too because he drew his carriage to a stop just behind the wagon and climbed down. And though Celeste desperately wanted to hear his exchange with her sister, she was interrupted by a crisp, "May I help you?"

Celeste spun back around to see a woman standing in the doorway.

She was tall and thin, with her silvery hair pulled back in a bun and partly covered with a frilly cap. "I am Madame Petit."

Forcing herself to ignore the scene in the street, Celeste introduced herself and explained that she was looking for someone to care for her sister, who was ill, just until she recovered. "I met your husband recently at the inn, where I work. He was quite kind and said he would try to help me figure something out."

The woman frowned.

"I can pay," she quickly added.

"Why us?" the woman demanded.

Celeste explained that her parents were French. "Huguenots. I was led to believe perhaps you were too."

She pursed her lips. "Stay here. I'll speak with my husband." The woman left, and Celeste returned her attention to the street.

Jonathan's companion was now sitting alone on the carriage bench, lips pursed and brow furrowed as she waited for him. He was standing near the back of the wagon talking with Berta, though it looked as if their conversation was wrapping up.

He turned abruptly and climbed up into the carriage, took the reins, and gave them a snap, never once glancing toward Celeste as he rode off. She looked to Berta, who fell back along the wagon bench as if heartbroken—and Celeste was stabbed with yet another pang of guilt. She should have been the one to tell her sister what had happened. Instead, the poor girl had obviously learned it from Jonathan himself. Clearly Berta was devastated for Celeste—and for her own future as well.

Without a man to pay for their contracts or to look out for them, the sisters were vulnerable. Berta didn't know how lucky she was to have Spenser's care. True, he could only do so much, but he'd saved them from harm over and over already.

A rustling sound drew Celeste's attention back to the cottage doorway. "Is your sister in some sort of trouble?" It was Monsieur Petit, standing beside his wife.

Celeste shook her head. "No, sir. She's merely ill." Celeste was the one in trouble, but she wouldn't tell them that.

"Why did you come to us?" he asked.

"I thought you might be *sympathique*." Celeste shrugged her shoulders and then turned away. No matter how desperate she was, she wasn't going to beg—at least not any more than she had already.

"Wait," the woman said. Then quietly, "Husband..."

Celeste froze. She couldn't hear the rest of the Petits' conversation. Finally madame said, "We'll care for her for a few days until you can figure something else out. It's our Christian duty, I suppose."

Celeste turned toward them, choking back her tears. "*Merci*," she whispered.

⸺

The Petits' home was well furnished, and they employed not just the maid but a cook as well. Spenser, carrying Berta, followed Madame Petit down a hallway to the back of the house to the sickroom. A cotlike bed with fresh linen nearly filled the room, along with a small table with a pitcher and basin. The accommodations were a castle compared to the horror of the shed she'd been holed up in. The maid stepped into the room with a clean petticoat and chemise.

"Strip off her clothes," Madame Petit said. Spenser followed the woman out, and as Celeste undressed her sister, the maid returned with water in the pitcher and a fresh cloth. Celeste bathed Berta, dressed her in the clean clothes, and then tucked her into the clean bed.

"Cook is heating some broth," the maid said. "I'm Judith, by the way."

"Thank you."

"The Petits are good folks," Judith said. "I'll be back with the broth in a few minutes."

Celeste had so much she wanted to say to Berta. She knelt beside the bed. "I'm sorry for all that's happened." Berta would be healthy and living in London if Celeste hadn't snuck down to the ship, causing her sister to follow her. True, Berta had made the choice to follow, but Celeste's sin of disobedience to their parents had led to unintended consequences for them both. "I'll do all I can to make sure you have a chance to get well."

"Thank you." Berta's voice was barely audible. "For all you've done for me. Caring for me on the ship, rescuing me from the Whartons. Bringing me here…"

Celeste's heart warmed at her sister's words. "Did Jonathan tell you what happened? When you spoke to him out on the street?"

Berta shook her head. "No. But I gather he betrayed you. Betrayed us." Berta's eyes filled with tears, though from whose pain Celeste wasn't sure.

"I'll figure something out. I promise." She almost added that at least Berta had Spenser, thinking it might comfort her to be reminded that there was still one decent man they could count on, but she held her tongue. That conversation could wait until Berta was feeling better.

Judith returned with the broth, and Celeste told Berta that she had to go. "I'll come back tomorrow to check on you. You'll be fine here."

In the salon, she thanked the Petits again and offered half the money she had left to the French couple, hoping the amount would convince them to care for Celeste longer than just a few days.

"Not now," Madame Petit replied, pushing Celeste's hand back and then walking her to the door. "We'll discuss the matter and let you know a fair amount."

"*Merci,*" Celeste said. "I'll have the physician come and take a look at Berta."

"Very well." Madame Petit saw her to the door and then told her goodbye.

Spenser was waiting for Celeste outside, and together they walked toward the street.

"I couldn't have rescued Berta without you, Spenser," she told him. "Once again, I'm indebted to you—"

He held up a hand to stop her. "I'm pleased to help, Celeste. I hope you know that."

She nodded. She did. Thank goodness he'd been taken with Berta during their voyage and had befriended Celeste as well.

Spenser frowned. "I'm sorry, I really am, about Jonathan. But don't you think it's for the best? A cad like that doesn't deserve you." His mouth turned up a little. "Things will work out for you." He appeared so caring and kind that, for a moment, a sense of warmth filled her heart.

But then he had to be on his way, and once again she was alone. Celeste watched him hurry up Queen Street. Berta had no idea how fortunate she was to have Spenser interested in her. On the ship, Celeste's thinking had been so misguided. In her mind, she kept comparing him to Jonathan, telling herself that while both men were kind and caring, Spenser was not the type to speak to the captain with authority on their behalf. He was of a class of men who had no power, who could not get things done. If Jonathan had been there, on the other hand, he would have set the record straight right away, she'd told herself. He would have convinced the captain of their true predicament and gotten that ridiculous contract torn up and tossed overboard.

She had been so wrong on all accounts. Here she was in the same village as Jonathan, and he'd done worse than not set the record straight—he had abandoned her altogether. Her heart heavy, Celeste trudged toward the inn. The rat-a-tat of the drums continued in the background. Somewhere, Jonathan drove on in his pretentious carriage with Miss Vines.

Loneliness nearly overwhelmed Celeste as she stopped by the physician's residence and left a message, asking him to examine Berta, and then continued on to the inn and around the side to the kitchen door. Her pace slowed with each step as she wondered how she could possibly manage to oversee Berta's care and fulfill her duties. Hope for any sort of meaningful life of her own was entirely gone. Forget her dreams of having a husband and children. She no longer even had herself, her own freedom. For the next four years, she was owned by another.

Celeste stopped for a moment outside the inn and thought of studying her catechism under her mother's direction as a young girl.

Her mother would ask: "*What is the true and right knowledge of God?*" And Celeste would answer: "*When He is so known that due honor is paid to Him.*"

"*What is the method of honoring Him duly?*" her mother would ask. Celeste would answer, "*To place our whole confidence in Him; to study to serve Him during our whole life by obeying His will; to call upon Him in all our necessities…*"

Celeste hadn't obeyed God when she took the ruby ring and fled to America. She'd dishonored both God and her parents and put her sister in a horrible situation. She didn't feel as if she had a right to call upon Him now.

"You're back." Mr. Edwards stood at the corner of the inn, a bucket of scraps in his hand.

"Yes," Celeste said. "I was just catching my breath."

"Well, catch it in the kitchen. Sary needs your help."

"Yes sir." But instead of heading that way, she paused for a moment, met his eyes, and thanked him for giving her the time off. "Mr. Horn had misspoken. It wasn't my sister who died but a different maid."

His eyes widened, and he actually seemed relieved on her behalf.

"Unfortunately, Berta is quite ill. But I was able to bring her back with me. Currently, she is being cared for in the home of Monsieur and Madame Petit."

Avoiding his questioning gaze, she dug at her waistband for the pouch under her skirt and took out the money he'd given her. Celeste had paid for their passage with the money from the ring instead. As she handed him back his loan in full, his bushy eyebrows rose.

"I had more resources than I thought," she explained, her face growing warm as she realized perhaps that didn't sound as she meant it.

He didn't seem to take it wrong. "Resourceful, you are." He put the money into his own pouch. "You remind me of someone I held very dear."

She guessed he was referring to his daughter, but she didn't want to bring up the girl's name in their conversation, not when he hadn't.

Celeste simply nodded. He handed her the bucket. "Take care of the chickens first. Be quick." He turned and headed back toward the inn.

Celeste called out, "Mr. Edwards?"

He stopped and took a step backward.

"I'd like to see my sister when I can."

"Of course. Just as long as you keep up with your work."

"I promise I will. Thank you."

Celeste started toward the coop. She was grateful for the man's help, but she needed to remember not to expect too much. He was kind, but he wasn't her father. She quickened her step. According to her parents, God was a Father who always cared. No matter what. Could she call upon Him to help?

She tried to form a silent prayer but nothing came. She didn't feel she had a right to ask for anything after what she'd done.

CHAPTER SIXTEEN
Maddee

When I arrived home from church, the smell of baked goods greeted me even before I opened the front door. Stepping inside, I spotted a tray of what looked like homemade crescent rolls on the stovetop, their flaky layers gooey with some sort of cinnamon fruit filling. I followed sounds of laughter to the living room, pulling back the curtain to see Miss Vida perched on the side of the bed and facing Nicole, who was sitting up against the pillows, her hair on top of her head in an elaborate updo. Beside them sat the rolling tray table, covered with an array of tubes and bottles and brushes and more.

My sister looked up at me and smiled, her face radiant if overdone in pink rouge, coral lipstick, and dark gray-blue eyeshadow. Gaping at her, I couldn't decide if she looked ready for a runway or a clown show. It was kind of halfway between the two.

"Good timing, Maddee. Miss Vida was just finishing up my makeover." Though Nicole kept a straight face, I could tell she was trying not to laugh.

"Wow," I replied, stepping closer. "That's all I can say. Just…wow."

"Hey, Maddee, did you see the rugelach we made in there?" Miss Vida asked, dabbing a thick brush along Nicole's cheekbones. "Help yourself."

"I will, once I've changed out of my church clothes. They smell amazing."

"They taste even better," Nicole replied.

Miss Vida gave one last swipe of the brush before turning to gauge my reaction, her eyes sparkling. "Well?"

"Like I said. Wow."

"Thanks." She seemed quite pleased with herself. "That was fun, doing makeup on a young woman. Your skin is still so perfect. At my age, all I can do is slap on some foundation and hope it fills in the nooks and crannies."

She rose and stepped back to take a final look, nodded in satisfaction, and then turned her attention to the table, rolling it off to the side and gathering up her supplies. I stepped closer to the bed, resisting the urge to reach out and tug on one of the ringlets in Nicole's hair.

"She looks great," I said. "Like something out of *Vogue*." Or maybe *Circus Monthly*.

"I told your sister if she'll keep off the crank for good, her skin will stay this beautiful a lot longer," Miss Vida said as she placed the items one by one into a large, zippered makeup bag. "Not to mention her teeth. She's lucky she caught all this nonsense in time. Trust me, there's nothing uglier than meth mouth."

Meth mouth? Crank? I glanced at Nicole, startled that not only had the topic of drugs come up between them, but that they both seemed so casual about it now. Leave it to Miss Vida to walk right up to the elephant in the room and call it by name.

"I was telling your sister that I did what she's doing, though to a much lesser degree, of course. Back in the eighties, when I had to have my gall bladder out, I decided to use that as an opportunity to quit smoking. I mean, why not? I knew that by the time I got out of the hospital I would have already gone a couple days without a cigarette, plus I was going to feel rotten anyway from the surgery, so I might as well get all the pain over with at once." She glanced at Nicole and gave her a smile. "Right, baby? You're just going to get all the pain over with at once, aren't you?"

"Sure am," Nicole replied, and in that moment she sounded utterly sincere.

"Seems like you two had a good time," I told her once Miss Vida was gone and I had changed into jeans and a comfy top. "I should have guessed y'all would get along. You're both blunt and hardheaded."

"Hey!" Nicole replied, scooting to the edge of the bed so I could help her out. "At least she knows how to make a girl feel pretty."

"Um, okay. That's one word for it."

We got her in the chair and then I rolled her to the bathroom, where I hoisted her up so she could see herself in the mirror, giving us both a good laugh.

Nicole seemed happy but exhausted from her busy morning of baking and a makeover, and I could tell she needed a nap. We shared a light lunch first, and then I gave her her pills. But before transferring her back into the bed, I insisted on snapping a few pictures first. She tolerated it, though she threatened to punch me if I posted a single one of them to Instagram.

Back in the living room, she grew quiet as I helped her into the bed and pulled up the covers. The windows were open, and a crisp breeze rustled the curtains and filled the room with the scent of leaves, of a hint of wood smoke, of fall.

"I meant it, earlier," she said softly.

"Meant what?" I replied, distracted by the electronic controls as I pushed the button to lower the head of the mattress.

"What Ms. Vida was saying, about quitting. I've been sober now for forty-eight days, Maddee. I want to stay that way."

My pulse surged. Those of us in Nicole's current orbit—me, Nana, our parents, the doctors—had been saying this since the accident, that her drug habit needed to end now, for good. And though she'd paid lip service to the notion, this was the first time she'd actually brought the matter up herself, or said it quite like this.

Like she actually meant it.

I knew sobriety was a tenuous thing, and that all the determination and commitment in the world still didn't guarantee success. But I also knew that if it were to happen at all, this was where it would have to start. She had to want it for herself, or she would never stand a chance.

My heart full as I met her eyes, the best I could manage was a quick, "Yeah?"

"Yeah," she replied, looking back at me, peaceful but determined. "I really do."

Nicole slept for the next two hours, time I spent up in my room, laying out my clothes and accessories for the week and generally getting organized. As I worked, my mind kept going over our conversation. I felt as though I were on a balance beam, teetering precariously between wanting to believe in my sister a hundred percent and knowing I had to remain skeptical at all times. Addicts could talk a good game. That's why the rule was to believe their actions, not their words. Even if I had to tell myself that over and over again, I was determined to remember it. I was also determined to see her get the treatment she needed. As a psychologist, I knew that the only way Nicole would ever stop doing the kinds of things she'd been doing on the outside was to first fix the ways she was hurting on the inside.

In the distance, I heard the children at the park. They must have been playing hide and seek, because one of them counted down loudly from ten to one then called out, "Ready or not, here I come!"

Ready or not, my sister had been handed a rare opportunity the night she survived that accident. The enforced sobriety. The reminder of her mortality. The very tangible love and support of her family. These things had all come in the wake of that disaster.

Truly, she might never be in a better position to change her heart and her life.

When Nicole awoke, she looked like a raccoon who had stuck her finger in an electrical outlet. And though I threatened to snap more pictures, I didn't have the heart. Instead, I just helped take down the updo, brush out her hair, and remove the makeup.

Deciding we could both use some fresh air, we spent the next two hours out on the patio, playing Uno, a favorite game from our childhood. Then we came back in and made goat cheese and spinach pizza for supper. Nicole was in high spirits, though as the evening wore on, I could see her growing weaker and more tired. We'd planned to watch a movie together after eating, but she was ready for bed by eight thirty and fell asleep before I could tell her good night.

I was just pulling her curtain closed when my phone rang from my purse in the kitchen. I didn't recognize the number on the screen.

"Hello?" I said softly as I climbed the stairs.

"Maddee? Hey. It's Austin. Austin Hill. Is this a bad time?"

I replied that no, not at all, this was fine.

"Great. Well, listen, it was nice running into you today. I was just calling to see if you might be free for dinner on Friday."

"This Friday?"

"No, the third Friday in August."

It took a moment to realize he was teasing me. "Ha-ha. Very funny."

"So what do you say? There's a new Cuban place I've been wanting to try. If it's a warm night, we could eat outside. *Tostones* with *mojo* sauce? *Camarones a la plancha*? *Pastelitos* for dessert?"

"Well, I don't know a *pastelito* from a *plancha*, but it sounds wonderful to me."

He chuckled. "Super. How's seven?"

I was about to say perfect when I remembered Nicole and realized it was out of the question. Disappointed, I reminded him of what I'd told him earlier, that my sister was living with me now. "I'm tied up with her every evening and on weekends. I'm sorry."

He was quiet for a moment, and then he asked if Saturday night might work any better. I thought about it and decided that as long as I could get her to an earlier meeting that day, I should be free to go out in the evening. I hated the thought of leaving her home alone on a Saturday night, but I felt sure I could find someone to keep her company while I was gone.

"Why not? I'm sure between now and then we can figure something out."

"Excellent. Saturday it is."

We made the arrangements and ended the call, and then I immediately went about setting a ringtone for his number. It didn't take much thought. I was just downloading the song I wanted, "He's a Dreamboat" by Shirley's Girls, when I realized Nicole was saying something.

"Maddee? Who was that?"

Phone still in hand, I headed down the stairs. "I thought you were asleep, nosy," I replied as I came around the curtain.

"How's a girl supposed to sleep when her sister is right upstairs, talking all mushy-gushy to some guy? Who was it? Spill the beans. I didn't know you were seeing anyone."

"All right, all right. Just give me one sec." The download complete, I assigned the new ringtone to Austin's contact page and then I tucked my phone away, plopped in the wheelchair, and rolled close to the bed. For a moment, as she leaned in toward me, it felt as though we were teenagers again, ready to gossip about the cute boys in youth group.

"That was Dr. Austin Hill," I said, a big grin growing on my face. "He asked me out. We're going to dinner on Saturday night."

Nicole's smile faded. "Dr. Hill? *My* Dr. Hill?"

I nodded, realizing I probably should have run this past her first to make sure it was okay. Ethically, he and I were free to date despite their doctor/patient relationship, but if my going out with him made her uncomfortable, I would need to respect that. "Is it a problem?"

Eyes narrowing, she stared at me for a long moment. "Well, no. But…yeah."

Oh, boy. "What do you mean?"

She grunted. "I mean, I don't care if you go out with him. I've only seen the guy two or three times since the operation. Once he takes the casts off, I can't imagine ever seeing him again."

"Okay. So…"

She shook her head. "So, no. You shouldn't go out with him."

"Why not?"

"He's too…perfect."

My head jerked back, as if struck. "Too perfect?" I asked, incredulous. Where had that come from? How could she say such a thing to me, especially knowing my history?

She shrugged. "I don't know how to explain."

"Wow." I pushed myself away from the bed. "That's harsh."

"You don't get it—"

"Oh, I get it. Leave it to you to turn something good into a negative."

"That's not what I'm trying to do," she said defensively. "Just forget I said anything. Never mind."

With that, she turned away and pretended to be asleep. I got up and left the room, not even bothering to close the curtain all the way.

Was she jealous? Was that it? I didn't know. I stomped back up the stairs to my room. What I did know was that even after a wonderful day of bonding, Nicole was capable of being cruel, of striking out in the exact way that would cut me to the quick. So I wasn't good enough for the handsome doctor? Of course I wasn't.

Once an ugly duckling, always an ugly duckling, right?

I dreaded the thought of dealing with my sister the next morning, but fortunately Inez arrived before Nicole was awake. Quickly but quietly, I showed the woman around and told her what she needed to know, and then I slipped out without ever having to interact with the patient.

It wasn't a good day. As I worked, I kept going over our weekend, wondering what I could have done to make my little sister say something so hurtful. By the time five o'clock rolled around, I wasn't ready to go, but I didn't really have a choice. The invalid with the razor sharp insults was depending on me.

I pedaled home in the gathering darkness and was out on the patio, locking up my bike and helmet, when I realized I could hear a man's voice coming from inside the carriage house. For a moment, panic seized me. This happened sometimes when I was greeted by unexpected things. A flashback to the cabin in the woods, the body on the cot, the horror of knowing, even at so young an age, that something was terribly wrong, that things would never be the same again. I took a deep breath and reminded myself that I was an adult now, that the murder was in the past.

Unless Nicole was entertaining an unauthorized guest in my home, in which case she'd be in big trouble.

"Hello?" I called sharply as I opened the door.

"In here," an unfamiliar voice said from the living room. A male voice.

I swung the door wide to see a man bending over Nicole. She was in her wheelchair, and he was doing something to her arms.

"Good," he told her. Then he released her wrists and gave her shoulder a pat. Looking up, he rose and extended a hand to me.

"Greg Fremont," he said. "You must be Madeline?"

"Maddee," I replied, taking in the logo on his navy polo shirt and realizing he was the new physical therapist Nana had arranged for Nicole. I breathed a sigh of relief. I'd been so worked up about last night that I'd completely forgotten he was coming today.

"I'm still doing my evaluation. But once I'm finished, I'd like to discuss her treatment plan with both of you."

"Sure. Just let me know when you're ready."

Turning, I spotted Inez in the kitchen, just pulling on her coat. I could tell she was tired and ready to go, so I resisted the urge to ask all about the day. Instead, I saw her to the door, whispered a quick thanks, and headed for the stairs.

Though I usually dressed to impress, tonight I wanted nothing more than to be comfortable. As they continued working downstairs, I changed into a long sweater and a pair of yoga pants and then pulled my hair into a ponytail.

I headed back down after that, trying to be unobtrusive in the kitchen as I heated up what remained of the chicken casserole Inez had made for dinner. It was delicious, and I ate quietly, observing them work and trying not to flinch as this man put my sister through her paces.

I had finished and was just washing up my dishes when Greg said they were ready for me. The three of us convened at the kitchen table, and though Nicole looked exhausted and in pain, she also seemed encouraged. Almost upbeat.

Greg launched right in, explaining that they would start by focusing on range of motion and lung health, including exercises to help prevent pneumonia, which was always a danger with excessive immobility. In two or three weeks, once the casts came off, Nicole would be moving around more, and their focus would shift to leg work and all-over muscle strengthening.

As Greg talked, I glanced at my sister and saw that she was gazing at him with rapt attention. He was terribly cute, all dark, wavy hair and deep-blue eyes, and it struck me as I looked from one to the other what Nana had meant when she called this particular therapist "special." Yet again, she was playing matchmaker for one of her granddaughters—only this time it was for Nicole.

Frustration swelled in the pit of my stomach at the very thought. Unlike me, Nicole was in no way ready to date, much less form a relationship with anyone. She had to get well first, both physically and emotionally. Until she did, a romance was the last thing she needed.

I couldn't believe it. I could tolerate Nana meddling in my love life, but to pull this with a recovering addict? Our grandmother should have known better.

Somehow, I managed to make it through the rest of the session, but by the time Greg was gone, I felt ready to explode. Nicole, on the other hand, seemed oblivious to my roiling emotions.

"I can't *wait* to walk again," she said as I went to the sink to dry my dishes and put them away. "You have *no* idea."

I took in a deep breath, held it for a long moment, and then let it out slowly, telling myself I could deal with our matchmaking grandmother later. For now, I would focus on my sister. She may have forgotten all about her hurtful comments last night, but I hadn't. We needed to clear the air. I set down the dishtowel and turned toward her, ready to speak my mind. But before I could say a word, we heard a knock at the door.

What now?

I swung it open a little too forcefully and then took a step back when I saw who it was, Detective Ortiz, here at the time we'd arranged the other day, yet another of tonight's appointments I'd forgotten all about.

She had come to share with us what she could of the file, to tell us more about the cabin in the woods, the disappearing victim, and the day that changed our lives forever.

CHAPTER SEVENTEEN

Maddee

For the next hour, Detective Ortiz, Nicole, and I sat and talked about the case over decaf coffee and yesterday's rugelach. In the face of more important matters, I decided to put my anger with my sister aside.

The detective started by explaining how one goes about attempting to solve a crime that happened twenty years ago. "First you review the existing information, which in this case wasn't very much. Just the single police report written up by one of the responding officers to the initial incident."

We were allowed to have a copy of that report now, which I skimmed eagerly. It had been written when I was just eight years old, yet here I was at twenty-seven holding a copy of it in my own hands. Reading it through, I didn't see that it told us anything new, but it still felt validating somehow.

I passed it over to Nicole and took the next item from the detective, which was a copy of the more recent report, along with our statements, which we'd given to police in July after the four of us returned to the cabin—this time as adults—and tested it successfully for blood evidence.

Ortiz went on to talk about that evidence, how their luminol tests had validated ours and how, by bringing several of the floorboards from the cabin into the lab, they had been able to extract enough DNA to run a profile. She let us see a copy of that profile now, though we weren't allowed to keep it. That didn't matter. It was mostly just numbers and terms and graphs, all of it meaningless to the untrained eye. The only part I understood was in the summary at the bottom, which identified the blood as having come from a "single source, male."

I handed that page to Nicole as the detective continued, explaining how that profile had been checked against all of their various databases but had come back without any hits. Meanwhile, she said, they had investigated in all the other ways she'd already told me about last week, to no avail.

"That's really about it. I'm sorry there isn't more. We tried to figure this one out, we really did, but I'm afraid that unless something new turns up, there's nothing more we can do."

I nodded, somber and disappointed but no longer angry, as I had been last week. Considering the lack of information and evidence, Detective Ortiz had done more than any of us had the right to expect, and I said as much now.

"Thanks, Maddee. I appreciate—"

"I don't understand," Nicole interrupted, her eyes on the profile she still held in her hands. "I thought DNA could tell you all sorts of things about a person. This just says he was a male. Where's the other info about him?"

Detective Ortiz sat back in her chair and provided a lengthy response, one that had to do with profiling and confidentiality and legalities, the long and short of it being that yes, DNA forensic technology was capable of predicting, with fairly reliable accuracy in many cases, not just gender but also race, hair color, eye color, age, various medical conditions, and even some physical features.

"But that's a different type of DNA report," she continued, "and one

I'm not at liberty to share. Though I will tell you this. On the way over here, I thought of one last thing we could pursue."

We both looked at her, suddenly encouraged. So maybe the case wasn't completely inactive just yet?

"There is a company that specializes in a new but really promising area of phenotyping," she continued. "Do y'all know what that is?"

We both shook our heads.

"Put simply, a genotype is the part of the DNA sequence that varies between individuals. That's what you're looking at, Nicole, and it's what we use to compare one person's DNA with another. But a phenotype is the *expression* of those genetic variants, the way they play out in the person's physicality. This company takes an individual's phenotype and uses it to generate an image similar to what he or she might actually have looked like. It doesn't always work, but in many cases, fairly accurate computer-generated likenesses of people have been created solely from their DNA phenotypes. The whole science is still new, but in situations of forensic identification it can be useful."

"But we already know what the guy looked like," I said. "We have Danielle's drawings."

"Oh, right, the drawings." Ortiz leaned over to pull a packet of papers from her case. "Here. We have to keep the originals as evidence, but I made copies for you."

I accepted the small stack of paper and shared it with Nicole, both of us flipping through slowly, taking in the various sketches of the man on the cot, the blood, the cabin, the knife. These pictures had been drawn by our cousin Danielle in the weeks following the incident at the cabin simply as a coping mechanism. And though she'd been only nine at the time, she was already quite talented, almost an artistic prodigy, and we all agreed her renderings were extremely accurate. Once the case was reopened, Danielle had dug up these old pictures and handed them over to be used in the investigation. They weren't easy to look at, but I was glad they existed, just one more validation of our claim.

"If you check closely," the detective said, "you'll see she never got all that detailed around the face. The hands and the knife are drawn repeatedly, but the face is always pretty much in shadow."

I nodded, understanding as a psychologist that the day it happened Danielle's eyes had been riveted on the shocking parts of our discovery, and those were what she'd later drawn in an attempt to work through the trauma. "So even without a good sketch of the man's face, you're saying this company might be able to create a likeness anyway, just from his DNA?"

Ortiz nodded. "It's worth a try. I can't keep actively working this case, as you know, but I can probably talk the chief into letting me run this one last report. I'll keep you posted. Sometimes a good image can open up new doors of inquiry."

"Thank you, Detective," I said. "Anything you can do would be deeply appreciated by all four of us."

We were wrapping things up, just chatting more generally about the situation, when I happened to glance over at Nicole and realized something was wrong. She had spread Danielle's drawings out on the table in front of her, and her eyes were darting from one image to the next, taking them in their entirety.

"Nicole? Are you okay?"

She looked up at me, her eyes wide, her expression one of horror. "I just…this is new to me. I can't explain it. I…"

Her voice trailed off. Watching her, I realized she was white as a sheet.

"What's going on?" I persisted.

"I…nothing…"

"It's not nothing. You look like you're about to pass out."

"Yeah, I need to lie down."

Hands trembling, she reached out and pushed herself away from the table. Because of her healing ribs, it hurt to wheel herself around in the chair, but at the moment she didn't seem to notice or care. She began propelling herself toward the living room.

"Wait, let me help," I said, rising from my seat.

"If you really want to help, you'll put those drawings away somewhere. Please. I don't ever want to see them again."

Confused and alarmed, I dashed around the table to stop her.

"What is it?" I asked, catching her chair and turning it toward me. "Did you see something specific? Something that could help the investigation?"

She shook her head miserably. "No. It's just…I wasn't expecting… Maddee, this is the first time I've ever seen those pictures."

I thought for a moment and realized she was right. We hadn't even known about them when we were younger, and though I had gotten a look this past July when Danielle dug them out for the police, Nicole was back in Norfolk by then, living the wild life as usual, oblivious to the progress of the investigation.

"I'm not like the rest of you," she said, crying now, tears streaming down her pale, pale face. "I was younger than y'all when it happened. I don't have any memories of that day, not really—or at least I didn't think I did. Until now. I was sitting there looking at them and…I don't know…they just…I *remembered*. I remember the blood, the knife. I remembered him. He wouldn't wake up. I shook him by the shoulder, but he wouldn't w-wake up."

Her words sent shivers down my spine, the memory of that encounter etched permanently into my brain. As we three older cousins stood and gaped at the fellow on the bed with the knife in his chest, we'd all known he was dead. But as a six-year-old, Nicole hadn't quite caught on. For some reason, despite the tremendous amount of blood, it just didn't click for her right away. Before I thought to stop her, she'd stepped forward and was tapping the man on the shoulder, telling him to wake up.

I could still hear her little-girl voice, could still feel the rising panic in my throat, could still smell the coppery stench of the blood. Within seconds, she seemed to understand what was actually going on, that the man was dead. Then she let out a bloodcurdling scream. She'd been standing in the sticky red liquid, but now she turned and ran away, her little white boots tracking the blood across the floor. I could still see it, vividly.

And even though I'd heard her say this before, that she didn't remember it much at all, I hadn't really understood until now. Undoubtedly the incident had stayed with her, but on a less-than-conscious level. All these years, while the rest of us had been able to think about it and process it and work through the trauma in our own ways, Nicole hadn't had that luxury. Though the incident was tucked away somewhere deep in her brain, she'd been left with the nearly impossible prospect of overcoming a trauma she couldn't even recall. No wonder she was so messed up.

My heart nearly breaking for her, I asked the detective to excuse us for a few minutes and then I helped Nicole the rest of the way into the living room. After pulling the curtain closed behind us, I knelt down and wrapped my arms around my sister and held on to her until her trembling eased. And though she didn't hug me in return, she buried her face against my chest and sobbed as she gasped, "That man in Danielle's drawings…that's how my nightmares always start. I never see the details of his face, but the image is the same, his dead body…just… lying there. In the dreams I see him exactly like that. Then I realize that whoever killed him is coming after me next. I run and I run, but he's always after me, always trying to kill me too."

My stomach lurched at the thought. These were details she had never shared.

"Oh, sweetie," I said, rubbing her back. "How awful. I had no idea."

Before the murder, when Nicole was a carefree child, we would tuck in our favorite dolls every night in their miniature beds, smoothing their blankets under their chins so they would sleep better. But then the nightmares started, and she wanted nothing to do with that ritual. Or much to do with me.

Those dreams kept us both awake, night after night. Her room was next to mine. I still remember her screams, the nightmares she would wake up from that would make her body tremble. I couldn't do anything to help her. Only our parents could calm her down. Soon I began to feel that I had done something wrong. I hadn't protected her at the scene of the crime. And I couldn't protect her from its aftermath either.

I hugged her tighter now, saying, "I'm so sorry. I'm so sorry."

Nicole eventually managed to calm down, and I was able to help her into the bed. After I'd tucked the covers around her, I stayed, sitting on the edge of the mattress and holding her hand until she fell asleep.

When I finally emerged from behind the curtain, I was afraid the detective might be gone, but she was still sitting at the table. I rejoined her, and though I tried to apologize, she wouldn't let me. She just gave me a sympathetic look and assured me that she understood Nicole had been through a lot—then and now. Glancing down, I noticed that Ortiz had gathered up the drawings and tucked them underneath my pile of papers.

"Thanks."

"No problem. Is she going to be okay?"

I thought for a long moment and then nodded, realizing this might actually have been a good thing. If part of her drug habit really was driven by the need to keep those memories at bay, now that they had broken through, maybe she could begin to deal with them at last.

"Lucky for her, she has a psychologist for a sister, right?" Ortiz flashed me a small but encouraging smile. "I mean, I know you can't work with her directly on this, but at least you're in a position to connect her with all the right resources."

"That's true. And trust me, I will make sure she gets the help she needs, no question about that."

It was late, and I knew the detective had to go. Antsy from the commotion as well as from all that had proceeded it, I grabbed a jacket from the hook and offered to walk her to the car. As we went, she asked me a bit more about Nicole's accident, which had happened southeast of here, far from the detective's area of jurisdiction.

I described the incident and answered her questions, but then I was surprised when she asked where things stood from a legal standpoint.

"What do you mean?" I pulled my jacket more tightly around me in the chilly night air.

"With the police. I assume at some point your sister will have to face charges?"

The thought surprised me, but even as she said it I vaguely remembered some discussion between my parents about this that first night at the hospital. I'd assumed the police would let it go because it was a single-car accident and no one else had been hurt. Yes, Nicole had been driving impaired at the time, which was no small matter. But given the seriousness of her injuries, I couldn't imagine the long arm of the law slamming down too hard on her. Only now did I realize how naive that assumption had been.

"So what's the worst that could happen?" I asked, not sure if I wanted to hear the answer.

"Well, clearly, no one's going to do anything until she's out of those casts and walking again. After that, it depends on the DA—and on other mitigating factors, such as whether or not she was in possession at the time, if she has any priors. Things like that."

She looked at me questioningly, but I just shrugged. I didn't know.

We stopped beside a dark Buick. "Best-case scenario," she said as she dug for her keys, "her attorney is already working on some sort of deal. He or she will probably try to negotiate for rehab in place of incarceration. Might even be able to get the charges dismissed entirely if she successfully completes the program."

"Do you think the DA may be more sympathetic if he understood the extenuating circumstances? The situation with the case you've been working on?"

She paused, seeming surprised by the question. "My investigation? That crime happened twenty years ago."

"Yeah, but you saw her in there just now. It's not hard to understand how she ended up going down the path she did. I'm not saying that early trauma excuses her actions now, not by any means, but it definitely makes them a little more understandable."

She seemed to consider my logic. "I suppose I could make a phone call. Whatever ends up happening is really between the judge and the DA, but they do have some leeway, so I guess it couldn't hurt."

Once again, I thanked the detective, not just for this but for all of her help. I also apologized for having been curt with her when we met at the school last week, but she just shrugged and said not to worry about it, that I'd been given some pretty disheartening news and my frustration was understandable.

"You're dealing with a lot right now, Maddee. I hope I didn't make things worse by asking about the charges. Please try not to worry about that right now. I'll help out if I can, but at this point your focus—and your sister's—should be on getting her well."

I agreed. "And keeping her sober."

"Yes," she replied. Then we shook hands and she was gone.

My walk back to the house was slow and deliberate. I needed to return to Nicole, but the night air was so quiet and peaceful, the coolness soothing to my frazzled nerves, the starry sky calming to my worried heart. Whatever needed to happen would happen. I just had to trust that God would work things out according to His plan.

As I turned the final corner toward home, I noticed an odd movement up ahead on the right, almost as if someone had ducked into the alley that sat directly across from the carriage house. The Fan district was filled with narrow, brick-paved lanes that had originally been created to facilitate coal deliveries to the rows of homes. These days, those same alleys were mostly used for trash collection—and for shortcuts. Maybe what I'd seen was just someone cutting through that particular alley to get home a little faster.

Still, it didn't hurt to be prudent. Picking up the pace, I immediately crossed to the other side of the street and gave the alley a wide berth. I didn't even look in that direction until I was at my door, but when I did, what I saw was a bit disconcerting. Sure enough, someone was there. It was a man, and he wasn't passing through. He was just standing there, leaning against the wall in the shadows, watching me—until I looked right at him, and then he turned away.

With a shiver, I let myself in and locked the door behind me. I wasn't sure what it was about the guy that bothered me, but he had definitely given me the creeps.

Wanting to get a better look at him, I took a quick peek at Nicole to make sure she was okay, and then I tiptoed upstairs and made my way in the dark to the window that faced in that direction. Knowing he couldn't see in, I knelt there on the floor and peered through the glass. He was still there, but at least now he was smoking a cigarette, which might explain what he was doing.

It was too dark to tell much about him, but then, for just a moment, he was illuminated by the lights of a passing car. The glimpse it gave was brief, but I'd been able to see that he wasn't some kid. He looked to be in his forties at least and was balding and paunchy, not exactly a common hood. Letting the curtain fall, I got up off the floor and headed back downstairs, putting him from my mind. Something about him had seemed odd, but I had bigger things to worry about than a middle-aged guy sneaking a quick cigarette in the alleyway. He was probably just hiding from a wife who didn't want him smoking.

The next day was supposed to be Nicole's first Narcotics Anonymous meeting, but after the drama of last night, I wasn't going to push it. I had a feeling she might need a few days to rally before entering this next phase of her recovery.

At work, I had a long talk with Debra, who thought that what had happened was a positive and necessary step. She said Nicole should definitely get some one-on-one therapy, and that more than likely, that would end up being one of the requirements of her sentencing. If not, she should look into it anyway, and Debra could help with some recommendations of therapists who specialized in childhood trauma.

Though I'd checked in with Inez during the day and had been assured that my sister seemed fine, I still didn't know what to expect when I got home that evening. Would she be weepy? Angry? Closed off and shut down? I was prepared for almost anything except what I got. A sister already dressed and in her wheelchair, ready to go to her first meeting as planned.

"You're sure you're up to it?" I asked her once Inez was gone.

"Hey, rules are rules, right?"

I hesitated, teetering between the need to maintain my boundaries and the instinct to extend a little grace. I decided to go with grace, telling her that yes, rules were rules, but that considering what a tough time she'd had last night, it would be okay with me if she needed a few days more to recover first.

"Nah, it's fine," she said, almost casually. She even attempted a little humor as she added, "Changing things around now would mess with your masterpiece of a schedule. I'd rather suck it up and go as planned than give you an excuse for hours of perverse pleasure with a pack of dry erase markers and a whiteboard."

I laughed, grateful that she really did seem okay.

Once again, the night was shaping up to be a chilly one despite the warmth of the day, so I grabbed both of our jackets and slid a thick pair of socks over Nicole's toes, which were exposed at the tips of her casts. In order to fit thirty meetings in thirty days, I had planned out an intricate schedule of gatherings at a variety of locations. Tonight's meeting was just a few blocks away, at an Episcopal church on Monument Avenue, so we decided to walk. As we headed off, her demeanor really did seem upbeat and not at all like the trembling, sobbing girl I'd held in my arms last night. I wanted to ask what had wrought such a change but held my tongue. Better to let her bring it up in her own way, in her own time. Tonight I would simply count my blessings and be grateful for this unexpected rebound.

I did ask her the one question that had been burning in my mind all day—did she know what the legal consequences of her accident were going to be? Without even sounding all that upset, she explained that they didn't know for sure yet, but her lawyer was trying to cut a deal with the DA that would keep her from behind bars. "He said it'll either be jail plus probation or some combination of probation, rehab, counseling, and drug testing. Things like that. Oh, and I'll definitely lose my driver's license for a year."

Just the thought of all that made my head spin—and reminded me how very different her world was from mine. "When will you find out?"

She shrugged. "With my injuries, they're not rushing it. He said I'll probably know by the end of next week. Then, depending on my progress, I'll have to start serving my time around the end of November."

The prospect was so terrifying, I couldn't believe how calm she seemed about it. I told myself it was probably the circles she traveled in, that a life of drink and drugs was one spent in the company of less-than-savory people. For all I knew, her best friend had done time at Chesterfield and her last boyfriend was on the FBI's Most Wanted list.

Trying to push such disturbing thoughts from my mind, I focused on our walk, which was lovely—except for the way others stared at her.

"What is wrong with people?" I asked Nicole after a while. "Haven't they ever seen a woman in a wheelchair before?"

"I think it's the Popsicle legs," she replied, not seeming bothered by it. "At least once I get to the meeting, all that staring can serve a purpose. I'll be a great cautionary tale for the other druggies in the room."

"Nicole," I scolded.

"Hey, sis, this ain't my first time at the ball, you know. I've been to meetings before. I know what they're like."

The revelation surprised me, though I supposed it shouldn't have. The key was to make it work this time in a way it hadn't had a chance to in the past.

"Is it hard, to go in there and participate?" I asked as we came to a stop near the door.

The answer she gave surprised me.

"Kind of," she said, turning to meet my gaze. "But you've been so good to me, Maddee, even if this meeting served no other purpose at all, I would still go through it just because of how important it is to you."

Chapter Eighteen
Celeste

The morning after Celeste installed Berta with the Petits, the physician stopped by the inn and told her that her sister did indeed have typhoid fever.

"She'll need care and rest for quite a while. She's fortunate to have survived. It will take some time until she's over the fever and regains her strength."

"Thank you." Celeste pulled her pouch from beneath her skirt. "Did you inform Madame Petit?"

"Yes. She and her maid are committed to caring for her."

Relieved, Celeste paid his fee, trying not to worry about how long her funds would last. And though she kept the money hidden away in her pouch, she later tucked the brooch from Jonathan under the pallet, where it would be safe. No one besides Sary and herself climbed the ladder to the loft. There was no reason for her to carry it around any longer.

August began even hotter than July. Celeste attended the service at the parish church the first Sunday of the month. Mr. Edwards had explained that attendance was compulsory, at least once a month, and she could be arrested if she didn't attend. She sat next to Aline through-out the Anglican service, missing her family and fighting back tears. She barely listened as the priest read from the Book of Common Prayer and then the Books of Homilies. Instead, her thoughts stayed on her family in England and on Berta. She also scanned the group of soldiers sitting closer to the front, but she didn't see Jonathan. Perhaps he'd trav-eled to the Vines's plantation for the day. Governor Nicholson sat in the very front pew.

When Celeste stood to leave at the end of the service, she saw Spenser slipping out the back. She quickly followed, but by the time she exited he was gone. On their way through the churchyard, Aline detoured toward a cluster of graves, making a quick sign of the cross as she passed by a more recent plot.

When Celeste asked who was buried there, she answered, "One of the maids." Then she pointed across the way. "Over there is Miss Anna-belle's grave."

Celeste shielded her eyes from the noon sun. All of the staff had had so many losses in such a short time. Life was brutal everywhere, but especially in this New World. Relief filled her, again, that she and Spenser had reached Berta in time.

That afternoon, Governor Nicholson came into the inn. He'd been out for a stroll and decided to stop in for a cup of tea and perhaps another serving of Sary's bread pudding. She'd made some the night before, and there were leftovers.

As Celeste served the pudding, the governor asked her how long her parents had operated their inn. She quickly explained that they had left France nearly twenty years ago and began operating the inn soon after.

"They arrived in London around 1685?"

"Yes, sir."

"Huguenots then?"

She nodded.

"What trade did your father have?"

"He was a printer. He still works as one at the *London Gazette*." As soon as it came out of her mouth, she felt she'd said too much.

"Goodness, child. Why are you working as a servant?"

Her face grew warm, and she didn't answer.

He tucked his lips together and then said, "Some sort of trouble, I presume?"

Her head bobbed, involuntarily, but she still didn't speak.

He picked up his spoon. "Well, please advise me if I can help." He probably heard all sorts of sad stories as governor. Celeste wouldn't burden him with hers.

She whispered her thanks and then quickly left the room, wishing there was something he could do. He seemed kind, considering what Aline had said about him, but he couldn't force Jonathan to marry her. And, at least for now, Berta was safe. That was what mattered.

Berta had grown weaker the first couple of weeks at the Petits, hardly speaking at all, but then she began to get stronger. The couple quoted Celeste an acceptable price for Berta's care. Celeste knew the increased work for the maid and cook and the extra cleaning and laundry that needed to be done all added up. She figured she could pay for another few months before the money ran out. She hoped by then that Berta would be strong enough not to need it. What she would choose to do after that, Celeste didn't know.

During the hot afternoons of early September, Celeste helped Benjamin in the garden, harvesting the ripening vegetables. The leaves of nearly everything—both the plants and the deciduous trees—were growing dry and golden. They also picked grapes off the vines. Benjamin explained that the plants were native to the area, and that the ones imported from France had died. Celeste's parents had talked some about the grapes that grew outside of Lyon, but she had never paid much attention. As she gathered the fruit, though, she did think about the Scripture from the Gospel of John her mother quoted, usually when Celeste was acting self-righteous toward Berta. Celeste whispered the words to herself, "'I am the vine, ye are the branches: He that abideth in me, and I in him, the same bringeth forth much fruit: for without me ye can do nothing.'" One time after her mother quoted the verse, she added, "Celeste, you're called to abide. Focus on that."

The memory brought tears to Celeste's eyes. Her mother had been right, of course. Sadly, Celeste wasn't sure she'd ever figured out how to abide. She'd been so pleased with herself for being responsible and trustworthy. It was as if she thought she didn't need to abide, as if she didn't need Christ's sacrifice.

One evening in the middle of September, on one of the first cooler days, Celeste arrived at the Petits' just as Spenser was leaving. He said hello but that was all.

Celeste asked Berta if he visited often, and she said he came when he could. She either didn't have the strength, or the desire, to say more. Later, Madame Petit told her that Spenser stopped by now and then but never overstayed his welcome. Celeste got the impression that the woman was quite taken with him.

Jonathan avoided Celeste and didn't come to the inn. A few times she saw him in the village when she was running errands for Mr. Edwards, but as soon as he spotted her he would do his best to disappear. Toward the end of September, on her way to the inn from the market, she saw him outside of the blacksmith shop, looking the other direction, and decided to catch him off guard. She approached and asked him if he'd sold his carriage.

His face fell. "Please don't be cruel."

She clutched her basket. "Could you answer my question?"

He sighed. "I haven't found anyone who's interested yet." He stepped closer, which surprised Celeste. She expected him to flee from her yet again. "There's something I should clarify with you though. About your sister."

"What about her?"

"I'm afraid she may have...fabricated a story about me."

Celeste shook her head. "What story?"

He lowered his voice. "She made false accusations the day you first brought her here, out on the street."

Celeste nodded. She remembered the encounter but hadn't been able to hear their exchange.

"Perhaps the young man with her told you what she said?"

"Spenser?" Celeste shook her head. "No. He didn't."

Jonathan rubbed his jaw. "That's interesting. I thought at least one of them would have said something."

Celeste again shook her head, annoyed that Jonathan had changed the subject. "Surely there is someone interested in your carriage."

He held up his hand. "Please, Celeste. I need you to know what your sister said in case she repeats her story. Or someone who overheard it says something. I don't want you to be misled."

She raised her eyebrows. He spoke slowly and quietly. "She claimed I asked her to come to Virginia because I had feelings for her. She said I told her I no longer cared for you."

A pain shot through Celeste's chest. "What?"

"Ridiculous, isn't it?"

Celeste took a deep breath. "When did she say this happened?"

"Before I left London. When I was so consumed with tasks I didn't have time even to see you." He leaned closer. "I cared about you, Celeste. I really did. I still do—"

Her heart lurched. "Please don't."

"I know you still care for me." He reached for her hand.

She jerked it away. "Don't." He was only making it harder.

His hand fell to his side. "I heard Berta is quite ill."

"Yes, she is."

"Perhaps her strange words were part of that. I'm wondering if she was delirious."

"Perhaps. Thank you for telling me." She wished she could be sure Berta would never do such a thing—imagine such a thing or, worse, fabricate or exaggerate—but it wasn't beyond belief. Her sister had been known to be both dramatic and deceitful. Exaggeration was her forte, which made her untrustworthy. And she had been intrigued with Celeste and Jonathan from the very beginning. Now that Celeste thought about it, Berta had always seemed taken with him. Sadly, it was believable she would make up such a thing—either that, or she actually thought it was true. Perhaps Jonathan had been too kind to her, and she'd misinterpreted his intentions. Maybe he'd mentioned coming to America, and she took it as an invitation. Whatever had happened, she needed to talk to Berta soon.

"I have to go," Celeste said. "Thank you for telling me."

Jonathan nodded. "I'm enough of a scoundrel from what I've done to you without adding more to it." His eyes hung heavy. "If only I'd known you were coming... Please forgive me."

"I do forgive you," she answered. He was sincerely sorry.

"I know you're in a difficult situation. Having to work harder than you're used to, and below your station in life. And, I promise you, I am trying to sell the carriage to help you. I feel horrible about what's happened."

"Thank you, Jonathan," she said again, turning toward the blacksmith shop. Sadly, she could understand him choosing the plantation owner's daughter. She'd been foolish to give her heart to him. As she hurried away, she still longed for him. Longed for what they had for that short time in London. She'd never felt so alive as she had during those wondrous, heady days.

Her forgiveness had been more sincere this time, and she expected to be filled with relief, but she wasn't. Instead, she found herself mourning the loss of Jonathan all over again. Soon her thoughts shifted to Berta. What would make her sister lie like that? Her illness? Jealousy? Either way, she was more worried about Berta than ever—but now for a different reason.

Even in her anguish over what Berta had done, Celeste questioned what Jonathan told her. What if, for some reason, he had made it up?

She didn't know what to believe.

Celeste couldn't get away from the inn that evening to see her sister. The next day, Benjamin was ill, and she had to start the fires and tend to them all day. It wasn't until an hour before it was time to serve supper that she managed to slip away. She would have to be gentle with Berta. From experience, she knew if the girl felt cornered she would grow silent and wouldn't respond at all. Or worse, she would lie. There were several times growing up that Berta had been punished by their parents for her lying. Not once, no matter how severe the punishment, did Berta confess. She could be the most stubborn person on earth.

When Celeste arrived, Berta was sitting in the salon with Madame Petit. She wore a housedress and her hair was pulled back in a bun, a white frilly cap on her head. She looked the best she had since they had left London, and Celeste couldn't help but smile with relief.

"You're up and about," she said in surprise as she entered the room.

"Only while Judith changes the bed," Berta replied, tiredly.

Celeste's smile faded. She took a seat in the chair Madame Petit indicated but didn't know what to say after that. She was hesitant to bring up Jonathan's claims in front of their hostess, but then Madame Petit excused herself to go check on the bed, perhaps sensing the sisters needed some time alone.

As the woman left, Celeste leaned closer to Berta and got right to the point. "I saw Jonathan yesterday. He said you made some disturbing accusations the day you arrived in Williamsburg."

Berta pursed her lips.

"Can you tell me more about it?"

Berta shook her head.

"This is important. Jonathan said that you—" Celeste nearly choked on the words. "—believed he had feelings for you."

Berta started to stand. "I can't talk about this."

Celeste pulled her sister back down. "I know we've had our differences, but could we please discuss it? I need to know what happened." She had to find out which one of them was telling the truth, which one she could trust. "Did you have feelings for him?" Celeste looked her sister directly in the eye.

Berta's eyes narrowed as she glared back.

Celeste leaned forward even more. "Did you believe he had feelings for you? You told me you'd been kidnapped..."

Berta's cheeks flushed a vivid red, and in that instant Celeste realized that she'd been duped. "You weren't kidnapped?" she hissed.

Berta shrugged, averting her eyes. "You assumed I'd followed you down to the dock out of concern. You assumed I'd been forced aboard that ship against my will. When you asked if that's what happened, I didn't challenge you."

"In other words, you lied."

"I let you believe what you wanted to believe. It seemed…easier."

"Easier," Celeste echoed, stunned. "You told me someone must have knocked you out or drugged you because the next thing you knew you were waking up on board the ship after we were out at sea."

"Again, it was your assumption. I just…elaborated a little."

Celeste couldn't believe it. Not only had the girl lied, but she wouldn't even accept responsibility for those lies. "How did you get on board?"

Berta met her eyes. "The same way you did. I signed a contract. I walked right on with my own two feet."

"But…why?"

Berta shook her head, her eyes filling with tears. "Because Jonathan promised to marry me once I reached Virginia, just as he did you."

Celeste exhaled loudly, unable to take it in. "You're my sister, Berta! You're saying you went out with the man I loved behind my back? How could you?"

"I admit I found him attractive from the beginning. I went out of my way to talk with him, and soon he was taken with me."

"Nonsense. I don't believe you."

"You think I'm lying, Celeste?"

"Yes. Why would he betray me like that?"

Berta folded her hands in her lap. "Why would I lie?"

Celeste could think of several reasons. Spite. Jealousy. Embarrassment. But she couldn't say any of those. Instead, she chose something much worse. "Why wouldn't you?"

Berta stared for a long moment and then whispered, "Yes, perhaps I have lied in the past. And I lied by letting you believe I'd been kidnapped, and by providing a few false details. But I swear to you I'm telling the truth now." Her voice grew louder. "I don't expect you to believe me. But, trust me, if I had known that you were going to be on board that ship, I *never* would have come."

Celeste was quiet, trying to take it all in. This whole time she'd felt guilty for Berta following her down to the dock that day and being abducted, but her sister had made that choice on her own, just as Celeste had. This changed everything.

Berta's face reddened. "You weren't spending as much time with Jonathan."

"He was getting ready to leave the country."

"I hoped you no longer cared for him."

Celeste shuddered. "Did you think to ask me if I did?"

"Honestly, I was so taken with him that I wasn't thinking much about you." Berta placed a hand on Celeste's wrist.

Her sister's touch burned Celeste's skin.

"I was so flattered by his attention..." Berta leaned closer. "God knows the truth, and I've confessed my sins to Him and He's forgiven me. But I still need your forgiveness."

Celeste yanked her arm away. "I wouldn't know where to start."

Berta sighed, closing her eyes for a moment. "Let's start with when you found me on the ship. Believe me, I was as shocked to see you as you were to see me."

Celeste pursed her lips, silent.

Berta continued. "I was so ill by then that I could hardly speak."

"And so you let me speak for you, let me make all the wrong assumptions. Why?"

"Because I had no choice! I needed you to care for me. How would you have felt if I'd told you the truth, that the man you thought you were going to marry had betrayed you for me? Would you have stayed by my side and nursed me across the Atlantic?"

"Of course I would have," Celeste whispered, even as Berta's words echoed in her mind. *He betrayed you for me.*

For me.

It couldn't be true. Berta had to be lying. Celeste stood, wanting to say more but having no idea what.

"I have to go," she murmured, grabbing her cloak and fleeing the cottage.

Outside, the wind blew, whipping the brown leaves from the trees. Dirt and debris pelted Celeste. The first storm of autumn was brewing as she ran down the front steps, her head bent, anger welling in her chest.

"Easy…"

She jerked her head up just before she collided with Spenser. He reached out and steadied her, his hands on her shoulders. "What's the matter?"

Only Spenser's strength could anchor her.

"I spoke with Jonathan yesterday. And then with Berta just now."

Spenser's face fell. "Does this have anything to do with what she said to him the day she arrived?"

She nodded, mute.

"I'm sorry, Celeste."

"Do you think she's lying?"

He grimaced but didn't respond.

"She's lied before, so this isn't that surprising. She was so ill, and I was so desperate to save her that I forgot what she could be like."

"Celeste," Spenser said, gently. "She seemed quite genuine when she confronted him. And heartbroken."

"And how did he seem?"

"Caught off guard. Surprised she was in Williamsburg. Flustered."

Celeste shook her head. "Well, of course. But he was honest with me about what Berta said, wanting to prepare me. She could be lying."

It was Spenser's turn to shake his head. "I don't think she is."

Celeste stepped away from him. Of course he didn't want to believe that the woman he loved was a liar. "I don't blame you for siding with her. You care about her."

"I care about both of the Talbot sisters."

She swallowed the tears welling in the back of her throat. "I need to get back to the inn."

"Can you pray about it?"

"Pray?"

"Yes. For the truth to be revealed."

She couldn't tell Spenser she hadn't prayed in the last half year. She stumbled past him.

"Celeste!" he called out, but the word was muffled by the wind

howling through the village. Ignoring him, she braced herself, marching down the street, the wind pushing her sideways. She held onto her
cap and increased her speed as much as she could. She'd forgiven Jonathan for not waiting for her. Could she forgive Berta for lying?

If Berta hadn't come, Celeste would still have the ruby. Perhaps she
could have bought her own freedom and then worked for her return
passage to London. Now it would be four years until she was free. Then
more years until she could save any money to return home. And then,
even if that all went smoothly, they couldn't risk Berta's health with
another voyage.

Celeste was destined to stay in this New World, penniless, with no
hope of marriage and no family of her own. And with a sister she most
likely couldn't trust.

That evening, after dinner was served and Celeste was scrubbing a
pot with her calloused hands, Sary asked her in French what was wrong.
Celeste could have tried to ignore her. Rain battered the window, and
the wind howled too, scraping a branch from the hickory tree against
the eaves.

But it was seldom that Sary asked Celeste anything, so she decided
to respond while avoiding an actual answer.

Celeste lifted her head. "Just a spat with my sister. Is it that obvious?"

Sary nodded over her shoulder as she tended the fire. "Must have
been a bad one."

Celeste merely concentrated on the pot.

Sary stepped to Celeste's side of the table and gathered up the leftover rosemary. "You're fortunate to have a sister close by."

Celeste murmured in agreement, remembering Sary mentioning
her own sister. She paused for a moment and then asked, "Did you ever
have conflict with yours?"

Sary's eyes grew misty as she put the herbs in a basket. "A few times.
But she was older than me and stronger. She was always praying—for

all of us, but especially for me. She was very protective of me. In fact, that's how she ended up dying."

Celeste gasped.

Sary nodded. "She put herself between me and a beating."

"What happened?" Celeste wiped her hands on her apron, moving slowly, hoping Sary would keep talking.

The woman paused and looked toward the kitchen door, even though they were speaking in French. "My husband had died the month before from malaria."

Celeste blinked, startled. This was the first time Sary had ever mentioned a husband.

"We tried to save him, but he never had a chance. Of course, I was distraught. Neither my sister, Orrinda, nor I wanted to leave what had been our home our entire lives. Our mother was ill with malaria too, and we asked to stay with her for just a few more days. I wasn't *not* cooperating—not intentionally. I just couldn't seem to move. Not only did Orrinda get whipped, but she was pushed and hit her head..."

"Sary." Celeste put her arm around her, pulling her close. Sary leaned against her but didn't say anything more.

"I'm so sorry." Celeste wanted to know exactly what happened, but the woman remained silent.

Celeste held her tighter, not letting go until Sary took a deep breath and pulled away, a dazed expression on her face. She seemed to have said all she was going to—at least for the moment.

Celeste hoped that someday Sary would feel safe enough to tell her the rest.

Sary put the basket on the shelf and then stepped back to the fire, bending down. "I suppose whatever happened was your sister's fault."

Surprised the woman had broached the subject of Berta again, Celeste simply replied, "I hope not, to be honest." She couldn't bear to think that Berta had betrayed her. Hearing just a bit of Sary's story made her even more desperate to find a sense of harmony with her own sister. But no matter what, Berta had been willing to steal Jonathan away from her, or else she'd lied about having done such a thing. Either option was horribly cruel. Celeste didn't know if she could forgive her for either, but she desperately wished there was a way to discern the truth.

"Can you make it right with her?" Sary asked.

Startled, Celeste glanced up from the pot. "Pardon?"

"Your sister. Can you make amends with her?"

Celeste pursed her lips together. Berta had asked for her forgiveness, but she wasn't going to tell Sary that. Instead, she answered, "Perhaps," and tackled the pot again. She'd been able to forgive Jonathan, but this was different. Maman had always claimed Berta and Celeste would one day be best friends. Now that day would never come. What Berta had done was unconscionable.

That night as Celeste tried to fall asleep over the rhythmic beat of the rain pounding the roof, she thought of Sary, her husband, sister, and mother. Then she thought of Maman, and of Berta.

She missed her mother more than anyone. Maman was always gentle. Always quick to pray about a problem. Always ready to forgive. Now, an ocean away, she realized that her mother had been her best friend, but she'd never valued the relationship as she should have. If only she could have the same with her sister now.

Was Celeste the kind of woman who could forgive a man who had jilted her but not her sister for lying to her? Or, perhaps, betraying her? A sister who was one of a very few people she had any relationship with at all in this New World?

And what if she didn't forgive Berta? Already she felt the threat of bitterness.

Would she grow more resentful for being stuck in Virginia with no hope of freedom for four years? No hope of ever going home? She and Berta would have to work together to survive, if her sister was willing.

But what was Celeste willing to do to embrace her sister?

Spenser had suggested she pray. She tried to, but all she could manage was *Lord, please help me.*

CHAPTER NINETEEN
Celeste

*C*eleste didn't return to the Petits' home for several days. She vacillated between wanting to distance herself from Berta to chastising herself for even considering such a thing. Could she really abandon the only family member who was on the same continent as she, the only one she could have a meaningful relationship with? That thought alone made Celeste feel as if she were on a ship without a sail.

At times she feared her grief might overwhelm her, but each day she rose from her pallet in the loft, washed her face and hands, and continued on with the life that she'd inadvertently chosen.

On the third day after she confronted Berta, Monsieur Petit came into the inn. Out of politeness, Celeste asked how Berta was doing.

"Very well. She seems to be recovering." Lowering his voice, he added, "I asked her what her long-term plans were, but she doesn't seem to have any."

"She'll have to find a position in the village. She'll need to work to pay her keep, like the rest of us."

"And where will she live?"

"I'm not sure…" As Celeste cleared his plate, she thanked him for keeping her sister. "It's been such a relief for both of us."

He sighed. "We're happy to have helped, believe me. I just don't want her getting used to being waited on."

"Of course. She should be able to secure a position soon." Perhaps one of the village families with children needed a governess. Berta had never been particularly good with little ones, but she was smart and well educated. Surely someone could use her services. Celeste couldn't imagine Berta working as a maid. She feared her sister would fall ill again under such a heavy load.

Perhaps Spenser would be in a position to marry Berta soon. She would be able to keep house for him, and maybe by the time any children came along, Berta would have grown strong enough and mature enough to be a good mother.

After thanking Monsieur Petit again, Celeste continued on with her work. She couldn't abandon her sister despite her betrayal. Berta was all she had now, though Celeste dreaded seeing her more than anything.

As the days grew cooler, Sary grew quieter. Several times she seemed lost in thought, staring into the fire when she should have been cooking. But a gentle reminder from Celeste, lest Mr. Edwards notice, seemed to bring her back. At least now Celeste had an inkling of what troubled her.

Celeste found a rhythm in doing her duties, and each day she seemed to gain more strength in carrying trays of food and dirty dishes, scrubbing pots, and helping Sary. Yesterday Joe and Benjamin had started picking the apples. The storm had knocked many to the ground, leaving them bruised. Sary and Celeste had spent the day making apple butter. Most of the others would be pressed into cider, except for enough to make apple tansy that evening for dessert. Celeste could practically taste the nutmeg and cream. It was a dish she'd had often back home in the fall when farmers peddled their apples in London.

The second week of October, eight days since she'd last seen Berta, Celeste readied herself to go and visit her again. It was late afternoon, and she was about to leave when Spenser stepped into the inn and motioned for her.

"What's wrong?" she whispered as she approached, afraid she'd waited too long to go see Berta and that her sister had taken a turn for the worse.

"Monsieur Petit sent me. Constable Wharton is at their home."

"Oh, dear." Celeste's heart raced, and she wished she had gone to see Berta sooner. "What does he want?"

"His servant back."

"I'll go get the contract." Celeste hurried toward the back door. "I'll meet you there."

After she retrieved the document, she kept it under her cloak as she hurried along. Another day of rain had turned the street into a muddy mess. Benjamin said by winter the mud would be a foot deep. Celeste was beginning to believe him. She held her skirts as high as she could, but there was nothing she could do about her boots.

When she reached the Petits', the front door was open, and Monsieur filled the frame, as if waiting for her.

She cleaned her boots as best she could and hurried into the house. Constable Wharton was on the settee, and Spenser stood beside Berta in front of the fireplace. Her coloring was good, and standing didn't seem to be an effort. Madame Petit was nowhere to be seen.

The constable stood as Celeste entered the room. He wore his wig this time, but it was a little lopsided, as if it had been whipped around by the wind. Monsieur cleared his throat and motioned toward the constable as he addressed Celeste. "Miss Talbot, this good man wants to ask you some questions."

"I can explain everything." She extended the contract.

Constable Wharton stepped forward, took the document from her, and then scanned it. "Where did you get this?"

"Madame Wharton. She made the transaction."

"And who stamped it?" he asked.

"She did," Celeste answered. "And Mr. Rawling signed it."

Constable Wharton glanced toward Spenser. "So you are now, allegedly, the owner of Miss Berta Talbot's contract."

"Yes, sir." Spenser spoke with confidence. "But I'll sign the contract over to Berta as soon as she is well."

"My wife had no right to do this. It's not legally binding."

Celeste hung her head. She knew that. She just hadn't thought he would come all this way to make the claim. Constable Wharton opened his hand. In it was the ring. "However, as an enforcer of the law, I'm most concerned about the payment. Is this what was used?"

Celeste couldn't look at Berta as she answered, "Yes."

"And where did you get it?"

"It was my mother's." Celeste eyes fell to the floor, not wanting to see her sister's reaction, but she couldn't miss Berta's gasp.

"Your mother's? I find that hard to believe," the constable said. "I think it's more likely that you stole it. Perhaps on the *Royal Mary* on the way over?"

Celeste shook her head. However, she *had* stolen it.

Berta found her voice. "You took our great-grandmother's ring?" she asked in French. "From Maman?"

Celeste could only nod and whisper, "I did." This time she met her sister's gaze.

Berta's face turned ashen, but in a calm voice she said, "She didn't steal it. It was our mother's, and her grandmother's before that. Maman had always promised it to Celeste." Berta frowned. "I didn't know until now that Celeste had used it to buy my freedom. That's not what it was meant for."

Constable Wharton turned toward Berta. "Perhaps both of the Talbot sisters need to be questioned about the ring. Perhaps you worked together to steal it."

"No! Berta didn't even know I had it."

He turned his attention back to Celeste. "Are you saying your mother gave it to you or that you took it?"

"She always told me it would be mine," Celeste said. "But she didn't know I took it when I did."

"I see." He made a fist around the ring and then crossed his arms, rocking back on his heels. He shook his head. "Perhaps you took it from someone besides your mother. Why would a girl with a ring of that value end up as an indentured servant?"

"I came to this country without my parents' knowledge or blessing.

I believed my contract would be purchased by my betrothed when I arrived in Virginia. I'd hoped to keep the ring in my possession. I only brought it with me to be prudent, in case something went wrong."

"There were a lot of thefts reported on the *Royal Mary's* last passage, including jewelry. Perhaps that's where you obtained the ring."

Celeste shook her head, wondering if she should mention that she herself had been a victim of theft during that passage. She decided not to bring it up, sure it would only serve to confuse matters. "I'm not a thief."

"I can confirm that Celeste had possession of the ring," Spenser said.

"Can you?" Constable Wharton shifted his gaze to Spenser. "Did you board the ship with her?"

"No, sir!" Spenser spoke with force. "But I can vouch for her integrity. She wouldn't have stolen the ring."

"She says she took it from her mother. Isn't that stealing? She admitted to that herself."

"She didn't steal the ring," Spenser said.

Constable Wharton snorted. "It looks as if we may have three thieves. Perhaps there's more jewelry hidden away."

"Of course there's not," Celeste said. "Don't be ridiculous."

He held his palm out again. "I had this appraised by a man staying in Norfolk at the Bayside Tavern. He's done extensive work in Europe and is thinking about buying land here. His credentials are solid. He said it's worth much more than your sister's contract. I can't fathom you would practically give it away to my wife if it was a family heirloom."

"My sister was *dying* in your care." Celeste's voice shook as she spoke. "I had no choice if I wanted to save her life."

Berta gave out another gasp.

"A relative of the Vines family was one of the first-class passengers who had jewelry stolen. I'm headed out to their plantation in the morning. In the meantime, I'll search all of your rooms." Constable Wharton nodded toward Berta. "Starting with you."

"Shouldn't you consult with the constable here first?" Spenser asked. "This is under his jurisdiction."

"How about if I consult with the governor himself? I'm well acquainted with him."

"He's out of town." Mr. Edwards had mentioned the fact to Celeste that morning. Otherwise she would have been tempted to seek his help directly. "He won't be back for a few days."

"With that information," Spenser told them, "I'll go fetch the Williamsburg constable then." He started toward the door.

"There's no need—" Constable Wharton began.

Monsieur Petit shook his head. "No. I agree with Mr. Rawling. Go ahead, son. Tell Jones to go to the inn."

Constable Wharton started to protest but then shrugged. "Fine. As long as he doesn't get in my way."

Spenser didn't look at Celeste as he hurried by.

Constable Wharton looked to Monsieur Petit. "I'll start here, with the younger Miss Talbot's room. Please direct me."

Berta and Celeste stood across from each other. "Thank you for defending me," Celeste whispered.

Berta frowned. "You shouldn't have taken Maman's ring."

"She always intended for me to have it."

"Yes, when you married George. She wouldn't have wanted you to take it to America with you, chasing after a British soldier."

Celeste didn't respond. She knew what her sister said was true. Her shame had been exposed.

Berta's voice wavered as she spoke. "And you shouldn't have traded it for me."

Surprised, Celeste locked eyes with her sister. "You're right about my taking the ring—but not about my trading it. You would have died."

Berta's eyes teared up. "Did you bring any other jewelry with you? Take anything else from Maman?"

Celeste shook her head. "All I have is a brooch Jonathan gave me."

Her sister's expression darkened, but before she could say anything, Madame Petit stepped into the room and to Berta's side. "What is going on?"

As Berta explained, Constable Wharton came back into the room.

"I'll follow you down to the inn," he said to Celeste. "Your sister isn't hiding anything, but I suspect you are."

"Tell him about the brooch," Berta said.

Celeste looked him directly in the eye. "I have a porcelain brooch that was given to me by a young man. It's not worth enough to hardly mention. It's under my sleeping pallet, but that's all the jewelry I have."

The constable harrumphed. "Who is this young man?"

Celeste's face grew warm. "Lieutenant Gray."

"Jonathan Gray?"

She nodded.

"Isn't he betrothed to Mr. Vines's daughter?"

Celeste shrugged, choosing not to answer the question.

The constable laughed. "Why in the world would you name him as the giver?"

"Because it's the truth."

"We'll see," the man responded. "Now lead the way to your room."

"I live above the kitchen at the Publick House Inn. Mr. Edwards is my—master." She tripped over the word. It was still hard for her to say.

"I'm acquainted with Mr. Edwards. I stay at the inn when I'm here for the General Court."

Celeste knew the Court was only held twice a year. If Constable Wharton decided to arrest her, would she be jailed until the next session? At least it was just over a week away. Still, her heart raced in fear. If only she could place her whole confidence in God now.

She turned toward her sister to tell her goodbye.

Berta's eyes warmed. "I'm praying for the whole truth to be revealed—and believed." Clearly Spenser had been influencing her.

"Thank you," Celeste said, wishing she could pray along with her sister. But her soul was a desert, dry and lifeless. Berta—a known liar—had more faith than she did.

Chapter Twenty

Celeste

Celeste led the way down the street, holding her skirts high and trying to navigate through the mud. The wind blew hard through the trees, and rain started to fall. She lifted her hood over her head and trudged on, Constable Wharton right behind her.

When she reached the inn, she scraped her boots on the front porch, entered the foyer, and left the constable on the porch. Mr. Edwards stood at the counter going over paperwork by the light of a candle, quill in hand. Aline stepped past Celeste, said a quick hello, and headed upstairs with a basket of clean linens.

Mr. Edwards glanced up. "What's the matter? Why aren't you in the kitchen?"

"There's a man on the porch who wants to speak with you."

Mr. Edwards raised his white bushy eyebrows. "What about?"

"Me."

His eyes narrowed, and with concern in his voice he asked, "What's happened now?"

"Nothing. It's all a misunderstanding. He thinks I stole a ring—but it had been in my family for years." She quickly explained what happened.

Mr. Edwards put down his quill.

"He wants to search my room for other jewelry. I told him about a brooch I have, that Jonathan gave me. Of course, he thinks it's stolen too—"

"Hello, Edwards."

Celeste turned her head. Constable Wharton stood behind her, his hat in his hands and his wig wet against his forehead.

"Goodness." Mr. Edwards stepped from around the counter and drew on his innkeeper personality, one Celeste had seen both mediate arguments and soothe distraught patrons. "It's good to see you, Mr. Wharton."

"Constable."

"Yes, that's right. Constable Wharton." Mr. Edwards extended his hand and the two men shook. "How have you been? We haven't seen you for a while."

"Not since the last General Court."

"You're here early, then, aren't you? It's more than a week until the Court convenes."

"I'm here on other business." Wharton scowled at Celeste.

Mr. Edwards kept his voice even. "What can I do for you?"

"Miss Talbot already told you. I need to search her sleeping quarters."

"She mentioned that. I'm just surprised, is all."

Wharton cocked his head.

"I haven't had a single problem with her."

"Not like your last maid?"

Mr. Edwards leaned against the counter. "What have you heard about that?"

Constable Wharton frowned. "That she got herself into some trouble."

Mr. Edwards's eyes saddened. "Perhaps we could talk about her later."

When Wharton didn't respond, he said, "Come along. Miss Talbot rooms with the cook, above the kitchen. We'll go around outside.

I don't want my patrons wondering what's going on." The innkeeper grabbed his hat and led the way. "Just remember that I cooperated with you, and I can't afford to lose my help right now. We're short staffed as it is…And the General Court *is* coming up soon." As he passed Celeste, he gave her a sympathetic look and then started prattling away again. "She's an honest girl, I can assure you. Like I said, I haven't had one problem with her."

Celeste appreciated his words but doubted they would do any good. She followed behind him out the front door. The rain blew sideways now, stinging her bare hands and face.

As they reached the kitchen door, Spenser arrived with Constable Jones. Clearly, he'd been apprised of what was going on because he said, "This is my jurisdiction."

Constable Wharton bristled. "Not so fast. If a crime was committed, it would fall under *my* jurisdiction."

Mr. Edwards opened the door, saying, "Just search the room."

As they traipsed through, Sary's eyes grew large.

"Tell her not to worry," Mr. Edwards instructed Celeste.

She spoke to Sary in French as quickly as she could, telling her what had happened and that everything would soon be back to normal.

Sary nodded, her eyes darting from man to man.

Celeste wondered how they would all fit in the small loft, but only she and the two constables ended up going up the ladder. Mr. Edwards and Spenser both remained in the kitchen. Once she reached the top of the ladder, she walked straight to her pallet and removed the brooch from beneath it. It was all she had from Jonathan, the only thing that was left of his promise. She handed it to Constable Wharton.

He eyed it and frowned. "I'll take this with me too." He slipped it into his pouch. "And show it at the Vines's plantation."

"You'll need to record it as evidence," Constable Jones said. "So it can be returned to Miss Talbot when the case is closed."

"Don't tell me how to do my job." Wharton flipped the pallet. Then he shook out the single blanket. Next he flipped Sary's bed. From there he went to the washstand and searched beneath the pitcher and basin, and then along the underside of the crate. His hands empty, he stepped to the clothes hanging from the pegs and searched them.

"I told you there was nothing here," Celeste said.

He turned toward her and held up his pouch. "This is quite enough, I assure you. So far it appears you've stolen from passengers on the *Royal Mary*, and then you fabricated a story that the ring originated in Paris and a soldier, who is betrothed to another, gave you a brooch. How can you, an indentured servant, have a family who is wealthy enough to own a ring worth more than you will ever see in your entire life? And how could you, an indentured servant, have managed to captivate the interest of a soldier—who, I'll say once again, is betrothed to another."

"I'm not lying. Both things are true. I was betrothed to him before Miss Vines was, back in London. He's the reason I came here."

Wharton looked at Jones. "Even you must admit this is highly suspicious."

Jones shrugged. "Do you have any evidence that she actually stole the items?"

"I'll go speak with the Vines family tomorrow. Surely I'll have evidence then. In the meantime, I'm arresting Miss Talbot on charges of theft."

"No!" Celeste gasped.

"*No* is right!" Mr. Edwards bellowed up the ladder. "You cannot incarcerate my kitchen maid."

"Of course I can," Constable Wharton responded.

Jones crossed his arms. "I need to question Lieutenant Gray."

"Fine." Constable Wharton jerked his head toward Celeste. "Descend." As she did, he said to Jones, "Send the young man after him and tell him to meet us at the jail."

When they reached the bottom, Jones directed Spenser to go to the barracks and summon Lieutenant Gray.

Spenser answered, "Of course."

Celeste reached for his sleeve. "After you do that, please check on Berta. And when the governor returns, would you let me know immediately?"

"Yes. I'll do everything I can." Spenser hurried toward the door.

Mr. Edwards folded his arms across his chest and confronted Wharton. "This isn't right. I've had no problems with her. Nothing has gone missing. She's not a thief."

Wharton grabbed Celeste's arm, squeezing it tightly, and hissed to Mr. Edwards, "This is none of your business."

"It certainly is. I cannot run my inn without her."

"That's not my problem. And if you interfere further, I'll charge you with harboring a criminal."

Mr. Edwards took a step backward, bumping against the shelf, a look of misery on his face.

"Send the boy with our meals," Jones said to Mr. Edwards. "We'll get to the bottom of this as soon as we can."

Celeste stifled a smile. Constable Jones's love of Sary's cooking was probably the only hope she had.

As Wharton dragged her from the room, Celeste quickly told Sary what was going on. "I'll be back soon," she added. "Don't worry."

But Sary clearly was worried.

Once they reached the street, Wharton kept his grip on Celeste's arm as they followed Constable Jones, taking the usual route to the jail.

The two men led her through the gate and into the courtyard. "Take her upstairs," Wharton said. After all these months of delivering food, this would be her first look inside a cell.

Daylight was fading as Jones unlocked the gate and led her through. A man shouted from the closest cell, "Where's my dinner?"

"Pipe down!" Jones called out.

"Who do you have there?"

"None of your concern!" Jones barked. He led Celeste through a doorway and then up a ladder to a trapdoor. He opened it and led the way to the loft. She knew that was where the women stayed, not that any had been jailed since she arrived in Williamsburg that she knew of. She crawled inside, dragging her skirt through a puddle of water that had come in through the open window. The room smelled of mold. It was cold and dark, except for slivers of light making their way through the bars in the window.

"I'll close the shutters." Jones reached for the wood panels. "There's a blanket in the corner, and I'll bring your dinner when it arrives."

"Will I be released as soon as Jonathan verifies my story?"

He hesitated. "I hope so."

"Thank you."

As he secured the shutters, the room fell dark. He started to descend the ladder but then stopped. "I'm sorry about this, Miss Talbot. I don't believe you stole anything either."

Before she could respond, he was gone. A moment later, Constable Wharton said something to Jones in a harsh tone, but Celeste couldn't make out the words.

She crawled across the rough floorboards, searching each corner until she found a musty blanket and a chamber pot. She pulled the blanket over her cloak, wrapping herself in it, and then collapsed on the floor, trying not to think of Berta.

She stayed awake for as long as she could, hoping Jonathan would arrive soon and wishing for some sort of dinner. By the yelling from the two cells below, none of the men had received their meals either. Celeste could imagine the chaos at the inn with Benjamin and Mr. Edwards serving. Aline was probably helping too.

As she waited, she felt more and more disoriented in the pitch-dark, and it wasn't long until she fell asleep.

A knocking sound woke Celeste. It took her a moment to remember where she was, and once she did she couldn't tell if an hour had passed or an entire night. Then it all came back. She was in the jail's loft. She pulled the blanket around her as she rose to her knees, wondering why no one had woken her once Jonathan was found.

The trapdoor creaked. "It's Jones," the constable said. "I have breakfast for you—and a visitor."

Celeste scooted over to the shutters and opened them, letting in more of the cold air, hoping Jonathan had come at last. No one was below. After straightening her cap over her disheveled hair, she pulled the blanket tighter, anticipating that Jonathan was on the ladder too.

The trapdoor popped up and then clunked heavily against the rough boards of the floor. Instead of Jonathan, Spenser appeared, holding a bucket.

For a moment disappointment washed through her, but Spenser's face reflected so much sympathy that she couldn't help but be thrilled to see him.

"Are you all right?" He looked as if he hadn't slept.

She nodded. "Where's Jonathan? Why didn't he come last night?"

"He took off to the east in his carriage yesterday morning. No one has seen him since."

Celeste sank back on her heels, speechless for a long moment. Once Spenser made his way through the hatch, she managed to say, "Well, if he's at the Vines's plantation, he's soon in for a big surprise." Celeste was certain Constable Wharton would mention her and the relationship she claimed to have with Jonathan. It wasn't her concern how Miss Vines would react.

"He'll tell Wharton about the brooch. And about his treatment of you, I'm sure of it." He handed her the bucket. "Sary made you biscuits and tea for breakfast." Lowering his voice, he added, "And she sent along some smoked pork for later."

She thanked him, taking the half-full pewter mug first. It certainly wasn't the way tea was usually served, but it was still warm. She wrapped her hands around it, grateful.

"I've made some inquiries into a solicitor for you."

"I don't have enough money to pay for one." Celeste still had some funds left, but she would need every bit to pay for Berta's care in the coming weeks.

He shrugged. "We'll figure it out. Hopefully, your case can be heard in the General Court next week. The sooner this is settled, the better, but it sounds like the judicial system here doesn't work the same as in England. Things don't seem to be as—uniform."

Celeste inhaled deeply, knowing it was pointless to ask any more questions. Spenser couldn't predict how things might turn out. "How's Berta?"

His face darkened. "Wharton took her with him."

Celeste gasped.

"He declared the contract void, of course. In his mind, he's reclaiming his property."

"Is he taking Berta with him to the Vines's Plantation?"

"Apparently so."

Celeste held the mug closer, as if she could find comfort in its warmth. She was terrified for Berta. And though Spenser surely was too, he had a calmness about him that she admired. Perhaps he'd prayed for Berta and had faith she would be all right.

She took a sip of tea, hoping it would calm her, as Constable Jones called up the ladder, "That's enough time."

Celeste thanked Spenser and then added, "Make sure to let me know when the governor gets back. He might help me." She wasn't sure that he would, but she had to try.

Spenser nodded. "We'll get you out as soon as possible." He turned to go.

"Wait." Reaching toward the bucket, Celeste removed the cloth covering to reveal two biscuits. She took one for herself, along with the pork, and then she slid the bucket toward Spenser and directed him to give the other to Constable Jones. "He's probably hungry."

"Good idea. I'm sure he'll be grateful." Spenser stuck an arm through the bucket's handle so he could grip the ladder with both hands.

"And you should take mine." She held her biscuit out.

He shook his head and grinned. "You keep it. Sary already gave me two."

Celeste couldn't help but smile back.

After he was gone, she scooted close to the window, wrapped the pork in the cloth, and tucked it away. Then she bit into the biscuit. Warm butter filled her mouth. "God, please bless Sary," Celeste whispered. Tears stung her eyes. She'd prayed without realizing it. She wiggled her toes in her boots. Mr. Edwards had known it would grow cold and wet and muddy. He'd cared for her too. "Thank You for Mr. Edwards and for the boots."

She thought of her parents teaching her that all good things came from God. She believed that. Then she thought of her catechism lessons, of what it meant to honor God. *To call upon Him in all our necessities, seeking salvation and every good thing that can be desired in Him.*

Honoring him was a simple thing, and yet all these months she hadn't been able to. She'd sinned against God, but she sensed He still wanted her to call upon Him for her necessities. For Berta's safety. For justice. For salvation. For life itself. But first for something else.

"Forgive me," she prayed. "I sinned against You and my parents." She would write to them again as soon as she could.

"Please help me," she whispered. "Please help *us*."

She had no right to ask for anything good from God—but she would anyway, especially when it came to the safety of her sister. "Please keep her safe. Please get me out of here and show me what to do."

She took another bite of biscuit and thanked God for that small blessing. Sary cared about her. So did Mr. Edwards. So did Spenser.

So did God.

She was not alone.

CHAPTER TWENTY-ONE
Celeste

Celeste woke later that afternoon to the rat-a-tat of the drums. As she stretched, voices came up through the window from the courtyard below. She crawled to where she could see through the bars, pulled out her little cloth packet, and nibbled on the pork as she watched what was happening below.

Mr. Edwards spoke with Constable Jones. "Don't make me hire a solicitor, who'll take the case before the governor."

"You know Wharton will have my job if he comes back and she's not here."

"He won't be back," Mr. Edwards said. "He has the ring and his servant. Wharton can try her in the General Court, probably in the spring session instead of this next one, if he has enough evidence. Making her stay in jail until then is pointless. She'll die from the cold when she could be helping me run my inn. Do you want her demise on your hungry conscience?"

"I don't see how I can let her go—"

"I don't see how you can't," Mr. Edwards countered. "Otherwise, no one is getting any food out of my kitchen, and a ship is docking in a few hours." Celeste had heard a ship was on its way with a big load of supplies. It wasn't that more ships wouldn't come during the winter, but sometimes they were delayed.

"Well, that would be a problem." Jones patted his belly. The sound of knocking distracted him, and he stepped from view. A few moments later he said, "I didn't think any food was coming from your kitchen."

"This is just for Celeste." It was Spenser's voice, and a moment later he stepped into view. "Sary sent it. It's some sort of soufflé."

"What?" Jones stepped back into view too. "No breakfast, and now no dinner either?"

Spenser shrugged. "I'm just following orders." Celeste couldn't see his eyes, but she could imagine the twinkle in them.

"You may have the soufflé if you let Celeste out," Mr. Edwards said.

"I can't do that." Jones sounded angry—and defeated.

"I'll just take this up to her," Spenser said, stepping out of view.

"Wait a minute!" Jones turned back toward Mr. Edwards. "You could pay bail."

"I'd rather do that than watch my business fall apart."

"It still might get me in trouble with Wharton…" Jones scratched the side of his head. "Do you trust her?"

"Yes, I do," Mr. Edwards said. "I already told you that last night."

Spenser rejoined the other men. "She won't go anywhere."

"How about back to Norfolk, to try to protect her sister?" Jones asked. "She seems awfully devoted to her. I've seen her going back and forth to Monsieur Petit's house and all."

"Sure, she would want to if she could," Spenser answered. "But she won't have any money to get down there. She'll stay here. Besides, she wouldn't betray Mr. Edwards and go without his permission. Not after all he's done for her."

Celeste scooted a little closer to the window.

"How about if Spenser lets her out while you and I talk through the bail amount? Then you can eat the soufflé."

Celeste guessed the two men had planned this encounter with Constable Jones, making sure it happened at dinnertime. That must be why the pork had been included with breakfast, so she wouldn't go hungry now.

Spenser handed Mr. Edwards the soufflé.

Constable Jones hesitated and then shrugged. "You'll lose the bail if she leaves the village."

"She won't," Mr. Edwards said. "I can assure you."

Finally, the constable handed Spenser the key. A few moments later, as she popped the last bite into her mouth, Celeste could hear him scurrying up the ladder, and then the trap door flipped open.

"The constable's letting you out on bail," Spenser said.

"I heard." Turning, she pulled the shutter closed, wanting the loft to be drier for the next woman forced to stay in it. She hoped it wouldn't be her again. Then she folded the blanket and placed it away from the window.

"Ready to go, then?"

"Yes!" Relief swept through Celeste as she followed Spenser down the ladder, blinking in the brightness. God was using him and Mr. Edwards to meet her needs.

As she stepped out into the courtyard, her employer told her to go on back to the inn, get herself cleaned up, and then get right to work. "Remind Sary we'll have extra people to feed this evening. Tell her to roast the ducks the hunter dropped by this morning and bake the squash. And also to make a compote."

"I will."

Spenser walked with her for the first block but then they parted ways. "Thank you so much," she called over her shoulder as he veered off. "And don't worry. We'll get Berta back here as soon as we can."

He nodded, waved, and disappeared into the trees.

She pulled her cloak tight and hurried on toward the inn, keeping to the edge of the street to avoid the worst of the mud. Dark clouds hung heavy in the sky, threatening more rain. Leaves drifted down from the trees, littering the ground with patches of orange, yellow, and red. She brushed a strand of hair from her face. As Mr. Edwards had said, she would take a moment to wash up and repin her hair. She felt as if she'd spent a week in the jail—not just a night.

After dinner was finished, she would write a letter to her parents, asking for their forgiveness. She hoped one of the sailors on the ship that would soon be docking would deliver it to London for her.

She went through the back gate of the property, through the orchard, and then toward the garden. As she passed the grape vines, she thought about what it meant to abide in Christ and vowed to pray and ask for His help each day.

As she came around the chicken coop, she heard voices yelling. First a man and then Sary. Even if Mr. Edwards were in the kitchen—and she knew he wasn't—he wouldn't have been so harsh. Celeste hurried to the door and flung it open. Benjamin cowered under the table, while Mr. Horn confronted Sary, his hand raised.

"What's going on?" Celeste cried.

Horn spoke without looking her way. "It's time someone taught her a lesson. Edwards has ruined her. She hasn't done a thing all day." He shifted just enough for Celeste to see the whip in his hand.

"Mr. Horn, I'm back now." She tried to stay calm as she stepped into the room. "Everything will be fine."

"That's right," Horn said. "And it will be better than fine after I'm done with her. I never should have leased her to Edwards. He's only made her worse. I'll never get what she could have been worth now."

As he pulled his arm back, Celeste rushed forward, throwing herself between the man and Sary. When the whip came down, it lashed across Celeste's face, along her cheekbone. Sary screamed. The whip came down again, this time on Sary's shoulder, sending her toward the fire. She banged her hand against the pot suspended over the flames, sending hot water across her skin.

Celeste started to pull Sary to the table to get a better look at her hand, but Mr. Horn raised the whip again. Celeste jerked up her free arm, blocking the man and sending him off balance. He stumbled and then fell toward the fireplace, screaming as he landed. He struggled in the flames, trying to get out. Celeste let go of Sary and reached for Mr. Horn. He grabbed her hands but then slipped away in a panic and fell back into the flames. Celeste stepped forward, reaching down again and grabbing him under his arms this time, yanking with all of her might. He wasn't a big man, but the angle was awkward, and he didn't seem to be cooperating.

Then he shifted his weight, and she dragged him onto the hearth, yelling at Benjamin to go get the doctor for Sary.

"Get the constable first!" Mr. Horn shouted. "This maid tried to kill me."

"Don't be ridiculous! I just saved you."

"*After* you pushed me into the fire!"

Sary began to shake.

"Mr. Horn, please wait outside," Celeste said firmly.

He grabbed his whip from where it had fallen on the floor. Celeste's hand went to her face, afraid for a moment that he planned to use it on her again, but his fiery gaze fell on Sary. Celeste stepped in front of her friend, spreading her arms wide. Mr. Horn glared at her before stumbling toward the door, his back bent. His outward appearance matched what Celeste imagined the inner life of a person who traded people would be like.

She turned her attention to the cook. She feared Sary's thumb and index finger might fuse together, so she dipped a rag into cold water and wrapped it around the thumb to keep it separate. If only the cupboard were unlocked and she could get to the honey. She grabbed a jar of linseed oil from a shelf and poured some onto the burn instead, and then she dipped another rag in water and wrapped it around the entire hand. Sary pointed to Celeste's face. It stung, but she didn't think it was bleeding much. Then Sary pointed to Celeste's hands. Both were red, singed while saving Horn, but her injuries were nothing compared to Sary's burn.

Celeste shook her head and said in French, "I'm all right. It's you I'm worried about."

Tears filled Sary's eyes as she stared at the cloth wrapped around her hand, but she didn't say a word, not even in French. How could Mr. Horn believe treating a person that way would change their behavior instead of scaring them to death, or at least into speechlessness?

Celeste knelt in front of her friend. "Has he beaten you before?"

The tears began to roll down Sary's face. She nodded.

"When?" Celeste asked, but Sary just shook her head and with her good hand wiped her tears.

A moment later Mr. Edwards banged through the door. "Mr. Horn said you pushed him into the fire!"

"I was trying to stop him from whipping Sary, but I certainly did *not* push him. I may have inadvertently contributed to him losing his balance, though." She turned toward Mr. Edwards.

He gasped. "You're bleeding."

"From the whip." Celeste lowered her voice. "Sary's badly burned, and she's not speaking. Not even in French. It seems he has beaten her before."

A look of anger quickly passed over Mr. Edwards's face. "I don't doubt it. She was in bad shape when he first brought her here." He shook his head. "Why can't these men leave us alone to run this inn? It's one thing after another." Keeping his distance, he asked, "How bad is Sary's burn?"

"Very bad," Celeste answered. "And it's her right hand. I sent Benjamin for the doctor."

Mr. Horn opened the door. "I sent him for the constable."

Mr. Edwards's face grew white as he turned his back to the man and addressed Celeste, "Am I to lose both of you in the same day? And my bail?"

Celeste shook her head. "I didn't do anything."

"You certainly did." Mr. Horn turned to show his singed shirt and pants.

"That's ridiculous." Despite Celeste's protest, a sudden feeling of helplessness threatened to overwhelm her. "You fell into the fire."

Jones didn't take her to the jail this time—he took her straight to the stocks and pillory, located in front of the courthouse. He forced her head and burned hands into the half holes of the pillory and then secured the upper piece over the back of her neck, pushing down until he could lock it. She wiggled as best she could to release the pressure on the back of her neck, but it was pointless. She could neither stand nor kneel. She had to bend forward awkwardly, and she had to keep her head pointed down. She couldn't see her feet, but she could feel her boots settling into the mud. She hoped she wouldn't sink too far.

She'd never felt so humiliated in her entire life, not even when Jonathan had rejected her. This was public. The entire village could see her.

"I'll be back." Jones stomped off, probably angry that his meals would be further interrupted.

Strands of hair fell from her bun and tickled her face, but she was helpless to move them. A couple of soldiers walked by—Celeste could only see their legs. A woman with two small girls passed next. One of the children pointed at Celeste and asked, "What did that lady do?"

Her mother hushed her and hurried along.

Celeste's hands burned and her back and neck began to ache. She hoped the physician had arrived to attend to Sary. He hadn't by the time Constable Jones had dragged Celeste away.

Other villagers passed by, but Celeste tried to ignore them as best she could. By midafternoon, someone stopped in front of her.

She knew it was Spenser by his boots.

He dropped to his knees and looked up at her. "Oh, Celeste." His voice was tender. "How much more can they expect you to take?"

She couldn't answer—tears clogged the back of her throat, preventing her from speaking.

"Benjamin came and told me."

She managed to ask, "How's Sary?"

He shook his head. "I don't know. I'll go by the inn next." He pulled a small jar from his leather satchel. "I brought salve for your hands. Benjamin said you were burned too. It's from back home and has seaberry oil in it."

Tears began flowing down Celeste's face and dripping off her chin as he carefully applied the salve to the back of her hands.

For a moment he didn't seem to know what to do, but then he dabbed at her tears with the sleeve of his shirt. "There, there. We'll get through this." Next, he tucked her hair behind her ears and then pointed to where the whip had cut under her eye. "Does it hurt?"

"Some."

"I'll come back with a cloth and water and try to clean it."

"Thank you. And check on Sary, please."

"Of course."

But as he started to go, she called him back, asking if his writing supplies were in his satchel.

"Yes."

"If I dictate a letter, would you write it down? To my parents? I don't want to wait any longer."

"Right now?"

"Please."

He seemed to hesitate, but then he sat in front of her and took out a piece of paper, a bottle of ink, a rag, and a quill. He had a small piece of wood that he put the paper on.

"Put, 'Dear Maman and Papa, I'm writing to ask your forgiveness for being deceptive about Jonathan, for stealing the...'" her voice faltered. "'The ring.'" She wondered what Spenser truly thought of her. "'And for leading Berta astray. I'm sorry for the despair I know I've caused you. I don't know my future or Berta's. I will write more when I can. In the meantime, please know that I miss you and you've done nothing to deserve the way I've treated you.'"

Tears began flowing down her face again. "'Your...your loving daughter, Celeste.'"

When Spenser had finished, he held the paper up to dry for want of sand. "I'm sorry for all you've gone through, Celeste."

She couldn't answer for a moment, but then she whispered, "You must think me a horrible person."

"No. I don't. Not at all." He met her eyes. "But I do wonder, have you asked the Lord to forgive you? And take your shame? His forgiveness is immediate. And it will give you the strength to go on."

"Yes. I did that last night."

"Then gather that strength. Without knowing your parents, my guess is they'll forgive you too."

She smiled just a little, not sure they would.

"I'll deliver this to the inn." He folded the paper. "Mr. Edwards will make certain a trustworthy sailor takes it to London for you."

As Celeste waited, the day grew colder and darker. She imagined the clouds gathering overhead, and a desperate loneliness swept through her. She'd felt so optimistic when she'd left the jail, so sure God would take care of her. But in one moment all was lost. Berta had been nothing but a foolish girl. She, on the other hand, had known full well that what she was doing was wrong. She'd known it when she stole the ring. She'd known it when she took off in secret.

She would ask Spenser to go check on Berta as soon as he could manage to get down to Norfolk. Thank goodness, despite the fact that Spenser was an apprentice, his kindhearted master allowed him a great deal of freedom with his time and to make up his lost hours.

As for Berta, in a sense she was in a pillory of a different sort, taken back to a household that didn't care for her with a cruel man as her master.

As good as his word, Spenser returned, carrying a small pan and a cloth.

"How is Sary?" Celeste asked as he approached.

"All right," he answered. "Her hand is badly burned, but the physician hasn't arrived yet. Mr. Edwards is doing the cooking."

"Oh, dear."

"Yes. He tried to recruit me to help serve the meal—just a vegetable soup he managed to put together."

Celeste wasn't surprised Mr. Edwards hadn't attempted to roast the ducks. That would have been too much of a challenge. "What's Sary doing?"

"Sitting at the table."

"Is she speaking French to him?"

Spenser shook his head. "She's not saying a thing. In fact she's just staring into the fire."

That didn't sound good.

"How long do I have to stay in the pillory?"

"Jones didn't say. He indicated he'd return sometime…"

She'd expected he'd be back by now.

"I'll go back and take him some soup. And perhaps there are a few leftover biscuits from this morning I can heat. Maybe that will warm him up…"

"Try to get him fed before it starts pouring. That will only make things worse." The air smelled like rain now. It wouldn't be long.

"I will."

"Is Matthew all right with your missing so much work?"

"I'll make it up. Don't worry about that. Right now I'll see if the physician has checked on Sary and come let you know. About Jones too."

"Thank you, Spenser."

The rain started soon after he left. Celeste's hair fell back against her face. The water rolled off her treated hands but soon the rest of her was soaked. She began to shiver, and as her body shook, her neck pulled against the wood, scraping against her skin. She tried to stay still, but over and over a violent shiver would overtake her. All of her muscles grew stiff and sore.

A few wagons went by. Then a trickle of people on foot, most likely passengers from the ship that had docked. Then a few handcarts pushed by sailors.

Spenser returned at last, out of breath. He knelt down in the mud in front of her again, and she raised her head as best she could to look at him. "The physician treated Sary's hand. He said you did a good job with it, but he's not sure she'll have use of it again, not enough to cook with, anyway."

Celeste felt ill. Sary wouldn't be worth anything to Mr. Edwards, nor to Mr. Horn, without her cooking skills.

"Jones was happy for the food and said he would head this way as soon as he was finished eating."

Celeste thanked him and then said, "You should get on home and get dry." She hoped he would be able to work in front of a fire this evening.

"I will. But I'll wait with you until Jones returns."

"Do you think he'll put me back in the jail?"

"He didn't say."

Celeste sighed. "Even if he does, it will still be better than this."

Spenser shifted closer and looked up at her with his deep brown eyes. "You'll be all right, Celeste," he assured her. "You're stronger than you think."

Before she could reply, two sets of legs came to a stop behind him.

"Celeste?" a man said, sounding incredulous.

Her head jerked up, only to bang against the wood. She lowered it back down, confused and disoriented. Something about that voice…

"Can I help you?" Spenser asked, standing up and brushing at his knees.

"Who are you?" the man replied.

Celeste couldn't see more than his shoes, but suddenly she knew. Without a doubt, she knew.

The voice belonged to her brother. To Emmanuel.

CHAPTER TWENTY-TWO
Maddee

Nicole's first Narcotics Anonymous meeting ended up going well. Though I could tell she was exhausted by the time we got home, she seemed in an upbeat mood. Later, once she was in bed, she asked for a piece of tape, which she used to mount her new key tag on the headboard. White with black print, the triangular plastic tag featured the word "Welcome" on the front and "Just for today" on the back. I knew the group gave out key tags for various milestones, but I'd always thought they were color coded.

"Why is it white?" I asked as I straightened her covers and helped her get comfortable. "Shouldn't it be red or purple or something?"

"The first one is always white. The international color of surrender."

The week flew by as my sister, her caregivers, and I fell into a rhythm. Inez arrived each morning just as I was leaving for work. On Tuesdays and Thursdays, she would stay until I got home in the evenings, after which I'd take Nicole to a meeting and then back home for dinner afterward. On Mondays, Wednesdays, and Fridays, Inez would take Nicole to daytime meetings instead, feed her an early supper, and then stick around until Greg arrived for his evening therapy sessions. It worked out great from the start, though that first week poor Nicole ended each day so exhausted that she fell asleep the moment her head hit the pillow.

The exhaustion I could understand, but what bothered me was the pain she had to endure, especially during physical therapy. Because of the ribs, it hurt her to breathe deeply, yet that's exactly what Greg kept making her do, over and over. He even had a mean little device that required her to blow into a tube hard enough to shoot a Ping-Pong ball up a cylinder.

Wednesday, it was so difficult to watch the two of them work that I had to go outside. I spent the time sweeping the patio and wiping down my bike till it looked shiny and new, all the while distracting myself by trying to come up with a ringtone for Greg's phone number. He was an interesting guy but a little hard to peg, and the best I could think of was the line "thick brown hair and a friendly smile," from a song by the Carolettes. I didn't love it, though, so I decided to wait. Something better would come to me as I got to know him.

On Friday night when he was there, it was too chilly to go outside again, so I headed upstairs instead. But with no door between us, I found it hard to block out my sister's deep, guttural groans as they worked. Soon a different ringtone came to mind, the Pink Umbrellas' "Can't Take the Pain," but I resisted the urge to download it, telling myself this was Greg's job, after all. If Nicole didn't resent how hard he was pushing her, I would try not to either.

But that didn't mean I was going to keep quiet about it. Later, as he was leaving, I asked if he had a few minutes and then followed him out the door and partway down the walk, where he and I could speak privately.

"I have to tell you, Greg, these sessions are brutal. Seems to me that you may be pushing my sister a little too hard."

"I know it looks that way, Maddee, but she's a tough kid. There's a huge amount of determination inside that tiny package."

I couldn't help but smile at the description. She had always been a tiny package, even before losing weight after the accident. Nicole had taken after our mom, who was short and petite—unlike Dad and me, who were Jolly Green Giants in comparison. When my sister and I were teens, standing next to her made me feel like a cornstalk beside a mini pumpkin.

At least Greg had some height to him, I thought now, his eyes just about even with mine as we talked.

"But the pain," I said, ignoring how blue and warm those eyes were. "She can't take anything for that except ibuprofen. Maybe you don't know this, but recovering addicts aren't allowed—"

"Oh, I know," he replied, cutting me off. "All of my clients are in the same boat, Maddee. This is what I do. I'm a certified addiction specialist."

I blinked. "You? I thought you had to be a psychologist for that." I didn't add that if I hadn't decided to work with children, I probably would have focused on addiction disorders instead and become a CAS myself.

"Not necessarily. The certification is open to other medically related professions as long as you meet all the requirements and put in the time."

And a lot of time it was, including several years of experience plus a bunch of additional training. He wasn't just helping Nicole heal from her injuries; he was helping her heal from her addictions as well. In that instant, an image of Nana popped into my head, and I realized what she'd meant when she called the PT she'd hired "special." She hadn't been trying to play matchmaker at all. She had just been bringing in the best of the best, once again—this time a physical therapist who also happened to be an expert in addiction and recovery disorders. Thank goodness I'd been too busy this week to call and fuss at her for something she hadn't even done.

"Anyway," Greg was saying now, "I agree that it's hard to watch Nicole suffer. If it helps, the groaning has as much to do with her lack of stamina as it does with actual pain. At seven weeks, she's on the home stretch with the ribs. They should be better soon. It just hurts to do the exercises because the area isn't immobilized like the legs are. You can't exactly put a cast over a rib cage."

"If it's that painful, though, how can it be good for her?"

He leaned one shoulder against the brick wall of the carriage house. "Treatment protocol requires movement and deep breathing. Without that, she could develop pneumonia, or even a collapsed lung. I know it's not fun, but it's a necessary part of the healing process."

I exhaled slowly, considering his words as he continued. "I do make sure to use moist heat before we start, and I always end with ice. You might try giving her a heating pad at bedtime to see if that helps." He went on to describe other options we could explore, including pain relief patches, a TENS unit, and even acupuncture. "Bottom line," he said, "there are many ways other than narcotics to ease her pain."

"Then ease her pain," I replied, trying not to sound snarky.

Saturday morning dawned cool and cloudy. Today was to be Nana's first visit since Nicole moved in, so I spent the morning baking my special caramel apple coffee cake while my sister kept me company. Our grandmother showed up shortly after eleven, as promised, and the three of us enjoyed the still-warm treat, along with coffee, at the kitchen table.

Fresh from her weekly women's group, Nana seemed to be in a much better, far less anxious state than she had been last Saturday. She'd even brought a little gift for Nicole, a tiny ceramic frog, which she said was in honor of her continued sobriety.

"It's supposed to remind her to F-R-O-G: fully rely on God," Nana explained to me. Turning to Nicole, she added, "That's one of the things they say at those meetings of yours, isn't it?"

"Yes," Nicole replied, studying the little figurine, and though I expected to see a familiar mix of scorn and amusement in her eyes, instead she seemed genuinely touched. "Thank you, Nana. This is so sweet."

Prior to the visit, we had both prepared ourselves for what we called the Onslaught of Nana, but our grandmother was on her best behavior, with not a criticism or insult to be heard. In fact, she went in the other direction, complimenting both the living room setup—especially my "very impressive" whiteboard schedule—and how well Nicole seemed to be doing.

Once we finished our coffee cake, I cleared the table, and Nana grabbed the manila envelope she'd brought with her, set it down, and pulled out its contents, explaining that these were the letters she'd told us about and that she'd made copies for each of us.

"As I said, these letters were written to Catherine Talbot by her daughters. The very first one was sent by Celeste in July 1704. The second one is from October of the same year. Those two are both short and to the point because back then the girls were both so occupied with surviving that they didn't have time for much else. Later on, they wrote more detailed letters, including all about what those first few difficult months in Virginia had truly been like."

Nicole held up the second letter. "The handwriting on this one is completely different. Are you sure it came from her?"

"Yes, but that's an interesting story," Nana said. "Someone else had to write it for her because she was…incapacitated. You'll learn more as you read. "

I stared down at the old-fashioned handwriting. "If the letters were sent to England, how did they end up back in America?"

"One of their younger brothers came over a few years later and brought the letters with him, along with other family documents, including the pamphlet that's now at the Smithsonian."

I nodded. That priceless pamphlet had been donated to the Smithsonian last July in a lavish ceremony, the same weekend our cousin Renee proved there had been blood in the cabin and sparked the official investigation into our old mystery.

"As I said before, I thought the two of you would really appreciate the story these letters reveal." Nana's expression growing intense, she turned toward Nicole, adding, "I especially want you to read them." By the tone of her voice, it sounded oddly important to her.

"O-kay," Nicole replied warily.

"Do you promise to read them?" she persisted, and again I detected some undercurrent I didn't understand. From the look on Nicole's face, our grandmother was making her uncomfortable.

"Yes, of course, Nana. I promise."

Nana wrapped up her visit after that, and then I walked her to her car. As soon as we were out of earshot, I asked what on earth that was about. To my surprise, she wouldn't tell me. All she said was, "That's between me and your sister, dear. Don't be nosy."

Whatever it was, I decided, maybe I would figure it out after I'd read the letters for myself.

There was no time for that now, however, so once I was back inside I tucked our copies safely away in the living room and helped Nicole get ready for today's meeting, which would be at a church in Carytown at one o'clock. I usually spent that hour sitting in the hall and just reading a book or catching up on email on my phone, but today I was feeling antsy, so I went window-shopping along nearby Cary Street instead. Known as the "Mile of Style," Cary Street offered an amazing array of stores and boutiques. And though I didn't buy anything, at least I managed to work off some energy.

Back at home afterward, Nicole and I set about making lunch, a beef-and-vegetable stir-fry with Tahini sauce. As she chopped and I cooked, I offered to put on some music.

"Are we talking about my definition of music or your definition of music?" she asked slyly, gesturing toward the stereo in the living room. "I'm sorry, Maddee. I love you, but I've never seen such a lame CD collection." Setting her work aside, she rolled herself over to the cabinet. "Just the 'ettes' alone are enough to make me queasy."

"The 'ettes'?"

"Yeah, let's see." Running a finger down the neat stack of CDs, she began reading off some of the band names. "We've got the Marvelettes, the Chordettes, the Ronettes, the Barbalettes, the Ikettes, the Jaynetts, the Royalettes, the Velvelettes, the Carolettes, the Marquettes, the Pearlettes, the Charmettes, and the Coquettes. Seriously?"

"Hey, now," I replied, shaking a carrot at her. "Don't judge what you don't know. Have you ever given any of them a try? You just have to get in touch with your own inner girl band."

"Yeah, okay," she said, rolling her eyes.

"Go ahead. Put on any one you want. I promise you'll find something you like."

"Fine." She began sorting through and pulling various CDs from the rack, reading the backs and then setting some of them aside.

"Find anything that looks interesting?" I asked, wondering what was taking her so long.

"Yeah. I'm putting together a medley of hits in honor of your date tonight," she replied with a mischievous grin. We hadn't discussed Austin once since our fight earlier in the week, but if she was willing to have a sense of humor about him now, I guessed I could too.

Her montage started off with the Quin-Tones' "Down the Aisle of Love." Considering that the song opened with a bridal march before moving into the melody, I feared things could only go downhill from there.

At least Nicole had fun with her musical torment, playing songs like "Tonight You Belong to Me" and "Born to Be with You" and "Then He Kissed Me." As I predicted, after a while she seemed to be getting into the music, bopping around as best she could without hurting her ribs to "Sweet Talking Guy," and singing along with the chorus of "Be My Baby." Over in the kitchen, I danced along as well, wrapping up the stir-fry to the Angels' "I Adore Him."

As I fixed her plate and carried it to the table, she put on her DJ voice one last time and announced we'd be ending today's girl band showcase with one final selection, dedicated "from Richmond's prettiest psychologist to the world's hottest doctor." Then she put on the Shirelles' classic, "Will You Love Me Tomorrow?"

"Very funny," I said, making my own, smaller plate as I sang along.

When it ended, she put the CD back in its case, turned off the stereo, and got herself to the kitchen. Watching her, it struck me that she really was doing better. This time a week ago, she couldn't have rolled herself two feet without collapsing in pain.

"So what happens next?" she asked once I said grace and we began to dig in. "We paint each other's nails and watch a Doris Day movie?

Because if that's how this is gonna play out, I'd rather do my taxes or get a root—"

"Oh, no you don't! Make fun of my music all you want, but do *not* malign the Great and Wonderful Doris."

We both laughed, and once again I felt a pang of something deep in my heart, a mix of joy and trepidation. How I had missed my sister! Until she came to live with me, I hadn't even remembered how much.

"Yuca?"

I glanced up from my plate to see the handsome man across from me holding out what looked like a small french fry dipped in mayonnaise.

"Go ahead," Austin urged. "It's really good."

I accepted his offering and popped it into my mouth, savoring the surprising flavors of the fried yuca combined with cilantro and lime. We were sitting outside on the deck of Casa Cubana, a downtown restaurant not far from the Canal Walk. It was a beautiful evening, the chill of the air negated by radiant heaters around the perimeter of the dining area.

Thus far our date had been going great, even if I had been a bundle of nerves at first. This afternoon, while Nicole napped, I had taken my time getting ready to go out. As I smoothed and dabbed and curled and styled, I kept trying to push from my mind the hurtful thing she'd said the other night, how I wasn't good enough for him. It wasn't easy, but in the end I was as ready as I was going to be. At least my outfit worked, a light sweater paired with a wrap dress, leggings, and my beloved stiletto boots.

For Nicole's sake, I had waited for Austin outside on the patio, chatting easily with Miss Vida, who had agreed to hang out with my sister while I was gone. I had enticed her with the offer of the pay-per-view movie of her choice along with, a party-size bag of M&Ms and a big bowl of popcorn with extra butter.

Austin arrived exactly on time, and his face broke into a broad grin the moment he saw me. I immediately felt more at ease. Perfect or not, I'd obviously passed muster. After that, I felt more confident.

He looked amazing in gray slacks, a fitted shirt, and an elegant tie, his smile a perfect white, not a hair on his head out of place. It was fun introducing him to my landlady, especially when she caught my eye behind his back and started fanning her face, pretending to swoon.

His relaxed and pleasant demeanor immediately put me at ease, and I enjoyed our drive to the restaurant in his sporty Infiniti. Once there, we were shown to the perfect outdoor table for two, where we had fun choosing our meals from the elaborate menu. We chatted easily, just getting to know each other a bit. He had a habit of straightening his tie every few minutes, a gesture some might find off-putting but that I liked. It showed he was neat and orderly, qualities I admired. He was also charming and pleasant, and we had so much in common the conversation never lagged.

Now it seemed we had made it all the way to the food-sharing stage. After enjoying the yuca fry he'd given me, I offered him one of my plantains in return.

"Sure," he said, though he didn't take it from me with his own hand. Instead, he leaned forward so I could feed it to him. The motion was oddly intimate, and I could feel heat rising in my cheeks as I slid it into his mouth.

By the time we made it back to my place, I was reluctant for the evening to end. He took my hand as we strolled to the door and kept holding on to it even once we came to a stop. Nerves fluttering in my stomach, I turned toward him and thanked him for a lovely evening. A cool breeze swept past, blowing at my hair, and almost immediately he reached up and tucked away a stray strand.

"Looking a little windswept there," he teased with a grin, his fingertips lingering at my cheek. Then he brought his lips to mine, warm and sweet, for one brief but impressive kiss.

Chapter Twenty-Three

Maddee

The next morning, I was awakened by a four-second clip of music proclaiming, "He's a dreamboat!" A text from Austin. Smiling, I grabbed my phone from the bedside table and checked the screen.

Sunny and warm today. Bike ride and picnic after church?

I hesitated only a moment before responding: *Love to. Will see if I can work it out.*

He replied: *Okay, but two incentives to keep in mind. Roast turkey sliders with garlic-basil mayo. Me in shorts.*

I burst out laughing—and found myself hoping he would deliver on both.

Miss Vida said she was happy to stick around and handle lunch, so I knew that as long as I got back in time to help Nicole in the bathroom and take her to her meeting, it wouldn't be a problem. My sister didn't seem all that happy about it, but I felt sure that had more to do with her reservations about my seeing Austin than spending an extra hour or so with her new buddy. After last week's makeover and last night's movie fest, she and Miss Vida were fast friends.

~

Austin and I ended up riding the James River Trail Loop, stopping to eat at a pretty spot along the water. As promised, he brought the food and drink, including not just turkey sandwiches but also fruit salad, fresh veggies, macadamia nut cookies, and a thermos of lemonade. We had fun, though he did tease me mercilessly about my "sissy bike," especially once I admitted I'd chosen it primarily for the color scheme. He also wasn't too happy about having to cut our time short, but what could I do? Caring for my sister was my top priority right now, and everything else had to come second—even time with this extremely handsome and charming man.

He was almost petulant on the ride back, though once we reached my place, he apologized.

"It's just that now that I've found you, I'd really like to spend time together, you know?"

His words made me blush, but I couldn't have agreed more. There was so much promise here, and not just of more fun afternoons in the park. When I looked at Austin, I saw a home, a family, and a whole brood of beautiful children. A lifetime together. I was still getting to know him, but there was already so much to like. The fact that he was this interested in me in return was enough to make my heart soar.

Before leaving, he asked me out for Saturday, to a party at a friend's house. I accepted, not exactly sure what I would do about Nicole, but with a whole week to figure it out, I should be able to come up with something. To my delight, we also made plans for lunch after church on Sunday, something I hoped would turn into a regular thing.

Maybe my dream of a family wasn't so far off after all.

~

Though we had to rush, I managed to get Nicole to a three o'clock meeting at a Baptist church on First Street. We didn't talk much on the way, but that was fine with me. I was off in my head somewhere anyhow, trying to picture what our future children might look like. Would the girls get my auburn hair? Would the boys have their daddy's broad shoulders and trim waist? Either way, they would be tall.

I brought along a book and spent the hour sitting on the floor in the hall just outside the room where the meeting was held. About halfway through, I peeked inside, checking on Nicole. The chairs were in rows, about half of them full, with a woman addressing the group from a podium up front. Nicole sat off to the side in her wheelchair, and though I couldn't see her face, I could tell from her slumped posture that she was either really bored or in a fair amount of pain.

It turned out to be the latter. By the time it was over, she looked miserable, her skin pale and beads of sweat forming along her brow. Once I managed to get her home and into bed, pills in her system and ice on her aching ribs, I asked if she knew why she was hurting so badly today. To my surprise, she confessed that she'd tried to go the bathroom this morning without help and had ended up falling hard against the handrail as she attempted the transfer.

"Nicole! You could have really been hurt. You know you're not supposed to do that alone."

"Yeah, but I also knew Miss Vida shouldn't do it, and you were off playing footsie in the park with Dr. Ken Doll."

"Hey, watch it," I snapped.

"Sorry. I'm just concerned about you, is all. You guys seem to be moving so quickly."

"Imagine that." I could hear the sarcasm in my own voice. "I guess he doesn't realize that he's too perfect for me. He even seems to like me. And I like him."

She sighed heavily, shaking her head. "He's not the one for you."

"Yeah, you made that abundantly clear the other night. I'm not good enough."

"What?" She pushed herself up from the bed and then fell back down again, wincing from pain. "No. It's not about who's good enough or not good enough. It's about you and this imaginary world you live in."

"Excuse me?"

"Why do you think you love fifties girl bands and Doris Day movies?

For that matter, why do you have a hope chest full of baby clothes you started making fifteen years ago? Because that's where the fairy tales are. The happily-ever-afters. The perfect life with the perfect house and the perfect husband and the perfect children. You've been dreaming that dream since you were a kid, Maddee, but you're not a kid anymore. At what point do you grow up and realize that life is ugly and messy and difficult? That it doesn't tie up in a neat little package with a perfect little bow?"

I gaped at my sister, realizing in that moment how far apart our life choices had brought us. Maybe her world was ugly and messy and difficult, but mine was just fine, thank you.

"What does any of this have to do with Austin Hill?" I asked, not even caring anymore where she was going with this argument.

"You want the things he can give you so badly that you're not even seeing who he is. You're blinded by the same hopes and dreams as always. Don't you get it? You two are too much alike, Maddee—in all the wrong ways. Being with him will only bring out the worst in you. All those tendencies and inclinations inside yourself that you ought to temper will instead just grow and grow until they take over."

"That's the most ridiculous thing I've ever heard!"

"Is it? Put you and him together and what have you got?" She counted off on her fingers. "Obsessively punctual, times two. Compulsively well dressed, times two. Perfectionistic and rigid, times two. Should I go on?"

My eyes narrowed. "No. These are stabs in the dark. You don't even know the man—"

"Exactly. And neither do you. Yet you live in such a fantasyland that after one date you're practically planning the wedding."

"Says who?"

She flashed me a knowing look, and I felt heat rush to my cheeks.

"Whatever," I muttered, leaving the room and ending it there. That was the problem with sisters, I decided as I mounted the stairs. Sometimes they knew you a little too well.

Over the course of the afternoon, we managed to come to a truce and recover at least somewhat from our argument. Still, the clash had left a bad taste in my mouth, and I had a feeling it had done the same for her. She took a brief nap, and that seemed to help, as did ending the evening in front of the TV together, something I rarely did but which seemed about all either of us was up to tonight.

As I was putting her to bed, I grappled for something to say, for the right words that would ease the lingering tension between us. But before I could think of anything, my sister beat me to the punch.

"You do know I love you, right, Stupidhead?"

"Yes. You know I love you too, right, Uglymug?"

"Yes."

We shared a smile, and I headed upstairs feeling much more at peace.

On Monday morning, I called Austin and told him I was sorry, but I wouldn't be able to go to the party with him on Saturday after all. Ever since yesterday, I hadn't been able to get the image of poor Nicole out of my mind, struggling to transfer herself in and out of her wheelchair while he and I were off sharing a picnic lunch in the sun. As much as I would have enjoyed another date with my handsome suitor, spending that kind of time with him was going to have to wait until my sister's casts were off and she could maneuver a little more easily.

"But I've already ordered our costumes and everything," he said, his disappointment tinged with anger.

"Costumes?"

"Yes, did I not mention that? It's a costume party." His sigh was audible. "Can't you get someone to watch her? A friend? Your parents? Hire an aide if you have to. I'll pay for it."

Something in his tone rubbed me the wrong way.

"Thank you, but no," I replied, trying not to sound sharp as I told myself he had a right to be peeved. "If it helps, you'll be taking her casts off in another week or two, hopefully. After that, caring for her will be easier. I'll have more flexibility." Even after the casts were off, I knew, she would continue to need a lot of care as she graduated slowly from wheelchair to walker to crutches to cane to eventually nothing at all. But there was still a big difference between tending to her needs now, which was difficult, and tending to them once her knees could bend and she was able to bear at least some weight on her legs.

We ended the call soon after, but it wasn't until I'd hung up that I realized he hadn't mentioned what our costumes were going to be. How odd that he would make arrangements for such a thing without even checking with me first. I chalked it up to his gifts for efficiency and organization. Better the kind of person who gets things done than one who dithers around until it's too late, even if that did mean making decisions for the both of us once in a while.

When I got home that evening, Greg was there working with Nicole, and I was pleased to notice that she didn't seem to be gasping and grunting quite as much as before, despite yesterday's near fall. Later, I found out why when she showed me her new TENS unit, a small device that helped control discomfort by sending electrical signals directly to the affected nerves.

"I still hurt," she explained, "but this thing dulls the pain somehow. It seems to make it more of an ache than a stab."

On Tuesday, she and I were just sitting down to supper when she got a call from our father, who said he'd heard from the lawyer and had the final word on Nicole's sentencing. She put the phone on speaker, and we listened together as he explained that the judge was giving her two options. The first was two years in jail—of which she would serve ninety days—plus two years' probation. The second was no jail but three to four months in rehab, plus five years' probation. Regardless of which option she chose, she was to undergo regular drug testing starting next week, she would be required to see a counselor for a minimum of ten sessions during the probationary period, she would have to pay a $1000 fine, and her driver's license would be suspended for one year. He suggested she talk to the lawyer herself tomorrow, just to get all the details, but that was basically it.

Nicole seemed to take the news well, though once we ended the call, she was subdued. She asked to go to bed earlier than usual, and I complied without comment. More than anything, she probably just needed a little space and privacy to process her fate.

On Wednesday, I got tied up at work and arrived home a bit later than usual. By the time I walked in the door, Nicole's PT session was pretty much over, and she and Greg were just talking. The curtain was half closed, and they didn't seem to notice me, so I hovered in the kitchen without disturbing them, thinking they would be finished soon.

I could tell by the conversation that she'd shared the news with him about the sentencing, which didn't really surprise me. They had been working together for a while now and had established a nice relationship, not to mention this was something he'd undoubtedly helped other people deal with before, considering his area of specialty.

What did surprise me—shock me, really—was when I realized she wasn't sure which of the two options she was going to choose. In fact, at the moment she actually claimed to be leaning more toward jail than rehab, just because the total time involved would be so much shorter.

"With jail, I get two years' probation," she said to him. "With rehab, I get *five*. I don't think I could do that, Greg. Five years of probation? That's horrible."

I couldn't believe it. I wanted to run in there and scream, *You're choosing punishment over the chance to heal, the chance for a new life?* But somehow I managed to hold my tongue. From the sound of things, he was handling it far better than I could anyway. For the moment I would stay out of it—though I couldn't listen to another word or I'd explode. Quietly, I grabbed my peacoat from the hook and slipped back out the door. Then I sat on the patio in the evening chill and simply waited.

About ten minutes later, Greg emerged, his backpack slung over his shoulder.

"Maddee?" he asked in surprise when he spotted me. "What are you doing out here?"

"I overheard part of your conversation," I explained in a low voice. "My choices were either this or go in there and clobber my sister."

He gave me a look of commiseration and then joined me at the little wrought iron patio table.

"Good choice," he said as he plopped onto the other chair and set down his backpack. "If I were you, I'd keep staying out of it for now. We have time. She said she doesn't have to give them her decision until next month."

We grew quiet as the night sounds surrounded us. A car honking in the distance. A garbage can being rolled to the street. A light wind rustling the treetops.

"What can I do in the meantime to knock some sense into her?"

"What you've been doing all along. Taking care of her and being here for her. I promise, Maddee, your part has a bigger impact than you know."

"Didn't sound like it to me."

He shook his head. "She's just reacting to the news right now, that's all. Did you know something like eighty percent of addicts pick jail over rehab when given the choice?"

My eyes widened. "Seriously?"

He nodded. "But Nicole is different. I think once she's had time to think things over, she'll make the right decision. I'll help her get there."

I thought about that for a moment, hopelessness swelling within me. Was it possible that I could go through all of this with her now, only to see her turn her back on rehab—her single biggest chance of ever staying sober—in the end?

"I'm so scared for her," I whispered, a catch in my voice.

Greg studied me, his eyes searching mine. "Love casts out all fear, Maddee, and faith moves mountains. I know you've been praying for her and that you love her very much. She loves you too. The way she talks about you—you're her hero."

I bit my lip, knowing I was anything but a hero. I'd been the one who had let her down all those years ago in the first place, the one who hadn't protected her at the cabin, who had caused the start of all her problems.

Still looking at me, Greg tilted his head. "You don't know, do you?"

"Don't know what?"

"How valuable you are in this."

For some reason, his words struck me hard. Tears sprang to my eyes. I brushed them away quickly.

"Sorry. I think I needed to hear that."

He didn't reply. He simply reached out and placed a warm hand on my shoulder. We grew quiet after that, just sitting there together, in silence, as I got my emotions under control. Something about his presence was so comforting, and I realized he was becoming a friend.

After he was gone, I went inside to hear Nicole in the bathroom, brushing her teeth. By the time I'd changed out of my work clothes, come back downstairs, and heated up a serving of Inez's lasagna, my sister was ready for bed.

She was quiet as we went through our routine, and I was glad. Tonight at least, if I couldn't talk to her about the things I wanted to, it was probably better not to talk at all.

It wasn't until the lights were out and I was leaving the room that she said, "I don't need it, you know."

"Need what?"

"I'll be fine without it. It will all be fine."

I wasn't sure if she was talking about rehab or meth, but before I could respond, she was asleep. It was just as well. I didn't know what I would have said anyway.

The next day, I was waiting to go into a county meeting when I heard from Detective Ortiz. She was calling to say she'd just received the results of the phenotyping report she'd told us about, the one that included a computer-generated drawing of what our victim probably looked like. And though a part of me didn't want to see that drawing for fear it would stir up old memories, a bigger part couldn't wait to get a look. Fortunately, she was allowed to share it, and by the time I got back to my office two hours later, it was sitting in my email's inbox.

My heart pounded as I downloaded the file and opened it up. Right there on the page was the image of a man's face, and I stared at it in fascination. Though I had vivid memories of that day in the cabin, I couldn't recall anything of the dead man's features, so whether this was accurate or not, I just didn't know. The artwork was definitely done by computer, the image looking like a character in *Sims* or *Call of Duty*. Beside it was a summary of the face shape: Narrower than average jaw, prominent nose and cheekbones.

Beneath that was more detailed information about each particular feature shown in the image. It said the man had been of Jewish ancestry with brown hair, either hazel or green eyes, a medium to olive complexion, and probably no freckles.

I'd asked the detective if I could call her back once I'd had a look, so I dialed her now and we went through the results together, starting with the fact that he'd been Jewish.

"'Of Jewish ancestry' is the more accurate term," she corrected me. "Why do you mention it? Is that significant to the case?"

"No, I just like the specificity of it. That narrows down the search quite a bit, doesn't it?"

"Yes, though not as much as you might think. Richmond has a substantial Jewish population, something like twelve or thirteen thousand people. Even twenty years ago, the percentage was relatively consistent."

She went through the rest of the form, but before hanging up she said there was one more thing, and by the tone of her voice, I could tell it was important.

"I made a few calls, like we discussed, to put in a good word for your sister."

"Thank you," I said earnestly. I was about to add that we'd received the final word on her sentencing yesterday when she continued.

"Anyway, I learned one thing I thought you might want to know. Hector Edgemont is back on the street. His parole hearing was last week. He got an extension on his parole but no jail time."

"I'm sorry, who?"

"Edgemont. The man who was in the car with Nicole when she had the accident."

"What? There wasn't anyone with her. She was alone—"

"No, Maddee. She wasn't. She claimed to be at first, but it was clear to the responding officers that someone else had been in the car with her but ran off before the police got there."

"How did they know that?"

"Blood, not hers, on the passenger door. Fresh footprints in the mud. They think he pulled himself out through the busted window."

I sucked in a breath. "Is that how they figured out who he was, from the blood?"

"Nope. Fingerprints provided a quick match. It was Hector Edgemont, all right. He goes by the name of 'Hedge,' and he's a twenty-five-year-old ex-con from Schooner Pass. Apparently, he's a friend of Nicole's."

"Why did he run away?"

"My guess is that he was committing some sort of parole violation—under the influence or maybe in possession—when they crashed, and he took off so he wouldn't get caught."

I closed my eyes, pressing a hand to my forehead. "He just left her there? To die?"

"Not completely. Turns out he was the one who made the anonymous call to 9-1-1 to report the accident from a gas station about half a mile away. He must have hitched a ride out of the area soon after that, though, because the police looked for someone on foot and never found him."

"Does she know the police figured it out?"

"Oh, yeah. She had to revise her statement in the hospital. The only reason her original lie didn't count against her with the judge was because it had been said in the immediate aftermath of the accident. They had to allow some leeway, though I'm sure she knew exactly what she was saying."

My mind was spinning. "I don't understand. Why did she lie about it in the first place?"

"He's a friend. She probably didn't want to get him in trouble."

I let out a deep breath. "Wow. I can't believe this."

"Well, I thought you might want to know that he's back out on the street just so you can keep an eye on things. You definitely don't want him sniffing around and getting Nicole into trouble, you know? She seems to be doing really well. I'd hate to see all that hard work derailed by some dirtbag."

That night I felt almost nauseated as I looked at my sister across the dinner table. When Ortiz and I finished our call, the detective had emailed me the man's mug shot so I would know whom to watch out for. I'd stared at the picture for a long time, memorizing his face. Hector Edgemont was in his twenties, skinny, with a scraggly black goatee. A real winner.

Sitting here now with Nicole, still astounded that she'd never mentioned him, a verse from Jeremiah kept coming to mind, *The heart is deceitful above all things and beyond cure. Who can understand it?*

Definitely not I.

Trying to give her the benefit of the doubt, hoping she would tell me about this guy on her own, I brought up the accident in conversation, asking for more details about how it happened and if it was scary and what it had felt like. She seemed perfectly willing to talk about it, almost overly so, the way people do when they're lying.

"That must have been terrifying," I said, "to go through something like that all by yourself."

Without missing a beat, she replied, "It was, Maddee. Thank goodness some good Samaritan called the police, or I probably would have bled to death."

For once, I was the one who wanted to go to bed early. My heart heavy as I went through our nightly routine, I never challenged her on her lie. I just let it sit there between us, like a dead animal rotting in the road.

Later, as I lay in bed unable to sleep, I told myself this was a sobering—and probably necessary—reminder of truths I'd already known:

Believe what addicts do, not what they say.

Addicts lie.

Never trust an addict.

Not even your own sister.

CHAPTER TWENTY-FOUR
Celeste

hat did you do?" Emmanuel asked Celeste, stepping closer. She still couldn't see his face, but she was overwhelmed with humiliation.

"Are you Jonathan?" a second voice asked, and then her humiliation was complete. It was George Barré, her old sweetheart, the man she'd lost all interest in the moment she met her handsome soldier. He and Emmanuel must have come here together in search of her and Berta. Unbelievable.

"No, my name is Spenser Rawling." He went on to explain that he'd met Celeste and Berta on the ship.

"He's been a good friend to us," Celeste added. "Especially to Berta."

"Nice to meet you then," George said. "I'm a friend of the family."

Celeste cringed at the thought of him standing there, witnessing her humiliation. He was another person she needed to ask forgiveness of.

"And I'm her brother," Emmanuel said. "The oldest son in our family."

"Right," Spenser said. "Emmanuel. I've heard a lot about you." As they shook hands, George ducked down to look Celeste in the face. She couldn't read his brown eyes, but she was dumbfounded by his presence. Why had he come too? Did he still care for her even after what she'd done to him?

George stood up straight. "Where's this Jonathan you wrote your parents about? Have you married him already?"

"No," Celeste answered as Emmanuel stepped closer. An unexpected sob shook her, followed by uncontrollable shivering. She was cold, yes, but her response was more of relief. Emmanuel had come after her, most likely sent by their parents.

"We need to get Celeste out of here." Spenser knelt down again and spoke directly to her. "Perhaps now that family has arrived, Constable Jones will treat you better."

Another sob shook her.

"There, there." Kindness flooded his eyes along with a sadness she didn't expect. "I'll go get Jones and tell him to hurry along. You have an advocate now. Two, in fact."

She'd already had two advocates—Spenser and Mr. Edwards. But maybe family would count for more with the authorities.

Spenser stood. For a moment, Celeste didn't want him to leave. Emmanuel and George felt so unfamiliar to her. Spenser was her rock, even though he'd been limited over and over by what he could do. She knew he would save her if he could.

Softly he said, "I'll be back as soon as I can." Then he hurried away.

Emmanuel and George both squatted down in front of her. Emmanuel wore a cap over his dark hair. Despite the circumstances, his eyes were as lively as ever. "What happened?"

"I defended the cook back at the inn." Celeste paused for a moment. "From a slave trader. He fell into the fire and then claimed I tried to kill him." She didn't have the energy to explain everything.

"Goodness, sister. I didn't think you had it in you to attack someone."

Celeste didn't answer. She hadn't attacked him, but clearly she wasn't the same person she'd been back home. So much had changed.

"So where's this Jonathan?" George asked.

"Away, probably at the plantation that belongs to the Vines family.

He intends to marry the Vines's daughter." She swallowed hard. It was good to say that right away, but it still hurt.

"I see." A hard look fell across George's face. The rain eased a little. It didn't matter. Her cloak was soaked through, and her skin was growing numb.

"How is Papa?" she asked Emmanuel. "And the boys? And Maman?" She choked on the last word.

"Worried. You can imagine how we all felt when you and Berta disappeared. Maman found your cryptic note, but we had no idea where Berta was."

"I didn't ask her to come along. At first I didn't even know she was on the ship…" She wasn't sure how to explain the rest.

"Then weeks later Papa received your letter." Emmanuel rubbed the stubble on his chin. "He was ready to come over after the two of you, but I volunteered to come instead. He wasn't so sure about that until George offered to accompany me."

"That was kind of you. Both of you." Celeste meant it.

"We can start back tomorrow when the ship returns to Norfolk. A few days after that it will leave for Carolina and then London," Emmanuel said.

Celeste wasn't sure what to say. Could she possibly return home so soon? She would see Maman. Papa. Alexander, Frederick, and William.

Of course she couldn't. "There's the matter of my indenture, the cost of my contract."

"What are you saying?" Emmanuel asked. "That you sold yourself as a servant?"

Her face burned in shame. "That was how I paid my passage. Jonathan said he would buy my contract once I arrived."

"But then he didn't," George surmised.

"He promised to sell his carriage and buy my contract that way—"

Emmanuel shook his head. "But he hasn't, correct?"

"That's right. And there's another issue too. Berta."

This time it was George who shook his head. "She's indentured as well?"

That situation was far more complicated than Celeste was prepared to explain while her head and hands were hinged.

"She was," Celeste said. "And perhaps still is. You'll probably have to hire a solicitor to help sort it all out."

"We have money to get you both home," Emmanuel said. "Plus some more."

"Enough to free us?"

"I'm not sure…" Emmanuel's voice trailed off.

George cleared his throat. "Will your masters sell your contracts at reasonable prices?"

"I don't know." Celeste couldn't guess how Mr. Edwards might respond. He was a kind man, but on the other hand he had a business to run. Perhaps it would depend on how bad Sary's injury was. If she couldn't cook again, neither Sary nor Celeste would be worth much to Mr. Edwards. As far as Constable Wharton, she had no idea what he would do.

"And then there's the matter of the attempted murder charge against me." Not to mention the accused theft of the ring and the brooch, but she would tell Emmanuel about both of those later when she was out of the pillory.

"I'll ask the constable to drop the charges," Emmanuel said. "Surely once everyone has cooled off we'll be able to resolve the matter."

Celeste believed Emmanuel could talk Jones out of it—maybe after Mr. Horn left the village. Emmanuel had a gift when it came to interacting with others. Plus, his optimism was contagious. "Once they let me out of this thing, you need to go get Berta and settle her contract with Constable Wharton. You have to get her away from there."

"All right," Emmanuel said. "Then we'll figure out how to buy your contract and head back home."

"There's one problem…"

"What is it?" Emmanuel squinted up at her.

"Berta nearly died coming over. I've never seen anyone so ill."

"Seasickness?" George asked.

"Yes. It nearly killed her. She came down with typhoid fever too, but she was already deathly ill from seasickness. I doubt she can make the journey back. I'll stay here with her. I can't leave her." No matter what Berta had done, Celeste wouldn't go home without her.

"Maybe she would do better on the trip back," Emmanuel said. "With home as the end goal."

"I doubt it."

"There would be three of us to care for her," George added.

"Spenser helped me with her on the way over, but she couldn't keep down much as far as food and water." Not that they'd had much food to give her by the end of the trip.

"You seemed quite fond of this Spenser," George said.

"I am. I'm very grateful to him. Berta is too." She exhaled. "And he's quite fond of her."

George showed his dimples. She'd forgotten how endearing he could be. He reached for her hand, but she cringed in pain.

He pulled away, rubbing his hand on his pants. "What's the sticky stuff?"

"Salve. I burned myself pulling Mr. Horn out of the fire."

"Is that the same fellow you pushed *into* the fire?" Emmanuel asked.

"I didn't push him!" she said loudly, but then she saw the teasing glint in her brother's eye.

"Where is this constable?" he asked. "Maybe I should go find him."

"He's probably at the jail. It's up the hill from the inn."

"Where's the inn?" George asked.

"Down this street, on the edge of the village." Celeste twisted her wrist painfully to point the way. "In fact, George, you should go there now to get a room for the two of you. It may fill up because of the sailors."

"Good idea," he said, sounding relieved, she thought, to be done with her and the whole situation.

She'd been about to add that he should order food as well before it was all gone, but she held her tongue. With that kind of attitude, he deserved to go hungry tonight. Then again, she realized, that meant Emmanuel wouldn't eat either, and she didn't want that. Besides, who was she to judge George, or anyone else, for that matter? She was about to speak up, but then she realized the man had already walked away.

"The two of you might be going hungry tonight unless you leave now," she warned her brother instead. "If you're lucky, you'll at least get a bowl of soup. Ask for bread and cheese too, after you tell Mr. Edwards who you are."

The thought of food made her stomach growl. Anything warm would be more than welcome. She didn't know how she would survive the night if she had to remain as she was. Every inch of her body hurt. Every inch of her skin was wet and cold. And it would soon be pitch-black.

Emmanuel interrupted her thoughts. "I'm not worried about food. I need to speak to the constable."

"Perhaps Spenser isn't having any success getting him down here. It might not hurt to go up to the jail instead."

A rustling distracted her. "No one needs to go anywhere." It was Jones's voice. "Miss Talbot, Spenser tells me you have company."

"Yes."

Jones came around so she could see his boots and legs.

Emmanuel stepped forward and introduced himself. Celeste searched the ground, hoping to see Spenser's legs as well, but it seemed he hadn't returned.

"Could you unlock me so we could talk?"

"I can't do that. You're sentenced to spend the night."

Tears stung Celeste's eyes.

"This is unconscionable," Emmanuel said. "You can't leave a lady out in the elements like this."

"Lady? More like attempted murderess. Liar. And thief."

"Thief?"

"She didn't tell you about the jewelry? The brooch? The ruby ring?"

Emmanuel sunk down to his knees in the mud, his face next to Celeste's. "You didn't."

She scowled, willing him to be quiet and wishing she'd brought up the ring before Jones returned. "Shhh," she hissed. "I'll explain later."

"I was afraid you took it," Emmanuel said, ignoring her admonition, "but Maman kept saying there's no way you would have done such a thing."

She was about to shush him again when she realized that his testimony could work to her advantage. "I already told the constables it was Maman's, and our great-grandmother's before that, but they wouldn't believe me. They claim it's too valuable to have come from the family of an indentured servant." She paused for a moment, realizing she needed to explain the rest. "I used it to buy Berta's freedom from Madame Wharton, in Norfolk. But then Constable Wharton came back and accused me of stealing the ring. At the same time, he reclaimed Berta as his property."

"I see," Emmanuel said. Then, to her surprise, he looked to Jones and asked the man if he would excuse them for a moment. With a huff, the constable turned and stomped off, his boots sloshing in the mud as he went.

From the sound of things, he didn't go all that far before stopping. Emmanuel leaned in closer to Celeste.

For a moment she wondered if she could trust him, but then she scolded herself. Of course she could. He was her brother, raised by her parents. He had her best interests in mind. He was certainly far more trustworthy than she was.

He lowered his voice to a whisper. "That ring is even more valuable than you think, Celeste. Are you aware that it originally came from King Henri IV? He gave it to our great-great-grandfather."

"How do you know?" she gasped, her heart sick.

"Maman has the note that came with it, signed by the king himself and embossed with his seal. Her grandmother sent it before she died. Maman showed it to me once she realized the ring was gone. It's a thank-you note for the handling of some very important legal matter, and it mentions the ring specifically. Along the lines of, 'I know you refused payment for your services on the basis of our friendship, but it is on the basis of that friendship that I give you this ruby ring as a gift of thanks.' Considering that his words provide provenance straight from the throne, I'd say that piece of jewelry is worth quite a lot."

Celeste's face burned, her guilt and shame only compounded by this new knowledge. "I don't suppose you brought that letter with you?" she asked meekly, thinking that if he had, they could use it in her defense as proof of ownership.

"Of course not. Why would I?"

"I don't know," she said miserably, her eyes welling with tears.

He leaned back on his heels. "I can't believe you stole it," he said with a shake of his head, no longer whispering.

"Yes, but I stole it from Maman, not from whom they are saying I did. You need to make them understand that—though they may not believe you, either."

"Of course they will." He put his head in his hands for a moment. "I just can't believe you no longer have it."

"Don't think about that now, Emmanuel. And you would have done the same, right? Used it to save a loved one?"

He nodded as he pulled his hands down his face, a glimmer returning to his eyes. "Of course." He turned and called out to Jones. "What my sister has told you is true. The ring belonged to our mother. Celeste stole it from her before she left England."

"Yes, well, you'll need to convince Wharton of that." By the tone of Jones's voice, Celeste realized, it sounded as though he still needed convincing as well.

"Invite him to supper," she whispered.

"And leave you alone? Like this? In the dark?"

"I'll be fine—well, at least not any worse than I already am. I need you to go and do what you do best."

This situation was delicate, and she knew that if her brother was to be believed, he would have to establish a relationship of sorts with the others first. That meant sticking around the inn, dining, talking, sharing tales, laughing, and making friends. George wasn't exactly gregarious, but everyone would love Emmanuel; people always did. If anyone could finesse this situation, given enough time, it was he. Meeting his eyes, she tried to communicate as much.

"Go on. I'll see you in the morning. Really, I'll be fine."

He studied her face for a long moment, silent communication passing between them. Then he looked over at Jones. "So, Constable?" he called out, "Can I buy you some supper at the inn?"

"Why not?" Jones replied matter-of-factly, as if he weren't thrilled on the inside. Relief flooded Celeste's veins, for she knew nothing on earth warmed that man's heart faster than food.

"Thank you," she whispered.

Still squatting in front of her, Emmanuel nodded but then hesitated before leaving. "I just wish I understood how you could have done such a thing in the first place."

Her eyes welled. "Maman always told me the ring would be mine one day." She blinked, sending tears down her cheeks. "But I know I was wrong to take it. I was wrong about so many things."

With a soft grunt, Emmanuel reached out and gently wiped away her tears. His hand lingered at her cheek, though whether in comfort or absolution she wasn't sure.

"I'll do what I can."

Then he rose and stepped to Jones's side. She listened to the smack of their footsteps in the mud as they left her, the sound receding into the night until only the patter of rain remained.

Please, Lord, help him win them over and soften their hearts toward me.

Celeste wanted to feel optimistic, but as the darkness continued to fall, she began crying again, hot tears streaming down her cheeks and mixing with raindrops. Her head hanging low, her body shaking uncontrollably, she licked the salt from her face and tried to think about happier times, but those thoughts only made her cry more.

Eventually, her tears came to an end, as did the rain. With her aching eyes fixed on the dark and muddy ground in front of her, she imagined the night sky above and what Spenser would say about it. How he would find the Big Dipper and then point out the North Star.

Where was her North Star? If Berta could bear the trip home, perhaps George would still marry Celeste. But then again, perhaps he hadn't come in pursuit of her at all but only as a favor to Emmanuel. He hadn't indicated in any way in their brief interaction that he still cared for her. She couldn't blame him if he wanted nothing to do with her ever again. It was clearly what she deserved. She owed him an apology. She knew now what it felt like to be jilted.

Celeste braced herself for the long night, knowing she wouldn't be able to sleep. Sometimes Papa would talk about how brave Maman was back in France, how she'd stood up to both dragoons and royalty. How she rode her horse into the wild to save her cousin. With pride, Papa spoke about how fearless Maman had been. How she never would have denied her faith, no matter the persecution. Maman would say, "That's enough, dear. I only did what anyone would have. What you did too."

"But you did it alone," Papa would say. "You were so brave."

Celeste knew she would never be brave like that.

She'd heard of Huguenots in France being tortured, often until death. She couldn't compare her circumstances to that or what her mother had survived either. She wasn't being persecuted for her faith. Only her stupidity. She'd brought it all on herself.

"*Stupide,*" she said, mimicking her mother.

She caught the flicker of a lantern out of the corner of her eye. "No," a voice said. "You're courageous."

"Spenser?"

"Yes, it's me."

"What are you doing?"

"I came to keep you company. I saw Emmanuel and George at the inn and told them to eat and rest, that I would watch over you."

Her tears started again and a sob shook her.

"Do you want me to leave?"

"No," she managed to say. "P-please stay."

He put the lantern down, took her wet cloak from her back, and spread a dry blanket over her shoulders, tucking it around her as best he could.

"Here," he said gently, unwrapping a cloth napkin to reveal a thick piece of bread, which he held to her lips. Despite her tears, she bit into it hungrily. She'd had nothing to eat for hours.

Her sobs subsided as she chewed. When she'd managed to down the whole piece, Spenser tried to give her some water as well, though the angle of her head didn't make it easy.

"Thank you," she whispered once she'd finally had enough.

"You're welcome," he replied, wiping her wet chin with the napkin and then tucking it away in his pocket.

Next, he spread an oiled cloth over the mud and scooted it under her feet. He moved the lantern closer and took out a book from under his coat, sitting down on the far edge of the cloth.

"What about your work?"

"I'll make it up later. For now, I've brought a book of prayers."

"Anglican?" she asked, expecting what she'd heard in the parish church.

"No," he answered. It was a small volume. "It belonged to my father. I thought reading would make the time go faster."

He opened the book and started with, "O, grant that we may willingly, and from the heart, obey Thee and become so teachable that what Thou hast designed for our salvation may not turn to our perdition."

"Who's prayer is that?" she asked.

"You don't recognize it?"

She forgot for a moment that she couldn't shake her head. "Ouch. And no, I don't."

"John Calvin."

"Really?"

He nodded. "My father was a Presbyterian."

"Oh." Presbyterians were Calvinists, through and through, a branch other than the Huguenots but from the same tree. *Salvation may not turn to our perdition.* Celeste asked, "Are you worried my salvation might become my eternal punishment?"

Instead of answering directly, he said, "You're hard on yourself, Celeste, but you've been hard on others too."

"What did Berta tell you?"

He shrugged.

"Probably how critical I was."

"And maybe a little self-righteous," he added gently.

Celeste frowned, but it was true. Every word of it. She'd been horrible. And then she'd reversed completely, deceiving her parents and stealing the ring.

"All that's left is for you to forgive yourself—"

"Stop. Please. This is enough." She couldn't think of forgiving herself, not now. Not when she didn't know how everything would turn out for Berta. Not when she didn't know if her parents would be able to forgive what she had done.

"Fair enough." He resumed reading Calvin's prayer.

Several times Celeste told him to go.

He politely declined, but the last time he said, forcefully, "I'm not leaving you here by yourself!"

"It's not as if anything will happen to me."

Spenser just shook his head. "No one should have to endure such a thing alone."

The light from the lantern began to dim. He'd probably used oil he needed to work by. It sputtered and then went out, but the night wasn't as dark as Celeste expected it would be.

"Did the clouds part? Can you see the moon?" she asked.

"No to the moon, but I can see some stars."

"Can you see the North Star?" Perhaps they were destined to never see the stars at the same time. They had never been on the deck of the *Royal Mary* at night together. And the night in Constable Wharton's field, she'd been too tired to crawl out from under the canopy of the tree to look at the stars. If only she had.

"No, the North Star isn't visible. All of the Big Dipper is covered with clouds."

They talked about the stars and then more about their families throughout the night. Spenser asked about Emmanuel. Celeste explained his position in the family as oldest son. Their parents hoped he could start a business that would employ the younger brothers. "They were working toward a paper mill," Celeste said. "Our uncle from France had some ideas." Now all of that had been put on hold thanks to her foolishness.

"And what about George?"

Her face burned as she spoke. "His father is a weaver, but he's not fond of the work. He'd much rather be involved in running an inn." George's family was poorer than hers, and not as educated, but they were good people.

"He seems quite fond of you."

"Seemed," Celeste corrected.

"Why do you say that?"

"It-it was assumed we would soon be betrothed."

"Oh."

Before daybreak, Spenser stood and began pacing back and forth until the sun rose. As the light transformed the world, Celeste heard the rattling of keys and then Jones asking, "How was your night?"

Celeste didn't answer him.

"Are you freeing her, then?" Spenser asked.

"Yes," Jones answered. "Horn left this morning. He was satisfied with one night in the pillory as punishment. He has no lasting wounds. He's not pressing charges."

"How is Sary?" Celeste asked.

"Probably worthless as a cook." Jones sighed. "Edwards bought her outright from Horn, which undoubtedly he'll regret."

Tears stung Celeste's eyes again. She was relieved that Mr. Horn no longer owned Sary, but she feared for the woman's future nonetheless. Could Mr. Edwards afford to keep her and take on another cook as well?

Jones jangled his keys. "Captain Bancroft scolded Horn last night for being so selfish to insist the kitchen maid be punished at the expense of feeding him and his sailors. He threatened not to return if such antics continued, and he said other captains will become leery of making the voyage up the James if we don't treat them well." The keys dangled from Jones's hand.

"That's true," Spenser answered. "And we wouldn't want that. We'd have even less food and goods."

Jones patted his stomach, the keys jangling again as he did.

"Did my brother speak with you?" Celeste asked, trying to turn her head.

"He did. Now he's with Edwards, negotiating your contract. He's concerned about how far his money will go." With that, Jones opened the lock and lifted away the heavy piece from her hands and head.

Celeste gasped. But as she tried to straighten, her relief evaporated into a dizzy haze. Immediately, Spenser jumped forward and caught her before she could fall. Her legs had long ago gone numb, and she couldn't manage to stand on her own. She leaned heavily against him as Jones left without even saying goodbye. If Spenser hadn't been with her, she would be crawling back home.

Home? The thought startled her. Home was in London, not Virginia. And certainly not above the kitchen of an inn.

Yet she longed to get back to Sary to see how she was doing, nearly as much as she wanted Emmanuel and George to begin their journey to free Berta. Sary had become important to her. Celeste couldn't imagine, come what may, leaving her behind.

Chapter Twenty-Five
Celeste

No one was in the kitchen when Spenser helped Celeste inside. A pot of corn porridge bubbled over the fire, and Spenser quickly dished up a bowl for her. At least the numbness was gone from her legs, though pain and exhaustion still radiated throughout her body as she sat down to eat.

Once she was finished with the porridge, Spenser asked, "Can you manage the ladder?"

"I think so."

"I'll wait until you're in the loft. Then I'll go find Mr. Edwards and tell him you're back but need to rest."

She nodded, too tired to thank him. He helped her up the first several rungs and then she continued on by herself. Once she reached the top, she stared at a sleeping Sary, wanting to check her friend's hand but not wanting to wake her. Instead, Celeste stripped out of her wet clothes and collapsed on her pallet, wrapping herself in her single blanket. The next thing she knew, the light in the room had shifted and it was afternoon. Sary knelt beside her with a glass of water, which Celeste quickly drained, and then Sary unwrapped a piece of bread from a clean cloth, which Celeste hungrily devoured.

"How is your hand?" Celeste asked.

Sary held it up. It was wrapped in strips of fabric.

"May I look?"

Sary nodded.

Celeste carefully unwrapped the rags. The burn was red, deeply blistered, and oozing puss. She had to tug on the strips of fabric, though she did that as gently as possible. She knew the pain had to be horrible.

"Did the doctor give you anything to put on it?"

Sary shook her head.

"I'll get some salve for you." Celeste wondered why the physician hadn't given Sary anything. The thumb and finger seemed to have fused together regardless of Celeste's efforts, and she didn't want to try to force them apart. She would talk to the physician to see what he recommended. Now that she was rested and feeling a bit better, it would take only a few minutes to go to his shop.

First, though, she needed to find Emmanuel and George. She hoped they had made plans to go to Norfolk for Berta.

Sore but steady, she washed, put on her other set of clothes, and took her dirty things down to the laundry. Linens were piled high. Obviously, Aline had been overwhelmed with the extra work from the sailors being in port, not to mention the extra work created by her absence and Sary's injury. She dropped her small pile on top of the sheets.

As she left the laundry, she caught sight of Mr. Edwards in the chicken coop, gathering eggs. He was probably considering making some sort of light dinner. Thankfully, they wouldn't have many patrons tonight with the ship leaving.

Celeste hurried toward the inn. Aline held a tray of empty mugs as she came out the door. "Oh, good! You're back."

"Give me just a minute," Celeste said. "I need to speak with my brother."

"Your brother?"

"Emmanuel."

Aline's eyes lit up. "He's your brother?"

Celeste nodded.

"How about the other lad?"

"A friend," Celeste answered. "From London."

"I see," she said. "Ten minutes. Then you take over the serving. I have laundry to do—and I'm running out of daylight."

"I saw. And added to it. Sorry." Celeste slipped through the door and into the inn and then called over her shoulder, "Oh, and I need to go to the physician's too. So maybe fifteen minutes."

Aline groaned. "Hurry!"

Celeste found Emmanuel and George in the dining room surrounded by men—soldiers, townspeople, and a few sailors. Perhaps she still would have a chance to thank the first mate of the *Royal Mary* for delivering her letter.

Emmanuel was talking about the recent elections in London and how fiercely they were fought. "There was mob violence in several areas."

"Excuse me," Celeste said.

George stood to greet her. Emmanuel kept on talking. "But the balance between the Tories and Whigs ended up being fairly even." He had always taken after their father in keeping up with what was going on in the world.

She cleared her throat.

Her brother noticed her then and stood too. Smiling, he said, "I see you survived."

"Yes."

"I can't finalize the amount I'm able to pay Edwards for your contract until I find out what the situation with Berta is. That means George and I will be staying in Virginia longer than we thought. We'll have to return home on a later ship, something other than the *Royal Mary*."

Celeste nodded, swallowing hard, pleased she wouldn't have to say a final goodbye to him yet. "When do you plan to leave for Norfolk?"

"Spenser is thinking he can go with us. He's making the arrangements."

"Oh," she said. Of course he'd want to go.

"He has a delivery to make," George added. "He'll combine the trips."

"Oh," Celeste said again. She contemplated apologizing to George for how she'd treated him but decided to do it later. She grabbed a piece of bread and a hunk of cheese from the plate on the table and hurried out of the dining room. She needed to stop by the physician's and then get back to the kitchen as soon as possible.

A few minutes later, swallowing the last of the food, Celeste ducked into the apothecary. The physician stood at the counter, pulling dried leaves off a stem. She quickly explained who she was and her concern for Sary's hand. "Will she have the use of it?"

The man shook his head. "The thumb and finger already fused. I'd have to cut them apart."

Celeste tried to control her emotions. "They were separated right after the accident."

He shrugged. "The dressing had to be changed."

"Then will you cut them?"

"No. She would barely let me touch her."

"She let me."

"Well, you should have stuck around to help," he said, a smirk on his face.

If Benjamin had been allowed to fetch him before going for the constable, she would have been there to help him instead of being in the pillory. "Do you have a salve I could use on her hand?"

"Lard will do."

"Do you have anything for her pain?"

The man shook his head. "She can handle it."

Tears stung Celeste's eyes. She was horrified by his treatment of Sary. "Good day," she said, quickly leaving before he could see her tears. She had no patience for his lack of empathy. She walked as quickly as she could toward the woods. Before she reached the creek, she could hear the hum of the mill. Matthew and the other man were feeding logs through the saw. She headed up the trail to the shop.

Spenser was arranging chairs in the back of the wagon as she approached.

"Celeste!" He jumped down. "How are you? I see your legs are working again."

She nodded, although they ached now from walking. "I heard you're going to Norfolk." Her voice wavered a little as she spoke. Perhaps she was still weak from her ordeal. And emotional.

"I thought I could help Emmanuel and George."

"And Berta."

"Of course. But you didn't come all this way for that. What do you need?"

"I know you probably don't have much of it, but the burn salve. Could you spare some for Sary?" She held out her hands to show him. "It helped me, and I'm hoping it will help her."

"Of course." He smiled. "I'll go get it."

She waited while he ran into the shop. When he returned, he handed her the little pot.

"What's in it?" she asked, grateful for his generosity but feeling guilty for using up even more of his limited supply.

"Mostly seaberries, from back home. It's what my father used for burns."

"Oh, dear," Celeste said. "Do those grow around here? Can you make more?"

He shook his head. "But I'll learn what's used here. Put more on your burns too. And tell Emmanuel and George I'll meet them at the dock."

Celeste nodded. "I will. Have a good trip." She turned and hurried away.

"Celeste!" Spenser called out.

She stopped and looked over her shoulder. "Yes?"

He hesitated. Then he said, "I'll see you when I get back."

She waved and continued on, walking into the wind. Berta would be with him when he returned. She felt pangs of something uncomfortable, something she didn't recognize. But as she continued walking, it struck her: jealousy. And not jealous in the sense that Berta had what she wanted, which was a good man like Spenser. She didn't want a good man like Spenser.

She wanted Spenser.

Was it possible she loved him? Her knees grew weak at the thought.

Why had he protected her through the night when he loved Berta? Why had he been so good to her? She sighed. He was only being kind. He had no idea how he'd endeared himself to her. How he'd nurtured her love.

She'd had no idea herself until this moment. How could she have done something so horrible as to come to the point of loving him? He would never return her feelings. She would have to live out her life watching him love her sister.

The pangs of jealousy quickly turned to heartbreak. Real pain twisted inside her chest. She loved him, but no one could ever know. Because of Berta, she had no choice but to swallow down this new-found realization, burying these thoughts of love somewhere deep inside. It didn't matter how much she loved him. She would never hurt Berta that way. She just hoped her sister would value him and treat him as he deserved.

A block from the inn, as Celeste turned the corner, her head down against the wind, she nearly plowed into a man in a red coat.

Hands fell to her shoulders to steady her as she stepped aside, landing in a puddle. "Excuse me." She looked up into Captain Bancroft's face. "Oh. It's you."

He chuckled. "I hoped to see you, Miss Talbot. I take it you've had a chance to discuss your circumstances with your brother?"

"Yes, I have."

"And your sister? Is she still at Constable Wharton's?"

"Yes." She had no desire to explain Berta's situation to him, how ill she'd been and that Celeste had purchased her contract, only to have it revoked. But she did owe him an apology for the lie she had unknowingly helped to perpetrate.

"The situation is complicated." She paused and cleared her throat. "But I'm afraid I was wrong about my sister's contract. Apparently, that was her signature, and she did board the ship of her own free will. She…

allowed me to believe otherwise for reasons that are far too difficult to explain here. I just wanted to say how sorry I am for all the trouble I caused. You're a fair man, and I appreciate that you didn't dismiss our claims outright."

There. She felt better. Berta might have had no problem lying, but Celeste wanted only to tell the truth, to clear up the messes her sister had left in their wake.

"I appreciate that, Miss Talbot," he said, and when she allowed herself to meet his gaze, she saw that his smile was genuine.

"I believe my brother will be traveling to Norfolk on your ship to tend to my sister," she said, looking away again.

"Very well." He bowed slightly. "Best wishes to all of you Talbots. Here and in London too. I found your father to be a delightful man."

She stuttered. "Y-you met him?"

"I did. At your family's inn and then when he accompanied your brother and his friend as they boarded the ship."

"Why did you visit the inn?"

He shrugged. "I was curious, is all, after Hayes told me your father was educated and of means."

"Oh," Celeste answered, still confused. A wave of homesickness nearly overcame her. "I have to ask you to excuse me. I need to get back to work."

Perhaps he hadn't heard her. "It's really a shame, all you and your sister have gone through. I'll be honest. I didn't expect, at first, that you came from a good family. You've had one self-inflicted trial after another—and for what?"

"Exactly," she said, brushing by him. He'd been kind to her, true, but she had no patience for his reflections, not at her expense. She was well aware of the situation she'd thrust her entire family into.

By the time she reached the inn, Emmanuel and George had congregated with a group of sailors around the bench on the other side of the fence. Celeste relayed Spenser's message and then told them goodbye. "Give Berta a hug." Tears sprang into her eyes again. "Tell her I love her and hope to see her soon."

It was true. She did love her sister. Beyond measure. That was one good thing that had come from their trials. It didn't matter if Berta had lied about Jonathan or consorted with him. Celeste would stand by her no matter what.

Emmanuel told her goodbye and George simply nodded to her. She paused a moment and then blurted out to him, "I shouldn't have treated you so badly, George. The least I could have done was be honest with you."

"You're right."

"Please forgive me," she said softly.

"Celeste…you have no idea how badly you hurt me."

Actually she did, but she didn't say so. "I'm sorry."

He nodded curtly and then stood when Emmanuel got up to head to the dock. The men walked away together.

She hadn't expected George to forgive her, but she couldn't help but wonder why he'd come. Obviously, it wasn't for her.

That evening, Mr. Edwards and Celeste managed to make savory cheesecakes for dinner with a little direction from Sary. She didn't speak, but she communicated with gestures and expressions until they got the recipe right. Then Celeste served it to the few patrons in the dining room. Among them was Monsieur Petit, who asked after Berta.

Celeste explained that their brother Emmanuel had come over from England, much to her surprise, and that he was now on his way to Norfolk to straighten things out with the constable there. The man seemed relieved to hear it, and from the way he talked, she could tell that both he and his wife had grown quite fond of Berta during her convalescence in their home.

Later, Celeste was in the kitchen when Mr. Edwards appeared.

"Lieutenant Gray is here to see you," he said, brows furrowed. "I told him I thought he should stay away, but he insists it's important."

She wiped her hands on her apron, weariness nearly overtaking her. "I'll talk to him."

"He's in the sitting room. And I'll wash these up. The water won't be good on your hands anyway."

Celeste thanked him for his kindness and trudged back to the inn. Jonathan was standing at the window when she entered the sitting room. Thankfully, he was alone. He turned quickly. "Celeste. How are you?" He appeared genuinely concerned.

"All right," she answered, wondering what he'd heard.

"Mr. Horn came out to the plantation this morning, ranting about what happened. But I'm guessing it was all an accident. I know you wouldn't hurt him on purpose."

"No. Of course I wouldn't."

Jonathan opened his hand and extended it, revealing the brooch. "Constable Wharton had this. I told him I gave it to you and that he had no right to it."

"Thank you, Jonathan."

He stepped closer. "Please take it."

"Perhaps you should give it to Miss Vines."

He winced, but Celeste didn't apologize. Nor did she take the brooch. He closed his hand around it again.

She asked if he'd seen Berta.

He shook his head. "I was told she was with Wharton, but I didn't see her."

Celeste squared her shoulders. "And what about the ring? Did Constable Wharton come to a conclusion about it?"

"What ring?" Jonathan asked.

"The one I used to buy Berta's freedom—the one he accused me of stealing. It was my mother's—"

"Goodness, he didn't ask me about that at all. I could have told him your family has means, that you wouldn't need to steal such a thing."

Celeste sighed, grateful for his words. "When did the constable leave?"

"Soon after he arrived. I saw him briefly, and we only discussed the brooch."

"I appreciate your coming to see me," Celeste said, "but I need to get back to work." Or collapse if Mr. Edwards would let her.

"Please wait a moment. There's something I need to tell you—and ask you."

Her heart lurched at the sadness in his voice. Even after all he'd done to her, she still cared about his well-being.

"First, I want to apologize again—for everything." He's eyes grew watery as he spoke. "I haven't been sleeping, Celeste. All I can think about is you."

She crossed her arms but didn't respond.

He blinked a few times, as if trying to rid his eyes of tears. "I sold the carriage. I finally have the cash to buy your freedom."

She gasped, her hand going to her throat. Emmanuel didn't have enough money to buy both Celeste's and Berta's contracts, but if Jonathan bought her freedom, then that would solve some of their problems. "Thank you," she whispered.

"I've been given orders to go to Carolina, down by Charles Town. This time a land grant has been guaranteed."

"Oh, Jonathan, that's wonderful! Will you marry before you go?"

"I've chosen to go to Carolina rather than remain here. And because of that, I will not be marrying. Unless…"

Celeste's heart lurched again.

"Unless you'll have me after how horrible I've been."

Celeste was too shocked to respond. Surely she hadn't understood what he said. Perhaps she was delirious.

He stepped closer. "I've loved you since the first time I saw you. I made a huge mistake not to wait for you. If I had, none of this would have happened. Come with me to Carolina. We'll start a new life together. I'll be a landowner again. You'll be the lady you were meant to be." He reached for her red, rough hand. Numbly, she let him take it. "I want you with me, Celeste. There's a Huguenot community there, including a church, where we can marry. I'll take care of you, I promise. I've never regretted anything in my life as much as I have not waiting for you."

She tried to speak, but no words came out.

"Please say yes." Jonathan's eyes now swam in tears. "I must leave tomorrow."

"Give me tonight," she managed to say. "I'll let you know first thing in the morning."

He slipped the brooch into her hand. "This is just the first of many gifts. You'll have far more than the ruby ring Constable Wharton took from you."

Celeste closed her hand around the brooch. There was still the matter between them of Berta's claims. Jonathan had already told her Berta was lying, but she simply had to be sure before things went any further.

"I talked to Berta about what you said. She insists that you asked her to join you in Virginia."

A pained expression passed over his face. "I gave this more thought after I last spoke with you about it. I saw Berta one time, late in the evening along the Thames. I was worried about her being out by herself and escorted her home."

Celeste cocked her head.

"Yes," Jonathan said. "I hardly gave it a second thought, but I remember she asked quite a few questions of me, including if you and I were still seeing each other. I evaded answering her, not wanting to discuss my relationship with you. Then she said she longed to go to the New World. I simply listened. But looking back, I wonder if she got the wrong impression somehow. Perhaps she's fanciful enough to have concocted something from that small exchange?" He shrugged. "That's the only thing that I can think of that would cause her to come up with such a story."

Celeste looked him in the eye. "I honestly don't know what to believe."

Jonathan reached for her hand, the one now clasping the brooch, and held it gently. "Please trust me. Please believe me. Please give me a second chance."

She exhaled deeply, the air catching in her chest.

"I heard about what happened to the cook. About her hand, and about Edwards buying her contract." Jonathan leaned toward Celeste. "I was thinking I could buy her too."

"Buy her?"

"Free her. As a gift to you. She can come with us. Mr. Edwards said the two of you have become close."

Celeste pulled her hand away, trying to think it all through. Jonathan wasn't Spenser, that was for sure, but he *was* offering to free Sary.

"I can speak with Edwards right now," Jonathan said. "I'll negotiate for both of you."

She could save Berta and Sary if she agreed to marry Jonathan. Yes, she'd been hurt by him, but he did genuinely seem to love her. And she'd be close to a Huguenot church. That was more important to her than she'd realized when she'd agreed to leave London.

What reason did she have for not accepting his offer? He said he'd acted in fear in agreeing to marry Miss Vines, and now he'd made it right. Celeste had forgiven him—so why not marry him? In another year the last few months would be nothing but a distant memory. All the hurt and pain would be gone. They would have a new start, at last, in this New World. And she wouldn't be reminded over and over, as she would be if she stayed with her sister, of her failures. In fact, Berta might be better off without Celeste around. And Celeste wouldn't have to watch Spenser devote himself to Berta. In time, she would forget her love for him.

"Celeste?"

She wrapped her arms around herself. "I was thinking, is all. I don't need the night to decide." She lifted her head and gazed into his blue eyes.

His voice wavered as he asked, "What is your answer?"

"Yes." She dropped her arms to her side. "Yes, Jonathan. I'll marry you."

A smile crept over his face, and then he swept her up in a hug, holding her close as he had in London so many times. As they pulled away, Jonathan swiped at his eyes. "I'll go talk to Mr. Edwards. I'll buy your contract and pay for Sary too. You have my word."

With the Court convening in a few days, and all the extra travelers that would bring to town, Celeste couldn't imagine Mr. Edwards would be happy about letting her go, but surely he already had plans in the works for finding a new cook.

Mr. Edwards and Jonathan negotiated in the sitting room while Celeste tackled the remaining dishes in the kitchen, even though the burns on her hands made the task difficult. Sary came down to help her put everything away, using her left hand. Celeste didn't dare tell her about Jonathan's plans lest she raise false hopes.

When they were finished, Mr. Edwards hadn't yet returned to the kitchen, so Celeste followed Sary up the ladder, where they both collapsed on their pallets without speaking. As exhausted as she was, Celeste couldn't fall asleep. She went over and over what Jonathan had said to her. He loved her.

She couldn't help but remember their passion in London when they were together, the intense longing she'd felt for him. She hadn't felt that tonight, not even an inkling of it when he held her. But she was exhausted. Surely, in time, those feelings would return.

She rolled toward the window, focusing on the shimmering stars against the black sky that she could make out through the warped glass, and fell into a fitful sleep.

CHAPTER TWENTY-SIX
Maddee

*T*he day after my conversation about her accident with the less-than-honest Nicole, I talked to Debra about the situation, and she helped me put it into perspective. She reminded me of various psychological studies that showed how lying could become habitual in a person, to a point where it was second nature.

"This is something that can be changed," she said. "She may not even necessarily be trying to deceive you about the accident. She's just doing what she always does, giving out half-truths and making omissions and generally obscuring reality through force of habit."

I had a feeling she was right. And though that didn't excuse my sister's behavior, at least it helped calm me down enough to let it go for now. As long as her chronic lying could be successfully treated with therapy, there was hope.

That night, I had just finished locking up my bike and helmet when Greg appeared in the doorway of the carriage house, a broad grin on his face.

"I'm glad you're here," he said. "We have a surprise for you. Are you ready?"

Before I could even respond, he swung the door open wide and stepped back to reveal Nicole, standing with the aid of a walker a few feet away, a smile on her face—and no casts on her legs.

"*What?*"

I guess that was the reaction she wanted, because she squealed and laughed in return. Then she explained how Dr. Hill's office had called this morning and said they'd had a cancellation and she could get her casts off a few days early. Wanting to surprise me, Nicole hadn't contacted me to let me know but instead had simply asked Inez to take her there, and that was that. Her bad leg, the one she'd had surgery on, was now in a canvas boot, but it ended below the knee.

As she spoke, she inched her way over to the wheelchair, Greg hovering nearby, and gingerly lowered herself into it. Judging by her movements, she wouldn't be running sprints anytime soon, but this was still a vast improvement. Now that the casts were gone, no longer would she be held prisoner by those two huge, obtrusive, pain-in-the-neck orange and yellow Popsicles.

Thinking of them made me think of Austin. I put down my stuff, crossed to the table, and flipped around one of the chairs so I could sit. Something was niggling at the back of my mind, something disturbing that I couldn't quite articulate.

"Explain this to me again," I said, checking out her legs more closely. "What happened to wearing the casts for nine or ten weeks?"

She shrugged. "Dr. Hill said it wouldn't hurt anything to take them off a few days early."

"*Five* days," I corrected. "Five days early. Today is Friday. They weren't supposed to come off till next Wednesday at the very soonest."

She shook her head, impatient for me to get with the program and just be happy for her. "Whatever. He was sweet and really careful, and once the casts were off he examined my legs and said they both looked great. I still have a ways to go, of course, and I'll probably be in this boot for a while, but otherwise it's all good."

I swallowed hard, hoping against hope that this was a coincidence, that her premature cast removal had nothing to do with me. I looked to Greg and asked if he concurred with Dr. Hill on the timing. "I mean,"

I added, "I'd hate to think he acted prematurely just because of a scheduling matter."

Or, more importantly, to free up his new girlfriend's dating roster.

"I'm sure it's fine," Greg said. He went on to explain about variations in the healing process and the pros and cons of limiting immobilization and so on, and though I had trouble paying attention to everything he was saying, I told myself he was the expert here, not I. If he wasn't worried about it, then I wouldn't worry either. Austin Hill was one of the best orthopedic surgeons in the country. It was ridiculous for me to think he might somehow endanger the health of a patient just to make it easier to date her sister.

I gave Nicole the smile and hug she'd been waiting for and said we should celebrate.

"One step ahead of you, sis," she replied. "Pizza for three will be here in fifteen minutes."

Once I decided to go with things the way they were, it didn't take long to become genuinely excited about this momentous change. Tiny as Nicole was, with the added weight and awkwardness of her casts, shifting her around had been exhausting.

As the two of them finished their session, I ran upstairs to change into my favorite sweatpants and an old but extremely comfortable flannel shirt. This was my secret only-when-I'm-home-alone outfit, but somehow it seemed fitting for tonight. I decided to take this as a sign of growth, that perhaps my antiperfectionist plan had begun to work well enough that I was now willing to look this way in front of others.

Back downstairs, the pizza arrived, we ended up having a wonderfully fun evening together. I was happy to see that Greg fit right in, laughing and talking and cracking us up with stories about his family. Between a hyperorganized mother, an absentminded professor father, and four rambunctious, practical joke-loving brothers, what he described sounded like one long, happy, rollicking childhood. As he talked, I found myself wondering how many children, if any, he hoped to have someday. With four siblings, chances were he would like a big family too.

Before leaving, he took a few minutes first to explain to me what this change would mean as far as Nicole's therapy and how they would be proceeding from here. Starting on Monday, he said, she would no longer need in-home visits but instead would come to his office during the days so that they could work in the gym there and take advantage of all the equipment. Though I was happy for her, the thought made me sad. Coming home to find Greg here three nights a week had grown into a very pleasant habit, one I now realized I was going to miss.

"How can I stay in the loop?" I asked, thinking of how helpful it had been to observe part of their sessions and talk afterward.

"You have my number, right? As long as Nicole leaves her release on file, I can continue to discuss her case with you whenever you want." He asked for pen and paper, and then he jotted down his schedule, marking the times during the week when he would most likely be free to talk. "Really and truly, don't hesitate to call," he said, sliding the cap back on the pen and handing it and the paper over to me. "Any questions, concerns, clarifications, whatever. I'm your man."

"Thank you, Greg," I said, and then I impulsively gave him a hug. He'd been such a blessing to both of us.

Later, in bed, I thought of him again and what a wonderful boyfriend he would make for Nicole. I still felt strongly that she wasn't ready for a relationship and wouldn't be for a long while, but when that time eventually came, if he were still available, they really should give it a try.

A line from a song by the Simpson Sisters came to me, "Say it again girls, good men are hard to find." Maybe that should be his ringtone. I'd need to give it more thought first, but if the sentiment fit anyone, it definitely fit him.

Nicole was excited for Nana to see her without the casts, and our Saturday visit started out well. She seemed genuinely pleased with Nicole's progress, and the three of us chatted happily around the table over coffee and a small fruit and cheese platter I'd thrown together. Unfortunately, our father had told Nana the news from the lawyer, and as soon as she brought it up, our pleasant conversation began to unravel. She and Nicole got into an argument about rehab versus jail, but I was determined to follow Greg's advice and stay out of it. As the fight went on, I actually left the room, slipping upstairs, where I stayed until they had calmed down.

I rejoined them with the hopes that things would get better from there. But then Nana asked if we'd read all the letters in the packet, the ones written by our ancestors, and we answered simultaneously:

"We haven't started them yet," I said.

"We're almost finished with them," Nicole said.

She shot me a glare, but what could I do? I wasn't going to lie, especially not to my own grandmother. I knew that she was eager for us to read them—and we were looking forward to it—but she would just have to understand that between physical therapy and daily meetings and my work and Nicole's doctors appointments and even my dates with Austin, things were a little crazy around here right now. I tried explaining that to her, and she seemed to accept what I was saying—especially when she heard that Austin and I had gone out not once but twice.

"Yes, I can imagine you are quite busy these days, Maddee. Caring for your sister is a full-time job, and then on top of that you *have* a full-time job." With a wink, she added, "Not to mention your new young man."

She patted me on the arm. I thanked her for understanding and assured her that we really did want to read them and would do so as soon as we had a chance.

"Thank you, dear. As for you, Nicole," she said, turning toward my sister, her brow furrowing, "there is no excuse. You promised you would read them. You've had them an entire week. What else do you have to do all day except lie around in a bed?"

A part of me wanted to jump to Nicole's defense, saying that things weren't all that easy for her right now either, that she'd been dealing with a lot of pain, and considering the shape her body was in, just the pace of getting to daily meetings was enough to wear her out, not to mention the physical therapy. But for some reason, I held my tongue. My sister was a liar, and she deserved to hang out to dry.

Nicole ended up giving a plausible enough excuse, but watching her was like watching an actor on a stage playing out a scene. I felt as removed from her as she was from the truth.

By the end of the hour, I was relieved to see Nana go. I loved the woman, and I did feel sorry for her in this, but her time with us today had simply worn me out. As I walked her to the car, I assured her that I would definitely see to it that Nicole and I made time this week to read the letters. Turning, she gave me a pat on the cheek and said, "Thank you, Maddee. I have no doubt that you'll follow through. You always do."

Nicole and I finally got to Nana's letters the next day, in the afternoon. Doing so required some juggling of our carefully planned schedule, starting with canceling my after-church lunch date with Austin, attending my church's early service instead, and getting Nicole to a 12:30 meeting across town rather than waiting for the much closer 4:00 meeting we'd originally planned on. Once again, Austin wasn't too happy with me, but I couldn't worry about that now. I was still feeling conflicted over Nicole's early cast removal, especially after he'd texted me the afternoon before and said, *Last chance. Sure you can't come to the party?* All I could think when I saw it was, why would he ask again? Because he'd engineered a change in my circumstances? After a long moment, I texted back, *Sorry. Wish I could. Have fun.* And that had been that. Before he and I went out again, I would need to do some serious thinking on this matter.

As for today, I assumed Nicole would be worn out after her meeting and need a nap, but she seemed fine, so once we got back home I made grilled cheese sandwiches for lunch and we settled in at the table. Because the letters were just copies and not the originals, we didn't even wait until we were finished eating but instead dumped out the whole packet and got started right away.

What we found were about thirty different letters, most of which were from Celeste.

We began with the first one, written by her on July 8, 1704. It was hard to get used to her handwriting, so it was slow going, but we managed to read through this short one. She had written that she and Berta were both safe, and that she was sorry for what she had done, but that she loved Jonathan and planned to make a life with him.

"Ooh," Nicole said. "A love interest. These could be interesting."

The next, from October 11, 1704, was the one that had been written in a completely different hand, that Nana said had been penned on Celeste's behalf because she was "incapacitated." I couldn't wait to find out more about that, though there was no explanation here. That short note consisted of just a few sentences, and it was a simple plea from Celeste to her parents, asking their forgiveness for "being deceptive about Jonathan," for "stealing the ring," and for "leading Berta astray."

I glanced at Nicole. "So much for our venerated ancestors. This girl sounds like a real piece of work."

"At least she's apologizing," Nicole replied, her eyes riveted to the page as she read the rest aloud. "'I'm sorry for the despair I know I've caused you. I do not know my future or Berta's. I will write more when I can. In the meantime, please know that I miss you and you've done nothing to deserve the way I've treated you.' See?"

We kept going through the pile, one by one, for the next several hours, immersing ourselves into our family's fascinating and faraway past. We wanted to reach the explanation of who had written the second letter but were relishing how the story unfolded along the way. Because they were handwritten, not to mentioned faded, it remained slow going, but we took turns reading the letters aloud to each other, and that seemed to help.

Despite the questionable start, the story the letters told ended up being one of tremendous determination and courage. We were also both impressed by the maturity of our young ancestors, particularly Emmanuel. By our calculations, he was only sixteen years old when he came here, yet he acted far more like a man than a boy. We credited it to the fact that people seemed to grow up a lot faster back when marriages often happened in the teens and life expectancy was less than forty years.

Several of the early missives referred to a ring, but it wasn't until we got to a later, longer, more explanatory letter that we were able to figure out what they were talking about. Apparently, King Henri IV of France had once given a ruby ring to Baron Gillet, Celeste's great-great-grandfather, back in 1607, and that ring had been passed down to her mother, Catherine, just before she left France for England. Then, prior to leaving for America, Celeste stole it from her mother's things and brought it with her.

Reading all about that now, I wondered where the ring had ended up. Considering its age and provenance, if it were still being passed down through the family today, it would definitely be worth a pretty penny. I made a mental note to ask Nana if she knew anything about it.

Nicole and I got through about half the letters before she began to fade, so I suggested we put them away for now and come back to them later in the week. Just to be sure we could make that happen, I grabbed a paper towel and a dry erase marker and rearranged a few things on the whiteboard until I got it to fit.

Thinking Nicole might want a late-afternoon nap, I helped her into the bed, but she never really drifted off. From what I could see, she just lay there, staring off in the distance. Whether her mind was caught up in the past or on her future, I didn't know, but I could tell she needed some space.

I used the time to pay a visit to Miss Vida.

The idea had come to me three days ago, when I'd first gotten the phenotyping report from Detective Ortiz. I still hadn't shown the computer-generated picture of the man's face to Nicole, fearing it might create within her an even more drastic reaction than seeing Danielle's drawings had. But I did want Miss Vida to get a look, so that meant sharing it with her when Nicole wasn't around. I had printed it out at work and was carrying the pages with me now as I headed next door.

Fortunately, the older woman was home and seemed happy to chat. I followed her to the kitchen, where she was in the middle of making cookies. She declined my offer of help, so as she measured and poured and stirred, I sat in her breakfast nook and explained why I had come. Of course, I had to start all the way back at the cabin in the woods and go forward from there, but she was quickly engrossed in my tale. By the time I got to the part about the report and laid it out for her to see, she eagerly wiped her hands on her apron and picked it up to give it a look.

The reason I was bothering her with all of this, I went on to explain, was because of the victim's Jewish heritage. To me, the next logical step in learning his identity was to contact local Jewish groups or resources or libraries to see if I could get access to their archives. If so, perhaps eventually I could unearth something that would reveal this man's identity. Miss Vida had lived in Richmond her whole life and was very active with her synagogue, so my hope was that she could offer some guidance here about my options and maybe make a connection or two.

"I'll do better than that, Maddee. Why don't you let me do some checking for you first? Before you bury your nose in a bunch of old papers and photos, I'll ask around in the community to see if any of this—the facts of the murder or a missing person from that time or this picture of the victim—rings a bell. It wouldn't hurt, and it would sure be a lot more pleasant than what you're talking about doing. You're already far too busy as it is."

I readily accepted her offer and couldn't thank her enough.

"Are you kidding?" she replied, shushing any further thanks. "This is exciting! I can't wait to get started."

Though I knew I shouldn't get my hopes up, I was feeling almost as excited myself by the time I left her place. If anyone could circulate info and get some answers, it was my personable and popular landlady. Whether she ended up succeeding or not, it was definitely worth a try.

I left her house the way I had come in, through the back door. It was fully dark now, but I let the glow of the light from my kitchen—visible over Miss Vida's back fence—guide the way. Breathing in the cool night air, I padded across the grass of her little yard and garden, but just as I pushed open the gate, something made me hesitate.

A person, a man, was standing outside my kitchen window, trying to see into the carriage house.

Chapter Twenty-Seven
Maddee

I gasped. At the window the man turned, startled by the sound. Time froze as our eyes met and held. Though he was mostly in shadow, I could see the gaunt face, the scraggly goatee, the tattoos covering every inch of his bare arms.

Hedge.

Before I could even decide what to do, he took off running. Stunned, I just stood there, frozen.

Then I ran after him.

He'd veered off to the left, so I did too. But it was darker in that direction, with more alleys and trees and a million places to hide. By the time I reached the end of the walk, he was nowhere to be seen. I kept going anyway, but then I stopped after half a block, knowing it would be foolish to continue. He could be hiding up ahead and ambush me. Even if he wasn't, and I managed to catch him, what would I do with him? A few years of karate class in middle school hadn't exactly made me a force to be reckoned with.

I turned toward home, thoughts of my sister suddenly flooding my mind.

Nicole. Was Nicole okay?

Adrenaline coursing through my veins, I ran all the way, slamming open the front door when I got there. She was in the bed, asleep, but the noise startled her awake.

"Maddee? What's wrong?"

Again, time seemed to freeze. In an instant, my brain went through the whole scenario, the call from Ortiz, the mug shot, the way my sister had lied to me, was still lying to me. I shook my head, avoiding the question.

"Sorry," I replied, trying not to sound breathless. "I didn't realize you were sleeping."

Needing privacy, I suggested she take a shower and afterward we could eat a light supper. I set up her shower chair and helped her get started. Then I went upstairs to make my calls.

I began with Ortiz but got her voice mail, so I left a message telling her what had happened and asking her to call me ASAP. I didn't know what to do, whether to call the police or file a restraining order or what, but I knew she could advise me, so I would wait until I heard back.

In the meantime, I thought about calling my father next but hesitated. Knowing him, he'd race right up here and insist on taking both of us back home with him. But even with Hedge out there "sniffing around," as Ortiz had put it, I didn't want that. Not only did I have to be in Richmond for my job each day, but changing things now would mess with every single element of our carefully constructed schedule, threatening all the progress Nicole had been making, both with her therapy and her daily meetings.

Hands shaking now from the aftereffects of adrenaline, I found myself scrolling for Greg's number instead. He answered on the first ring, sounding pleased to hear from me even though it was a Sunday night and not a workday.

Speaking in a low voice, I explained the situation, adding that I'd called my detective friend and was waiting to hear back from her, but in the meantime I just wanted his opinion on whether I should tell Nicole about this or not.

He sighed heavily, and I could picture his thoughtful expression, his concerned eyes. He asked a few questions to clarify—this was the first he'd heard about the existence of a second passenger in the car who had run off after the accident—and then he concluded that maybe for now it would be better if she didn't know. His thinking was that if she realized the guy was coming around, she might find a way to connect with him, and that was something none of us wanted to happen. For all we knew, Hedge wasn't just her friend but her dealer as well, and he had come here with drugs in hand.

"There are a few things we need to do security-wise," Greg added. As he went on to talk about doors and windows and exterior lighting and even some instruction in self-defense, all I could think of was how he'd used the word "we." Things *we* need to do. Something about that made me feel safe yet empowered. Proactive. I thought of a line from a song by the Miralettes: "Always there when I need him, he's such a stand-up guy." That was Greg to the core. Maybe that should be his ringtone.

We made plans and ended the call. I listened to make sure the shower was still going and then quickly dialed Miss Vida next. Not only did I want her to know that I'd caught an unsavory friend of Nicole's snooping around, but I needed help in getting Nicole out of here for a few hours tomorrow night so Greg and I could work unobserved. As usual, the older woman sounded more than happy to help. She came up with a grand plan for the evening, including what she would make for dinner and how she just might use the opportunity to teach Nicole mah-jongg. We were interrupted by a beep, so I ended our call and answered, glad it was Ortiz.

We didn't talk long. I'd made several decisions since leaving the message, and she concurred with those decisions now. She offered to do one favor, saying she would contact my local precinct to let them know what was going on and who the guy was so they could "up the patrol" for a while. "You know, they'll establish a presence and keep an eye on the place. Make a point of being seen. It won't take long for Hedge to notice, and then he'll probably hightail it out of there. One more parole violation, and he's back behind bars. He's not going to risk that."

Before going to bed, I sat by the upstairs window for a while and peered out into the darkness, watching for anything suspicious. Instead, I was thrilled to see a police car pass by on the street, slowly and deliberately, not once but twice in a half hour period. Thanks to that, and to the three friends who had come to my aid tonight, I ended up sleeping well despite my scary encounter.

The next day was to be my sister's first day on the job, and the timing couldn't have been better. Now that she was somewhat ambulatory, no way did I want her at home and in a position to connect with anyone from her past.

Because Nicole was still recovering from her injuries, Debra started her out slowly, giving her simple duties she could perform while seated. She told her that as long as she tracked her time, she was free to take as many breaks as she needed and even call it a day once she'd had enough. Debra showed her the family meeting room across the hall and explained that she was welcome to treat it as her own personal break space. Set up more like a living room than a counseling office, it held a long couch that would be perfect for putting her feet up and taking a nap. And because it was only used in the evenings, for family counseling sessions, it was always empty during the day.

Once her orientation was done, Nicole jumped right in, and she seemed to catch on to things quickly. She'd dropped out of college halfway through her first year, but she was a sharp kid, and I had no doubt she could handle whatever anyone threw her way. Had she not gone down the wrong road back then, she'd be out of school and in the workforce in some professional capacity by now, I felt sure. Perhaps at some point, if she stayed clean, she could try again.

As Debra and I had expected, Nicole ran out of steam after just a few hours and spent the afternoon sleeping in the family meeting room. By the time we headed home, she still seemed exhausted, but she was in good spirits. I wasn't surprised. Work was a great thing, a healthy thing, and I had no doubt this little job was going to have all sorts of positive effects on my sister. Too bad it would only last for four weeks, until her sentence kicked in and she would have to head off to rehab—or to jail.

On the drive home, I told Nicole that Miss Vida had invited her over for dinner, followed by a mah-jongg lesson. And though she was tired, she actually seemed pleased at the idea.

"Just me, though?"

"Yeah. I have some things I need to do. I figure at least this way you won't be bored while I'm gone."

She grunted. "In other words, Miss Vida is babysitting me again—though why over at her place this time?"

"It's not babysitting."

"Oh, wait," she said, ignoring my objection. "I get it. You're wanting a little private time with Dr. Ken Doll."

I glanced at her. "Actually, we did have a date tonight, but I canceled it. Too much else going on."

"You canceled on him *again*? Better be careful, Maddee, or you just might make his plastic hair fall out with worry."

I couldn't help but smile. "What's it to you? You don't like him anyway."

"I like him fine. I just don't like him for you. In fact, if you think about it…" Her voice trailed off, leaving silence between us.

"If you think about it, what?"

"Well, it's just…if you're willing to skip a date with a sexy hunk like him just to run errands or whatever, then maybe you're not as into him as you think you are."

I hesitated, not wanting to sound defensive but wishing I could make her understand. "Austin and I want the same things," I said finally. And we did. Family, kids, stability.

"Whatever you say, sis," she replied. Then she turned and gazed out the window, silent the rest of the way home.

～

Greg led me across the squishy mat, one hand on my elbow for stability. We were at his physical therapy clinic, after hours, in the main gym, which was a large, impressive space lined with fancy equipment. Along one wall was a huge blue floor mat, and that's where we got into position now.

After spending more than an hour at the carriage house, checking and fixing the locks on all windows and doors and installing two exterior motion detector lights, we were at last embarking on the self-defense portion of the evening. As a former instructor, Greg had said he could show me a number of moves and techniques I could use to protect myself in dangerous situations.

"The most important thing to remember when you're under threat is this," he said, and then he counted off on his fingers. "Eyes, throat, groin, knees. These are some of the most vulnerable parts of the body, and that's what makes them your four primary targets. Injuring your attacker, even briefly, in one of those places may give you enough time to get away."

"Okay, I'm ready." Stifling a grin, I raised both arms and one leg in the air, assuming the classic crane pose from *The Karate Kid*.

Greg smiled. "Intimidating. But remember, it's not about karate—or taekwondo or krav maga or anything else, for that matter. It's just basic self-defense, where anything can be a weapon. You don't need perfect form or special knowledge."

"But what if I have some smooth moves?" I asked, digging deep in my middle school martial arts memory and executing an impressive side snap kick.

This time he didn't smile. He walked over to me and placed his hands on my upper arms, looking me deeply in the eyes. I had previously thought we were the same height, but with both of us face-to-face and barefoot, I realized he was a good two inches taller.

"You need to take this seriously, Maddee. I want you to be safe."

I could feel the warmth of his hands through the thin fabric of my shirt. Goose bumps lifted on my forearms.

"I'm sorry," I said, meaning it. "I'll behave. Guess it's just easier to be silly than to admit I actually need to know this stuff."

He gave me an understanding nod, let go, and returned to his previous position on the mat.

"Basically, you want to use your elbows, fingers, feet, car keys, cell phone—anything you have at your disposal to cause pain to your attacker, which will momentarily distract him. Whatever it takes."

I nodded. "Cause pain, escape. Got it."

"Good. Okay." He stepped back a few feet and turned to one side. "Let's say I'm you, and you're the attacker."

I wanted to make a joke, something about if he were me, then he would definitely not be wearing that shade of orange, but I held my tongue. After all, I'd promised to behave.

"Are you ready?" Greg asked, interrupting my thoughts.

"Ready for what?"

"I want you to come at me, but in slow motion. I'll show you what you should do in response."

"All right."

Concentrating now, I did as he said, moving toward him and grabbing his left upper arm with both hands. As I did, he raised that arm in a wide circle, breaking my grip, and then he quickly spun toward me and pretended to jab at my eyes with his other hand.

I stepped back, surprised at how easily he had managed to defend himself.

"Good. Let's try it again, this time from the back."

I did as instructed, moving forward and flinging an arm around his throat, but before I could even blink, his foot was at my kneecap. Had he actually kicked, I would have been on the ground in agony.

We spent the next hour trying different techniques, changing roles, learning and experimenting until I began to feel confident. It was strenuous, both of us growing sweaty as we worked, but it was fun too. More than once, I found myself marveling at his surprising physique. Having never seen him in anything other than his standard uniform of navy polo shirt and khaki pants, I hadn't realized how fit he was.

If that day ever came when he and Nicole actually did start dating, she wouldn't just be getting a good man, I realized. She'd be getting a buff one too.

"Think you're up to it?" I asked Nicole the next day after work as we stood side by side gazing up at the walking bridge that led across the river to a small island known as Belle Isle. Now that her casts were off, Nicole was supposed to walk a little bit each day, but after spotting Hedge at the window the night before last, I'd decided we wouldn't be taking those walks in the neighborhood, where we might cross paths with him. Instead, we'd do it here.

"We won't walk the whole thing today, of course," I added, sensing her hesitation. "But I thought it might be nice, especially on a day like this."

The temperatures had been dropping lately, but today was wonderfully clear and warm, even now at just an hour before sunset.

After a little more thought, she agreed to give it a try, and she took hold of her walker as the two of us set off toward the switchback ramps that would bring us up to the bridge's entrance. Suspended below an interstate, this footbridge and the island beyond were quite popular with tourists and locals alike.

As she moved slowly up the ramp, I realized that perhaps the slope was too much for her at this stage. But she persisted, and eventually we made it to the top. Once we were actually on the more level bridge, she seemed to rally.

We started across, Nicole concentrating on her gait as I walked beside her, ready to catch her should she start to fall. Far below, the James River churned and swirled in a beautiful flow toward downtown Richmond, which rose majestically in the distance.

We went perhaps twenty feet before she had to turn around. By the time we got back to the car, she was pale, out of breath, and limping.

"That might have been too much," I admitted as I helped her get comfortable and handed her a bottle of water.

"Let's try it again tomorrow," she replied, the determination and resolve in her voice a lovely sound.

Nicole continued to do well at work over the next few days, sleeping a little less each time. Not only did they seem pleased with her performance, but I could tell she was liking it too. She'd always been an intuitive person, instinctively tuning into others' needs, so it didn't surprise me when I caught her reading some of the psychology books in the treatment room during her breaks. Perhaps she was hoping to figure out some of her own issues.

We returned to the footbridge daily for our walk, going a little farther with every visit. By Friday, we made it more than halfway across before we had to turn around because of the time. Not only would it be dark soon, but tonight's agenda was to finish reading the letters before our grandmother's weekly visit.

That was, of course, the first thing Nana asked about as she came in the door the next morning, and for once I was relieved to answer yes, we'd read them all and we loved them. We sat and talked about some of the various elements—from Celeste's misfortune in love to Berta's health to Emmanuel's sudden appearance—for at least ten minutes before I realized that Nana and I were doing all of the talking. Even though Nicole had read the letters too and found them quite fascinating, she now sat hunched in her chair, looking as though she would rather be anywhere than here.

That was odd enough, but then Nana did something even odder. As I poured her some more coffee and set it on the table in front of her, she looked up at me and asked if I would mind giving her and Nicole some time alone.

Again with the weird thing that was none of my business?

I was vaguely offended but could hardly refuse. I managed to mutter, "Sure," and then asked how much time they would need.

"Oh, I suppose the rest of the hour," Nana replied. "So you and I can say goodbye now. Then you'll be free to run out somewhere if you'd like."

Ouch. Talk about a dismissal.

I glanced at Nicole, but her eyes were trained on the floor, her cheeks a vivid pink. Whatever this was about, I realized, maybe I didn't want to know.

Considering that I'd been told to vacate the premises, I decided to go for a bicycle ride. Because of my sister, I'd been forced to take the car to work all week, and I'd really missed my little blue sissy bike.

Though the day was cold and cloudy, I ended up having a lovely time, pedaling in a big loop that took me all the way to Maymount Park and back. By the end of my ride, I was hungry for lunch and curious to learn how the rest of Nana's visit had gone.

I was slowing things down, about two blocks from home, when I noticed a man sitting in a parked car up ahead. I didn't give it much thought, assuming he was just waiting for someone or texting on his phone. But as I pedaled past, motion from inside caught my eye, and I glanced over to see him bringing a camera to his face and taking a picture.

With all of the gorgeous historic homes in the Fan district, it wasn't unusual to see people snapping photos, but I'd gone another half a block when it struck me that something was different with him. His camera had had a telephoto lens—which he'd been pointing directly at the windows of the carriage house.

My heart pounding, I looked both ways and then swung out into the street, making a U-turn on my bike and heading directly back toward the car. In seconds, I heard the ignition spring to life, and then the vehicle pulled out and began speeding in my direction.

At first, I thought the driver intended to hit me, but he veered around me instead, just trying to get away.

"Hey!" I shouted as he flew past. "Stop!"

But he didn't. He kept going, barely even pausing at the corner before continuing on.

At least I'd gotten a look at his license plate, and I quickly pulled out my phone and typed in the number. After that I pedaled for home, trying to gather my wits about me as I went. My mind was spinning, however, with the most disturbing realization of all. This was the same older, balding, paunchy man I'd seen lurking suspiciously in the alleyway almost four weeks ago, two days after Nicole first moved in.

Chapter Twenty-Eight
Maddee

Between a known ex-con who lurked outside my house, peering into the windows at night, and some random older guy, who seemed to be keeping a watch on the place from afar, I couldn't decide which was creepier. All I knew was that this business had to stop.

Not surprisingly, Nana was gone by the time I arrived at home, but otherwise things seemed normal. Nicole was napping in her bed, so I went back outside to call Detective Ortiz. I felt really bad burdening her yet again with matters that more than likely had nothing to do with her, but she was gracious, taking the license plate number and saying she would follow up, including making a second call to the local precinct on my behalf. I asked if she thought this could have anything to do with her investigation, but she sounded skeptical.

"I can't imagine why. Let me run the plate first, and then we'll know more."

"Do you think Nicole and I are in danger?"

She was quiet for a moment before answering. "I don't know, Maddee. Not necessarily. Spying on people and doing harm to them are two different things. That guy today could be anything from a pervert to a federal agent. There's no way to know for sure without more information. Your getting the license plate number was key. Hopefully, that'll lead us to some answers."

We ended the call, and I felt a little better—until I went back in, heard a soft whimpering noise in the living room, and realized my sister wasn't napping. She was crying. With all that had just happened, the realization made my heart lurch.

"Nicole?" I ran to her. "What's the matter?" Had that man been inside the house? Had he hurt her somehow?

She twisted around in the bed to look at me, her eyes puffy, her nose red. "I'm fine. It's just been a difficult morning. You know how Nana can be."

Relief flooded my veins. Nana, I could handle.

"Would it help to talk about it?"

She shook her head and reached for another tissue. "I really just need to be alone right now. Thanks."

Pitiful as she was, I gave her some space. Whatever was going on between her and our grandmother was not my affair—Nana had made that abundantly clear. If Nicole was choosing to shut me out as well, I would just have to live with it.

After all the drama of the morning, the rest of our day was blessedly quiet. We made it to a meeting, but otherwise Nicole spent the afternoon and evening withdrawn and subdued, lost in her own thoughts. It was just as well. Her mood freed me to retreat to the sanctuary of my room and get some much-needed alone time. As I sat in my chair by the window and listened to the children in the park, I found my heart softening toward Austin. Surely the early cast removal had not been intentional. Any man who wanted a houseful of children the way he did would never endanger another person's health just for his own selfish gain. Feeling better, I texted with him for a while, and we made lunch plans for the following day.

The next morning, for the first time since moving in, Nicole went to church with me. When the service was over, Austin was waiting for us at the curb as planned. Prior to this, I had intentionally kept these two parts of my world separate so Nicole wouldn't feel awkward. But now that her status as his patient was nearing an end, it seemed appropriate to transition into a different sort of relationship.

Austin drove the three of us to a restaurant he had chosen, a lovely little Italian place on the south side of the James. I liked it immediately, and the food tasted even better than it smelled. Best of all, Nicole's funk from the day before seemed to have lifted, and at lunch she was witty and engaging.

At one point, Austin surprised me by asking her about her plans for the future. I was going to kick him under the table, thinking, *Duh! Rehab or jail. Take your pick!*

But then he added, "The real future, I mean. The one that's waiting for you on the other side of all of this."

I settled back down. What a lovely way to put it.

"It's a little soon to know for sure," she replied, "but lately I've been thinking about going back to college and actually finishing this time."

"Excellent idea," he said. "Any thoughts on a major?"

She glanced shyly at me. "To be honest, I'd really like to get a master's in social work and become a counselor."

I tried to mask my surprise, but I knew she saw it. Worse, she surely saw my skepticism as well. Going back to college was one thing, but sticking it out all the way through grad school? Working as a counselor? Those were lofty goals, and I doubted she had it in her. Nicole never finished anything she started. What made her think this time would be any different?

The conversation went on from there, but her words came back to mind a while later, over a dessert of blueberry mascarpone tarts. She and Austin were talking about books and reading, and it struck me that when I'd seen her with a psychology text at the office, she hadn't been trying to solve her own problems. She'd been exploring a topic that deeply interested her, one she might even want to make a career out of. She had the right to dream and plan and hope—even expect. I should allow myself to do the same on her behalf.

Watching her across the table now, I couldn't believe this lovely young woman in the Stella McCartney blouse with the elegant makeup and expensive highlights was the same kid who, just a few months ago, had sported bleached-blond scraggly hair with dark roots, torn jeans, dirty shoes, and the jittery intensity of a hard-core meth user. If only she could see what I saw, the emerging of a beautiful butterfly from a dark and dingy cocoon. It wasn't even about appearance, though the difference was striking. It was about the person, the clarity of mind, the gleam of hope and promise that had begun emanating from her more and more each day. With every thought that stretched beyond the next hit, every memory that emerged painfully from the fog, every day of sobriety that built on the previous day, Nicole was finally becoming the woman God intended her to be.

I couldn't wait to see what He had in store for her.

As I sat at my desk doing my regular calendar review the next morning, I was reminded that it was exactly two weeks to the day when Nicole would have to give her decision to the judge on whether she'd be heading to rehab or jail. I realized I hadn't prayed nearly enough about that and made a mental note to start ASAP.

I also noticed that a week from tomorrow would be Nicole's thirtieth meeting in thirty days, just as she had agreed to do when I moved her in with me. The thought filled me with such joy that I decided to commemorate the accomplishment with a surprise party. With just a week to prepare it wouldn't be anything fancy, but a small gathering of those who had been walking alongside us in her recovery—Nana, our parents, Miss Vida, Austin, Greg, several PT assistants from the gym, Debra, a few of our coworkers—would be fun and might even help push her ultimate decision in the right direction.

The only damper in my week was the news I received from Detective

Ortiz about the license plate results. She said the vehicle was registered to "Franklin and Associates," a name so generic she wasn't even sure what kind of business it was. All she knew was that it was a private company out of Richmond, with only a rented postal box for an address.

"So what happens next?"

She sighed heavily. "Nothing, at least not on my end. If you'd caught the man actively committing a crime—like breaking into the house rather than just snapping a photo of it—I'd have more leeway. But as it is, I'm sorry, Maddee. This is all I can do for now."

The day of the party, I took Nicole to her regular 6:30 meeting on Monument Avenue and then raced home in time to let my parents in, help unload and set out the food trays they had brought, hang up decorations, and greet the other guests as they trickled in. Half an hour later I headed back to the meeting to pick up my sister. Sometimes these gatherings could be emotional for her, but when she came out of this one, she had a big smile on her face.

In the car, I could tell she was hinting around about why tonight's meeting had been a special one, and she even went so far as to mention a "new addition" for her headboard. I knew she meant her milestone key tag, but I pretended to be completely obtuse, changing the subject every time she tried to bring it back up. At the house, everything seemed perfectly normal, just a regular Tuesday night in November.

Until we opened the front door.

Pandemonium ensued as everyone jumped out from their hiding places, yelling "Surprise!" and blowing noisemakers and applauding. Nicole was dumbfounded, and it seemed to take her a minute to recover from the shock. Then she turned my way, tears brimming in her eyes, and wrapped her arms around me.

"I don't deserve you," she whispered in my ear.

In that moment, all the pain and worry and fears of the last month lifted out of me, and I was again with my little sister, the most important person to me in the whole world. Truly, having her here and sober and on the road to health and recovery were beyond all I could have asked or imagined.

As we pulled apart, the noise began to fade, and then everyone seemed to be looking at Nicole expectantly, as if they wanted a speech. I was about to rescue her when she held up a hand and addressed the group.

"Just one question," she said, her eyes scanning the small crowd. "This is a real party, right? I mean, y'all aren't here to do an intervention, are you?"

Her joke was met with a burst of laughter. After that, everyone begin talking and milling around and coming up to congratulate her and give hugs. I directed them toward the food, and once the crowd finally cleared in front of my sister, I went over and presented her with a piece of tape. She looked at me quizzically for just a moment before thrusting a hand into her pocket and coming out with her new orange key tag. On the front was the same NA logo, and on the back were the words, "Clean & Serene for Thirty Days."

"You stinker," she scolded, "trying to act like you didn't know. I couldn't believe it. That was mean."

"I know, right?" I grinned.

Together, we went to the bed, which I'd managed to turn sideways and push all the way against the wall, and hung this second tag beside the first.

"You did it, kid," I said softly. "Now go get some food and enjoy your party."

I was still standing there when Greg came over, a plate piled high in his hand. Gesturing toward the key tag, he asked if I knew why it was orange.

I shook my head.

"That's the color of caution. At thirty days, they stress being cautious and avoiding old playmates, old playgrounds, and old playthings."

We shared a look, knowing the battle was far from over.

Austin joined us then, placing one hand on my back in a casual yet possessive way. Feeling oddly uncomfortable, I ignored it as I launched into the story of Nicole's progress walking to Belle Isle. Then, spotting

Nana across the room, I excused myself and went to her, greeting the woman with a hug and a smile despite the fact that the last time I'd seen her she had been kicking me out of my own house. My feelings were still a bit hurt, but I tried not to let that show. Without knowing what the issue was, I couldn't say whether she'd been justified or not. I did ask what she had said to upset my sister so, explaining that the poor girl spent half the day crying. Without missing a beat, Nana met my gaze and replied, "Believe me, dear, so did I."

About halfway through the evening, Greg was taking out a bag of trash for me when he texted from outside. I still hadn't given him a personal ringtone, so I wasn't sure who it was until I saw his name on the screen above his message: *Ask your grandmother how she got here tonight.*

Confused, I did as requested then sent my response: *Silver Lincoln, driver is Jerome. (She doesn't drive after dark, uses Windsor Transport.) Why?*

His reply was quick: *Tell you in a few.*

By the time he got back inside, I had a feeling I knew what this was about. Sure enough, he explained that he'd spotted a man sitting in a car and had become suspicious until he noticed the small driving service logo on the back windshield and realized that was probably what it was. After texting with me, he'd gone over and introduced himself, and the two men had chatted for a bit.

"Your grandmother really makes him sit out there alone all night?" he asked, incredulous.

"I guess. That's his job, isn't it?"

"Yeah, but the least she could do is invite him to join the party."

I smiled, thinking Greg surely hadn't grown up in Nana's kind of world.

"'It's just not done, dear,'" I said, with enough primness for him to catch my sarcasm.

"I see. Well, if you don't mind, I'm going to pull together some food for him."

"Be my guest."

With a smile, I watched as Greg went down the buffet line, a paper plate in hand, filling it up and topping it off with a second plate turned upside down. Then he grabbed a napkin and some plastic utensils and headed outside.

"Where's he going?" Nicole asked, appearing at my elbow.

I explained his little errand and she chuckled. "What a guy. This one, on the other hand…"

She subtly gestured toward Austin across the room. He was engaged in conversation with our grandmother, looking handsome and debonair and totally in his element.

"Watch this," Nicole added under her breath. Then she called out, "Hey, Nana, should I invite your driver in for some meatballs and macaroni salad? Looks like we have plenty extra."

Nana looked at Nicole in bewilderment, and then she said, stiffly, "I'm sure he's fine."

"I don't know. He might be hungry. Austin? You want to take him a plate?"

He gaped at her blankly, as if she'd asked him to bring a pig to a cotillion.

And though I didn't think it was very nice for her to set him up that way, her little stunt had its intended effect. Standing there, watching him, it was as if the veneer cracked just a bit. Did I really want to spend my life with a man who was better looking on the outside than he was on the inside?

A short while later, I managed to get him alone out on the patio, where I asked the question that was really on my mind, if he'd taken Nicole's casts off early so I would be free to go to that party with him.

He seemed amused at first, perhaps at my naïveté. He wouldn't come right out and admit it. He just kept saying that the removal "was within acceptable medical limits." In other words, whether he had or not, it wasn't something that would get him in trouble or could cause him to lose a lawsuit. That still didn't make it right.

"Can I ask you something?" Taking a deep breath, I turned toward him. "Which do you like more? Me, or the fact that I want to settle down and have a big family?"

He was quiet for a long moment, the smile now gone. Finally, he let out a sigh. "I could ask you the same question, Maddee."

Our eyes met, and I could see that we both knew the truth. Though we'd wanted this to work, we didn't have the kind of connection that was going to lead to love and marriage and family. The whole thing looked good on paper, but despite our similarities—especially when it came to our dreams for the future—we weren't a good match and never could be.

After a final congrats to Nicole, Austin left. Nana had to go soon after, but as we said our goodbyes I told her something I knew would please her, that Nicole and I were planning to visit Williamsburg the next day, just as she'd been urging us to do. Thanks to some new computers my office was having put in, I explained, our workday was to end at two. We'd been talking about going ever since we'd finished reading the letters, so this seemed like the perfect opportunity.

"Of course," I added, "the village as it's presented is from 1775, not 1704 when the sisters first arrived. But it will still be fun to see the different places they talked about."

Nana seemed delighted—though almost overly so, as if this was the best news she'd heard in her life.

"Have your sister call me as soon as you get back home," she said intensely before turning to go.

I nodded, not even bothering to ask what that was about because I knew she wouldn't tell me.

Once everyone else was gone, Greg stuck around to help clean. We ended up with a few more bags of trash, so this time I went out with him. We made our way around the back of the carriage house to the cans along the alley.

"Austin seems like a nice fellow," Greg said.

"Yeah, we broke up tonight."

"Good. He's not the guy for you."

I chuckled. "You sound like Nicole."

"Thanks. I tell you what. She has an uncanny sense of what makes people tick. I'd listen to her if I were you."

We reached the cans and set our bags inside, and then as we walked back I found myself telling Greg the story of Nana's matchmaking with me and Austin and how, when she'd called Greg "special" soon after, and then he'd shown up that first time all handsome and sweet, I'd assumed Nana was at it again, but this time for my sister.

"Nicole's not in any position to date anyone," he said, clearly startled. "The timing couldn't be worse."

"Oh, I totally agree. That's why I was glad when it turned out the 'special' thing Nana was talking about was your certification, not your being dateable. I'd jumped to the wrong conclusion."

He smiled, gesturing for me to go first once we rounded the building.

"Though I have to say," I added, "a few years from now, if it happened to work out…"

"What?"

"Just that she could do a lot worse."

He came to a stop halfway up the walk. "I'm confused."

"I'm just saying that once Nicole has a year or two of sobriety under her belt, if you're still single, you ought to give it a try."

"Give what a try?"

"Dating Nicole."

He blinked. "Nicole."

"Yeah."

"Try dating Nicole," he repeated.

"If you want," I said.

He didn't respond. Instead, he walked me the rest of the way to the door in silence. Then he simply mumbled that he needed to go and took off without another word.

CHAPTER TWENTY-NINE
Celeste

*T*he next morning, Celeste slipped down the ladder to find Benjamin building up the fire in the kitchen. The boy wore a raggedy coat and a scrap of cloth wrapped around his neck.

"Mornin'," he said. "Mr. Edwards wants you to go see him at the inn."

Celeste thanked him and hurried out the kitchen door and up the back steps. Mr. Edwards sat at the counter, going over his ledger. He looked as if he hadn't slept at all.

"Good day to you, sir," Celeste said softly.

Without looking up, he asked, "How are you?"

"Better."

He made another mark on the page and then looked up. "Lieutenant Gray spoke with me last night."

"He said he planned to, sir."

"Are you in agreement with him?"

She nodded. "As long as Constable Jones doesn't try to stop us."

Mr. Edwards rubbed his temple. "We spoke with him last night. He returned my bail, saying he's convinced Constable Wharton manipulated the situation to his benefit—getting his maid back and keeping the ring. He doesn't think he'll pursue matters with you. If he does, he'll tell him to go after you in Carolina."

Celeste grinned for the first time in days.

"But avoid him in Norfolk. Don't bring attention to yourself. Understand?"

"Yes. Of course."

"I hoped you would go home with your brother. If you don't, you may never see your family again."

"I-I realize that." A hollow feeling settled in the pit of her stomach.

"Do you trust Lieutenant Gray?" He raised his eyebrows again. "In spite of what happened?"

She swallowed hard and then spoke, forcing her voice to sound convincing. "Yes." Celeste steadied herself against the counter.

"And you'll take good care of Sary?"

"I will." That she knew without a doubt.

"Even if it turns out she'll never be able to cook again in her life?"

"Yes, I promise, but what will you do with Sary and me both gone?"

He sighed. "When Mr. Horn was here, I asked him to find another cook and another maid. Hopefully, he'll be back with them before the General Court starts. I'll ask him to bring an additional maid when he can. Eventually, life will calm down around here." He gazed at her intently, his eyes full of concern. "Go tell Sary and get ready to go. You'll need to hurry down to the dock. There's a boat leaving soon."

He turned the document around so she could see. "Here are Sary's papers. Lieutenant Gray asked me to sign them over to her as a gesture of good faith on his part. She's free."

Filled with joy and relief, Celeste thanked him as she took the document. "I'm eternally grateful, Mr. Edwards, for everything. You've gone far beyond your duty in kindness."

Mr. Edwards's eyes grew watery. "You remind me of my daughter, Miss Talbot. You're determined. Resourceful. I just hope Lieutenant Gray is worthy of being your husband."

"Oh, the situation is quite the opposite. I hope I'm worthy of being his wife."

Mr. Edwards paused for a moment, and then he said, "Go on now." He waved toward the back door. "Go on."

Celeste walked slowly through the passageway, glancing into the empty dining room, silently telling the inn goodbye. When she reached the kitchen, Benjamin was stirring the porridge in the pot. She waited until it thickened and then filled two bowls.

"Come eat with me," she said, nodding toward the table. When they had finished, she told him that she and Sary were leaving.

Tears filled his eyes.

"You're safe here with your father."

He nodded.

"A new cook will come, and new maids. Mr. Edwards will take care of all of you."

He nodded again and wiped at his eyes. Once she had cleaned their dishes, she climbed the ladder to the loft.

Sary was awake, and Celeste quickly explained what had happened, handing the woman her papers. Sary, her expression blank, turned toward the window as she clutched the document.

Giving her time to adjust, Celeste grabbed her extra set of clothes, spread them flat, and then rolled the garments into a parcel, tying it with the strings of her extra apron. She was embarrassed she had no trousseau, thinking back to her chest of clothing, linens, and other household goods in her parents' house. Jonathan would need to buy her a new wardrobe, eventually, and all of their household goods too. Gratitude swept over her for his generosity. Surely the passion she'd felt before would return.

She knelt down beside Sary. "Are you all right?"

The woman nodded.

"You are free to go wherever you want, although I don't have any money to give you right now to travel. You can stay with me until I can secure the money, or you can stay with me for the rest of your life."

Sary twisted her mouth, but she didn't speak or move from her pallet. Celeste didn't know what she would do if the woman refused to come along. Sary couldn't stay with Mr. Edwards if she couldn't work.

"Celeste?" It was Aline, coming up the ladder. "I just heard you're leaving with Lieutenant Gray."

"I am," Celeste responded as the maid's head came into view. In the distance, the rat-a-tat of the snare drum began.

Aline stepped up to the floor. "Do you remember that day outside the laundry when I started to tell you about the maid before you? And Mr. Edwards interrupted us?"

"Yes," Celeste answered, moving across the room to her own pallet.

"I don't know if I should have said anything then—or if I should say more now. But she was acquainted with Lieutenant Gray before she arrived."

"Oh?" Celeste concentrated on folding her blanket.

"Yes. And they had a row one night outside. I couldn't quite make out what it was all about though."

"She was indentured?"

Aline nodded as the drumming grew louder. "But she wasn't poor like I am or most servants are. She was from the gentry, like you."

Celeste cocked her head as she clutched her blanket to her chest for a moment. "Really?"

Aline nodded.

"I'll ask Jonathan about her." Celeste placed the blanket on the floor. Perhaps she was someone he'd once known in London who had fallen on hard times.

Aline shrugged. "I just thought you should know. In case…"

"Thank you," Celeste said. "I appreciate it, truly. And what a good friend you've been to me too."

Aline smiled at that. "Will your brother be back?"

"I don't think so." There was no reason for him to return to Williamsburg now that she was no longer in need of being rescued.

Aline's face fell. "He seems like a good man."

Celeste nodded. "He is. I hope to see him in Norfolk one more time." She choked on the last word. He could return directly to England with George if a ship was sailing from Norfolk in the next couple of days. She'd go on to Carolina with Jonathan. And Berta would come back to Williamsburg with Spenser if all went as planned.

"I don't mean to be forward, but I only have a few more months on my contract," Aline said, blushing. "It's just that so many things seem possible here that never would have back home."

Celeste nodded, thinking how far her own ideas had come about such things. Spenser had turned out to be more than good enough for Berta. Why shouldn't Aline be with someone like Emmanuel? Too bad he was leaving, for both their sakes.

"Give him a farewell for me?" Aline asked sadly.

"I will." Celeste flung her cloak over her shoulders and clasped it closed with the brooch. Then she turned her attention to Sary. "We need to go."

Sary put her cloak over her shoulders. Then she rolled her papers in her extra skirt and chemise and tucked the bundle inside the waistband of the skirt she was wearing. With that they were ready.

"We'll follow you down," Celeste said. Aline led the way, then Sary. Celeste inched down the ladder last. By the time they reached the street, Jonathan was waiting for them. They paused a moment as the soldiers marched by, the drum beating her farewell to Williamsburg. Celeste doubted she'd ever be back, but she knew she wouldn't miss the drumming.

The trip down the James on the cargo boat was uneventful. The sun had come out, and Celeste felt as if she was shaking off the cold of the night out in the elements. How quickly her life had changed once again. Jonathan chatted happily as they went, but Sary just stared at the trees along the bank. Celeste wished she could know what was going on in the woman's mind.

Thinking ahead to their stop in Norfolk, Celeste hoped to be able to tell Emmanuel to pay as much as needed to free Berta and not to worry about the ring. Yes, she very much wanted to have it back in the family, but it wasn't worth risking Berta's life over, even though it had come from Henri IV.

She hoped to have a chance to apologize to Berta too. There was no need to go over the past again, no matter what Jonathan had revealed the day before. She simply wanted to be at peace with her sister.

It was late afternoon by the time they reached Norfolk. As the *York* docked, Celeste could see George and Spenser on the wharf. Walking toward them were Constable Wharton, Emmanuel, and Berta. She looked steady on her feet and as beautiful as ever. Relief swept through Celeste. Their brother must have secured her release. Spenser spoke briefly with Emmanuel and then said something to the constable.

They needed to transfer to the *Royal Mary* to take them on to Charles Town, but Celeste didn't want to disembark when Constable Wharton could see her.

"I'll go see what the problem is," Jonathan said.

Celeste wasn't sure if it was her imagination or not, but Constable Wharton didn't seem surprised to have Jonathan butt into the conversation. He just looked annoyed—especially with Spenser. Then he threw up his arms and marched toward the village.

Celeste exhaled, glad to see him go. She rose as Jonathan approached, chuckling.

"What's going on?"

"Spenser was trying to trick Wharton out of your ring."

"Why?" But as soon as she asked she knew. Spenser wanted it for Berta.

Jonathan shrugged. "He says it's worth more than the contract. That Wharton swindled Emmanuel."

"Is there hope Spenser will be able to get the ring?" She hated the thought of Wharton keeping it.

"I doubt it," Jonathan answered, a sly smile on his face. "It seems Wharton is now claiming that the ring was fair trade for Berta's contract."

Celeste puzzled over the problem of the ring. "Did you tell Emmanuel that you bought my contract?"

"Not yet. He wants to speak with you."

Of course he did. "Will you come with me?"

Jonathan nodded.

Celeste told Sary to stay put. Then she followed Jonathan to the dock, stepping around the hogshead barrels full of tobacco that had come off the *York*. They would most likely be loaded onto the *Royal Mary* for her eventual return trip to England.

Emmanuel greeted Celeste with a kiss, but Berta held back. "Sister," Celeste said, moving toward her.

Berta didn't budge.

"I'm sorry, Berta."

"What are you sorry for?"

"Not listening. Not trying to understand."

Berta nodded toward Jonathan. "What's he doing here?"

"He bought my contract. We're headed to Carolina. We plan to marry in Charles Town."

Berta's brown eyes flashed. "He's using you, Celeste."

"Why do you say that?"

"He's a scoundrel."

"No, there was just a misunderstanding—"

Berta shook her head. "He doesn't do anything that doesn't profit him. He wants something from you. Just wait and see."

Celeste hesitated, not wanting to sound prideful. But then she said, "I'll be his wife. He loves me."

Berta shook her head. "He only loves himself."

Celeste held her tongue. Clearly, Berta still had feelings for Jonathan, feelings that hadn't been returned. She couldn't blame her sister for that, no matter how hurtful Berta's lie had been.

Yet...staring into her sister's fiery eyes, Celeste had a moment of doubt. What if she hadn't been lying? No, Celeste couldn't dwell on that. She had wagered her life, and Sary's too, on Jonathan. It was essential she support her soon-to-be husband.

Celeste turned toward Jonathan, who was speaking with Emmanuel and explaining that he had bought Celeste's contract. Spenser shot her a concerned look. She nodded at him, trying to communicate that she was in agreement. Even as she did, her heart lurched in longing for the man she really wanted, the one she would never marry. This kind of torment was a new emotion for her—one she feared she might be living with for the rest of her life.

She stepped forward to reassure her brother. "Now you have no concerns about money, Emmanuel."

He didn't answer but turned back toward Jonathan. "Where did you say you're going?"

"Carolina."

Emmanuel looked to George, who shrugged in answer to an unasked question.

"So are you married, then, already?" Spenser directed the question to Jonathan.

"No. We'll marry once we reach Charles Town, in the Huguenot church there."

Spenser's face grew pale. He turned toward Celeste. "Can we speak privately?"

She nodded and followed him a few feet away.

He whispered, "So you don't love George?"

She shook her head.

"And you still love Jonathan?"

She didn't answer. It didn't matter whether or not she still loved Jonathan. She'd already sacrificed everything she had for him. He was the only pragmatic choice left for her.

Spenser cleared his throat.

"It's none of your business," Celeste whispered, taking a step back. As soon as the words were out of her mouth, guilt surged through her. "I'm sorry." She met his gaze. "That was unkind of me. You deserve better."

He shrugged, the hurt clear on his face.

"You have Berta." Celeste's voice faltered. "You'll be fine."

"I have Berta? Is that what you've thought all along?"

Celeste nodded, her heart aching so badly she feared it might break. Why did he have to have such kind eyes? Such a caring face? Such internal strength? All she wanted, in all the world, was to step into his embrace.

Spenser's eyes narrowed. "Is that why I went to the jail to try to win your freedom? Is that why I stayed at your side while you were in the pillory?"

Celeste nodded again.

"For Berta?"

"Yes," she answered, keeping her voice as low as she could, trying not to cry. "Isn't that why you want the ring back in the family? So you can give it to Berta?"

Spenser gazed past her, out toward the bay, his jaw set. "You're certain you no longer have feelings for George."

"I am."

They both looked at George, who had stepped to Berta's side. Perhaps, in retaliation for Celeste not believing her about Jonathan, Berta had shifted her affections, hoping to hurt Celeste again. It wasn't going to work. She had no feelings for George whatsoever.

But Spenser did care about Berta. Suddenly, Celeste's heart ached in a new way, for poor Spenser and how badly this must be hurting him. Berta was a fool, spurning a man like him, with all his depth and sweetness and wisdom, for a clod like George.

She glanced again at Spenser and saw that his eyes were blank, his expression drawn.

"You'll take Berta back to Williamsburg with you, then? And Emmanuel and George will return to England?"

Spenser shook his head. "No, we'd all planned to go back to Williamsburg, at least for the time being…"

That made sense. Emmanuel would want to make sure Berta was settled first before he left the New World for good, even though he no longer needed to go to Williamsburg on Celeste's account. Feeling awkward but not knowing what more to say, Celeste was relieved when she saw Captain Bancroft approaching the group. Without another word, she turned and moved back to the others.

"Lieutenant Gray," the captain called out. "How fine to see you again. And with Mr. Talbot. I didn't realize you two were acquainted."

"We are now," Jonathan said. "In fact, he will soon be my brother-in-law."

"Oh. Well, then. You must not be marrying the plantation owner's daughter after all."

"No, that's behind me, thankfully. I've been given a land grant in

Carolina. Miss Talbot and I will wed in Charles Town. We'll be joining you on the *Royal Mary*."

"Really? Which Talbot sister did you decide on?"

Berta cleared her throat. Celeste shot Jonathan a look, but he either didn't see it or chose not to acknowledge it. Surely Captain Bancroft was jesting and had no idea he was inadvertently supporting Berta's claim.

Jonathan smiled. "Both Talbot sisters are beautiful, and honestly I'm not worthy of either. That said, I've only ever had eyes for the elder."

The amusing tone in Captain Bancroft's voice disappeared. "Is that so?" He glanced at Celeste and then back at Jonathan. "Would you walk with me, please?"

As the two went to the end of the wharf together, Celeste excused herself, stepped away, and then began retreating back toward the boat. She was suddenly eager to be apart from all of them—Spenser with his broken heart, Berta with her cruel ways, George with his…Georgeness.

She needed to move their things and Sary to the *Royal Mary* anyway before the *York* left on its return trip up the James. Once she'd done that, she would collect herself and go back and tell Emmanuel and Berta farewell in a more rational frame of mind.

When she boarded the boat, Celeste saw that Sary had gathered her bundle and was holding it in her good hand. With a nod, Celeste grabbed Jonathan's bags and led the way to the *Royal Mary*. First Mate Hayes greeted them. Celeste thanked him for delivering the letter.

He nodded. "You come from a good—and wealthy—family."

Celeste bowed her head, not wanting to discuss her parents' means.

"I was surprised you would venture so far away when you would be so well cared for at home."

When Celeste didn't answer, Hayes shook his head in disbelief. Then he directed Sary to a spot on the starboard side.

"I'll bring you back some food," Celeste told her, turning to go.

"Wait." Sary spoke in English.

Celeste spun around. Sary hadn't said a word since the incident in the kitchen, the day she was burned.

Sary motioned for Celeste to step closer. In a whisper she said in French, "That captain isn't a good man."

Celeste hesitated, confused. "He's been helpful to me. He was sympathetic about Berta." Granted, his comments just now on the dock were a little odd, but he was being facetious, she was sure. Someone must have told him about Berta's lie. She didn't understand the ways of men, but Jonathan seemed to get the joke.

Sary shook her head. "That Wharton is a bad man too. In fact, they seem to be in on things together. Maybe with Mr. Horn. And maybe even…" Her voice trailed off and she tightly pursed her lips, as if to hold in the rest of her words.

"In on things?" Celeste repeated. "What things?"

She expected Sary to be embarrassed, but instead the woman leaned forward, her expression growing determined as she spoke in a low voice. "They trick girls to get them on the ship. Then once those girls arrive here, they have no choice but to work. There's good money to be made in the buying and selling of contracts. Of young women— whether they actually want to come here or not."

Celeste felt an odd fluttering in her stomach. "What are you saying?" she asked, her mouth suddenly dry. "They trick girls? How?"

"They lie to them. In some cases, they even kidnap them. Whatever it takes to get the girls over here. And then they are stuck. Just like you."

Celeste's head began to spin. She reached for the railing to steady herself. "How do you know all this?"

Sary shrugged. "I listened. You'd be amazed at how much one can hear from a well-placed drying hut."

Celeste frowned. The drying hut? She thought for a moment and then it struck her: The bench where the men liked to congregate and smoke and talk was well within hearing distance of Sary's hut. Often she would gather her dry herbs after a meal when conversations were taking place on the bench just over the fence.

"Didn't anyone ever see you over there, listening?" Celeste asked, aghast that Sary would take such risks.

"People don't really see slaves in that way. Besides, everyone knows I speak only French. As long as they conversed in English, I'm sure they thought they were free to talk about whatever they wanted, even if I was nearby."

Celeste wasn't surprised. She'd figured out some time ago that Sary understood English far better than she let on.

"Anyway," Sary continued, "not only have I heard the men talking, but I actually know a couple of Irish girls in the West Indies who never stopped insisting they were kidnapped. Then there was an English housemaid who ran away from a plantation near Jamestown a few months ago, claiming she'd been tricked into coming here. Mr. Horn found her and beat her badly, and then he took her down here to Norfolk. Last I heard, she'd been forced to work as a maid for Constable Wharton himself."

Of course. That must be the same girl she'd met in the Wharton's house that night she and Spenser spoke to the constable's wife and traded the ring for Berta's contract.

"And there's your situation with Lieutenant Gray, and him getting you over here on false pretenses."

Celeste bristled. "Our love was not false! Didn't he prove that in the end by buying my contract? By asking me to marry him?"

Sary again pursed her lips, offering no reply.

"He even bought and freed you," Celeste added defensively.

Sary looked away, a glimmer of hurt in her eyes, probably at the thought that Celeste would believe Jonathan's word over hers. "Most likely he's hoping I'll be able to cook again. I don't doubt, if I stay, he'll figure out some way to take my freedom away too. And he'll buy slaves, probably here in Norfolk, before we leave."

Celeste shook her head, more in disbelief than disagreement. She'd been a fool to think a plantation in Carolina wouldn't need slaves to make a profit. It seemed most business ventures in the southern colonies did. Why hadn't she broached the subject with Jonathan? She felt as if she might be sick. She tried one more time to convince herself she'd made the right decision. "But Jonathan is kind and—"

Sary's eyes watered. "Charming?"

"Yes."

"Those are the ones you need to watch out for," Sary countered. "It seems he used that charm as bait, luring innocent young women from all over to come to the New World. No doubt he receives a cut of the profits for every one of them. Even your sister."

Celeste's eyes narrowed. She'd never told Sary about Berta's claims. "Who else?"

Sary hesitated only a moment before speaking. "The maid before you, who died. The one Aline was trying to tell you about. She came over on the same ship as Jonathan this last time. My heart broke for her. She stayed up in the loft with me, and she didn't know I could understand her words as she prayed aloud, night after night, whispering, 'Please, God, forgive me for the sins I committed on that ship. Show me what to do before I can no longer hide my condition. Please soften Jonathan's heart toward me and our child.'"

Celeste's knees nearly buckled, and she gripped the rail harder, fearing she might collapse. "What happened to her?" she whispered.

"She died a few weeks before you got here. Something went wrong with the baby. It was tiny, not ready for this world at all. She bled to death."

"Did anyone try to help her?"

"I tried." Sary's eyes filled with tears. "I lost a baby, a girl, in such a way. She was bigger than the maid's, though, just a couple of months from being ready. And mine was healthy—until I was beaten."

Celeste gasped. "Mr. Horn did that to you?"

Sary nodded.

"And he's the one that beat your sister too?"

She nodded again. "He beat Orrinda the day we left the West Indies, causing her to hit her head. She died on the ship. Mr. Horn was so furious with my wailing that he turned on me."

Celeste remembered the fear in Sary's eyes in the kitchen that day. Now she knew what the slave trader was capable of. "I'm so sorry." Celeste put her hand on Sary's arm.

The woman nodded, her chin down. "There was nothing I could do for my baby or for that poor girl's baby either."

"Did the physician come?"

"Eventually." Sary raised her head a little. "But there was nothing anyone could do. She was dead by morning. She's buried in the churchyard."

Celeste nodded. Aline had shown her the grave. "You don't think Jonathan had anything to do with her death, do you?" Celeste felt ill.

Sary considered the question for a moment. "No. Except for breaking her heart. And filling her with shame."

"And you think he talked her into coming? Into indenturing herself?"

"She never said, but I wouldn't be surprised. She was smart, like you. Except for believing in a man like him." Sary sighed. "I'm sorry."

"No." Celeste clasped Sary's forearm. "Thank you for telling me. You are a true friend."

Sary placed her good hand over Celeste's and squeezed. "As you are."

Their eyes met, and in that moment they seemed to share the knowledge of how truly dire their situation was.

"You're not married yet," Sary whispered. "We can still get away."

Celeste shook her head. "I can't. He owns my contract. But you can go with Emmanuel and Berta. You're free."

Sary frowned. "No. Where you go, I go."

"Sary, please—"

"No," the woman replied firmly. "I'm not leaving you alone with that man."

CHAPTER THIRTY
Maddee

My conversation with Greg the night of the party stayed with me all the next morning. I just kept trying to figure out what I'd said that had upset him. I was sitting in my office, trying to put him out of my mind and focus on the file in front of me, when I received a call from Miss Vida.

"Taavi Koenig!" she cried as soon as I answered.

"Excuse me?"

"That's his name. Taavi Koenig, from Cleveland, Ohio."

I gasped. "The man in the cabin? How do you know?"

"Well, I don't for sure. But nineteen years ago last July, a Jewish man with brown hair and green eyes named Taavi Koenig came to Virginia for a visit—and he was never heard from again."

The next hour was insane as I connected Miss Vida with Detective Ortiz and then waited nervously to hear back from one of them. In the meantime, I gave Nicole the news, and then together she and I

317

conference-called our cousins Renee and Danielle. All four of us were so excited that to an outsider we might have seemed disrespectful, but we weren't celebrating a man's demise; we were celebrating the fact that we had our first real lead since the case was reopened in July.

We were still on the phone when I heard back from Ortiz, so I conferenced her in as well and we all listened as she gave us an update. Apparently, the man's son was ready to hop on the next plane and fly here from Cleveland, desperate to know, at long last, what had happened to his missing father all those years ago. Ortiz had told him to wait for now, but when he mentioned he'd once had his own DNA tested as a part of an ancestry project, she had him scan and send that report, and then she ran a comparison.

"And sure enough," she told us now, "Koenig's our guy. The case is back on."

She warned us that we were probably still a long way from finding the whole truth, but at least this was a big step in that direction.

When two o'clock rolled around and the office closed for the rest of the day, Nicole and I took off for Williamsburg as planned. It felt odd to leave town in the wake of such exciting developments, but there was no reason to stick around and nothing we could do to further the case—Ortiz had been firm about that.

"You did well, Maddee," she'd said at the end of our call, "but your time for playing detective is over. Don't poke around any further, or you might actually mess things up. Understand?"

"Understand," I said, happy to relinquish that role. I had enough going on in my life as it was.

We reached Williamsburg at four, paid at the visitor center, and headed toward the village. A canopy of yellow and orange blazed above us as we walked, our feet crunching through dried leaves along the path.

I'd been here several times before, but never in the fall. I couldn't help but think of Celeste trudging through town in a storm, braving both the wind and the mud. Thankfully, we had a paved path to walk on, and the day was clear and bright.

I was also grateful for all of the walking Nicole and I had been doing lately. Although she seemed quiet and lost in her thoughts, she was moving pretty well. We brought along the wheelchair for when she'd had enough and would need to switch, but at the moment she was fine just rolling it in front of her, using it like a walker.

When we reached the village, we both stood in awe for a long moment at the top of the green. The fall colors were absolutely spectacular, framing the entire place in reds and oranges. It struck me that this was where Celeste first stopped when she arrived in Williamsburg to search the crowd of soldiers for Jonathan. As if right on cue, the rat-a-tat of a snare drum started, and a group of soldiers began to gather.

"Let's keep going," Nicole said.

At her leading, we wandered east toward the jail. It was larger than it had been in Celeste's time, but we could easily imagine her up in the loft, longing for Jonathan to arrive—only to have Spenser appear instead. Nicole shivered as we stood there, but she didn't say anything. In fact, she'd been oddly quiet almost since the moment we arrived.

Before moving on from there, I told her it was time to shift to the chair, and she did so without protest.

"Mr. Edwards's inn was this way," I said, turning right at the next street. Nana had told us the original inn was torn down nearly two hundred years ago and replaced with several smaller buildings, but we found the property and even the spot where the bench would have been. I imagined Sary standing in her drying shed on the other side of the fence, listening in on all the gossip and deals being made within her hearing. I squinted, picturing the garden and orchards, the kitchen and laundry. If only we could step back in time.

We continued on, passing several "villagers," all dressed as if they belonged in 1775. And though the styles would have changed from Celeste's era, the layers of clothing—shift, chemise, petticoat, skirt, apron, cloak, and cap—were probably quite similar.

We came upon the blacksmith shop, which made me think of poor Celeste and the heavy pot. Next was a row of houses, one of which was white with green trim, not unlike the Petits'. Up ahead, I spied the sight I'd wanted to see most, the pillory.

When we reached it, we stood silently for a long while, staring at the brutal contraption of wood and metal, thinking about that horrid night of Celeste's.

People were allowed to try out the pillory and take photos, so I asked Nicole if she wanted a turn. "We ought to take at least one picture for Nana."

Nicole shook her head, and when I really looked at her, I realized she was visibly upset. Her face was pale, her shoulders slumped, her hands trembling.

"Hey, what's wrong?" I asked, startled. "Are you in pain? Why didn't you say something?"

She shook her head even as her eyes filled with tears. By the anguish on her face, I just knew this had to do with Nana and whatever big secret it was they shared.

"Let's go," she said suddenly.

When I hesitated, she rose, grabbed the handles of her wheelchair, and took off on foot toward the green.

I stared after her for a moment. "Wait. Nicole! What's wrong?" I strode forward to catch up.

"I need a meeting," she said, and then she gestured in the direction of the parking lot. Apparently, we were going back home.

I hesitated a moment, glad at least that she had recognized her need and made the healthy choice. "Okay. But let me push you. You're going to hurt yourself."

With a heavy sigh, she complied.

As she sat down in the wheelchair, I turned back to look at the pillory one last time, thinking of the brave and determined Celeste who, much like me, had just wanted to love and protect her little sister but ended up hurting her instead—or so she'd thought. In the end she learned that Berta's plight had not been her fault after all.

Perhaps, I realized, that was a truth I needed to grasp as well.

Nicole said not one word the whole way back to Richmond. She just sat there, hugging herself, eyes closed, head leaning against the door. We'd been doing meetings for so long now that we both knew the schedule by heart, so when we got into town at 6:25, we headed straight to the 6:30 one on Monument Ave.

I pulled to the curb out front and let the car idle as she gathered her things.

"I hope you know how proud I am that you recognized the need for a meeting—and then made sure we got you to one," I said. "That's exactly how the program is supposed to work."

She nodded, one hand clutching her bag, the other reaching for the door handle.

"Can I ask you something?" Her voice sounded sad. Lost.

"Sure."

She turned and met my gaze. "You would love me no matter what, right?"

Her question floored me. Of course I would, but why had she asked? Was she on the verge of doing something she knew was going to hurt me? Something so big she feared it might even make me stop loving her?

Swallowing hard, I replied, "No matter what."

I prayed all the way home even as my mind wrapped around every possibility. Was she on the verge of using? Had something—or someone—from her former life shown up in the here and now? I hadn't seen any more of Hedge, but that didn't mean he wasn't around. With a shudder, I let myself into the carriage house and headed for the stairs.

I was so lost in thought, it wasn't until I placed a hand on the banister that I realized I wasn't alone. A man was in my living room, gaping at me in surprise, his hands buried deep in a pile of Nicole's belongings.

I gasped at the sight, realizing in an instant that this was the paunchy, balding fellow from the alley and the car. Now he was inside my home, rooting through our things? The very thought made me so furious I forgot to be scared.

"Freeze!" I barked. Without any sort of weapon, I had no way to enforce my command, but he obeyed just the same. "Who are you? And what are you doing here?"

He didn't answer but instead just stood there, his mouth shut tight, his expression blank.

My anger now being quickly replaced by fear, I glanced toward the door, wondering if I could make a run for it and get out before he caught me. Given our positioning, I didn't think so.

Greg's words filled my mind.

Elbows, fingers, feet, car keys, cell phone—anything you have at your disposal.

My keys were in my front right pocket, but before I attempted to arm myself, I held up my phone for him to see.

"I'm calling the police," I said as calmly as I could. I began to tap out 9-1-1.

"Wait."

Something in his voice made me pause.

"Before you do that, you might want to call your grandmother first."

CHAPTER THIRTY-ONE
Celeste

Celeste left Sary on the ship and hurried back down the gangplank to the dock. Beyond Jonathan, on the pier, stood Emmanuel, Berta, Spenser, and George. All of them watched her.

Celeste focused on Jonathan as she reached him. He took both her hands. "I have a few errands to run. Say goodbye to your family and then ask to be shown to our cabin on the *Royal Mary*. I'll be back soon."

Celeste watched him go, turning left when he reached the wharf, heading away from town. "What's down there?" Celeste asked a sailor walking past her.

"The slave auction. It's not open until tomorrow, but it doesn't hurt to look beforehand."

When Jonathan reached the end of the wharf, Captain Bancroft joined him, and they kept walking, conversing as they did.

A wave of nausea swept over Celeste. She hurried to the end of the wharf and went the same direction. She called out Jonathan's name, but he didn't turn back. Perhaps the wind had whipped her voice away.

"Jonathan, wait!" she cried out again. She lifted her skirt and ran after him.

Slowly, he turned toward her, shielding his eyes from the lowering sun.

"Don't go," she said, rushing toward him. "Please don't buy slaves. Perhaps we can open an inn in Charles Town. We can hire local help. I'll make it work, I promise."

Jonathan shot Bancroft a look. The captain chuckled and shrugged his shoulders.

Jonathan directed his attention back to Celeste. "This is none of your concern."

"I beg to differ. If we are to be partners in marriage, we must be in agreement."

Jonathan pursed his lips together. The captain took a few long steps forward as if to allow them some privacy.

"Please don't buy slaves." Celeste tried to keep her voice steady. "I can't bear it."

"I can't manage the land without them. You and I will never make a living in Carolina without cheap labor."

"*Cheap*? It's *free* labor."

"No, Celeste. Clothing, housing, and food aren't free."

"Not paying wages means the labor is free!"

He shook his head. "It's more complicated than that. Besides, I'll take good care of my property, I promise."

Property. Again she felt as if she might be ill.

"Do you want to plant, tend, and harvest hundreds of thousands of tobacco plants on your own?" he asked.

She didn't want any tobacco plants. Celeste didn't answer him.

"I didn't think so. We need scores of laborers to make a profit." He reached out for her hand as a plan began to form in her mind.

She jerked away. He just laughed. "You'll get over this, I promise. And in time you'll ask your family to help us. We'll need them to make a living here. I hadn't realized the true wealth your father had until Emmanuel showed up, flaunting his money." He glanced toward Captain Bancroft again, and Celeste couldn't help but think of what he

had said about his assessment of her family's means after visiting them.
It seemed likely he'd had an influence on Jonathan on this matter too.
Jonathan's voice grew louder. "After what I've done for you, you'll owe
me their help. That's how we'll truly be partners."

And there it was, the moment Sary had just been warning her about.
Thank the good Lord this man had shown his true colors before it was
too late.

Celeste tried to smile. There was no point arguing with him or trying to convince him that her family wasn't as wealthy as he thought. Or
that her parents would never agree to send money so Jonathan could
purchase human beings. "Do you have a little money now?" she asked.
"So I can buy some food for tonight, for when you get back?"

He took a few coins from his pouch, more than she needed, and
gave them to her, seemingly relieved to have her thinking about something else. "Put all worries from your mind, my love. We'll be in Charles
Town in no time. We'll marry and get situated on our land—and then
I'll take care of everything. I promise."

Celeste felt as if a half smile had frozen on her face.

"I know slavery still seems foreign to you," he said, "but it's how
things work here. Even among the Huguenots."

Celeste simply took the money from his hand, thanked him, and
then told both men goodbye. If Celeste ignored what Sary had said
about Jonathan and also what Berta had claimed, what else would she
have to ignore in the future? She'd be coerced into asking her parents
for money but not telling them what it was for. She'd end up tricking
them into going against their beliefs because her husband felt she owed
it to him. If she thought she'd lost her faith in God before, in the future
she would be absolutely stripped of any hint of faith if she agreed to
lead such a deceptive life. She wouldn't be able to live with herself at
all. She would end up dead in a churchyard like the maid before her,
stripped of all dignity and hope.

Aiming for the other end of the wharf, she held her head high—
only to see Berta coming toward her.

"Sister," Celeste called out. "I was wrong."

Both quickened their steps, and when they met, Celeste wrapped her arms around Berta. "I believe you now. I'm so sorry I didn't before."

Berta pulled away. "Don't go with him."

Tears flooded Celeste's eyes. "When is the boat to Williamsburg scheduled to leave?"

"Soon."

"I need to go get Sary. I'll meet you on the wharf. Don't let the *York* leave without us."

Celeste raced back up the gangplank of the *Royal Mary*. Sary sat with her eyes closed and Celeste simply took her hand, whispering, "I'll explain in a bit."

Sary's eyes flew open.

Loudly Celeste said, "We need to go buy food before Lieutenant Gray returns."

Celeste had to force herself to walk, not run, along the deck of the *Royal Mary*. When they reached the wharf, she could hear Spenser and Emmanuel talking about the ring. While Spenser sounded adamant that they simply had to get it back before leaving, Emmanuel insisted it was impossible, that Wharton wasn't going to budge.

Celeste stepped forward, interrupting them. "What's going on?"

"Spenser wants me to go to Wharton again and demand the ring back," Emmanuel told her. "He said if that doesn't work, he's willing to sell himself to the man in exchange for it instead."

She gasped. "Spenser, no!"

His cheeks turning bright red, Spenser kept his eyes on Emmanuel as he spoke. "There's one other option. What if we got the man who appraised it before to officially verify the value? If we prove that the ring is worth far more than Berta's contract, Wharton will have no choice but to pay the difference in cash or relinquish the ring. Considering its worth, I feel sure he'll be forced to do the latter."

"Great idea," Emmanuel said, "but is the appraiser even around anymore? I thought he was just passing through."

"I don't know. He was staying at the Bayside Tavern, so I'll start there." Immediately, Spenser turned to go.

"Don't!" Celeste cried. "We need to get out of here."

"Stay out of this!" he snapped in return. He'd never been harsh with her before, or with anyone else—not that she'd seen, anyway. "I'm getting that ring back."

Before she could respond, he marched toward the end of the wharf. Emmanuel threw up his hands and hurried after him.

Celeste yelled at them to stop, but they both ignored her and continued on. Her eyes filled with tears of frustration. As much as she mourned the loss of the ring, she had more important matters to deal with right now—starting with leaving before Jonathan returned. The issue of her contract could be handled later, from a safe distance, with her brother's help.

Celeste took the money Jonathan had given her and paid for her and Sary to board the cargo boat. A few minutes later, George and Berta also came on and sat beside each other. The boat *had* to leave before Jonathan got back—but not before Emmanuel and Spenser returned.

Celeste thought through what actions she needed to take and decided to go to the governor once they were back in Williamsburg. He had jurisdiction over all the men involved, including Constable Wharton, Captain Bancroft, Jonathan—and even Mr. Horn, if it turned out he was in on the treacherous doings as well.

Captain Doane strolled the deck, looking impatient.

"My brother will return shortly," Celeste told him, hoping that was true.

"I'll wait a few more minutes, Miss Talbot, but we need to be on our way soon. The tide is coming in."

She scanned the wharf, praying Spenser and Emmanuel would appear. Instead, Jonathan did without Captain Bancroft. Celeste ducked, yanking her hood over her head as she pulled Sary down with her.

Jonathan boarded the *Royal Mary* without stopping to say anything to Berta.

Celeste asked if she could see Emmanuel and Spenser coming. Berta shook her head and put a finger to her lips.

A minute later Jonathan returned to the boat. "Where's your sister?" he barked at Berta.

She stared straight ahead, lips pursed.

"You will answer me," he commanded.

Berta didn't budge, but George gave a furtive glance.

Jonathan boarded the boat and grabbed Berta's chin with his hand, tugging her face toward him.

"Leave me be," she hissed. "You treated me horribly. You have no right to expect anything from me now."

"Where's your—" Jonathan stopped, and then he turned toward Celeste and Sary, both hunkered down in their cloaks. He stepped toward them and yanked the hood from Celeste's head.

"I'm not going with you."

"I own your contract, Celeste. You have to come with me."

"I'll scream—"

He grabbed her by the arm and lifted her to her feet. "No one will help you, especially not Constable Wharton."

Berta lunged for Jonathan, but he jerked to the side.

"Get Spenser!" Celeste begged her sister. "Please!"

Berta scrambled from the boat with George trailing behind.

"Hurry!" Celeste yelled.

"Come on, Sary," Jonathan said.

"No! She's free. You can't force her."

Sary stood and grabbed Celeste's hands. "I'm going with you," she whispered in French.

"No," Celeste said. "Run. Follow Berta."

Sary shook her head.

Celeste reeled around toward Jonathan. "I'll report you to the governor."

He laughed. "On what grounds?"

"Kidnapping. Coercion. Colluding with Captain Bancroft and Constable Wharton. Berta and I aren't the only ones you people have done this too."

"He won't believe you over me. Over *us*. Besides, the governor is back in Williamsburg. The Court starts in a few days."

"No, he's here on business. I know he'll listen to me."

"You're bluffing."

She was bluffing, but in that moment she realized it might be true. Considering that the governor had to be in Williamsburg when Court convened, at this point he'd be either there or here. If he were anywhere else, he wouldn't make it in time.

"Come on!" Jonathan jerked her arm again.

"Is everything all right?" Captain Doane asked, stepping toward them.

"No." Celeste gritted her teeth against Jonathan's grip. "He's trying to kidnap me."

"That's impossible," Jonathan said. "I own her contract."

Captain Doane shook his head. "I can't get involved, then."

"Can you search for Governor Nicholson?" Celeste asked. "I'm acquainted with him. He'll know how to help."

Captain Doane shrugged. "I have no idea where to look."

"Ask at the tavern," Celeste suggested. "Someone there is bound to know." It was worth a try.

He seemed reluctant but did as she asked, stepping down the gangplank to the wharf and then hurrying along.

Celeste called after him. "Please keep looking—"

"Be quiet!" Jonathan yelled, yanking her down the gangplank with Sary still hanging on to her.

Celeste tried to resist him as much as possible and felt Sary doing the same, but Jonathan kept pulling them until they reached the gangplank of the *Royal Mary*. Celeste sank to her knees and spread her upper body flat, her face down on the wharf, still clinging to Sary's good hand.

"Celeste!" It was Spenser.

Jonathan kicked at her, his boot digging into her side. "Get up! Now."

"No!"

He kicked her again.

"Stop it!" Sary let go of Celeste's hand to lunge toward Jonathan, but Celeste managed to block her by quickly scrambling to her feet and positioning herself between them.

Behind Jonathan, Spenser—followed by Emmanuel, George, and then Berta—ran toward her, their boots drumming against the wooden wharf.

Jonathan turned and held up his hand. "There's nothing you can do to stop us. I legally own Celeste. She belongs to me."

Celeste shouted, "He's a criminal! He's kidnapped girls. Coerced others. Misled more than just Berta and me. He's working with Constable Wharton and Captain Bancroft. Perhaps Mr. Horn too." Several sailors from the *Royal Mary* stopped their work to gawk.

"She's lying." Jonathan wrapped his arms around Celeste and held her in front of himself. "She tricked me into buying her contract, and now she's trying to run away." Celeste raised her head, banging it against his chin. He cursed and tightened his hold.

Spenser stopped a few feet from them, followed by Emmanuel and George. Celeste searched out Berta. Right behind her was Constable Wharton. Far behind him, just coming out of the tavern, was a small group of men that included Captain Doane and the governor.

"I know what the three of you have done, Wharton!" Celeste shouted as she tore Jonathan's brooch from her cloak. "You and Lieutenant Gray and Captain Bancroft. I'll tell the governor."

Constable Wharton's eyes widened. "Let her go," he said to Jonathan. "She's not worth it."

Jonathan loosened his grip and then pointed behind Constable Wharton, but he didn't catch the warning. Free from Jonathan's grasp, Celeste turned and thrust the brooch toward him, but he didn't even notice. He was too busy trying to signal his cohort to stop talking.

"She won't tell the governor," Wharton said, oblivious. "She'll stay quiet, won't you Miss Talbot?"

"Stay quiet about what?" the governor asked.

Wharton spun around. "Governor."

Time seemed to freeze in that moment. Wharton was speechless, his face turning an odd shade of purple as he stammered and sputtered under the governor's suspicious glare. All Celeste could think as she looked from one to the other was, *Thank You, Lord.*

She turned to see Spenser stepping toward her, but then suddenly Jonathan exploded in a rage.

"I won't be brought down by you!" he shouted, grabbing Celeste's waist and jerking her backward. The brooch flew from her hand into the water. And when Jonathan abruptly released her, she fell over the edge of the wharf as well.

She tried to catch herself, but she was already falling into the bay between the wharf and the *Royal Mary*. The cold dark water swallowed her as she sank toward the bottom. She didn't know how to swim, but she tried to propel herself toward the surface. Yet no matter how hard she kicked, she was thwarted by the weight of her cloak, skirts, and boots. She flailed around until she faced the ship. Barnacles against the dark wood made her think of the stars.

Now she never would see the nighttime sky with Spenser.

She tried again to move upward, using her arms and legs with all her might. Her eyes still on the barnacles, she prayed, *Lord, don't let my time here be done.* She couldn't bear to think of her parents. Of Emmanuel. Of Berta.

Or Spenser. *Let them be happy. Bless them.* Feeling as if her lungs might burst, she prayed, *Forgive me, please. Accept me. I surrender everything I've been and am, to You. Everything I've done.*

She'd been so self-righteous all those years, doing the right thing, feeling as if she were better than Berta, feeling as if she was worth more to her parents. But then she did the wrong thing, and it had enormous consequences. Both dispositions had been so misguided.

A peace bubbled through her as the water began to churn. God truly had forgiven her. *He that abideth in me, and I in Him*…she did abide in Him, and He in her. *Now.* In her mother's voice, she heard her ask, "What is the method, of honoring Him duly?"

To place our whole confidence in Him…to call upon Him in all our necessities…to acknowledge Him both with heart and lips, as the sole author of all blessings.

Holding her breath with all her being, she felt all of her guilt and shame slip away. She'd be in heaven soon, she was sure, above Spenser's stars. Her sense of peace grew as the darkness around her deepened. Nothing mattered now. Berta was going to be all right. Surely her siblings would care for Sary.

But then, as if in a dream, Spenser appeared between her and the barnacles. For a moment she thought perhaps she'd died and the barnacles were actually stars and Spenser was an angel sent to take her home. Except that the pressure in her lungs was unbearable.

Spenser was stripped to his breeches and wore no boots. His mouth was pressed closed, his eyes wide, and his hair floated around him. He grabbed her arm with one hand and began flailing the other one. She tried to help. He shook his head.

Her arm hurt as Spenser rose faster than she did. The water grew brighter. His head disappeared. Unable to hold her breath another second, she let it go as he yanked her to the surface. Both air and water exploded through her.

Over the pounding in her ears and the rush of the water, Celeste could make out Berta screaming a prayer, "Dear Lord, please save my sister!"

CHAPTER THIRTY-TWO
Maddee

Standing in my living room, I did as my intruder suggested and called my grandmother. Unfortunately, I couldn't reach her and had to leave messages. Still holding on to the phone, I looked at the man across from me.

"Who are you?" I repeated. "And what are you doing here?"

He sighed heavily. "I'm a private investigator. I do jobs for Mrs. Talbot's lawyer."

My mind reeled. A private investigator? Hired by my own grandmother?

"What's the name of your company?" I asked, and when he said Franklin and Associates, I felt pretty sure he was telling the truth.

"All right," I said, slipping the cell into my pocket. "Before I turn you over to police, tell me what's going on."

"Yeah, about that. I'll tell you, but only if you'll ignore this little, um, indiscretion."

My eyebrows raised. "Breaking and entering is hardly what I'd call an indiscretion."

He shrugged. "Whatever. Do you want to hear what I have to say or not?"

I exhaled slowly. "Fine."

"Can we sit down first?" He gestured to the kitchen table and I agreed, though I pointedly ignored the longing glance he cast toward the coffeemaker. If he thought I was going to fix him a cup after he'd broken into my home, he was crazy.

I took the seat across from him and listened as he began his tale.

"Two days before your sister's car accident, she paid a visit to your grandmother, during which she stole a couple pieces of jewelry."

My eyes widened.

"That night, your grandmother discovered that the items were missing and knew immediately what had happened to them. She contacted Nicole, who insisted she knew nothing about it. Not wanting to involve police in a private family matter, Mrs. Talbot called her lawyer instead to ask for his advice. That's when I came into the picture. He hired me to go to Norfolk and recover the stolen items—or at least one of them, which he made clear has tremendous sentimental value. Although I suspect there's more to it than just that."

My pulse surged. "Not a ring," I whispered. "A ruby ring?"

He raised bushy eyebrows. "Yeah, how'd you know? Have you seen it?"

I shook my head. "No. Keep going."

His story became more complicated from there and involved tracking down Nicole, keeping her under surveillance, putting the word out to the local pawnshops, and more. But at some point, he said, she must have "gotten wise to him" because she "pulled a tricky maneuver" and managed to slip away. He was still on the job two days later, trying to track her down again, when he learned she'd been in a serious car accident. According to police, there was a man in the vehicle with her at the time who had climbed from the car and escaped.

"What I subsequently found out," he said, "is that when the accident happened, she and that man, a friend named Hedge, were driving to Newport News to meet with a known fence—which tells me they had the stolen items with them and were on their way to make a sale.

At first, I figured Hedge took off with the jewelry after the accident for his own purposes. But I've been watching him for a while now, and I've decided it's more likely he took them and ran as a favor to your sister, so she wouldn't be caught with stolen goods when the police came."

I sat back, my mind reeling.

"Where is the ring now?"

He ran a hand down his face. "I'm pretty sure Hedge still has it. He's been trying to reach Nicole. I figure he wants to give it back to her, or he wants to know if he should sell it for her."

At his words, my mind filled with the image of my sister at the church tonight, one hand on the car door.

You would love me no matter what, right?

I leaped to my feet. "Don't go anywhere," I commanded.

Then I ran out the door, not even pausing to explain.

I made it to the church just minutes before her meeting was to end. I raced inside and down the hall, bursting into the room.

A handful of startled addicts all turned to look at me.

"May we help you?" asked a man at the podium.

My eyes scanned the room.

Nicole wasn't there.

I dialed Greg's number as I rushed back out. Thankfully, he answered on the second ring and, after my tumble of words, said he was on his way. Frantic, I looked around until I spied an older woman on a porch across the street. Running toward her, I described Nicole and Hedge and asked if she'd seen either one, but she simply shrugged.

Moving up and down the block, I questioned everyone I could find. Finally, just as Greg arrived, a college-aged couple told me that yes, they had been in a lounge on the next block where they had noticed a guy who sounded like the one I was describing.

We took off at a run. Sure enough, as soon as we stepped inside, I spotted Hedge in the dim light at the end of the bar. He was alone, head down. Greg and I walked over and took the seats on each side of him.

"Where's Nicole?" Greg asked sharply.

Startled, the man looked at him. Then he turned my way, and understanding filled his eyes.

"Don't know." He pulled his drink a little closer.

"Did you see her tonight?" I asked. "Did you talk to her?"

He hesitated for a long moment before mumbling, "Yeah, at the church."

"And?"

"And I returned some of her stuff to her. Then I came over here. What of it?"

"Where is she now?"

Hedge shrugged. "No clue. She had to go. Somebody picked her up." His voice sounded bitter.

I glanced at Greg. "Picked her up? Who?"

Hedge shrugged. "I don't know. Some guy. I didn't recognize him. She just said thanks for holding on to her things and meeting up with her tonight, and she guessed she'd see me around."

"What did the guy look like?"

He shrugged. "I dunno. That's when I took off."

"What kind of vehicle was it?"

"Like I said, that's when I took off. I've been trying to connect with her for weeks, and then she just ditches me? Forget her."

He gulped from his drink and then hung his head again.

We'd gotten all we could from him tonight.

Greg and I raced back to the carriage house, hoping desperately that the PI was still there and that he could tell us who this other man Nicole left with might possibly be. We opened the door to find him still at the table, a cup of coffee in hand.

Stepping inside, I glanced to the right and was startled to see Nana in the living room. She was folding a shirt on the bed, but when she leaned forward to place it inside the Louis Vuitton suitcase, her movement revealed someone sitting behind her.

Nicole.

"What's going on?" I demanded, moving toward them.

Nana looked up in surprise, and then she smiled. Her eyes were red, as if she'd been crying, but she certainly seemed happy now.

"We're packing up your sister's things."

"What?" I continued forward, looking to Nicole. "Why? How did you end up back here?"

My sister's eyes were also red, but on her face was a mix of sadness and relief. "I called Nana to come and get me from the church. I needed to return some things that belonged to her."

"But we were told you left with some guy." Even as I said it, I realized Hedge's misunderstanding. That "guy" had been Jerome, Nana's driver.

Suddenly, more pieces of the puzzle clicked into place. Nana insisting Nicole read those letters. Nana urging us to go to Williamsburg. Nicole standing and looking at the pillory—the same place where Celeste first learned the royal origins of the ruby ring—and then suddenly insisting we leave so she could go to a meeting. I realized that had been our savvy grandmother's plan all along, to make Nicole understand the history of the ring, the importance of it to our family, the value of what she'd taken. And it had worked too. Between reading the letters and visiting the site in person, Nicole had become overwhelmed by guilt for what she'd done—which in turn had led her, finally, to contact Hedge and have him bring her the ring and then hand it over to Nana along with a full confession.

"So why are you packing now?" I asked, the one part of this picture I still didn't understand.

"I made a decision, and I don't want to wait," Nicole replied. "I'm going to rehab. Tomorrow."

CHAPTER THIRTY-THREE
Celeste

Celeste coughed, Berta's prayer still ringing in her ears, as Spenser rolled her to her side. Water sputtered from her throat. Spenser held her head as Berta knelt beside her.

"Is she going to be all right?" Berta asked.

Spenser nodded.

Berta sprang to her feet. "I'll go tell the governor what happened. Everything."

Celeste struggled to speak. "Tell him about Constable Wharton's maid too." She coughed. "The one who spoke with Spenser and me. The governor should interview her and any others in the house. Make sure he knows Mr. Horn is probably also involved."

Berta agreed and then scurried away, and Sary took her place. Celeste reached for her good hand as she turned her head toward Spenser and whispered, "Thank you." He'd saved her, once again. For the last time, she was sure.

"You need to get warm," he said. "Can you stand?"

She nodded. She struggled to her feet with Sary and Spenser both supporting her. The wind felt icy now, biting fiercely at her wet skin.

They passed the governor speaking to Berta. His assistant and several sailors, including First Mate Hayes, had Jonathan in custody, and a group of soldiers was marching down the wharf toward them.

Captain Bancroft wasn't in sight, but Constable Wharton had a scowl on his face and was keeping quiet. He frowned as Celeste slipped past him onto the boat.

"Help her get dry," Spenser said to Sary. "I'll try to find a blanket for her."

"We have one," Sary said in English. "But you should find another one for yourself."

Spenser gave her a smile and a nod. "Will do."

It was nearly dark by the time the *York* set sail for Williamsburg. Celeste, in her other set of clothes and wrapped in a blanket, was wedged between Berta and Sary.

Celeste turned to her sister. "I'm sorry I didn't believe you about Jonathan."

"I wish you had. It would have saved you so many troubles." She paused, and then she added in a lower voice, "I can see why you didn't, though. I wasn't very trustworthy. But I've learned my lesson, believe me. I've both repented and reformed."

After all that had happened, Celeste truly believed her sister. She'd been deceitful too, and Berta had long ago forgiven her. They both understood the consequences now. They both also understood what it meant to be forgiven by God, and what it meant to seek His guidance, to trust His care.

They were silent for a long moment, but then Berta said, "I'm honestly not doing what I did with Jonathan. I mean, I'm not trying to steal your beau."

"What are you talking about?" Celeste asked. She didn't have a beau.

Berta whispered, "George."

"Oh," Celeste said. "I wondered…" She smiled. "I'm happy for you."

"I don't want to encourage him if you're interested…"

"No, I'm not. Truly. But you're fond of him, then?"

Berta smiled. "Yes. It turns out I'm the reason he came with Emmanuel. He was concerned about me and wanted to make sure I was safe."

Celeste laughed. "He seems to have gotten over me rather quickly."

"Apparently so." Berta smiled.

Celeste patted her sister's arm. "You have my blessing. And my prayers for a good life."

Berta managed to thank her before the motion of the water sent her to the edge of the boat. This time it wasn't Celeste or Spenser who went to her aid. It was George.

Poor Spenser, Celeste thought. *If only he'd known about Berta's feelings for George before getting so worked up about the ring.*

The ring! Where was it?

She searched the deck for Emmanuel and Spenser. They stood near the hull, the still-damp Spenser wrapped in a blanket of his own. The two men were deep in conversation. She would wait until they were finished before asking.

In the meantime, she turned to Sary and whispered to her in French. "Clearly you understand English." She smiled at Sary's cunning. "And I imagine you're better at speaking it than you let on. Why did you pretend not to?"

The woman was silent for a moment, and then she matched Celeste's low tone, "I wanted Mr. Edwards to find someone who spoke my language. I needed a friend."

Touched by her words, Celeste gave the woman a warm smile and a nod.

As Sary rested, Celeste turned back toward her brother. When he eventually glanced at her, she waved him over.

"I have a question for you," she said as soon as he sat down beside her. "What happened with the ring? Did Spenser find the appraiser?"

Emmanuel winced. "I'm afraid he's much more intuitive than I am. Yes, Spenser found the appraiser. Once he heard our story, he confronted Wharton, who had stopped at the tavern for a drink. It turns out the ring is worth far, far more than Wharton revealed. There were enough patrons around that once the story was out quite a scene developed against Wharton. We were negotiating when Berta and George arrived, followed by Captain Doane. The governor, once he was aware of what was going on with you, suggested we all move to the wharf, while he consulted with the appraiser. Spenser led the way, of course. He's quite something, you know. A man of rare character."

"I know," she replied, hoping her voice didn't reveal her longing. She cleared her throat. "So where is the ring now? Still with Wharton?"

"No." Emmanuel patted his side. "I'm happy to say it's in my pouch. The governor sorted it all out while you were changing out of your wet things. The appraiser verified its worth and even gave me a copy of the document he'd made for Wharton—of course Spenser was right. I was a fool not to push Wharton on the matter."

"What counts is that you have it back." Gratitude swept through her. "Thank you," she whispered, closing her eyes for a moment.

"Don't thank me. Because I've been thinking seriously about keeping this thing myself—for my future bride or maybe one of my future daughters. You had your chance, and look what you did with it."

She opened her eyes and saw that he was teasing, but she shook her head vehemently. "You're absolutely right, Emmanuel. I don't deserve to get it back. I want you to keep it."

He put up a bit of a fight, insisting it was still hers and that he had only been kidding, but she stayed firm.

"Keep the ring," she insisted. "More than anything, I want it to be passed down, through the Talbot family line, for generations to come."

He thought for a moment and then spoke. "You know what? Considering its value, I could use it as collateral. How fitting, actually, for this ring to end up being the very thing that secures a future for all of us."

"What do you mean?"

"I've been doing a lot of thinking," Emmanuel said, and from the way he looked at her, Celeste realized he was about to tell her something important. "And I've decided to stay. For good."

Her eyes widened as he continued.

"If Berta can't survive the trip home, then I won't go either." He smiled. "I'm guessing George will stick around too. We'll buy a piece of land and build and run an inn, far enough away from Mr. Edwards's that it won't impact his business. And eventually we'll start a sawmill as well."

Celeste's heart pounded. "What about Maman and Papa?"

Emmanuel's eyes grew serious. "We talked this all through before I left. Uncle Jules sent more money for a business, but we've still made no progress as far as a paper mill or even a print shop. There are too many obstacles to overcome in England. Papa said if I found a business opportunity here, I should stay. The eventual goal is a print shop, just like the old family one back in Lyon, or a paper mill like in Le Chambon. Neither can happen here for a while, of course, but that's all right. They will eventually. In the meantime, we'll start with an inn. And like I said," he added with a grin, "if we need any loans now and then as we grow, we have the ring."

Celeste returned his smile, but her head was spinning with surprise and possibilities. "Tell me your idea as far as labor. For the inn and the sawmill."

"Well, Spenser for sure."

She ignored the surge in her pulse. "Who else?"

"George, Berta. And we'll have to get some workers for the inn—"

"Not slaves, though," Celeste said quickly.

"Of course not. We'll hire from whatever community we end up near, maybe bring in an indentured servant or two if necessary. And then there's Sary, if she's interested. Spenser said she's the best cook around."

"She was, before she got injured. Now there's a lot she can't do."

"But she could direct others, no?"

Celeste glanced at Sary and then back at Emmanuel, a smile teasing at her lips as a vision formed in her mind. "Of course." She could hardly believe what she was hearing.

Emmanuel cleared his throat. "Papa was all right with my staying, but he wanted me to send you girls back if you hadn't already married. Clearly, Berta would never make it. From what she said, I can't imagine how she survived the first crossing. So I'll see to her, along with George, but you should go back to London."

Celeste shook her head. "I want to stay with Berta too. She'll need me. Plus, I'm committed to helping Sary. She and I can cook in the inn." Her voice choked as she said, "I'll write to Papa and Maman. I'll explain everything that happened. Everything." Her gaze drifted across the river to the west, where the sun was setting over the trees. "What about our little brothers? What opportunities will they have?"

"Perhaps they will venture over here in a few years," Emmanuel said. "Or at least Alexander, once he's old enough. He's the adventurous one. Frederick and William will probably end up staying in London and see to Maman and Papa in their old age."

Celeste mourned not being able to care for her parents, but she couldn't fathom doing anything else besides staying here with her brother and sister. Spenser began pacing along the side of the boat. He'd probably noticed that George was tending to Berta. Poor, sweet Spenser. She could almost feel the breaking of his heart.

A glimmer of hope warmed Celeste for a moment. Maybe, in time, he would see the good in her. See that she could put her family and Sary first and what was best for others. Her heart constricted again. No, if Spenser was going to care for her that way, he would have by now. He never would. He'd seen her at her very worst, over and over.

Emmanuel cleared his throat. "Instead of going on to Williamsburg, Spenser and I are going to head up to Manakin Towne and talk with the Huguenots there. We've heard there's land available at a much better price than around Williamsburg."

"It's on the edge of the frontier, though," Celeste said. "So far from everything."

"It won't be for long. And we'd be part of a community there. As more people move west, we should get enough business to support ourselves."

Celeste nodded. "Where will Berta, Sary, and I stay while you're gone?"

"At the inn. Tell Mr. Edwards to put it on my bill."

"Is George going with you?"

Emmanuel shook his head. "He'll stay with all of you." He stood. "Try to get some rest, Celeste. And keep warm." He headed toward the railing, where George was huddled next to Berta.

Night fell and overhead the stars began to appear. Celeste huddled closer to Sary, hoping to keep them both warm. Celeste leaned her head back and watched the stars, her breath sending vapors up into the air.

For the first time, she and Spenser were seeing the same stars at the same time. Celeste glanced toward the hull. He stood with his back to the railing, wrapped in a blanket. But he wasn't looking at the stars. He was looking at her.

They told Emmanuel and Spenser goodbye at the dock and wished them a good trip up the river to the falls and then on to Manakin Towne. As George, Berta, Sary, and Celeste started the journey to Williamsburg, Berta again was able to ride in a wagon while the rest of them walked. Thankfully, the trail had dried out some. As the sunlight streamed through the trees, the changing leaves glowed against the evergreens. Celeste breathed in the fresh scent of the forest. No longer did the lack of people bother her. She found hope and harmony in the beauty of Virginia.

By the time they reached Williamsburg, Berta was barely able to climb down from the wagon. George carried her into the inn as the soldiers began to march on the green. The drumming was distant, and for the first time the sound actually calmed Celeste. She never thought she'd return to Williamsburg, but she felt relieved that she had. She was as safe as she would probably ever be, with or without a husband.

Mr. Edwards greeted them cordially but with surprise. After they all ate bowls of porridge, Sary returned to the loft while Aline showed Berta and Celeste to a room, where they collapsed on the bed. When Celeste woke in the afternoon, she ventured to the kitchen. Mr. Edwards and Benjamin were building up the fire and putting water on to boil.

"I can help cook," she said.

"Bless you, Miss Talbot," Mr. Edwards responded. "Mr. Horn promised me a new cook and maid by now, but he hasn't shown up with them."

"He may not show up ever again. He's most likely under investigation." As she explained what Jonathan, Captain Bancroft, and Constable Wharton had been doing, Mr. Edwards's face grew pale.

He sat down. "To think I've bought the contracts of women who have been tricked. Coerced. Peddled like objects."

"You didn't know," Celeste said.

"Well, I do now. Even if Horn isn't convicted, I'll never trade with him again." He winced. "I've tried to avoid trading, except for contracts. I made an exception with Sary, telling myself that her being here didn't make me a slave owner because she was leased rather than purchased. But that was a lie. It's essentially the same thing."

Celeste frowned, confused. "But you're a slave owner, regardless."

He looked up at her questioningly.

"Joe? Benjamin?" she prodded.

He blinked, surprised. "No. They're not slaves. They're free."

"Really?" Celeste was shocked. All this time she'd assumed his workers were enslaved.

"Yes. I pay them a wage. They choose to stay, at least for now." He sighed. "Finding good labor is a constant challenge."

Celeste's heart warmed even more toward this man who had been so kind to her. "Perhaps you could advertise up north. Or I could write to my mother to find out if there are any young women she knows who want to come to Virginia." Celeste couldn't imagine women from their congregation yearning for an adventure across the sea, but her mother had taken many girls under her wing through the years from all sorts of different situations. "You could pay their passage so they wouldn't be at the mercy of a sea captain or middleman."

"I'll think about that," Mr. Edwards said, standing. "In the meantime, I'll gratefully take you up on your offer of cooking, with Sary's help." He smiled. "We don't have many patrons tonight, but when the Court convenes, it will be a different situation."

A half hour later, Sary joined them in the kitchen, and with her advice, Celeste managed to make a game pie from some rabbits a hunter had sold Mr. Edwards that morning. Then she helped serve the meal to the handful of soldiers and others in the dining hall. She was surprised when the governor came in with Constable Jones, wanting to speak with Celeste in private. She joined them in the sitting room, wiping her hands on her apron.

"Are you well?" the governor asked.

She nodded.

"That was quite an ordeal yesterday."

"Yes."

He nodded in the constable's direction. "I filled Jones in on what is going on. He'll be interviewing maids here and then assisting in the investigation down in Norfolk."

Celeste looked at the constable, though she didn't say anything. Then she sighed. Despite all he'd put her through, she was grateful for his help.

The governor continued. "The investigation is ongoing, and there is plenty of evidence—falsified contracts and eyewitness accounts, including several from sailors on the *Royal Mary*. Even the first mate. All three of the perpetrators are being detained in Norfolk. They will most likely be sent to London for trial." He leaned forward. "However, although I suspect Mr. Horn knew what was going on, there's no evidence he participated."

"Thank you for checking," Celeste said, dabbing at her face with her apron. "Thank you for everything." It was far more justice—and kindness—than she'd expected.

"Thank *you*, Miss Talbot. You did a brave thing in standing up to Lieutenant Gray."

She nodded. Leaving home had been brash, but confronting Jonathan had taken far more courage.

"Are you two hungry?" Celeste asked. "There's more game pie in the kitchen."

Constable Jones said, "Well, Benjamin already brought me my dinner—"

"Please join me anyway," the governor said. "A second serving is in order today, don't you think?"

"You should interview Sary before you go to Norfolk," Celeste said. "She has some additional information."

"About the maid who died not so long ago?" Constable Jones asked.

"Yes. You would be surprised at all the things she knows."

The men moved into the dining room, and Celeste headed to the kitchen, thinking about Spenser suggesting that she pray, all those weeks ago, for the truth to be revealed.

She whispered a prayer of thanks now. "You are the sole author of all blessings. We called upon You, and You met our needs. Thank You, dear Lord."

Celeste spent the next week helping around the inn in gratitude for all Mr. Edwards had done for her as she waited for Emmanuel and Spenser to return. The Court convened and the inn was busy, but with Aline's help, the kitchen crew kept pace with the meals that needed to be served. Berta recovered from the boat ride and helped too. Sary's hand continued to heal, although the finger and thumb remained fused together. A few times, Celeste spied Sary using her hand while working in the kitchen to help balance a cooled pot, but she stayed away from the fire.

Emmanuel and Spenser returned after being gone for ten days, enthusiastic about what they'd discovered. They called Celeste, Berta, and George into the sitting room and gave them the details of their trip. Emmanuel did all the talking. He'd purchased land on the James, well past the falls, and on the other side of the river from Manakin Towne. However, there was a ferry where they could cross to attend the services that were conducted in French. Many in the Huguenot community lived nearby as well.

The property Emmanuel had purchased was covered with trees, had a wide and fast creek that flowed through the land that could be used for the sawmill, and had a knoll that was a perfect site for an inn. Plus, it was on a road, rough to be sure, but passable. Those traveling through would be able to see the inn and would be eager for a place to rest and obtain a hot meal.

Emmanuel and Spenser had already drawn up papers to be sent to the Netherlands to order the parts for the mill, and the men were hopeful the things they needed would arrive within the next year.

Celeste couldn't help but be proud of her brother. His leadership qualities and sense of adventure allowed him to quickly adjust to this new way of life. She was grateful for his personality that fit so well in the New World.

Emmanuel turned to George. "There's a parcel of land next to mine. It's rumored that it will be for sale soon. If our endeavors are successful, perhaps I could help you purchase it."

"Thank you," George said, all the while gazing at Berta.

She blushed and smiled, just a little.

Celeste wondered if Emmanuel had a similar sort of plan for Spenser.

"The other thing all of you should know is that Spenser and I have formed a partnership," Emmanuel continued, as if reading his sister's mind. "I couldn't build an inn or run a sawmill without him. I've spoken with Matthew Carlisle, and we settled Spenser's obligation to him."

Celeste was surprised to hear the news but ever so grateful to her brother. Where would any of them be without Spenser?

"How will you build an inn before you have a mill?" Celeste asked.

"We'll mill the lumber here," Spenser answered, "and then take it as far as the falls. Then we'll portage the lumber around the falls, put it back on a boat, and continue on to the property."

"I see," she said. Because Spenser was now in partnership with her brother, he would be linked to her in an even more tangible way—a thought that both thrilled and saddened her. She would be forced to spend the rest of her life in frequent interaction with the one person she truly wanted but couldn't have. And that would be sheer torment.

That evening a different broker arrived with a new cook and maid, both indentured servants, as Celeste dumped out the wash water under the ash tree. A cold autumn wind blew, and she took a moment for herself, placing the bucket on the ground. She stepped around the garden and out from under the trees. Then she shivered and leaned her head back, gazing up into the sky. Clouds hid the moon, but in the far sky stars shimmered brightly. She squinted, trying to find the North Star.

"Celeste?"

She jumped, startled until she realized it was Spenser.

"Yes?"

"May I speak with you?"

She turned toward him, "Of course."

He took off his coat and wrapped it around her. She shivered again at his touch. "I wanted to ask you a question."

She nodded, wishing he'd kept his hands on her shoulders.

Spenser leaned closer, his arms at his sides. "I don't want to make any assumptions, but I'm wondering if, perhaps, in time…"

Her heart began to race. "In time…what?"

"I'm wondering if you might come to love me someday. I'd like a marriage, if possible, like my parents had."

"Love you? Why?"

He sputtered. "B-because—"

"Spenser. You love Berta, I know that. You'll find someone else."

"No." He took a deep breath. "I care about Berta. I wanted her to be all right, and it's true I was drawn to her. At first." He smiled down at Celeste. "But as your trials grew and Berta recovered, as I came to know both of you better, you are the one I fell in love with."

"But what about the ring? I know you thought Emmanuel should recover it, but wasn't that fuss you made for Berta's sake? Didn't you hope she would wear it someday?"

He shook his head. "No. I mean, you're right. I didn't think Emmanuel should leave it behind, but I wanted it for you. I wanted you to have it back."

"Because?"

"Because I love you."

She looked into his eyes, suddenly seeing that it was true. He did love her. How could she not have realized it before?

"I love you too!" Tears filled her eyes. "I thought I would have to go the rest of my life without your ever knowing."

She collapsed against his chest, just as she had all those months ago on the ship, but this time she breathed in the scent of wood and smoke and the cold autumn night. Chuckling softly, he wrapped his strong arms around her and held her tight. She began to cry softly, tears of happiness, tears of relief. He loved her. They would have a life together. A marriage like his parents had. Like her parents still did.

Finally composing herself, she pulled away. He wiped her tears and then tilted her head toward his. As their lips met, the clouds parted and the light of the moon shone down from the starry sky.

Chapter Thirty-Four
Maddee

*L*ifeWalk Rehabilitation Center was beautiful and impressive, with sweeping lawns, colorful gardens, towering trees, and even a small brook. This would be a lovely place for Nicole to stroll each day, I thought as we eased up the drive, but then I felt a pang of sadness as I reminded myself that she'd be doing so without me. Once Greg and I dropped her off, in fact, I wouldn't be allowed to see her at all for at least ten days. And though I knew that was a necessary part of the rehab process, I was going to miss her terribly.

This wasn't like her first day of kindergarten when I was the big sister looking out for her on the playground. This time, she'd be on her own. As Greg pulled into a parking space, I wanted to say something encouraging to my sister, but my heart was too full to speak.

The people at registration had been expecting us, and that made the process go smoother. Obviously, Nana had spared no expense choosing this place. Greg had recommended it, not for the cushy accommodations and gorgeous grounds, but for the excellent treatment programs they offered, the faith-based focus, the physical therapy element, and the better-than-average recovery rate. Now he was talking to the resident PT, laying out his thoughts on that part of her treatment, and I was glad to know my sister's medical progress would continue to receive attention even while she was focusing on her mind and heart.

When everything was set, they let Nicole walk us back outside so we could say our farewells in private. She gave Greg a big thanks and a hug, telling him he'd become like a brother to her and that she hoped they would remain friends. When they were done, he stepped away and she turned to me.

"Guess this is it," she said.

I could only nod in return. In that moment, she seemed far stronger than I. How I wished I could go the rest of the way with her, but this next step had to be done alone.

"You're my hero," I whispered, tears filling my eyes. "I'm so proud of you right now."

"And you're my rock," she said, also starting to cry. "You always were."

We fell into each other's arms and held on as long as we could. Finally, reluctantly, we pulled apart. Then, with a soft "Thanks" and a tiny wave, my sister turned and went inside.

Tears were pouring down my face as Greg reached for my hand and led me to the parking lot. In the car, he slid an arm around my shoulders and simply held me as I cried.

When I was down to mere sniffling, he smoothed the hair from my cheeks, tenderly kissed my forehead, and handed me a pack of tissues.

The first few miles we rode in silence, but once my emotions were under control, I pulled out my phone and called Detective Ortiz. I wanted to tell her the good news about Nicole going to rehab as well as explain all that had unfolded last night and the many puzzles that had been solved. She'd been so helpful of late, she deserved to know about Hedge and the private investigator and what had really been going on with both of them.

As expected, she sounded thrilled with the news about rehab and relieved to get the facts behind our recent troubles. She thanked me for calling to tell her, but then our conversation took a disappointing turn when I asked how things were going with her investigation.

"Have you figured out yet what Mr. Koenig was doing here? Any ideas on how he might have ended up in the cabin?"

She paused and then spoke. "I'm sorry, Maddee. Maybe I wasn't clear enough on this yesterday. Learning the victim's identity was a huge step, and we're actively working the case again. But don't expect everything else to fall into place anytime soon."

My heart sank.

"I promise," she added, "I will work as hard as I can to find answers, but it could take weeks, maybe even months, before we get to the bottom of this."

Once we'd ended our call, I relayed her part of the conversation to Greg.

"Well," he said thoughtfully, "at least you can feel good about having solved one piece of the puzzle. Your cousin Renee did her part, now you've done yours."

I smiled. "Yeah. Next time, it's Nicole's turn to step in and help."

We grew quiet after that and rode along in companionable silence. Finally, with a sigh, I tucked my phone—and my expectations about the investigation—away for now and turned my attention to the man at the wheel.

"Speaking of Nicole," I said, "I can't begin to thank you for all you've done for her—and for me. You've been such a blessing to us both, more than you can ever imagine."

He humbly waved off my praise, saying he'd enjoyed every minute of our time together. But then it struck me that with Nicole gone, he and I no longer had any need to interact.

And for some reason, that thought filled me with a deep and profound sense of loss.

Turning away, I tried to act casual, but inside my mind was spinning. Was it possible that I cared for this man as more than just a friend? Startled by the thought, I kept my eyes on the passing scenery. My ancestor Celeste came to mind, how one day she had an equally startling realization. She was in love with Spenser.

And I was in love with Greg.

"So you know the other night at the party," he said, interrupting my thoughts, "when you mentioned all that about me dating your sister at some point in the future?"

I nodded, hoping he couldn't hear the pounding of my heart.

"Well, here's the thing, Maddee. Nicole's not the one I want to date. You are."

His words hung there between us as I processed what he'd said.

He wanted to date me?

I wanted to date him. I wanted to spend time with him, learn all about him, explore the possibilities of what we could be to each other. But I wasn't going to jump in blindly as I always had in the past. Instead, with eyes wide open, I would allow our friendship to evolve into something deeper—but only if that was God's will for our lives.

"Well?" he asked, and when I looked at him I saw apprehension written all over his face.

"Stop the car," I said.

"What?"

"Stop the car." I glanced around and spotted a small church up ahead on the right. "Turn in there. You can use their parking lot."

He did as requested, slowing and then making a right into the wide, empty space. Crunching on gravel, we rolled to a stop.

Greg put the car in park, rolled down the windows, and then turned toward me in the silence, exhaling slowly. "I just ruined a perfectly good friendship, didn't I?" he asked with a grimace.

"No, you didn't."

His eyes met mine, the apprehension fading.

"In fact," I added, "I think you've brought that friendship to where it's been headed all along."

Relief and joy flooding his features, he reached out and cupped my face in his hands. Then after a long, heady pause we drew together in unison, our mouths seeking each other hungrily, our hearts pounding the same rhythm. Our kiss was more passionate, more wonderful, more *right* than any I could ever have imagined.

When it ended, we shared a startled smile, as if both surprised at the intensity that had been there under the surface all along.

"Ah, Maddee, you have no idea," he said sweetly, pulling me to him and holding me tight.

I went willingly, resting my head against his shoulder in a spot made just for me. As we held our embrace, it struck me why I hadn't been able to choose a ringtone for this man. As Nicole had said, life didn't always tie up in a neat little package with a perfect little bow. Sometimes it was messy and complicated. People were complex and surprising. And Greg just had so many different levels to him, so many layers, that no way could I squeeze who he was into a single line from some song.

Just as I'd needed to let go of my perfectionism, I saw now that I had to stop categorizing people. I had to stop hiding behind labels and thinking I could control things by putting them into tidy compartments. Mostly, I had to stop escaping into unrealistic dreams of how my life would be "someday." Life was already here. It was all around me.

And, messy or not, I was ready for it.

C eleste and Spenser were married in the parish church three months later, after all of the lumber had been milled for the inn and loaded onto the boat. George and Berta were married soon after. Together, the two couples and Sary traveled with Emmanuel up the James to their new home. Within a year the inn was profitable. Soon after, the parts for the mill arrived from the Netherlands and that business grew too.

Emmanuel's work brought him to Williamsburg fairly often. Then, on one very special trip, he delivered the first of their milled wood to a plantation on the way—and returned home with Aline as his bride. Besides being a good wife to him and a friend to Celeste and Berta, she proved an asset to the running of the inn.

Through the years, Emmanuel did use the ring as collateral several times, to acquire more land and supplies. But even when it wasn't tied up that way, the women in the family rarely wore it. As it turned out, they all worked far too hard for such finery.

The Talbots kept their promise not to own slaves and managed to make a living off hospitality, timber, and the humble beginnings of papermaking and printing that would later evolve into the family fortune. Although Sary was free, she chose to stay and work at the inn, doing her best with her lame hand.

Celeste never saw her parents again, but she'd been assured of their forgiveness after she fully confessed in the letter written for her by Spencer. Alexander came to Virginia a few years later, which delighted them all, especially Celeste. He brought all of the letters she had written to Papa and Maman thus far, with instructions to pass them down so that future Talbots would know the hardships their forebears endured to forge a life in the New World. He also brought the note certifying the ruby ring's origins, which gave it even greater worth as a guarantee for financing. Alexander eventually returned to England, where he joined his two brothers in London as printers, just like their father.

All three of the couples who stayed in Virginia had children of their own, and love flew back and forth across the Atlantic, in both letters and prayers, throughout Celeste's lifetime.

Her heart belonged to Virginia, but she never forgot her family's history in France and then England, her journey to the New World, and God's steadfast presence through it all.

DISCUSSION QUESTIONS

1. Maddee knows that Nicole needed to fix what was damaged on the inside to begin healing on the outside and recover from her addiction. What in the story contributes to Nicole's healing? What do you think her chances of staying in recovery are?

2. Maddee has a difficult time getting past thinking of herself as an ugly duckling. Do you have a negative impression of yourself from your childhood that you have carried with you? If so, how have you dealt with it?

3. Nicole recognizes that Maddee's perfectionist tendencies are an effort to control everything around her and asks her when she's going to grow up and realize that life is "ugly and messy and difficult, that it doesn't tie up in a neat little package with a perfect little bow?" Was there a point in your life when you realized it would never be tied with a perfect little bow? How did you handle it? What advice do you have for someone who is a perfectionist?

4. Celeste leaves a good family to chase after a man and ends up halfway across the world. Have you (or someone you've known) made rash decisions in the heat of the moment that changed the course of your life? How did it turn out? What advice would you give someone contemplating such an act?

5. Lying comes easily to both Berta and Nicole. Maddee's supervisor reminds her that lying can become habitual but can be corrected through therapy. Do you think Berta and Nicole lie for the same or different reasons? Why? Do you believe this habit can be corrected?

6. How did Nicole's age and personality contribute to the long-term emotional impact of the murder scene the girls stumbled upon? Did you feel it was believable that her nightmares created an even deeper emotional wound?

7. At Mr. Edwards's inn, Celeste was forced to work harder than she ever had in her entire life. What prepared her, in her past, for the difficult labor of a kitchen maid and serving girl?

8. Celeste finds, for a good part of the story, that she cannot pray. Have you ever have had a time in your life when you found it difficult to pray? What got you through? What made you able to pray again?

9. Sary tells Celeste that the charming men are "the ones you need to watch out for." Jonathan and Dr. Austin Hill are the most charming men in the story. Even though they are separated by more than three hundred years, how are they similar? How are they different?

10. Are there stories about your ancestors you've learned from? If so, what are they and what did you learn?

Acknowledgments

Mindy thanks

John Clark, my husband, best friend, and partner in work and life.

Emily Clark, my daughter and all-important behind-the-scenes helper and collaborator.

Lauren Clark, my daughter, idea person, and wise advisor in ways big and small.

Tara Kenny, my assistant, who helps keep me on track.

Joey Starns, my brother, who really went above and beyond on this one. Thanks, bro!

Kay Justus, who graciously provided a wide range of medical information.

Tonya N. Lawrence, MD, who generously shared her expertise in psychiatry.

Tracey Akamine, Hannah Campbell, Jennifer Clark, Andrew Cooper, Marc Engeron, Suzanne Scannell, Daniel Scannell, Andrew Starns, Shari Weber, and everyone else who gave input and answers on various book-related questions.

The helpful staff and volunteers of Historic Huguenot Street in New Paltz, New York.

The helpful staff and volunteers of the Virginia Historical Society in Richmond, Virginia.

Leslie thanks

Peter Gould, my husband, research partner, and all-time biggest supporter in both life and writing. I couldn't do this without you.

My children—Kaleb, Taylor, Hana, and Thao—who all inspire me and support me in ways they could never imagine.

Laurie Snyder, for her encouragement and helpful ideas concerning this story.

Linda Morell, a reader and friend, for sharing about her Huguenot ancestry and inspiring me to "do a little research."

Dr. Ann Woodlief, Huguenot Society of Manakin national librarian; Bryan S. Godfrey, Huguenot Society of Manakin library assistant; and the Huguenot Society of the Founders of Manakin in the Colony of Virginia, for their help on the early history of Huguenots in Virginia.

The staff of the Manakin Episcopal Church and the Huguenot Memorial Chapel, Midlothian, Virginia, for allowing us to tour the buildings.

Bill Barker, archivist, the Mariners' Park and Museum, Newport News, Virginia, for his help with details about the James River in the early 1700s.

Allison Heinbaugh, circulation and reference librarian, John D. Rockefeller, Jr. Library, Colonial Williamsburg Foundation, for her help on historical details concerning early Williamsburg.

Any mistakes in the story are ours.

Mindy and Leslie thank

Chip MacGregor, our agent, for all of his work on our behalf.

Kim Moore, our editor and friend, for her expertise and encouragement.

And all the fine folks at Harvest House, for their hard work, dedication, and much-appreciated support.

Don't Miss

My Daughter's Legacy

Book 3 in the Cousins of the Dove Series
Coming Soon to Your Favorite Retailer

Continue the discovery of what truly happened all those years
ago at the cabin in the woods, and meet a new generation of
Talbots who along with their community, must face the challenges
and heartbreaks of the Civil War-era Virginia.

ABOUT THE AUTHORS

Mindy Starns Clark is the bestselling author of more than 20 books, both fiction and nonfiction (over 1 million copies sold) including coauthoring the Christy Award-winning *The Amish Midwife* with Leslie Gould. Mindy and her husband, John, have two adult children and live in Pennsylvania.

~

Leslie Gould is the author of 22 novels. She received her master of fine arts degree from Portland State University and lives in Oregon with her husband, Peter, and their four children.

~

To connect with the authors,
visit Mindy's and Leslie's websites at
www.mindystarnsclark.com and www.lesliegould.com.

One night
four lives entered the world
by the hands of an Amish midwife,
just outside North Star, Pennsylvania.

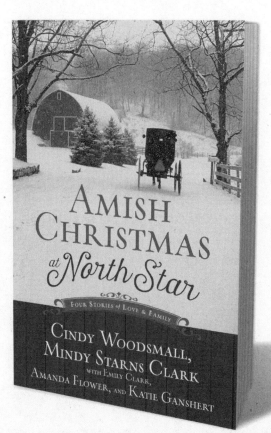

Rebekah's Babies, as they are called, are now grown adults and in
four heartwarming novellas each young person experiences a journey
of discovery, a possibility of love, and the wonder of Christmas.

To learn more about Harvest House books and
to read sample chapters, visit our website:

www.harvesthousepublishers.com

HARVEST HOUSE PUBLISHERS
EUGENE, OREGON